GUARDING SAVAGE

A Peter Savage Novel

D1057358

GUARDING
SAVAGE

A PETER SAVAGE NOVEL

DAVE EDLUND

Light Messages

Durham, NC

Copyright © 2018, by Dave Edlund
Guarding Savage (Peter Savage, #5)
Dave Edlund
www.petersavagenovels.com
dedlund@lightmessages.com

Published 2018, by Light Messages
www.lightmessages.com
Durham, NC 27713
SAN: 920-9298

Paperback ISBN: 978-1-61153-243-2
Ebook ISBN: 978-1-61153-242-5
Library of Congress Control Number: 2018939637

This is a work of fiction. All characters, organizations, and events portrayed in this novel are either products of the author's imagination or are used fictitiously.

For my buddy Gary. Thank you for your deep friendship, encouragement, and support over the past four decades.

ACKNOWLEDGEMENTS

WRITING AND PUBLISHING A NOVEL is not the work of a single person, and there are many who have contributed greatly to the completion of *Guarding Savage*. First, I want to thank Elizabeth Turnbull, my editor, for her countless suggestions and prods that *always* make the Peter Savage novels better. Also, a huge thank you to Betty and Wally at Light Messages Publishing for making these books possible. And a special thank you to my former publicist, Kylee Wooten, for all her hard work in promoting the Peter Savage novels as well as helping to guide me through the art and etiquette of social media marketing, as well as the many fabulous graphics she's created. I'm sad to say "former" because Kylee has moved on to a new marketing position with a sports equipment startup. All the best wishes, Kylee.

I want to express my gratitude and appreciation to the many advance copy reviewers, and a special thank you to Gary Stout and Gordon Gregory for your many good suggestions and constant encouragement.

Guarding Savage has many nautical scenes that required knowledge of U.S. Naval terminology, especially the phrasing of orders onboard warships. For help with this topic, I turned to my good friend and Navy veteran, Bill Shank. Thank you, Bill, for patiently guiding me through this specific terminology, seemingly arcane to a landlubber like me.

Last, but far from least, my heartfelt appreciation to you, the readers of these novels. It is a joy to read your emails, and the occasions when I have an opportunity to meet Peter Savage fans are always special moments. Please know that I read all emails sent in through my web site, or contacts through Light Messages:

www.PeterSavageNovels.com

dedlund@LightMessages.com

AUTHOR'S NOTE

FOR YEARS I'VE BEEN WANTING TO WRITE THIS TALE. The inspiration began to germinate following numerous trips to Asia beginning three decades ago—mostly to Japan and China, but also to Korea. It was through these visits that I began to appreciate the magnitude of Asian culture on the development of human society.

Then, more than fifteen years ago, I heard a story on National Public Radio about an author named Iris Chang, and her book *The Rape of Nanking*. This historical account retells events from December 1937 and into early 1938, as the Imperial Japanese Army occupied Nanking, the ancient capital of China. At the time, the population of Nanking was around one million. The atrocities that occurred over a period of several months, leaving more than 300,000 civilians dead, are well documented, yet little known.

The Rape of Nanking chronicles the Japanese blood lust, with civilians murdered by a variety of grisly methods, women raped, families destroyed. Historians call this rampage the Nanking Massacre, or the forgotten holocaust. Iris Chang's book spent ten weeks on the *New York Times* bestseller list, and it served her purpose of keeping the memory alive.

It is difficult to imagine, let alone understand, the depth of barbaric cruelty that humans inflict on one another. At times, such behavior seems motivated by hatred stemming from religion, race, or ideological factors. At other times, it seems to be purely for entertainment or sport. And so I found myself trying to understand the Twentieth Century conflict in Asia and the impact those events still have on the modern world. Make no mistake, the impact is very real.

It may be difficult for some Americans to understand the deep resentment that exists to this day between Chinese and Korean populations on one hand and Japanese populations on the other hand. The forgotten holocaust and the Korean comfort women—women who were forced into sexual slavery by the Imperial Japanese Army—certainly provide graphic examples for the animosity. But the analysis needs to go deeper, as there is much more at play.

The fact that the government of Japan has never apologized for its role in precipitating war on the Chinese and Korean populations during the middle part of the Twentieth Century, and the crimes against humanity that ensued, keeps the resentment alive. Recall that Germany has worked hard to make amends for the actions of the Nazi government, including public apologies, a staunch pro-Israel policy, and a program of paying reparations that dates to 1953.

In contrast, the Japanese government refuses to publicly apologize or pay reparations. Furthermore, unlike Nazi Germany, Imperial Japan was never held fully accountable for war crimes by the victorious allies in the years following the close of WWII. This is a fact not lost on Chinese and Koreans, who see Japan as unrepentant. This image is strengthened when Japanese politicians visit the historic Yasukuni Shrine, a memorial to Japan's deceased soldiers, including those who committed class-A war crimes.

Perhaps the words of the late Iris Chang say it best: "If the Japanese government doesn't reckon with the crimes of its wartime leaders, history is going to leave them as tainted as their ancestors. You can't blame this generation for what happened years ago, but you can blame them for not acknowledging these crimes."[1]

History is inescapable, and both China and Japan have long histories of advanced civilization and culture. In both countries, this rich cultural heritage spans millennia. Exploring the National Museum in Taipei, Taiwan, affords a glimpse at this Chinese cultural heritage and wondrous works of art that demonstrate not only the remarkable ability of craftsmen, but also an exhibition of advanced science and technology in the form of exquisite pottery and glazes. And let's not forget gunpowder, paper, printing, and the magnetic compass—all invented in China.

Chinese were also excellent navigators and cartographers, having explored the world's oceans long before the famous Italian, Portuguese, and Spanish explorers of the Elizabethan era. With a vast supply of historical maps, it's easy to understand why many Chinese honestly believe they have a legitimate claim to much, if not all, of the East China Sea and the South China Sea. Indeed, even many Western historians acknowledge the seafaring prowess of Chinese sailors under the government of Emperor Zhu Di in the early Fifteenth Century.[2]

Fast forward to the present day, and we have many disputes over islands dotting the seas from Malaysia northeast to the Kamchatka Peninsula. For the most part, these islands are uninhabited, and yet they are provoking strong international disagreements, bordering on hostility. Competing claims of

---

1   *www.IrisChang.net*
2   *1421, The Year China Discovered America*, by Gavin Menzies, 2008, Harper Perennial

sovereignty rely on historical claims. But without consensus on the legitimacy of those historical records, resolution remains elusive.

Is history bound to repeat? Is another war between two Asian giants—China and Japan—inevitable? Until old wounds heal, and past wrongs are repented, my fear is that we are locked on a course that will place the United States in the middle of a major conflict.

Perhaps, when all is considered, the root cause is nothing more than pride—a powerful emotion, one that drives people (and nations) to illogical actions. It is time to place rational thought ahead of national pride; to admit past transgressions and pledge to a peaceful path forward; to negotiate, in fairness and good faith, resolutions to overlapping historical claims. This is not a one-sided equation, and to succeed, cooperation of all parties is required. However, history also shows us that military victories never truly conquer national pride.

There is a lesson here for all nations—including ours. Something to think about...

DE

PROLOGUE

Nanking
January 4, 1938

THE SKY WAS GRAY with a thick cloud cover. A soft, intermittent drizzle was just enough to dampen the street and drive in the chill. But the weather made no difference to Wei. For the past two weeks, ever since the Japanese soldiers had beaten her and raped her, she felt nothing.

This dreary afternoon, she was stoically working the kitchen of the small noodle shop owned by her husband's family. Wearing the humiliation and shame of not only herself, but also that of her husband and family, Wei silently boiled noodles and chopped meager portions of duck.

There were only a few ducks left, and nearly all the pigs had been shot and butchered by the invading army. That which the soldiers did not gorge upon was left to waste. To the invaders, it made little difference if the population of Nanking slowly starved. There was still an abundance of men and boys for bayonet and sword practice and a seemingly inexhaustible number of women and young girls to satisfy the soldiers.

The reign of terror had begun twenty-three days earlier when the Japanese Imperial Army entered Nanking and swept through the civilian population like a plague, only the suffering was far worse than could be wrought by any disease. The unimaginable brutality inflicted on the defenseless Chinese left most, like Wei, emotionless—hollow shells devoid of feeling other than physical pain, and there was plenty of that. They simply functioned, doing what was necessary to survive from one minute to the next.

Three elderly men and a small boy sat around one of five tables in the main room adjacent to the cramped and tiny kitchen. Only a waist-high partition separated the kitchen from the dining tables. The front of the store was open, the roll-up metal door raised as it always was during business hours, which stretched from morning to late in the evening.

The despair felt by the population of Nanking was amplified on this dreary day, as the dull natural light provided meager illumination within the shop. There were no decorations on the walls to brighten the space. This was a business, and Wei and her husband, Pei-Ming, scraped out a paltry living by serving as many customers each day as they could. There was no profit in encouraging people to prolong their meal—they could go elsewhere to visit.

The four patrons waited patiently as Wei stirred the noodles in a large boiling caldron of broth. Guan-Yin, her daughter of seven, busied herself washing laundry by hand in a back corner of the kitchen. Later she would wash the tables and mop the floor. She also fed the poultry—what was left of them—and cleaned the pens.

After no more than two minutes in the bubbling broth, Wei scooped out portions of the noodles into four bowls. Then she used the cleaver to chop half of a roasted duck into four portions, placing one in each of the bowls. Pei-Ming carried the servings, two at a time, to the table. Not a single word was spoken. Even the boy, who was no more than six years of age, was silent.

Outside the shop, an elderly woman, bent over at a severe angle and supporting the weight of her torso on a crude crutch, shuffled by, disfigured by decades of stoop labor. Residents were peddling large tricycles through the cobbled streets, hauling a variety of loads strapped onto the back. Their loads were mostly merchandise for the tiny family-run stores and businesses, occasionally junk—material to be recycled in some creative fashion—sometimes garbage. Other people were walking this way and that, a seemingly random movement that was, in reality, filled with purpose. No one wanted to loiter on the streets. Japanese soldiers, carrying military rifles with long bayonets fixed to the muzzle, were everywhere. Always two or more, never a single soldier by himself.

The soldiers milled about casually. Military protocol was absent except when a ranking officer passed by. For years, the invincible Japanese Army and Navy had advanced throughout Southeast Asia unchecked. Now that Nanking had fallen, the army viewed their occupation as a time to rest and relax, to enjoy the spoils of war with impunity, as they had done before, following their conquests.

Pei-Ming returned to the kitchen and was washing some bowls when four soldiers entered. The elderly men kept their heads bowed, not daring to make eye contact. Wei stiffened at the sight of the solders—she recognized two as the men who had attacked her. She lowered her head and moved farther back in the kitchen, but there was nowhere to go where she would not be seen.

For the moment, the soldiers' attention was on the patrons, who continued to display their subservience. An officer—Pei-Ming thought him to be a captain—reached out and pulled the bowl away from the boy. The boy remained silent as the captain raised the bowl, sniffed, and then threw it to the floor and made a gagging sound. This amused his subordinates, who collectively laughed.

One of the old men gently pushed his bowl of noodles to the boy, but immediately one of the soldiers snatched it and threw it to the ground. Then the other remaining bowls were also swept off the table to the concrete floor, the ceramic bowls shattering.

Pei-Ming winced while Wei turned her back to avoid recognition.

Their household dog and Guan-Yin's close companion, an old and skinny Shar Pei, strolled over to the table and began lapping up the food that had splattered around the table and chairs. Tears appeared on the boy's face, but he refused to whimper.

The captain, one hand resting on the hilt of his katana and the other on the holstered pistol on his hip, spoke in Mandarin. He was well educated and stationed in Manchuria in part because of his language abilities. "What is wrong with you old man? See… the dog eats this. It is not fit for people." Then he said the same in his native tongue for the amusement of his soldiers, who endorsed his taunting with more laughter.

The Shar Pei finished lapping up the noodles and settled down to gnaw on part of the duck when the captain lashed out with his boot, planting the stiff toe in the dog's ribs. It yelped in pain, backing away, torn between maintaining a safe distance or daring to approach danger to eat.

The Japanese officer did not wait. He drew his pistol and calmly shot the dog. The old Shar Pei twitched and then died, bringing more laughter from the soldiers.

"There," the captain spoke in Mandarin. "There is food more suitable for you. We have been told you like to eat dog. Feast!" And two of the soldiers each grabbed a leg and threw the carcass on the table. Their mirth lasted only seconds before it was stopped by a scream from Guan-Yin.

Hearing the gunshot, and seeing her companion dead and tossed on the table, the young girl cried out in anguish and rushed from the kitchen. She threw herself over the dog and sobbed. The soldiers retreated a few steps and fell silent, unsure how they should react in the presence of their superior officer.

The captain blinked twice as he considered the girl's reaction. Raising his head, he glanced around, eyes settling on the woman in the kitchen. Then recognition came to him. He had been in this shop before, a couple weeks ago. Reflexively his lips formed a thin smile as he remembered.

"Hello, pretty one," he said as he started to move to the kitchen.

Wei shook her head and backed up until she had nowhere to go. "No, please," she pleaded, her hands behind her back and her head bowed.

The captain rounded the short partition and stepped into the kitchen. He continued his deliberate advance, enjoying the power he felt as the woman trembled in fear before him.

Pei-Ming closed his hand around the cleaver. As he charged, the heavy blade raised, weeks of pent-up humiliation and rage escaped his body in a visceral scream. He swung down but the steel edge clanged against the Japanese katana. With speed and grace from years of practice, the captain slashed the katana across Pei-Ming's stomach.

Wei's husband dropped the cleaver and placed both hands across the deep gash. Looking down at the blood seeping between his fingers, he never saw the katana fall across his neck, cleanly severing his head.

Pei-Ming's body fell to the floor in a grisly heap. No longer fearing for her safety, Wei rushed forward, tears already running down her face. She threw herself across her husband's body, convulsing as she wept uncontrollably.

With his soldiers watching, the captain raised his katana

again and brought it down with strength and precision, leaving Wei's head resting near her husband's.

Having just witnessed the murder of her parents, Guan-Yin started to run for the kitchen. She made two steps before one of the Japanese soldiers grabbed her arm and threw her to the floor. He then viciously kicked her in the face and head until she stopped moving. Blood trickled from her nose, leaving a stain where her face was pressed against the cold concrete floor.

Stepping around the prostrate girl as he returned to the table, the captain surveyed the pitiful creatures cowering before him. One of the old men was backing into a corner, shielding the boy, who was crying.

Neither of the two men still seated at the table would look up at the Japanese officer. The captain reached out and casually grabbed a cloth napkin from underneath the dog's leg. He wiped the blood off his katana and then stuffed the bloodied rag in the breast pocket of one of the old men.

As he led his soldiers away, the officer spoke briefly to his men. "Maybe tomorrow we come back and recruit these volunteers for bayonet practice," he said, once again earning jovial laughter from his subordinates.

CHAPTER 1

XO LAWRENCE FOLLOWED THE MH-60R Seahawk as it passed the bridge on a direct heading toward its mother ship, the white airframe sporting a red circle on the side. The helicopter was hunting an American submarine, part of his task force. Training, as realistic as practical, was one of the tactical goals of this three-day joint exercise. And then there was also the political objective.

"Do you think they'll catch the *Tucson* sir?" Lawrence asked.

"They're good, but not that good," replied Captain Wallace. "I know the *Tucson's* skipper. He runs a tight ship. Never lost yet, even against our own offensive forces."

Lawrence lowered the high-powered binoculars and swiveled his head to the port side of the bridge, marveling at the gray silhouette several-thousand-yards distant. "She sure does look like a carrier, sir. Reminds me of a World War II era flat top. Significantly smaller than our Nimitz class."

"It's all in the classification. She was designed to carry fourteen helicopters, primarily for antisubmarine warfare. But as you know, she can also land and launch Ospreys."

Lawrence was nodding. "Not to mention Harriers and the new F35. I suspect our Japanese friends are sending a message to China."

Wallace nodded agreement. "No doubt. The name they selected for the flagship isn't a coincidence."

"*Izumo*?" Lawrence said. The XO was young for a naval officer of his rank, a full fifteen years the junior of his captain. Raised in upstate New York, he had excelled in the ROTC program at Cornell University, graduating top of his class. With sharp intellect and an easy personality, Lawrence advanced quickly to his current position on the *USS Shiloh*, a guided missile cruiser.

Standing to the side of his XO, Captain Wallace was also admiring the *Izumo*, a helicopter destroyer and recent addition to the Japanese Maritime Self Defense Force. Wallace lowered his binoculars and glanced at his XO, a slight smirk on his otherwise hard face. He enjoyed coming out on top in what most would consider inconsequential trivia.

"You are familiar with the principal ships of the Imperial Japanese Navy?"

Lawrence hesitated.

Captain Wallace decided to let him off easy. Returning to his binoculars, he added, "The flagship of the Imperial Navy's Third Fleet was also named *Izumo*. The Third Fleet helped fuel Japan's expansion into China in the 1930s. They didn't teach you that at Cornell?" The smirk had grown to a grin as he watched a pair of helicopters take off from the expansive open deck of the *Izumo* while the one that had just flown past his bridge was hovering, preparing to land.

"Uh, no sir, not that I recall." Lawrence cast a sideways

glance at his captain, trying to determine if this was important or just banter. He had been serving under Captain Wallace for only five months, and he still felt uncomfortable in the man's presence. Was it the age difference, or gap in experience— maybe something else?

Lawrence said, "The tension between Japan and China seems to consistently ratchet up, not down. I guess choosing that name is like rubbing salt in an open wound."

"The meaning has not been lost on the leaders in Beijing, I assure you. Just be aware, Mr. Lawrence, that there is much at play in this exercise, and perhaps the most dangerous maneuvers are transpiring in political circles, not out here on the East China Sea."

They were well into day two of the joint exercise, conducting maneuvers and anti-submarine warfare training in a large area of ocean between Okinawa and the disputed Senkaku Island chain. In addition to the *USS Shiloh*, the fast-attack submarine *USS Tucson*, and two guided missile destroyers, the *USS Lassen* and the *USS McCampbell*, the joint task force was also joined by the *Izumo*, *Atago*, and *Kirishima*. So far, the weather had been excellent, with a thin overcast and mild seas. The forecast was for more of the same tomorrow.

Without warning, the klaxon blared, quickly followed by a message over the ship intercom. "CO, XO, report to CIC. Incoming threat detected." The voice was disarmingly calm, consistent with routine drills carried out hundreds of times before.

Lawrence shifted his optics, scanning the sky, not knowing what he was looking for, or where. Captain Wallace pivoted smartly and in two long strides he was at an instrumented console. His hand slapped down on a flat, round knob, activating the com.

"Wallace. What do you have?"

The Tactical Actions Officer, Lieutenant Commander Copeland, answered immediately, "Probable incoming ballistic missile, approaching apex now."

"Target?"

"Premature to say. Once it passes through the apex we'll have a good lock on trajectory."

"Sound general quarters, battle stations, and inform the other ships in the task force. I want a primary and backup firing solution, Mr. Copeland, by the time I get to CIC."

Without wasting another second, Captain Wallace and Executive Officer Lawrence swiftly left the bridge and descended several ladders before entering the dark, high-tech cavern of the Combat Information Center. Located deep within the hull of the *USS Shiloh*, this was the nerve center controlling the advanced weapon systems of the Aegis-class cruiser.

Lieutenant Commander Copeland was peering intently at a large, clear, vertical projection screen displaying a regional map with a grid overlay indicating longitude and latitude. The task force was positioned in the center of the map, indicated by a blue triangle, and a red trace was steadily advancing toward the blue symbol. The map was visible from either side and located in the center of the CIC, surrounded by banks of sophisticated electronic equipment for operating the highly complex and powerful Aegis radar and control of weapons systems.

The CIC was air conditioned to a cool sixty-eight degrees, a necessity to avoid overheating the multitude of computers and electronics. Long gone were the days of large-bore naval guns slugging it out with surface ships miles away. The state of naval warfare had evolved to long-range aircraft and radar-guided missile systems.

Wallace stopped just behind Copeland, while the XO detoured to a radar console and conferred in a low voice with the seaman manning the station.

Sensing the captain was behind him, Copeland explained, "The launch was from this area," he pointed to the lower left of the map, "near the Spratly Islands."

"Too far from our position to be a theater weapon… short-range ballistic missile?"

"Affirmative, sir."

"Submarine launch?"

"I assume so, unless there is a land-based launch facility there that we don't know about. Unlikely though, as any such facility would have been picked up by satellite imagery during construction."

By now the XO had joined Wallace and Copeland. "Captain, the schedule does not show a drone missile attack."

Wallace removed his cap and brushed a hand through his silver-white hair, still focused on the screen. "Wouldn't be the first time they threw an unscheduled action at us." Silently he ran through several training scenarios in his head. "Okay, power up the see-wiz and Sea Sparrow defenses, but keep them locked down. I don't want to shoot up one of the helos by mistake. And bring the SM3 battery on line.

"Our goal, Mr. Lawrence, is to make sure the computers record the proper response to the threat. I don't know how close launch control will allow the ballistic missile to come before auto destruct, but certainly not close enough to engage with Sea Sparrows. However, we might get to conduct a live fire with an SM3."

The XO understood. The entire training exercise was recorded by the ship's computer system and would cross-reference with the missile launch and other ship's logs, as well as ship-to-ship communications. This would then be parsed in minutia and critically reviewed for response time, type of response to match threat level, and so on. The see-wiz—30 mm Phalanx CIWS—was a last measure for extremely close-range ship defense and not a viable defense against a ballistic missile. It was, however, effective against other anti-ship missiles—the same for the Sea Sparrow missiles. In real combat they would be activated and placed on automatic response, but the danger of doing so in this exercise was not justified. So Captain Wallace signaled his awareness of the proper defensive moves without actually endangering the Japanese helicopters still on anti-submarine maneuvers.

"Do you have a primary firing solution?" Wallace said.

Copeland nodded. "Yes, sir. We can engage with SM3 missiles in seven seconds at the mid-course flight correction, just after the incoming bogie passes apex."

"Lock on, simulated launch." Wallace remained silent, watching the red trace continue to extend across the screen, advancing toward the symbol representing the task force, mentally counting down the seconds.

XO Lawrence was doing the same and was the first to break the silence. "Simulated launch recorded, Captain. Recommend we signal the *Izumo* of impending threat."

"See to it, Mr. Lawrence." Then, turning to Lieutenant Commander Copeland, "Have you coordinated radar search and fire control with the *Lassen* and *McCampbell*?"

"Affirmative, sir."

"Very good. Updated point of impact?"

Copeland turned and leaned in close to the sailor at the targeting radar console. It only took two seconds before he replied to his CO. "Still targeting this task force, sir." There was a brief pause. "It doesn't make sense. The mid-course correction should have altered the flight path so the missile drone would overfly our position."

Wallace pinched his eyebrows, trying to digest the volume of incoming information. No, it didn't make sense. The drone should travel well beyond the task force where it could be engaged by anti-missile defenses without endangering the ships and aircraft with debris.

"Mr. Lawrence, send a message to COMPACFLT. Ask if this is an unscheduled drill. Inform command that bogie has not altered course and remains on target for this task force."

"Yes, sir."

"Mr. Copeland, distance to bogie?"

"Uh, just cleared 200 kilometers. Accelerating into reentry."

"Very well. Inform *Lassen* and *McCampbell* of target solution and advise that we will fire one SM3. Request confirmation of bogie strike. Then make sure the *Izumo* knows we are preparing for SM3 live fire."

"Aye, Captain."

With every passing second the tension increased. The CO was still concentrating on the map and mentally running through his options. Now that the bogie was closing, the map automatically zoomed in, revealing the task force as a spread of six surface ships. It was still impossible to tell from the display exactly where the missile drone was aimed. Based on current trajectory, it would most likely strike open water somewhere between the group of ships unless it was destroyed.

What the hell is going on? Captain Wallace had been engaged in many live-fire drills of the SM3 anti-missile defense system, and they never aimed the missile drone even close to another ship or land mass. Furthermore, why hadn't this been scheduled as part of the exercise?

With the bogie entering terminal phase, Wallace decided not to wait any longer. Whatever idiot programed the flight path to terminate amongst the task force ships would take the heat for causing him to fire a multi-million dollar missile in an unscheduled drill.

"Confirm target lock," Wallace ordered.

"Target lock confirmed."

"Fire missile."

"Fire missile," Copeland relayed the command to the fire control operator.

The sailor pressed a red-illuminated button and the ship shuddered as the powerful SM3 missile launched, sending a plume of white fire and reddish-gray smoke into the air surrounding the aft deck.

Immediately, the tactical map showed a green line arcing from one of the blue symbols representing the *Shiloh*. The line looked like it would intersect with the red line, continuing to extend to the collection of six blue symbols.

"Time to intercept?" Wallace said.

"Twenty seconds," Copeland replied.

A second passed, and then another. Eyes focused on the tactical map and the merging lines.

"Make that ten seconds, sir. Bogie is accelerating." Copeland paused for a moment, then added, "It's accelerating like nothing I've ever seen before. Must have a re-entry booster. Speed is now... seven kilometers per second... still accelerating... now ten kilometers per second... intercept in three seconds..."

The CIC was dead silent, there was only the electrical hum as Wallace breathed shallowly, rapidly, eyes locked on the green and red lines.

The lines intersected!

But rather than terminating, the green line and the red continued on, past each other.

"What happened?" Wallace demanded.

"Checking, sir." Copeland checked the status at the fire control computer, confirming what the map was already showing. "Clean miss, sir."

"Mr. Lawrence. Any word from command?"

"Just a moment, sir, I have the admiral's aide on the line."

Copeland said, "Sir, *Lassen* confirms miss, requests permission to fire."

"I need an answer Mr. Lawrence! Tell *Lassen* and *McCampbell* to hold. What's the terminal location for the bogie?"

"Uh... checking now... the *Izumo*, sir. Bogie is closing at twelve kilometers per second. Still accelerating! Impact in seven seconds!"

"Get me confirmation on the bogie's trajectory!" Wallace barked. "Mr. Lawrence, inform the *Izumo* of incoming threat and recommend immediate activation of close air defenses. And tell them to land those birds or move them out ten kilometers!"

A second later Copeland replied. "Confirmed by *Lassen* and *McCampbell*!"

Suddenly the CIC transformed into a hive of frenetic activity. Captain Wallace had never participated in a live anti-missile exercise in which a task-force ship was targeted. His training kicked in, even though in the back of his mind he knew the bogie would self-destruct at any moment.

Multiple voices, each conveying deadly professionalism, overlapped resulting in a cacophony of noise. And yet over this sound Lawrence was clearly heard by everyone. "Command says no missile drone was launched. This is not an exercise!"

"Three seconds to impact, tracking true."

Wallace issued his orders. "*Lassen* and *McCambell* cleared to fire... Mr. Copeland, cleared to fire!"

Even as he was giving his commands, Wallace knew it would be insufficient if the bogie did not self-destruct. Still, he watched the green lines trailing from the two destroyers aimed directly at the leading edge of the incoming red line. It was going to be very close.

The sky was rent with a brilliant white streak of superheated and ionized air from far above. It looked like a ball of lightening thrown down from the heavens, and it moved at such incredible speed that it appeared to be a continuous line. Then it struck the large Japanese ship.

There was a blinding flash of white light, brighter than the sun. From a distance, all appeared to be normal—but that soon changed.

Onboard the pride of the Japanese Navy, the situation was anything but normal. The projectile struck amidships. With phenomenal speed, it penetrated through the vessel like a hot poker through Styrofoam. Steel was instantly vaporized as energy transferred from the projectile to everything in its path. Along the way, electrical lines and pipes carrying aviation fuel were severed, sparking an inferno that erupted in a large fireball. The ensuing flames quickly spread to the hangar deck and beyond.

A minor ammunition store was in the path of destruction; the white hot metal and shock wave generated by the projectile detonated tons of surface-to-air defensive missiles. The combination of explosives detonating and ignition of solid rocket propellant served to extend the radius of destruction and further compromise the ship's structural integrity.

The hardened and dense warhead continued through the many decks, wreaking havoc. In less than a hundredth of a second, the kinetic projectile exited through the ship's keel, leaving a near vertical channel twenty feet in diameter—within this channel there was nothing. Surrounding the channel for another thirty feet in all directions was twisted, fused, and broken metal that once constituted the ship, its structure, and its support systems.

Automatic fire suppression systems kicked in, but the extensive collateral damage to the ship's infrastructure disabled the sprinklers and Halon systems where the most intense fires blazed. Seawater pushed upward through this gaping wound into the ship. Watertight bulkhead doors closed automatically throughout the decks, a futile attempt to stem the incoming flood.

Fires, raging out of control even before fire suppression crews were able to respond, rapidly overheated the steel bulkheads. Quickly the fire spread across the hangar deck in a conflagration that consumed the parked helicopters.

With the keel severed and the associated devastation to the upper decks, the structural integrity of the *Izumo* was compromised beyond the point of recovery. Two minutes after impact, the mighty ship—the pride of the Japanese Maritime Self Defense Force—broke in two and slid beneath the waves.

CHAPTER 2

IT WAS THE TYPE OF CENTRAL OREGON DAY that visitors raved about and locals loved. Peter Savage and Todd Steed had just finished a long mountain bike ride that took them through miles of forested trails on the western boundary of Bend. After making a quick stop at Peter's loft residence in the Old Mill District to pick up Diesel, they peddled into downtown Bend, Diesel trotting by his master. It was late afternoon, and they had no trouble finding a shaded table on the west side of Wall Street, led there by their hunger and thirst.

While Peter tied Diesel's leash to the table leg, the waiter placed two glasses of water in front of the men, which they each consumed in a single, long gulp. Then they ordered local microbrews and a couple appetizers.

"You gave me quite a workout," Todd said. "Next time, I get to be in front and *you* can eat my dust."

Peter laughed. "You could've passed me any time."

"I thought you'd say something like that." Todd shared a

rare grin. Standing just shy of six feet and with broad shoulders, a chocolate-brown goatee, and short-cropped hair of matching color, he almost always wore a don't-mess-with-me look.

In contrast, Peter was quick to smile and laughter came easily. Slightly taller than his friend, and of medium build, Peter sported brown hair in a conservative cut. But his most distinguishing feature was his eyes—steel gray and determined.

"Okay, next time you can have the lead," Peter said. They were more than just good friends. Todd was also the Chief Engineer at Peter's company, EJ Enterprises. Following engineering designs Peter created, Todd was responsible for building the prototypes of unique magnetic impulse weapons—small arms used primarily by Special Forces—that the company sold to the U.S. military.

The waiter brought a bowl of water for Diesel, who was lying quietly under the table. He stuck his tongue in the water, took a few laps, then returned to lounging, completely ignoring the pedestrian traffic. Peter slunk lower in his chair, sipping his ale and people watching from the partial anonymity of his ball cap and sunglasses. A steady flow of locals and visitors occupied the sidewalk, rivaling the volume of street traffic.

"That's something you don't see here often," Todd said, nudging his chin toward the silver and black Rolls Royce cruising by slowly.

Peter agreed. "I saw a Bentley once, and a few Ferraris, but never a Rolls. That's a Phantom model, if I'm not mistaken. Watched a Discovery Channel show about the factory in England."

The waiter arrived with their order just as the luxury limousine turned at the corner. "What do you figure a car like that costs?" Todd asked.

"A lot. Maybe half a million or more."

"Huh. Do they also build trucks?"

Peter laughed. "Nope. You're outta luck."

As they were enjoying the sushi roll, two young women emerged from the restaurant and stopped at the curb. Their merry laughter carried through the background noise and attracted Peter's attention. He watched while one of the women spoke into her phone. By appearance, she was Asian. Her companion, who was blond, fished her phone out of a pocket and began scrolling through messages. A couple minutes later the Rolls came into view a block away, and the Asian woman raised an arm and stepped into the street like she was hailing a taxi.

The limo double-parked in front of the restaurant, and the driver stepped out and hustled around the rear of the car to open the door. Another car halted behind the Rolls Royce, which was blocking the lane. Two men jumped out and rushed the limo driver and his passengers.

Diesel emitted a deep, reverberating growl, his body taut and alert.

Both men were tall and very muscular—they could have been professional wrestlers, or body builders. The lead guy had a Fu Manchu mustache and his black hair pulled back in a ponytail. Wearing a white, sleeveless T-shirt, his brawny arms and shoulders rippled in the sunlight as he tackled the limo driver from behind, sending the unsuspecting man to the pavement.

Startled, the two young women stepped away. The blond screamed. Immediately, the second man, who wore a light-weight checkered shirt with the sleeves torn off at the shoulder, was on the Asian woman, his massive hands gripping her arm and shoulder. He pulled at her, but she resisted, screaming as she planted her feet and struggled to get away. She managed to land a hand on his head, trying to get a fist full of hair, but he wore it very short, military style, and there was nothing to grab.

As she pulled her hand away she dragged her nails across the side of his face. He back-handed her viciously, and a trickle of blood appeared at the corner of her mouth.

Peter was already moving toward the commotion. He grabbed a wine bottle from a neighboring table without breaking stride. The blond was now on Checkered Shirt, pummeling him with her balled fists, but to no avail. He swung a right hook at the blond, connecting with her chin and sending her tumbling to the ground—out cold.

Diesel launched after Peter, but came up short on his leash, still secured to the table. The table tilted and then crashed to the sidewalk, becoming wedged against a tree as Diesel pulled to protect Peter. He barked and growled in protest, the leash taut and his collar constricting around his thick neck.

Todd squared off with Ponytail, who had completed a rapid series of punches that left the limo driver unconscious. Todd took the first swing, a solid jab to his chin. His head rocked back, but otherwise he was unfazed. Todd punched again—a hard right fist to his nose. The blow drew blood, but Ponytail shook it off, and then unleashed a torrent of blows on Todd.

Peter ran up behind Checkered Shirt and swung drown hard with the nearly-empty wine bottle. The green glass slammed against his head, breaking around the middle of the bottle. He staggered for two heartbeats and then loosened his grip on the Asian woman. He fell first to his knees, then toppled to the side.

Peter wasn't sure if he'd killed him or not, although he knew the former was certainly a possibility.

"Are you alright?" he asked the woman. She was shaking, her arms wrapped around her chest and her eyes moist with tears. "Are you hurt?" Peter repeated. She shook her head no.

Peter turned to his friend, who appeared to have become a punching bag for Ponytail. Todd was bleeding from a cut above his left eye and from a split lip. His arms were tucked in to protect his body and face as much as possible; he was fighting a losing battle. As Peter looked on, Ponytail leaned back and extended his leg in a powerful kick that connected with Todd's leg. He fell to the side.

Still holding the bottle by the neck, a razor-sharp, jagged edge where the bottom should have been, Peter ran forward. Ponytail held Todd down and reared back with his right arm, ready to slam a massive fist into Todd's face for a killing blow.

Peter lunged forward with the broken bottle at the same time Ponytail accelerated his fist toward Todd. But the pummeling blow never arrived. The ragged edge of glass connected with his meaty forearm. The combination of Peter thrusting the bottle forward while Ponytail swung his arm toward Todd, ended in a gruesome spectacle as the razor-sharp glass peeled away nine inches of muscle and flesh from his wrist to his elbow, and all the way down to the bone.

Ponytail screamed in agony and retracted his arm, blood spurting from the hideous wound. He pulled away, wrapping his left hand on the wound in a vain attempt to staunch the flow of blood. Without pause, Peter swung the broken bottle, aiming for Ponytail's face. Upon contact, the remainder of the wine bottle exploded into a hundred fragments, some embedded in his face. Peter placed both hands behind the stunned man's head and pulled his face downward while raising his knee forcefully. The collision of knee into nose did the job, and Ponytail also went down like his partner.

By now the blond had come to and was sitting with one hand to the back of her head while her Asian friend held her other hand. A crowd had gathered and cell phones were out, no doubt filming the conflict. Peter hoped someone had called the police.

"Are you okay?" he asked Todd, extending a hand to help his friend to his feet.

"I'll live," Todd answered. He moved his jaw from side to side. Convinced it wasn't broken, he asked, "What about these guys?"

"I don't know about those two," Peter indicated Checkered Shirt and the limo driver, "but Ponytail is bleeding badly."

Sirens screamed, but they were still distant. "I hope that's not only the police," Peter said. Then he grabbed several linen napkins from a table. "Someone call an ambulance! We need medical help!"

A murmur worked through the crowd of gawkers. Diesel's barking had subdued to a whimper, and the growling had also ceased once the two assailants were incapacitated. Peter wrapped a couple napkins around Ponytail's ravaged forearm, and then used two more to tie it off. It wouldn't due for long; blood was already soaking through the bandage.

"Check for a pulse on the other guy," Peter said, nodding his head toward Checkered Shirt. "I'll check the limo driver."

Todd leaned down and pressed his finger against the man's neck. "He's alive."

The sirens were much louder now.

"Same here," Peter said. The driver was a stocky man. Peter estimated his weight at 240 pounds. He was older than his two women passengers, maybe late 30s or early 40s. He was wearing a light tan suit, and the jacket wasn't buttoned, revealing a handgun secured in a shoulder holster. "Looks like this guy's also a bodyguard. He's packing."

The Asian woman had approached Peter. She said, "Yes, he's my driver. He's also here to protect me. His name is Robert."

Two police cruisers came to a stop, lights flashing. The officers approached with service weapons drawn. Moments later the first of several ambulances arrived.

"Hands on your head! On the ground!" the officers commanded with guns pointed toward Peter and Todd.

They did as ordered. "They're alive," Peter said, the side of his face on the asphalt. "But that one is bleeding badly. The man in the suit has a pistol in a shoulder holster."

The medics rushed to Pony Tail and got to work. One medic started an IV while another replaced the make-shift dressing on his arm.

A second ambulance arrived and medics began to administer aid to the other two unconscious men.

"They assaulted the limo driver—he's the suit—and the two women," Peter tried to explain. A third officer had appeared and was questioning the Asian woman and her blond friend.

"He's telling the truth!" the Asian woman shouted.

After being searched for weapons and having their ID checked, Peter and Todd were each placed in the back of separate cruisers while the patrol officers questioned the witnesses. "That's my dog over there," Peter told one of the officers. "He's leashed and follows my commands."

The officer nodded. "I'll keep an eye on him. He looks calm now, and we should be done once we get a little more information."

Diesel sat quietly, but never took his eyes off his master. After about thirty minutes, Peter and Todd were told they could leave. "If we have further questions, someone from the department will get a hold of you," the officer informed them.

The EMTs transported all three men to St. Charles hospital. Robert, the driver and bodyguard, was the first to regain consciousness. At first he refused further treatment, but the EMTs explained the importance of a complete and thorough examination for head trauma by the emergency room physicians.

"Robert, you should follow their instructions," the Asian woman told him. He relented and was loaded on a gurney into the ambulance. The other two remained under armed-police supervision while being treated and transported to the hospital.

"I'm Jade," the Asian woman said, extending her hand to Peter. "And this is my friend Amanda. Thank you for saving us." She spoke with a hint of a British accent.

"Do you know those men?" Peter asked.

Jade shook her head. "I've never seen them before."

"Well, they seemed to know you. Any idea why they'd want to kidnap you?"

Jade stared back in silence. Her straight, raven hair extended to the middle of her back. With eyes the color of black coffee, full lips, and a rounded nose, her facial features looked more consistent with Malaysian or Indonesian heritage.

"Do you live here?" Peter asked. The police had the street closed and were still busy taking photos and measurements. They sat at one of the tables, waiting for the investigation to conclude.

"No. We are just visiting. Robert was going to drive us to Portland; we were planning to spend the night there." Jade went on to explain that she and Amanda were students, attending Stanford during the school year. They were presently enjoying a vacation traveling through the Pacific Northwest.

"I don't know what to do with the Rolls," she said. "I don't have a driver's license."

"Just a few blocks away is the Oxford Hotel, and they have valet service. We can see if they have a vacancy, if you like."

Jade smiled, and was typing into her cell phone, but Amanda found it first. She dialed the number and booked a room.

"I'd be happy to drive your car over to the hotel once the police open the street."

"Oh, thank you," she said. "I didn't get your name?"

"Peter. Peter Savage. And this is my friend, Todd Steed."

Amanda said, "I hate to think what would have happened if you didn't help."

"I don't know how I can thank you," Jade added.

"Not necessary," Todd answered.

Jade smiled at the dog standing next to Peter. "Is this your dog?"

Peter nodded. "His name is Diesel." Jade and Amanda both reached down and rubbed the big, blocky head of the red pit bull. He closed his eyes and raised his nose to the attention. "He's so cute! But what happened to his ear?" The canine's left ear was half gone.

"Long story," Peter answered. "He saved my life. Up in the mountains," he nodded his head toward the west, toward the Cascade Mountains.

Jade's eyes widened. "Oh! A bear attacked you?"

"Well, it was big, furry, and black." Peter didn't want to elaborate on the deadly contest that had taken place near the Tam MacArthur Rim.

"Oh my! The bear bit off Diesel's ear!" Clearly Jade was fine with filling in the gaps using a bit of her own imagination.

A uniformed officer approached and thankfully interrupted the conversation. She told Jade that they had finished and she needed to move her limousine. "I've got it," Peter said. The officer glanced at Jade, who nodded approval, and then gave the ignition keys to Peter.

"Never ridden in a Rolls before," Todd said. "Mind if I come along?"

With Peter behind the wheel, Todd took the front seat and Jade and Amanda sat in back with Diesel in the middle. The Rolls Royce Phantom was long, offering a roomy back seat. The interior was upholstered in luxurious leather and exotic wood veneer door panels matched the wood on the dash.

The drive was only a few blocks, and Peter deftly navigated the car to a stop in front of the Oxford hotel. An attendant was immediately opening the rear door and Jade stepped out, followed by Amanda.

Peter gave the valet ticket to Jade and then walked the women into the hotel lobby. With Diesel healing obediently on leash, Peter and Todd hung back in the lobby, making sure they checked in without any problems.

Jade walked up to Peter and extended her hand again. "Thank you. In the morning I want to visit Robert at the hospital. But afterward, would you accept my invitation to lunch? It's the least I can do for both of you."

"I'll have to pass," Todd said, shaking Jade's hand. "I have some drawings to finish in the morning and then an important conference call."

"Why don't you call me after you visit your driver?" Peter gave Jade his business card.

Jade's smile engulfed her face causing her dark auburn eyes to sparkle. "Okay, Peter. I'll take that as a yes."

CHAPTER 3

JADE ARRIVED AT THE HOSPITAL EARLY and helped Robert check out. Following a CT scan and overnight observation, the attending physician thankfully concluded there was no indication of a concussion, notwithstanding the large bruise and associated lump on his forehead.

A few minutes before noon, the silver and black Phantom pulled into a visitor parking spot in front of EJ Enterprises. Jade signed in at the front desk. The receptionist, a middle-aged woman named Nancy, paged Peter and he met his guest in the lobby.

"Hello. You're looking well today," he said. He offered his hand and Jade accepted it, wrapping her left hand around the clasp. Peter felt his neck warm as he slipped his hand back.

"Thank you. I must confess it was a restless night. I should have been exhausted, but I just couldn't fall asleep."

"How about Amanda and Robert?" Peter asked.

"Amanda is fine. She has a small bump on her head, and

I helped her stay awake until late in the evening. That's what the EMTs asked me to do, just to be sure she was okay. I let her sleep in while I went to the hospital. The doctors said Robert is also fine, and he was released this morning. He drove me here."

Peter craned his neck and saw the Rolls parked out front. "Todd is still tied up with business, so it's just the two of us for lunch. When you phoned from the hospital, I took the liberty of making a reservation. The restaurant is not far away—just a five-minute walk, if you don't mind."

"Of course not. It's so beautiful here."

Peter held the door open as Jade walked out, and he cast a quick glance back at Nancy. She had a sly grin and Peter shook his head and mouthed the word "no." That only caused her to giggle.

Robert stepped out of the Rolls and approached Peter and Jade. "Thank you for your help yesterday. Those guys got the jump on me."

"Don't mention it. I'm Peter."

"Robert Schneider," he replied as they shook hands. Then, turning to Jade, he said, "I'll stay nearby. Not expecting any trouble, but just in case."

"Okay," she said. As they walked, Robert a few steps behind, she looped her arm around Peter's. He glanced at her, but she remained looking forward, her expression a slight grin. Although Peter felt uncomfortable—not only because of their age difference, about two decades he estimated—he elected not to push her arm away.

The blue sky and warm weather was very inviting, and it looked like everyone had the same idea of getting away from work for lunch. The lucky ones were already occupying sidewalk tables under brightly colored umbrellas.

"The restaurant is just ahead. I reserved an outdoor table, close to the river." Peter waved his hand to the right indicating a large expanse of green, manicured lawn and beyond that, the blue waters of the Deschutes River. A half dozen people were standing on paddleboards moving in rhythmic strides up and down the lazy river.

"Oh, that's gorgeous!" Jade exclaimed.

"Come on, I'll show you." Peter led his new friend to a wooden pedestrian bridge crossing the river. He stopped in the center of the 100-foot span and pointed out the ducks and geese floating amongst the paddle boarders. "This part of Central Oregon was explored by French fur trappers, and they named this river Deschutes. It means rapids or falls."

Jade was drinking in the natural beauty, her head slowly turning from side to side as she leaned on the weathered wooden railing. "This is so different from my home. I mean, you have mountains, and rivers, and so much open land with wild animals!"

Peter chuckled at her unbridled enthusiasm. "Well, I wouldn't consider the ducks and geese wild animals. They're pretty tame."

After a few more minutes admiring the river and local waterfowl, Peter said, "We should get our table before it's given away to another party. It's just ahead," he pointed and encouraged Jade to walk with him. A wide walkway made from cobblestone-like pavers joined the wooden footbridge to the restaurant courtyard.

Sitting in the shade of a large red and white outdoor umbrella, Peter and Jade ordered iced tea.

"Are you ready to order lunch?" the waitress asked.

Jade leaned forward eagerly. "I'll have a salad, please, with bay shrimp."

"Make that two," Peter rejoined. He glanced to the side and saw that Robert had shouldered his way to a stool at the outdoor bar. Still wearing dark sunglasses, he turned his back to the bar so he could covertly keep an eye on Jade.

Many minutes passed in silence, and Peter was beginning to feel awkward. "You are so quiet," Jade finally said.

"Am I? I was just thinking that you are a mysterious woman."

"Oh really?" she said, and raised her eyebrows in mock surprise.

"Yes, really. I've never had lunch with anyone who had a personal bodyguard."

She frowned. "Let me tell you, it's not all that great."

"So where is home? I mean, when you're not attending classes at Stanford."

Just then their salads arrived and Jade took a bite before answering. "A tiny country in Southeast Asia. You may have heard of it: Brunei."

Now it was Peter's turn to be surprised. "Yes, I have, as a matter of fact. A tiny nation indeed. Ruled by the Sultan, who is very rich." He wondered if Jade was related to the royal family, but decided not to ask.

"Actually, my country is the fifth richest country in the world, and with a fairly small population, that means we enjoy a high gross domestic product per capita."

Peter raised his eyebrows. Jade said, "I'm an economics major," and she smiled. "My mother works in shipping. She's in charge of logistics at Hua Ho Holdings. It's a joint venture between a major Chinese container-shipping company named Sino Global and Brunei Royal Petroleum Company."

"And your father?" Peter asked.

"He died… when I was a little girl."

"I'm sorry." Peter's eyes turned to the Cascade Mountains not far to the west, and for a moment his mind conjured images of Maggie, his late wife. He still felt the pain of loss—it didn't seem to diminish with time.

"It's okay," Jade said matter-of-factly, refocusing Peter's attention. "I never really knew him."

"Do you have other family in Brunei?"

"Why are you so curious about my family?" Jade paused. "Okay. I don't have any brothers or sisters, but I have a lot of cousins. My mother—her name is Lim Eu-meh—thought I should attend university in America. She says that with a degree in business and economics, I could work at her company."

"Her name sounds Chinese."

"Yes. Are you surprised?"

"No." Peter knew that many Chinese had settled in Southeast Asia. "So, let me see if I have this correct. Following the Chinese custom, her first name would be Eu-meh?"

Jade smiled. "Yes, very good. The family name is given first. You know something of Chinese culture and customs?"

"A little." He paused for a moment, and then added, "Eu-meh sounds like a very wise lady."

The talk continued between bites of salad. Jade described her homeland, how it was always warm and humid. She talked about the mix of Malay, Chinese, Indonesian, and British cultures and people. Brunei was very much a melting pot.

The small talk was interrupted by the ringing of Jade's phone. She dug into her small handbag.

"Hello?"

She looked at Peter and handed the phone to him. "It's for you."

Peter pinched his eyebrows and cocked his head. "I don't understand..."

Jade pushed the phone to him.

"Hello, this is Peter."

"Ah, Dr. Savage. My name is George McIntire. I'm the Customer Service Manager for Rolls Royce." The British accent was thick.

Peter laughed. "This is a joke, right? Rolls Royce?"

"Yes, sir. Rolls Royce. The factory at Goodwood, U.K. Quite the contrary, this is not a farce at all. I was asked to call you and arrange for your visit."

Peter was still smiling, figuring this was a pretty good prank. He played along. "And just who asked you to call me? A young lady named Jade?"

"No, sir." The voice betrayed mild confusion. "Her uncle, His Majesty the Sultan of Brunei. He requested that I personally call you to schedule your visit so you can configure your automobile. The Sultan suggests a Wraith, but naturally you may select any model you wish."

"A Wraith. That would be—"

"Our newest model, sir. It *is* rather sporty."

Peter shifted his eyes to Jade. She was nodding as if she was also a party to the conversation.

"So let me get this straight. I'm supposed to fly to… Goodwood, or wherever… and pick out the paint color for my new car."

"Well, Dr. Savage, that is a bit simplified. Every automobile we build is bespoke. The owners have many selections to make and the Sultan suggests that Miss Jade accompany you. She may offer helpful advice, but of course the selections are yours to make."

Peter shifted the phone and nodded to Jade. "He says your uncle is the Sultan."

"Yes, that's right," she nodded.

"And he says you're to accompany me to the factory, where I will pick out the options for my new car." Peter's eyebrows were raised in amusement, still not believing this was more than a good prank.

She nodded enthusiastically.

Peter spoke into the phone again. "Okay, George. My

schedule is rather full this afternoon, so how about we hop on the Sultan's jumbo jet and fly across the pond tomorrow morning."

"Well sir, I'm sorry to disappoint, but the Sultan's 747 is being fitted with a new interior. However, I'm told the A340 is available; the engine overhaul was completed only yesterday. I should imagine the aircraft can pick you up tomorrow, before noon. You're on the west coast of the States?"

"Yes, close enough anyway. Hey, isn't it evening in the U.K. now?" Peter thought he had the prankster trapped.

"Yes, sir, shortly after eight in the evening. May I have my assistant call you directly after we confirm the travel schedule?"

Peter was still scrutinizing Jade's expression and only saw satisfaction and pleasure, perhaps mixed with a bit of excitement.

"You're not kidding, are you George?" Peter said it as much to Jade as the voice on the phone.

"I beg your pardon, sir. I would never joke about these matters. The Sultan is a very good client."

Peter relayed his cell number and ended the call. He was completely flabbergasted. He handed the phone back to Jade. She took it as if this was as normal a conversation as friends agreeing to go to the movies.

"So, if your uncle is the Sultan of Brunei, that would make your mother his sister."

"Yes, that's right."

"And what is your mother's position at Hua Ho Holdings?"

Jade shrugged. "She's in management like I said, an executive with the company. Why?"

"Young lady, you could have told me all this earlier."

"Oh, but that would have ruined the surprise! Besides, I wanted to make sure you were truly the nice man I thought you were and not just someone interested in my family's money."

"That's why you've been flirting with me, to see how I would react?"

Jade just shrugged and cocked her head to the side.

"Now I understand the bodyguard." He glanced to the bar. Robert was ever vigilant.

"So tomorrow we fly to London?" Jade said.

"Well, let me get back to my office and clear my calendar. But…" Peter had a huge grin as the realization finally sunk in. "I think I can make time for this. I would have to bring Diesel. Is that okay? He doesn't do well at a boarding kennel and I don't have time to book a dog sitter." The American Pit Bull Terrier had been rescued from a dog-fighting ring and adopted by Peter through the Humane Society of Central Oregon. Although the visible scars on the dog's face and nose had largely faded, the emotional scars had not. The sounds and smells of any kennel never failed to trigger terror in the dog, causing him to shake and refuse to eat.

Jade smiled. "Diesel is welcome—after all, he saved your life, right? He must be a good dog, and I can tell he's pretty close to you."

"It won't be a problem on the Sultan's jet?"

"Oh, not at all. My uncle has two Rhodesian Ridgebacks, and they often fly to London for the Westminster dog show."

Peter nodded. He was about to step foot into the world of the rich and famous, and everything was new and different.

"This will be fun! But you should allow two full days at the factory. There are so many choices to make."

"It sounds like you've done this before?"

"Of course! My uncle owns more than 600 Rolls Royce automobiles. I think his total collection is close to 7,000 cars. He gave me my first Rolls when I turned eighteen. I picked out everything myself, including the silver and black paint color. It's not too masculine for a woman, is it?" She went on before Peter could answer. "I think it's classy."

Peter was laughing again. "Jade, you are a remarkable young lady. And please tell your uncle thank you. But if we are to travel to the U.K. tomorrow, there are certain things I must get done."

"Yes, you should go, and I'll finish my salad. Besides, I can't think of a lovelier place to sit and enjoy this view of the river and mountains."

Peter rose from the table. "I'll be at work at least until six tonight, but call me later and I'll let you know what our travel schedule is."

"Oh, no need. George knows to make sure I get the schedule, too. I'll meet you at your office in the morning. Robert will drive us to the airport. Be sure to pack for five days."

"I thought you said it would only take two days at the factory?"

She laughed lightly. "Silly man. We can't go to London and not see a couple shows, now can we?"

CHAPTER 4

THE HULKING STEEL MACHINE had an ungainly appearance with its high bow and centrally-positioned trio of towers. The calm seas lapped at the water line, and three bilge pumps discharged a steady stream of water from the side. Orange streaks of rust stained the gray-painted hull, conveying an appearance of neglect. Aft of the towers, many dozen lengths of pipe lay neatly stacked, ready to be lifted into place by the deck-mounted crane, a necessity to extend the drill bit deeper into the seabed.

Opposite of oil tankers, the superstructure of the drilling ship was located close to the bow. From his forward-looking perch seven decks above the water line, the captain controlled the propulsion and navigation of the vessel. In stark contrast to the exterior hull, the bridge was state-of-the-art: packed with modern electronics and comfortably air-conditioned. Bridge windows facing aft afforded a panoramic view of activities on the deck below.

Presently, the ship was making headway at a steady ten knots. Almost illegible due to flaking and peeling paint, the name *Royal Seeker* was displayed in block letters on the stern.

"Maintain course and speed," the Captain ordered. In his early fifties, Captain Rei Jianming was an experienced seaman, having worked first on cargo ships under the employ of Hua Ho Holdings. His neatly trimmed hair was still jet-black, despite the pressures of his duties. He sported a short mustache, brown eyes, and deep wrinkles across his forehead. By faithfully using the well-appointed exercise facilities, one of the many perks afforded the crew, Captain Rei maintained a trim physique even though he worked a relatively sedentary job.

Although the *Royal Seeker* looked like an aging drilling ship, oil exploration and production was not her mission.

Captain Rei examined the folded paper from his pocket again. The message was clear and economical in its use of words. He addressed his First Officer. "Instruct the crew to begin preparations for a second launch. The missile is to be on the pad and ready to fire in thirty-six hours."

"Yes, Captain. It will be done."

The Captain nodded. "I will provide launch instructions later. Let me know when the missile is ready, but do not move it to the pad until I give the order."

More than 9,000 miles to the east, President Taylor was meeting with Secretary of State Paul Bryan, Secretary of Defense Howard Hale, and Director of the National Security Agency, Colleen Walker. The President was pacing in front of the Resolute Desk, his arms folded across his chest, as he listened intently to the report.

Paul Bryan had just finished sharing the cryptic message forwarded from the U.S. Embassy in Tokyo. "That's all there is to it."

"Brief and to the point," Hale commented.

"So, whoever is behind the attack wants a complete withdrawal of U.S. forces from Japan," Taylor said.

"And," Bryan added, "they are also demanding the Pacific Fleet be withdrawn to American ports along the West Coast and Hawaii."

The President stopped at a side table, staring at a bronze replica of the Vietnam Women's Memorial Statue resting on the polished wood surface. He ran his hand over the cool metal, reverently touching the figure of the wounded soldier receiving critical aid from a nurse while a second nurse looked upward to an imaginary approaching helicopter. Finally, he said, "It would take months to execute a redeployment of that magnitude."

"Sir!" Hale objected, sliding forward in his seat. "We can't remove our military from the region. In the ensuing power vacuum, the entire Asia-Pacific region would be thrust into turmoil."

"Relax, Howard. I'm not agreeing to anything." He turned to face his team. "No idea who left the message?"

"No, sir," Bryan said. "It was found by the night cleaning crew taped to the mirror in the men's room."

"Okay. So what are we dealing with?" The President addressed this question to his intelligence and defense advisors.

"Our information is still very preliminary," Colleen said. "And we don't have any physical evidence yet. It could take months before we are able to have heavy salvage ships on site to raise sections of the *Izumo*. Maybe weeks just to explore the wreck with robotic submersibles. Even then, there's no guarantee we'll be able to retrieve any useful evidence given the depth and the effects of prolonged exposure to seawater."

"How deep is the wreck?" Taylor asked.

"Based on the location of the *Izumo* at the time she was sunk, we estimate the debris to be under 3,000 feet of water, plus or minus."

"Why the uncertainty?"

"Because debris can be scattered widely as a result of the forward momentum of the ship and the irregular hydrodynamics of the major sections. Eyewitnesses report she broke in two as she sank. Sonar data from the *Tucson* is consistent with major hull failure."

"So the two halves of the ship could have settled far from each other."

"Yes, sir. That's assuming there are only two major sections. It's possible, maybe even likely, that further structural failure occurred in the weakened sections, resulting in other large sections of the ship breaking off."

President Taylor frowned and shifted his gaze to Secretary Hale, sitting at the opposite end of a Chippendale sofa from Colleen Walker. "Howard, how soon can you have an exploration vessel onsite?"

Howard Hale had served the President throughout his first term and was widely expected to remain Secretary of Defense until the end of Taylor's second term. A slim man, his sandy-brown hair and blue eyes contributed to his appearance of youth, even though he was in his early sixties.

"Fortunately, the *Pioneer*, an Avenger-class Navy minesweeper, was in port at the White Beach Naval Facility in Okinawa. She's equipped with a CURV-21 ROV—it's the largest and most capable ROV the Navy has and well suited to underwater exploration and limited salvage operations. With the *Pioneer's* towed side-scan sonar we'll get a detailed map of the sea floor in order to locate and map the wreckage, then the ROV will investigate. We'll get high-res video, and the pincher arm can even grab samples for further analysis. Admiral Baxter has ordered the ship to put to sea and she's en route now—should be on station within a day. Still, as Colleen has already explained, it could take some time just to locate the debris field."

"I understand. Any concern of interference from other navies?"

"You mean the Chinese? No, sir. The wreck is in international waters. Plus we have the other Japanese and U.S. task force ships from the exercise remaining on station. Captain Wallace of the *Shiloh* has overall command authority. The area is secure."

"What about air power?" Taylor asked.

"Kadena Air Base is nearby, also on Okinawa. The Eighteenth Wing is based there and can launch F-15s at any time, backed up with tankers. Plus we have an E-3 Sentry over the site 24/7 for long range surveillance. If necessary, the Sentry would also coordinate defensive and offensive air combat."

The President nodded his approval. "You'll let me know if we should move a carrier group into the vicinity."

"Of course, sir. But at this time the Joint Chiefs do not feel that is a necessary redeployment. And I concur."

"Okay, so the next question, then, is who did this. Paul?"

The Secretary of State was Taylor's most trusted advisor. Short and rotund, Paul Bryan was a brilliant statesman who had guided the administration through many trying times.

Bryan cleared his throat. "No party has claimed responsibility. It is very odd. Logic dictates that it must be a government that carried out the attack, since no terrorist groups have access to ballistic missiles."

"Is that true, Colleen?" Taylor asked.

"Yes, sir. The best that any known terrorist group can field are shoulder-fired heat seekers. But those are short range weapons—maybe five miles or so—usually used against aircraft."

The President had resumed pacing and swirled his index finger in the air, a habit when he was trying to recall an important fact. "What about those Russian long-range anti-aircraft missile batteries that were used in Ukraine. I recall the militia used one to down a Malaysian airliner. Could some terrorist group—maybe one we've haven't heard of yet—have gotten hold of a ballistic missile? Maybe from Russia?"

Colleen and Paul Bryan exchanged a glance before she replied. "We've considered that possibility, sir. But it just doesn't hold water. First, the radar tracking from the *Shiloh* indicates the missile was fired, most likely, from the South China Sea. The trajectory indicates this was a medium range weapon system. That's a big candle, sir, and it takes a well-trained crew and sophisticated facilities to carry out a launch."

Bryan said, "Taken as a whole, the possibility that a terrorist group could have executed this attack is so remote as to border on the impossible."

"That leaves governments, then," Taylor said. "I can think of several regional states that don't care for Japan, for one reason or another."

"That's assuming Japan was the intended target." Bryan raised an eyebrow, causing Taylor to pause in contemplation.

"Okay. And you're suggesting that maybe we were the intended target, and they—whoever 'they' is—simply missed?"

"Why not? It's a valid possibility. I think it is important to be precise in our choice of wording and avoid interjecting assumptions into this discussion unless it is clearly understood what the assumptions are."

"Very well. Please, continue."

"Japan and the U.S. were engaged in joint naval exercises. And since we are close allies, I suggest we look at all regional governments who have a dislike for the U.S. and Japan, as suspect."

"That puts China at the top of the list," Hale said. "Or North Korea."

Colleen and Paul Bryan nodded agreement.

"The trouble is that we have nothing linking China, North Korea, or any other country to the attack. I have personally called ambassadors from the countries ringing the South China Sea, and none have betrayed even a hint of prior knowledge—not that I expected them to."

"Very well, keep at it. Colleen, be sure to pass along any relevant intelligence—and I mean any."

"Understood, sir. We're working on it, top priority. I've also reached out to the intelligence agencies of our allies. So far, nothing."

Taylor took his leather chair and leaned forward, placing his elbows on the historic wooden desk and rubbed his temples. "Okay then. On to the final question. What type of weapon did this?"

Howard Hale leaned forward as he answered, "Based on the eyewitness reports and radar tracking data, we know it was a ballistic missile. But the terminal velocity exceeded anything we know of. It actually accelerated just prior to impact, perhaps to avoid our SM3s—"

"Our ships tried to shoot it down?"

"Yes, sir. High-velocity guided missiles designed to take down ballistic missiles and anti-ship missiles."

The President nodded, and Hale continued, "Like any object falling from the sky, a warhead will enter the Earth's atmosphere at high velocity and then either maintain that speed or slow somewhat due to friction with the air. But this warhead accelerated to phenomenal velocity—probably by a rocket motor of some kind—reaching Mach 15 just before it struck the *Izumo*."

Colleen said, "And it was still accelerating, sir, when it struck the Japanese destroyer. Best guess is that the warhead was a kinetic penetrator, not an explosive payload. It would have passed through the ship in less than six milliseconds."

"I'm not following," Taylor said.

"Think of it this way, sir," Colleen explained. "A kinetic penetrator is like a giant, hyper-velocity bullet."

"The warhead that sunk the *Izumo* struck her at more than 18,000 feet per second. To put that in perspective, a rifle bullet leaves the muzzle at less than 3,000 feet per second."

"But still, that was a modern steel warship. How could this, this... penetrator... cause such extensive destruction?"

Colleen held the President's gaze. "Our analysts suggest it is made of an extremely hard alloy, much harder than steel, and very dense. They calculate that if the warhead is only ten inches in diameter and three feet long, at this speed it would have the equivalent energy of nearly three tons of TNT. And all that energy would be focused upon a ten-inch circle as the warhead passed through the ship. Anything in the direct path would be vaporized. Extending out from the direct path of the warhead, metal would melt—steel decks and bulkheads would offer no more resistance than plywood. The shock wave would shatter structural plates and rip electrical conduit and fuel lines just as if it were a high explosive detonating within the ship."

Hale said, "The extremely small size of the warhead combined with its super-dense construction means this thing is virtually immune to our anti-missile weapons. A proximity explosion and shrapnel can't destroy it. And getting a direct hit with an SM3 on the kinetic warhead is very low probability, especially given the hyper-velocity of the attacking kinetic penetrator."

"And if *our* assets are targeted next time?"

Hale drew in a breath and exhaled before offering his answer. "We have no defense."

"My God..." Taylor replied.

CHAPTER 5

THE *ROYAL SEEKER* WAS MAKING MINIMUM headway at about six degrees north latitude and roughly 115 degrees east longitude. It was just after 1:00 a.m. and Captain Rei would have preferred to be sound asleep in his cabin. Instead, he busied himself overseeing the project. He consulted the radar display again. There were no green blips, no reflections. Within a radius of sixteen nautical miles, they were alone.

The captain exited the dimly lit bridge and stepped out onto the port wing. The air was cool and humid. Looking up, thousands of stars stood brightly against the blackness of space. He shifted his attention below, to the business at hand.

Below on the central deck, the Hwasong-12 missile body, payload absent, was already erected in the midst of the three towers. The second stage, employing a modified solid-propellant motor, was still lying horizontal on the deck. Workers were attaching a lifting cable to hoist it into place.

The three towers normally supported long sections of pipe for drilling into the seabed in search of oil. Now, the interlocked grid work of steel provided ample access to the rocket as it was being erected and the multiple stages assembled. Up close, one could see that portions of each tower were scorched from intense heat, the type of short-lived heat from a rocket plume.

The cylindrical missile body, about five feet in diameter, was barely visible through the crisscrossing steel girders and beams. *An effective camouflage*, Rei thought. Diffuse lights provided minimal, but adequate, illumination for the workers. The sleek missile was painted the same shade of green as the towers, and devoid of markings that would indicate nationality or manufacture.

The First Officer approached Captain Rei. He was taller than his captain, muscular, and twenty years younger. He spoke with confidence and strength. "Soon the second stage will be installed. I estimate that the warhead will be in place within twelve hours."

The captain didn't respond, his gazed fixed on the activity below.

"Captain. The first-stage fueling process is underway. What are your launch orders?"

After a long pause, Rei turned. "I will inform you at the proper time. Just keep the technicians on schedule."

"Forgive me, Captain, but sunrise is only a few hours away. The sky will be clear, and we could be detected by aircraft or satellite imagery. The towers provide camouflage, but that is no guarantee that the missile will remain hidden."

Rei nodded, and then resumed watching the swarm of technicians and engineers busily at work. The First Officer turned to leave.

"Chang," the captain said, "you must trust me. Our mission is of historic proportions, but we have a difficult and dangerous journey ahead. When we succeed—and we will—China will emerge as the dominant global power, and those who have attempted to conquer and enslave our people will become nothing more than dogs who lay at our feet."

Within an air-conditioned and dark control room, a Navy technician was skillfully driving the CURV-21 ROV over the suspected debris field. Only a few hours ago, the side-scan sonar had detected the first elements of wreckage. Within ninety minutes, the entire field was mapped. The most noteworthy features were two large reflections, initially interpreted as the fore and aft sections of the *Izumo*.

After descending 2,773 feet, the ROV—or remotely operated vehicle—was hovering only a few dozen feet above the silty sea floor. Trailing behind the unmanned submersible was the umbilical line, a collection of steel cable, electrical power, and fiber-optic communication conduit.

Powerful lights provided illumination, piercing the blackness. The operator turned the machine slowly 360 degrees, taking in the immediate area, while multiple monitors around the control room displayed the high-definition, black-and-white video. As the light beam traversed the depths, a shark-like creature suddenly darted across the field of view. But otherwise, there was nothing noteworthy to see.

Captain Stoddard stood behind the technician, his arms folded, watching intently. Before the ROV operator were two screens: One displayed the video feed from the submersible and the other was the sonar map of the debris field. Superimposed on the map was an arrow point. This was the location of the robotic craft.

"Start with the largest piece of the wreck. Let's take a closer look," Stoddard instructed the technician.

He moved a joystick and the CURV-21 picked up speed and cruised forward. After many long seconds, most of the superstructure and the bow section of the Japanese warship appeared—first as a dim, ghostly image. Quickly it took shape as the distance decreased and the remains fell under the intense lights.

"It's resting upright, on her keel," the technician observed. "We're lucky—the decks didn't pancake—so we should be able to explore the inner structure. I'll move the ROV closer toward the aft where the ship fractured in half."

Stoddard nodded and watched as the video panned alongside the hull. Suddenly, the smooth lines were abruptly halted by a jagged line of bent and torn steel, cables, and pipes. Maintaining a safe distance to avoid entangling the umbilical cable, the ROV traversed to the gapping maw and pointed toward what was once the interior of the *Izumo*.

"Start on the top deck," Stoddard ordered. "Let's see where the warhead struck the vessel first. Then work your way down toward the keel."

"Looks like the keel is buried in silt, sir."

"Nothing we can do about that now."

"Yes, sir." The submersible moved in and soon was amongst the steel remains projecting from the fractured hull. He zoomed in the video to get a clearer image of the top deck and successively lower decks as the ROV descended toward the sea floor. The deck plates were buckled downward and rent by a tremendous force.

"I don't see any significant impact holes from shrapnel," the operator said. "If there had been an explosion, we'd see evidence of the blast sending substantial fragments through bulkheads and deck plates. That's totally absent."

"Hold your position and zoom out. I want a perspective across the beam from port to starboard."

On the monitor they could see the extent of the damage. The path of the warhead was marked by downward-bent deck plates. In comparison to the beam of the ship, it appeared direct damage followed a vertical channel about forty to fifty feet across in some areas deep into the hull. Stoddard let out a low whistle.

"I've never before seen any damage quite like that, have you?"

"No, sir," replied the technician.

"See if you can maneuver in without entangling the umbilical. Get me several samples. Later we can have them tested for explosive residue."

The technician deftly propelled the ROV in closer and then engaged the manipulator arm. At the end of the arm was a sophisticated titanium pincer. He eyed a piece of metal that appeared to be mostly fractured from an inner deck plate. It was several inches wide and a little over a foot in length but held in place by only an inch or so of steel. He locked down with the mechanical hand and then reversed the thrusters. The craft backed away a foot and then stopped. The sliver of steel was still holding fast.

"I'll see if I can work it loose," he said. "It's already mostly broken away." He moved the manipulator arm up and then down. Through the video feed they watched as the sliver of steel moved back and forth. He repeated the process several times; each time the sample moved farther. Then he gunned the thrusters in reverse and the robotic craft shot backwards. With a jerk, the sample broke free. The technician moved the arm and released the specimen into a basket at the front of the ROV. The open-top basket was designed for heavy specimens such as rock and metal. Then he moved on to another location.

This time, it was a piece of conduit, electrical cables fanned out from the conduit like spaghetti. He locked the titanium pincer on the conduit and then engaged a second arm fitted with a guillotine-like cutter.

"Hopefully, the cutter will slice through this tube," he said as he worked another joystick equipped with a spring-loaded grip. When he squeezed the grip the tool snipped off a section, including electrical cables. He repeated the process several more times and after nearly an hour had collected five samples from various decks within the shattered hull.

"Let's move on to the stern," Stoddard ordered.

The CURV-21 turned and propelled to the second main section of the *Izumo*, only a few hundred yards away. It was laying at a right angle to the bow section, and was resting right side up, but tilted about thirty degrees to port.

The operator moved the submersible in so they could get detailed video of the deck surface. Immediately, he understood the importance of the images, and he stopped the ROV, hovering it in place. "See, the deck is buckled downward." He was pointing at part of the video image. If the warhead had been high explosive, the force of the explosion below deck would have pushed these plates out and upward."

Stoddard leaned in closer. "You're assuming detonation was below deck. But what if the fuze was defective and the warhead detonated on contact with the deck?"

The operator was shaking his head. "No, sir. That scenario doesn't fit the evidence. Had that been the case, the radius of destruction would have been significantly greater at deck level. But we don't see that. In fact, it looks to me that the warhead passed entirely through the *Izumo*, leaving a roughly cylindrical channel of primary devastation. If anything, I'd estimate the radius of primary destruction might be slightly larger about halfway through the vessel."

"Like a bullet passing through a target..." Stoddard muttered.

"Sorry, sir?"

"Nothing. Gather samples like you did from the bow section. Half a dozen should do it. Then bring the ROV up topside so we can get your treasures off for analysis. If it was an explosive warhead, there should be trace residues."

"Aye, sir."

CHAPTER 6

THE LUXURIOUS ACCOMMODATIONS onboard the Sultan's private jet were beyond anything Peter could imagine. Totally absent were the rows of seats found on commercial passenger planes. Instead, the cabin was divided into large rooms that one might expect to find in a luxury home or hotel suite. The cabin door opened onto an entry that connected to the sitting room, furnished with chairs and a large sofa, all upholstered in ivory leather and well padded. The paneling was maple, the floor covered in teal carpet, and a large flat screen with the latest electronics was centrally featured on the bulkhead.

Farther aft was the dining room, and the centerpiece was a polished cherry table that could seat twelve. Beyond the dining room were three bedroom suites.

Somewhere over the North Atlantic between the southern tip of Greenland and Ireland, Peter wandered to the bar located at the front of the cabin. The bartender, in his late twenties and neatly groomed, looked expectantly to Peter. "What is your preference?" he asked with a decidedly British accent.

"How is your selection of single malt Scotch?"

"Quite extensive. May I suggest the 18-year-old Talisker?"

Peter scrunched his nose. "A bit too peaty for my taste. Do you have Oban?"

"Certainly. We have the 2001 Distiller's Edition, but if you'd like to have an extraordinary Scotch, I'd recommend the Oban Bicentenary."

"Sounds interesting."

"It's quite remarkable, really. Aged sixteen years in sherry casks. Quite rare, but we managed to obtain several bottles."

"Well, you sold me. I'll give it a try. Neat, no ice."

As the bartender was pouring, Robert stepped in next to Peter. "Club soda, please. No ice," he said.

Peter warmed the glass in the palm of his hand, transferring the warmth to the richly-colored whiskey. He turned and leaned against the bar. "I could get used to flying this way," he said to Robert.

The big man smiled and nodded. His blue eyes, the color of glacial ice, twinkled with amusement.

Peter sipped his Scotch. "Ex-military, I'm guessing."

"It still shows, huh?"

"Short cropped hair is the first clue. But it's mostly the way you carry yourself—confident, disciplined."

"Once it's drilled into a guy, suppose it just can't be untaught," Robert answered. "Navy. Twelve years."

"How did you end up in this job?"

"Long story. The short version is I was in the right place at the right time."

Peter raised his eyebrows. Perhaps another time he would ask for the long version.

"You have an interesting history," Robert said.

"Oh?" Peter took another sip of the Oban Bicentenary,

enjoying the warmth as the whisky went down his throat, and the aftertaste that hinted of sherry, but without any sweetness.

"Ran a background check on you. Standard procedure, of course."

"Of course. And?"

"Graduate of the University of Oregon; reside in Bend, Oregon. Founder and owner of EJ Enterprises. You develop and manufacture unique magnetic impulse pistols. Never had the pleasure of using one myself, but I hear it's a nice piece of hardware."

"Thank you."

"Anyway, you have high-level security clearance with the U.S. government despite the fact that you have never served in the military or intelligence community. You had a run-in with local law enforcement recently. Apparently, they had reason to believe you were responsible for several murders in Bend."

Peter clenched is jaw. "And you want to know if I was. Is that it?"

Unblinking, Robert held Peter's stare. His implied question demanding a response.

"The answer should be self-evident," Peter said. "But if you're uncomfortable with my past, I'll just get on the next flight home."

Robert pinched his eyebrows together. "Okay. I just wanted to hear it from you. Consider it a test."

"Did I pass?"

"Yeah—for now, anyway."

"Remember, I didn't go looking for Jade. I just happened to be there when things got ugly."

Robert gently rubbed his fingers over the bruise on his forehead. It was still painful.

"Wrong place at the wrong time? Is that it?"

Peter nodded. "It seems to be a habit of mine."

"Some guys are like that. I've known a few. They generally don't live long."

"Gee, thanks. Up until now, I was really enjoying this flight."

"It's my job to know who Miss Jade is associating with. I have to be suspicious of everyone. Don't take it personally."

Peter downed the last of his Scotch, then slid the glass across the polished bar.

As he turned to leave, Robert placed a hand on his shoulder. "Hey. Thank you. If you and your friend hadn't intervened the other day, I hate to think of what might have happened."

"Sure," Peter said with a shrug. "It's what I do."

Peter completed the flight in his seat—feet up, headphones on and cat napping. He felt tired, but restful sleep was elusive. His mind kept going back to the encounter in front of the restaurant on Wall Street, when the two thugs attempted to kidnap Jade and Amanda. *What if I hadn't been there?* His thought echoed Robert's question. The possible outcomes were frightening. Although he'd only met Jade a few days ago, he was developing a paternal bond with her. Still innocent and sheltered from the dangers that could appear at any time, Jade reminded him of his own daughter, Joanna—before she had a brush with a homicidal maniac. Fortunately, that encounter had turned out well. *Life is so precarious. One moment everything is fine, and the next moment disaster upends it all.*

The trio—Peter, Jade, and the ever-present Robert—arrived at London City Airport, just east of the city center and taxied to a large, private hangar. It wasn't long before customs officials boarded the aircraft, stamped everyone's passport, and cleared them to debark. Even Diesel was allowed to leave, having avoided quarantine on the basis that he was represented to be one of the Sultan's canines. Robert hung back to make a phone call and hurried down the stairs to meet Jade and Peter. They were engaged in casual conversation while waiting next to the assembled luggage. In short order, a Rolls Royce Phantom drove into the hangar and stopped opposite the trio.

While Robert held the door open, Jade slid across the backseat. The leather upholstery was the color of ripe tangerines, and it was supple and soft, a demonstration of the exquisite legendary quality of the company. The door panels, dash, and center console were finished in polished black walnut burl with highlights of inlaid ebony and Birdseye maple marquetry in a classy geometric pattern.

Peter sat next to Jade, and Robert closed the door with a satisfying and solid thud. Diesel rode shotgun, earning a slight grin from Robert.

"Do you ever travel in anything other than a Rolls?" Peter asked.

Jade laughed. "It's my uncle's. What can I say? He likes the brand."

Peter raised his eyebrows and gently ran a hand across the seat, his eyes darting around the interior, attempting to absorb the meticulous artisanship—and opulence. "Well, I can see why."

Robert was behind the wheel with the engine purring. "To the Ritz, Miss Jade?"

"Yes, Robert." Then she looked at Peter. "I need to take a long nap; I never sleep well on an airplane. But tonight, we should go to the theatre. Have you ever been to a show in London?"

"No, I haven't. It'll be another first for me. No doubt one of many on this trip."

"Robert," she said, "after we check in, please see the concierge for tickets. Whatever is new and popular will be fine."

He nodded as he maneuvered the big car to exit the airport. Soon, Robert had the Rolls motoring on Newham Way and then the A13, headed for the heart of London.

Peter glanced at Jade. She was looking forward, seemingly lost in thought. "I'm curious," he said. "The Sultan's name is Omar Muhammad Shah. Why didn't he keep the family name of Lim?"

"Checking up on my family?" she replied with a smile.

"Maybe—a little bit. It only seems proper I should at least know the name of the man who is giving me a Rolls Royce."

"I see. Well, when he became Sultan, my uncle chose to honor the first Sultan of Brunei by adopting the same name. My mother and my grandmother prefer to use their Chinese family name and given names."

"Your mother—Eu-meh—was she born in Brunei?"

Jade nodded. "My grandmother came to Brunei as a refugee following the end of World War II. She was very beautiful, and one day Sultan Omar Ali Saifuddien happened to see her walking out of a shop in Bandar Seri Begawan—that's the capital city. The Sultan's palace is a few kilometers south of the city, on the banks of the Brunei River. Anyway, he saw my grandmother and instantly fell in love with her."

"Sounds like a fairy tale come true. Are your grandparents still alive?"

"Grandmother is. She lives in the palace and occasionally still advises my uncle."

"Really? She must be very sharp."

"Well, in case you hadn't noticed, the women in my family are quite intelligent and very head-strong. Unfortunately, my country still clings to old customs." Jade frowned.

"Meaning, there is no place in government for women."

"So how much do you know about my home?"

"Not very much. I know Brunei is surrounded by Malaysia and has a coast on the South China Sea. I hope to learn more."

"My country is tiny, although at one time Brunei ruled

much of what is now Malaysia and the Philippines. We have ancient ties to China, both cultural and trading. In 1984, my country won independence from the United Kingdom.

"My uncle, the Sultan, rules over the government. But like Singapore, the influence of British law and system of governance is still evident. For example, we have a Parliament, but we also abide by Sharia law in some instances."

"So I gather that Islam is the predominant religion in Brunei?" Peter asked.

Jade nodded. "Sunni Islam, but we also have Buddhists and Christians. Does that concern you?"

"I have no qualm with Islam. In fact, I believe Islam and Christianity have a great deal in common."

Jade leaned forward, twisting in her seat until she caught Peter's eyes. "Do you believe in the God of Abraham?"

"I do."

Jade waited for elaboration, but Peter declined to speak further.

"You are uncomfortable discussing religion?" she asked.

"Yeah, you could say so. I hold my beliefs private because the last thing this world needs is another person advocating for one religion over others. Too much violence has been justified by religion—too many people have been killed in the name of God."

"A lot of good has been done, too."

"Sure. But I don't support Sharia law. I'm sorry if that offends you."

Jade reached out and touched Peter's hand. "Not to worry. You do not offend me. I know you are a good man."

CHAPTER 7

THE DOORMAN AT THE RITZ PICCADILLY held the rear door of the Phantom open as Jade slid out, followed by Peter. Robert was at the curb and followed Jade into the ornate lobby of the grand and historic hotel. Peter expected one of the hotel staff to object to Diesel, even though he was leashed and healing beside his master. But none did. *Must get a lot of celebrities traveling with their pet dogs.*

Peter leaned toward Jade as they approached the registration desk. "Another favorite of you Uncle?"

She gave Peter a curious look. "Oh, no. He would never stay in a hotel. He usually stays at Buckingham Palace when he visits London."

Peter raised his eyebrows. *Of course.*

The bellman motioned toward the elevator. Jade led the way as they exited on the second floor and entered a wallpapered hall with crystal wall sconces.

"Looks like she knows her way around the hotel," Peter said to Robert.

"She's a regular here, and she always stays in the Prince of Wales Suite."

In three quick strides the bellman passed Jade, reaching the carved mahogany door first. He slid a keycard into the lock and turned the latch, holding the door as his three guests entered. A butler, dressed in a traditional gray suit, was waiting in the entrance hall. "Welcome back, Ms. Lim."

She returned a warm smile.

"Champagne?"

"Yes, thank you." She studied the butler's face only for a moment. "Roger, yes?"

He bowed slightly. "Thank you, ma'am. You remember my name."

They passed through the entrance hall into the spacious living room with Chippendale sofas and armchairs. A large bay window overlooked Green Park below. Jade sat near the fireplace.

"Krug Grande Cuvée," the butler said as he lowered a silver tray holding three flutes. Jade and Peter each took a glass, but Robert passed, preferring to walk through the adjoining dining room and three bedrooms, just to be sure everything was in order.

Peter felt refreshed and energized after walking Diesel through Green Park, followed by a three-hour nap. He had taken position in a generously padded leather armchair, the color of dried tobacco, and was reading that day's edition of *The Times*.

Robert had disappeared to the kitchen, mumbling something about wanting to make sure Roger prepared a hearty breakfast in the morning. The drive to Goodwood in West Sussex would take close to two hours, longer if there was traffic leaving London.

Peter stood as Jade entered the room. She was wearing casual business attire—pressed indigo-died jeans and a silk blouse under a suede vest. Having previously confirmed that the theater did not require coat and tie, Peter was dressed in slacks, a button-down Oxford shirt, and a navy blazer.

Jade had suggested they dine at Myung Ga, a trendy Korean restaurant nearby on Kingly Street. Peter was looking forward to bulgogi—a dish of thinly sliced beef, marinated and grilled on a barbeque. Roger had kindly offered to keep an eye on Diesel—it seemed the canine had made a new friend.

The Rolls was waiting at the curb in front of the main entrance on Arlington Street. After Peter and Jade climbed into the spacious rear seat, Robert started the engine and pulled away from the hotel. It was early evening, and the Rolls merged into a steady stream of traffic when Robert turned right onto Piccadilly. His eyes were alternating between the cars in front and the rearview mirror.

After five minutes, they'd travelled about a half-mile. Robert turned the Phantom left onto Regent Street. He was now devoting more eye time to the traffic behind him than he was to the cars in front. The wrinkles on his forehead seemed more pronounced.

Peter noticed but decided to trust Robert. After all, he was the professional and Peter was merely along for the ride—figuratively and literally. Another five minutes and two more turns, and Robert eased the Phantom to a stop in front of the restaurant.

"I'll keep an eye on the Rolls, Miss Jade."

"Are you sure? You're not hungry?"

"Don't worry, I'll be fine."

"Okay. If you say so. But if you change your mind later, be sure to ask Roger to cook up a late night meal. He's an accomplished chef, you know."

Peter hung back while Jade strode into Myung Ga as if she owned the place. "Something on your mind?" he said to Robert.

"Just doing my job." Robert leaned against the big sedan and crossed his arms.

"Couldn't help but notice you spent a lot of time focused on the rearview mirror. A tail?"

"Maybe. Maybe not. I'll hang out, just to be sure."

"Want me to order something for you?" Peter asked with a grin.

"You worry too much. I'm fine. Now you better hustle inside before Miss Jade gets suspicious."

They sat in a corner of the restaurant far from the entrance, at a table for two. The waiter introduced himself and took their drink order—a bottle of sparkling wine from France.

"Did you notice that look from the waiter?" Peter said. "He probably thinks we're dating."

"Are you embarrassed?" she asked with a sly grin. Clearly, she enjoyed the attention.

"First of all, we're not dating. I'm old enough to be your father."

"Maybe I like older, more mature men?"

"Flirt all you like, this is not a date. I have a daughter about your age."

Peter's protest drew a laugh from Jade. She leaned forward, chin cradled in her hands. "Ever the gentleman. But tell me—you don't have a rule against being friends, do you?"

Peter blushed. "Not at all."

"I'd like to meet your daughter someday. Tell me about her—please."

"Her name is Joanna, but she likes to be called Jo."

"Hmm. I like her already; she has character."

"She's an interior designer. She's always been very fond of drawing and almost everything art related."

The waiter returned with the bottle and presented the label for Peter's scrutiny. Then he untwisted the wire cage, popped the cork, and poured a sample in one of the flutes. Once Peter tasted and approved the selection, the waiter topped off both flutes and placed the bottle in a silver ice bucket.

"Are you ready to order?" he asked.

Peter motioned to Jade, and she expertly relayed her meal preference. Then Peter order the bulgogi.

"Thank you. Let me know if you need anything."

Peter smiled, and returned his attention to Jade.

"Does Jo also live in Bend?" she asked.

"Yes, she does. And we get together often. I also have a son, several years younger than Jo. His name is Ethan, and he's a student at the University of Oregon."

"Does he also like art? Or maybe, he'll follow in his father's footsteps?"

"Too early to say. But there's a place for him at EJ Enterprises if that's the direction he chooses."

Jade's eye widened in sudden realization. "Oh, now I get it. EJ Enterprises is named for your children."

The corner of Peter's mouth widened into a smile. "You are correct, young lady."

Several minutes passed in silence as each enjoyed the sparkling wine. Peter refilled Jade's flute.

She looked into his eyes and hesitated. "You haven't mentioned your wife."

Peter silently stared back, his eyes unfocused and his face devoid of expression.

"I'm sorry. I shouldn't have pried. It's none of my business."

Peter felt a lump in his throat as he tried to swallow, and his eyes moistened. He turned his head as if there was a spot on the far wall of immense interest.

"So," Jade stumbled, searching for a topic to discuss. "Are

you excited about visiting the Rolls Royce factory tomorrow?"

Peter had a far-away gaze when he answered. "She would have liked you."

Jade didn't answer.

"Her name..." Peter cleared his throat. "Her name was Maggie. She'd have thought you were charming, and funny, and smart."

"I'm sure I'd like Maggie, too."

"She died a while ago." Peter forced a smile and looked at Jade. "I'll never get used to saying that. I miss her."

Peter's hands were wrapped around the base of the Champagne flute, and Jade reached out and laid her hand on his. "I'm sorry. I didn't mean to—"

"It okay. You didn't know."

"My mother once told me that our wealth is measured by the love of our family and friends. And that love doesn't end when someone passes, but it continues as long as they live on in our memories and are cherished in our hearts."

"Then, by that measure, I am the richest man in the world."

They sat in silence as Peter drew his mind back to the present, and Jade saw another layer of mystery in this man she'd met only a few days ago. Just as the silence was reaching a point of awkwardness, their dishes arrived. The mixed aroma of spices and a variety of scents was enticing, and signaled the promise of a memorable meal. Jade commented how she had heard rave reviews of the restaurant from Roger, their butler. Peter sized up the bulgogi and concluded the slices of barbequed beef were too large to easily handle with only chopsticks, and he asked the waiter to bring a fork and steak knife to slice the meat into manageable chunks.

As they enjoyed their dishes, Jade steered the conversation to lighter subjects. Peter had many questions about what to expect at the Rolls Royce factory, and Jade was happy to go into exquisite detail about the process of selecting first the model of car, and then the interior and exterior finishes. Listening to Jade, Peter was left with the distinct impression that almost every aspect of the coachwork was customized to the owner's specifications.

After they'd finished the main course, Peter left his fork on the plate and laid his linen napkin on the steak knife. Before the waiter arrived to remove the plates, he slid the folded napkin to his lap.

"Would anyone care for desert?" the waiter asked.

Jade waved away the request, and Peter politely declined.

With raised eyebrows, the waiter asked, "Coffee or espresso?"

"Espresso, please," Jade said.

"Make that two. Thank you."

The espressos arrived in short order, and Jade discussed the theater, shopping, and art galleries while they sipped. When the waiter brought the bill, Peter insisted on paying. "We can arm wrestle if you want to, but I'm confident I'll win. This is the very least I can do," he said.

Peter followed Jade out to the sidewalk and the waiting Rolls. Robert was leaning casually against the wall of the restaurant, watching everyone coming and going. He quickly opened the rear door to allow Jade to climb onto the back seat. Peter paused for a moment and asked in a low voice, "Anything?"

"Nothing confirmed," Robert replied. "All things considered, fairly quiet."

CHAPTER 8

THE OLD STREETS WERE RELATIVELY NARROW for the big luxury car, but Robert was adept at maneuvering around parked vehicles and pedestrians who seemed to display little regard for the hazards of crossing in traffic.

"You should have let me bring you something to eat, Robert," Jade said.

"After the play, I'll have a snack. I'm sure Roger can help me out. How was dinner?"

"It was great," Peter answered before Jade got a word out. "The Korean barbeque was fantastic."

Robert slowed to pass around a small delivery van double-parked outside a pub. The name above the doublewide entry doors proudly proclaimed THE QUEEN'S HEAD in gilded letters. Through the large windowpanes, Peter noticed an animated crowd clustered near the bar.

Traffic was light, with only three cars keeping a steady pace behind the Rolls. The road was clear to the front for more than a block. Peter felt his body pushed into the seatback as the Phantom powered forward. Robert gripped the wheel with both hands, his eyes darting between the road and the rearview mirror.

Peter leaned forward. "Is there a problem?"

"We'll know in a few seconds," Robert answered without breaking his focus.

Jade was looking out the side window and nearly banged her head on the glass when the car took a sharp turn at a speed that bordered on reckless. "Robert?"

Through the rear window Peter saw two motorcycles accelerating quickly down the unobstructed street toward the Rolls. The spirited engine of the big car roared, and the pursuers fell back, but only briefly. Despite the racing heritage of Rolls Royce, the Phantom was no match for the acceleration and maneuverability of the experienced motorcyclists.

Robert covered another block and whipped around a corner, tires squealing, leaving rubber on the pavement. Jade was thrown into Peter by the centrifugal force, the high-pitched whine of the bikes rising above the refined, throaty rumble from the V12 engine.

"Where are the police when you need them?" Peter mumbled, not expecting an answer.

"Hang on!" Robert said as he turned the wheel sharply, the rear fishtailing before he straightened their trajectory.

The two cyclists closed the distance and bore down on the Rolls. One of the bikes shot past the car. "They're trying to box us in," Robert said.

A car pulled out in front of Robert, forcing him to brake and swerve into the oncoming lane. He oversteered and clipped the sideview mirror on a parked car before regaining control and passing the car. A second later the pursuing motorcyclist was right behind them again.

Ahead, the motorcycle had stopped and the rider, clad in black leather and full helmet, raised a pistol. Robert cranked the wheel, sending the Rolls into a drift as it cornered onto a cross street. As soon as Robert made the turn, he knew it was a mistake. The street narrowed, and with cars and vans parked along the side, there was only space for one vehicle to pass—it was a trap.

Peter felt the car surge forward as Robert floored the accelerator. Jade had both hands clenched on the seatback in front of her, eyes wide in fear.

"We have to get to a public location," Peter said.

"Working on it," Robert answered and he poked a display on the front console. For the first time, Peter noticed it was a GPS display, currently showing their route through a myriad of side streets. "If we get into the traffic too soon and stopped at a light, one of those street bikes can just drive up alongside and it's game over."

"What can I do?"

"Just hold on."

Peter heard the familiar click of electric door locks engaging. He reached across Jade and grabbed the shoulder harness, strapping her in before buckling his own seatbelt.

The motorcycle was still close on their tail. Fortunately, the rider hadn't displayed a gun, although Robert believed it likely that both riders were armed. The distance to the next cross street shortened, and it looked to Peter they would make it. But his hopes were short lived—a car turned onto the road, headed directly for them. "Hold on!" Robert said. "It's gonna get rough!"

He turned the Phantom into a gap in the string of parked cars, narrowly missing a fire hydrant. The sidewalk was wide and served as outdoor seating for the many restaurants and pubs. He slowed only a little and laid on the horn.

Terrified patrons leaped from their chairs, scattering to both sides to the relative safety of the parked cars and doorways. The heavy limousine plowed through tables, chairs, and colorful umbrellas. Robert cut sharply to the left to avoid hitting one of the patrons, preferring to careen off the side of a beat-up VW minibus with a large peace symbol painted on the side.

He stayed on the sidewalk for another thirty yards and then emerged onto the cross street to the angry blare of car horns as he cutoff two drivers. He glanced at the GPS display and swore. He was caught in a seemingly endless maze of side streets that more closely resembled old cow trails than a city grid. The way the streets intersected at odd angles and took sweeping turns made it nearly impossible to maintain his bearings.

Both motorcycles were again on his tail, and he seriously doubted he'd see any police unless he got onto one of the major roadways or arrived at a popular public location. But he also feared that he'd get bogged down in traffic if he tried either. For now, at least, he was able to keep the car moving.

In the rearview mirror, Robert saw a van pull in behind the motorcycles. It accelerated, and pulled even with the two bikes. In front of the Phantom, two blocks away, a sedan turned and approached, only to skid to a stop sideways, blocking the road.

"Looks like this is it," he said. "We've run out of road. Call the police and keep down!"

"I don't know the number!"

"It's nine-nine-nine. Tell them someone's trying to kidnap Jade!"

Peter dialed the number and was waiting for it to connect when Robert slammed on the brakes. As the Rolls stopped, Robert opened a panel in the driver's door and wrapped his large hand around a Walther PPK pistol. He shoved the door open, and was halfway out when he abruptly changed direction and dove across the front seat. A second later the van barreled alongside the Rolls, ripping the driver's door from its hinges.

"What's the nature of the emergency?" The voice had a decidedly calm British accent that Peter would have found amusing under less dire circumstances.

A swarm of men, all dressed entirely in black, poured out of the van and surrounded the Phantom. Like fictionalized outlaws from Western movies, they wore bandanas to cover their faces.

"We're on a street. I… I don't know where. There's a group of people attacking us!"

Peter heard the door handles being worked as the black-clad men struggled in vain to open the doors. He had his arms wrapped around Jade, drawing her close and covering her head while cradling the phone in one hand. He had it on speaker.

"Sir, please calm down. I need to know your location. Are you safe for the moment?"

"We're in the car—a Rolls Royce. The doors are locked, but the driver's door is gone. They smashed it with a van!"

"What is your location, sir? I need to know where to send the police."

One of the men produced a pistol with a suppressor fixed to the barrel making the weapon appear unnaturally long and muzzle heavy. He slammed the butt against the rear window, attempting to shatter the glass. After the third strike, and without the desired result, he pointed the barrel at the forward edge of the glass and fired. The bullet shattered the window into thousands of tiny fragments.

A black-gloved hand reached in and was fumbling for the door latch. Peter leaned to the opposite side of the car and kicked at the groping hand. The first strike was ineffective, but the second worked, and the arm retracted.

Then the window behind Peter shattered.

Jade screamed. Peter shifted to the middle, seeking distance from the attackers. He dropped the phone, but the connection remained live, and he could hear the distant voice, "Sir? Sir? What is your location?"

In the front seat, Robert was also fighting back. Through the gaping breach where the door used to be, one of the attackers was leaning over Robert, wrestling to control the Walther pistol still firmly in his grip. The tight confines of the car made it difficult for Robert to push the man off him—the seatback, dash, and top of the car boxed them in. He had to get a leg drawn up so he could plant his foot against the attacker—preferably in the stomach or groin.

The passenger-side glass shattered, covering Robert in fragments. And then an arm reached in and placed a Taser against his neck.

Peter heard the buzz of the Taser and knew what that meant—time was running out. "I don't know where we are!" he shouted, hoping the phone on the floor would pick up his voice. "Close to Piccadilly Circus! We were at a Korean restaurant called Myung Ga!"

Both rear doors opened and a torso thrust in, grabbing Peter's arm, attempting to pull him out. Through the passenger side, another assailant had latched onto Jade. Peter held tightly, refusing to let her go. But it was a losing battle against the swarm of men.

And then Jade slipped from his grip.

In desperation, Peter reached inside his jacket to the steak knife he'd lifted from the restaurant and discreetly tucked inside his waistband. His left arm was locked in an iron grip and he was being dragged out of the car. He thrust the knife across his chest, slashing the forearm of his attacker, causing him to release his hold and withdraw.

The fight wasn't over, and with Jade out of the way, more men grabbed Peter through the open doors. He lashed out with a clenched fist, but there wasn't enough power behind the blow to be effective. The attacker shook off the punch and latched onto Peter's wrist with both hands. Frantically, he stabbed with the knife, but missed and instead sunk the blade deep into the leather upholstery. Unrelenting, the assailant was yanking on Peter's arm, using a leg as leverage against the rear seat. At the same time, hands came from the other side and were struggling to get control of the knife.

Peter swung his elbow into the nose of the attacker, and then brought the knife forward and down. He narrowly missed the man's face, instead, slicing through his ear. He screamed in pain and broke off.

Off balance, Peter toppled to the side and was pulled from the limousine. A boot slammed into his ribs, and he grunted as the wind left his chest. Another foot came down on his arm allowing the knife to be taken from his grasp. He heard Jade scream again, and he turned his head just in time to see Jade being pushed into the rear of the sedan. The next sensation that filled Peter's mind was one of intense, all-encompassing pain as the Taser was pressed into his flesh.

CHAPTER 9

THE STRATEGIC GLOBAL INTERVENTION TEAM, commonly called SGIT, operated under the authority of Colonel Pierson of the DIA, or the Defense Intelligence Agency. SGIT headquarters, affectionately called The Office, was located in a discrete, high-security building in McClellan Business Park at the former Strategic Air Command (SAC) base in Sacramento. The business park was home to a mix of private-sector and military tenants, including the Defense Commissary Agency's regional office and the Defense Department Microelectronics Center. But the primary reason SGIT was stationed at the McClellan Business Park was to have direct access to the 10,600-foot-long runway and secure hangars to house its specialty aircraft.

Although many teams within the diverse U.S. intelligence agencies were working hard to provide any, and all, new information on the attack that sunk the *Izumo*, the small and highly capable SGIT team was devoting 100% of their attention to finding answers. Lieutenant Ellen Lacey, Senior Intelligence Analyst, was leading the effort.

With wavy red hair and fair complexion, Lacey was true to her Irish roots. She was widely recognized as one of the most gifted minds in the intelligence community and had a file full of commendations and accolades that was scheduled to remain classified "secret" for at least fifty years.

"We don't have anything other than the initial reports." Analyst Mona Stephens made no attempt to hide her frustration, or fatigue. They'd been at it non-stop for close to sixteen hours, and she needed a break. Petite and blond, her attractive looks often led her male counterparts to grossly underestimate her brainpower. In fact, she had proven instrumental in problem solving and quickly rose to be second in charge of the analyst team. Like her boss, she was confident, but not cocky, and brilliant at synthesizing theories based on disparate and seemingly random facts.

"Many of the analysts over at the DIA think the attack may have been a one-hit wonder," she added.

"You mean a one-trick pony," this comment from David Sanchez, the junior-most analyst, having been assigned to SGIT only a year ago.

That earned him a glare and sharp rebuke. "No, I meant one-hit wonder. That's why I said it."

"That's enough," Lacey ordered. "Stay focused. I know we are all tired." She ran her eyes around the room, taking in her collected team. Stephens and Sanchez sat across from each other at the conference table. Mark Williams and Beth Ross rounded out the team. Including Lacey, five of the best minds at intelligence gathering, interpretation, and problem solving—and they were striking out.

"Okay, people. Take a break. Get some coffee; check your emails. Back here in fifteen."

"How about some Chinese take-out?" Sanchez asked with a lopsided grin. "I'm starving."

Stephens looked over her shoulder on her way out of the conference room. "Yeah, it's been a whole three hours since your last feeding."

"Hey, I'm a growing boy. I can't think on an empty stomach."

"Relax," Lacey said. "I'll call the front desk and have Sergeant Wells order in some food."

An hour later and with hunger satiated, Lacey's team was back at it. The secure conference room had the spicy aroma of ginger and garlic, but at least the faces looking back at her showed a level of vigor that had been lacking for the last several hours. A fresh carafe of steaming hot coffee was on a table at one end of the room. Lacey was filling her mug.

"Do we have any updates yet from the Navy?" she asked to no one in particular.

"Not yet, ma'am," Beth Ross replied. "Although my last email exchange was earlier this morning. I can ping them again."

Lacey nodded, and Ross tapped away at the keyboard of her laptop.

"Based on the trajectory analysis from MOTHER, best guess is that the missile was launched from one of the many small islands in the South China Sea. Most likely in this area," Sanchez had a satellite image projected onto the large color monitor, and he was pointing to a circle overlaid on the geography. SGIT's super computer—nicknamed MOTHER because it always seemed to have an answer to every question—had crunched the radar data from the *Shiloh*, *Lassen*, and *McCampbell*. Constructed using massive parallel optical processing and rated at 158 petaflops, it seemed no problem was too difficult for MOTHER. And now, with three separate perspectives on the trajectory, MOTHER calculated the probable flight path of the missile and extrapolated back to the likely launch coordinates. Unfortunately, it was still a very large area that encompassed dozens of tiny islands in the Spratly chain—some no more than rocky outcroppings barely large enough for a small flock of seagulls.

Eyes were still focused on the screen when Ross spoke up. "Excuse me, ma'am. Just received an update from Navy."

"Go on," Lacey answered.

"It says the *USS Pioneer* arrived on site at the location of the *Izumo*, and she has just completed an examination of the wreck using the Navy's most advanced ROV. The debris field is relatively contained, and the ship did break in two sections, confirming the eyewitness reports. The bow section and stern section are only separated by about 300 yards. Let's see," she was leaning close to the computer monitor and summarizing the email as she read. "Looks like the ROV collected video. I have a link so we should be able to put it up on the monitor." Ross pointed to the large wall-mounted display. "Also, they collected a dozen samples—pieces from deck plates, bulk heads, conduit and electrical cable, and small pipe. Samples have been flown to Okinawa for lab analysis."

"Let's take a look at the video," Lacey said.

Ross entered a few keystrokes. The large monitor flickered and then video of an underwater scene replaced the color map of the Spratly Islands.

The analysts watched in rapt attention as the sharp image revealed first the bow section of the *Izumo*, then the broken decks, and finally the fractured stern section. The entire video, lasting less than three minutes, had been spliced together to provide a concise visual summary.

Sanchez was the first to react, letting out a soft whistle.

"I've never seen such destruction." It was the first comment from Mark Williams since the team had completed their meal. "But it doesn't look like it was caused by an explosive warhead."

Lacey had been studying the video from the far side of the room, near the coffee carafe. She walked to her chair and seated herself, her eyebrows pinched together. "Play it again. And when you get to the broken hull sections, freeze the image so we can take a closer look."

Ross moved the slider at the bottom of the video to advance to the frames of particular interest, then played the video at one quarter normal speed. "There!" Lacey said, and Ross paused the playback.

Both Williams and Lacey approached the monitor for a closer inspection. Williams shook his head. "The primary damage is largely buckled deck plates and bulkheads."

"And the damage is not localized," Lacey added. She pointed with her index finger. "It continues all the way through to the keel. In my opinion, the damage is more consistent with a kinetic penetrator and not an explosive device."

"I've read about such a weapon," Stephens said. "But I didn't know any military had actually deployed it. Mark? You seem to be the most familiar with this weaponry."

Williams returned to his seat and faced Stephens. "Well, there's not a lot to report. You're correct. Only the Chinese are believed to have developed an operational version. But Uncle Sam has funded development through the Department of the Navy for almost a decade now. Still, there isn't much support among the top brass for the weapon system."

"I'd have to agree," she replied. "I mean, why go to all the trouble when a thousand pounds of high explosive can do the job equally well?"

"Or a well-placed torpedo," Sanchez added.

Lacey leaned back. "The Chinese call it the ship killer. It's a key part of their strategic plan to forcibly retake Taiwan, if it ever comes to that."

"I still don't get it. Like I said, place a Mark 48 torpedo against a ship's hull, or detonate the warhead under the keel, and even the largest warship is in serious trouble."

Mark Williams had folded his hands, listening intently to the discussion. East Asia was his specialty, and lately that meant he stayed very busy. "It's a simple doctrine, when you think about it. China knows they must have a standoff weapon system that neutralizes our carrier strike groups. They accept that they will never win a prolonged naval conflict with the United States, and they don't have the patience to build a blue-water navy that does pose a formidable threat to the Pacific Fleet. Furthermore, they can't risk using tactical nuclear weapons, even in a limited theater dominated by open ocean."

Sanchez waved his hand in objection. "You haven't answered the question. Why deploy a weapon system as complicated as a ballistic missile when a cruise missile or torpedo can do the job equally well, maybe better?"

"The answer should be self-evident." Williams cast a curious glance at Sanchez. "Standoff distance. A theater ballistic missile has range that cannot be met—not even close—with anti-ship missiles and torpedoes. A plus is that the weapon may be fired from fortified positions, or from mobile launchers, within mainland China."

"And as we all know," Stephens said, "if a ballistic missile is not intercepted in the boost phase, the probability of taking it out during reentry is very low."

Lacey pointed to Williams. "You take point on this Mark. You've studied Chinese military doctrine longer than anyone in the group, and probably longer than any analyst at the DIA. I want every theory you can come up with, or have ever heard about, put forward. And then arguments for and against. You have the entire team at your disposal."

Williams returned a curt nod.

"Okay people. Let's get to it. I want answers!"

CHAPTER 10

IT WAS NEARLY MIDNIGHT, but despite the tasing and bruises from the beating, Peter was wired. He knew exhaustion would set in once the adrenalin rush wore off.

After hours of questioning, and long phone conversations with the Brunei Foreign Ministry and the U.S. State Department, the London police released Robert and Peter. They politely declined to return the Walther, citing the strict laws in the U.K. concerning ownership of handguns. "That's not your property," Robert objected.

"And I suggest your government take it up through diplomatic channels," a stern officer replied.

"Come on, Robert," Peter said. "Let's go back to the hotel."

He nodded. "How about having one of your patrol cars drop us off at the Ritz?" The Rolls had been impounded as evidence.

"I beg your pardon," the officer replied. "We are public servants to ensure safety and enforce the law. We are not a taxi service."

Robert's face flushed. Peter placed a hand on his shoulder. "It's fine. Riding in a London taxi will be another first for me."

Back in the Prince of Wales Suite, Diesel greeted Peter and Robert with wagging tail as they walked through the door. "Good heavens," Roger said as he laid eyes on the two men.

"Yeah, you should see the other guys," Robert quipped.

Roger raised an eyebrow, not sure if Robert was serious or his comment was just an example of odd American humor. "May I prepare something to eat and drink? Perhaps tea and cookies?" he asked.

"Thank you, Roger, but I'll require something stronger than tea," Peter replied.

"Champagne? I always keep two bottles chilled for Miss Jade."

"Yeah, well, Miss Jade is not here," Robert answered morosely. "She's been taken."

"Taken? You mean Miss Jade has been kidnapped?"

"Yeah." Robert walked away from Roger and leaned over the fireplace, his meaty arms anchored against the marble mantle.

Peter gently stretched. His entire body ached, no doubt from the muscle spasms caused by the 50,000 volts from the Taser. He gently lowered himself into one of the leather armchairs, the padding softly cushioning his back. Diesel curled on the Persian rug at his feet.

"Know much about whiskey, Roger?" Peter asked as he stretched his neck.

"Hmpf. Scotch, Irish, Canadian, or American?" Roger straightened his back and puffed out his chest as he replied, causing Peter to grin.

"Scotch. Oban, 18-year-old. Do you think they have a bottle at the bar?"

"Of course. I have no doubt."

Sensing Peter and Robert wanted privacy, Roger closed the

door as he exited the living room for the kitchen.

Robert had his phone to his ear, waiting as the call went through. Peter could tell that he was being transferred from one person to the next, finally connecting. "Yes ma'am, I'm sorry to bother you, but I have bad news."

The conversation was short, not more than a minute. Robert spared Mrs. Lim the details, informing her only that Jade had been kidnapped.

After the call ended, Peter asked, "What now?"

"We have to get her back."

"Yeah, okay. And just—"

A knock at the door interrupted Peter. Roger entered carrying a silver tray holding two tumblers, a bottle of Oban single malt Scotch, and a small ice bucket. "Would you care for anything else?"

Peter shook his head. "Thank you."

When Roger reached the door, he hesitated and turned to face Peter. "Sir, I hope Miss Jade will be all right."

"Me too, Roger, me too."

It was the first time Peter had witnessed Robert have a drink. After two more phone calls and a generous glass of Scotch, he looked Peter squarely in the eyes. "We've been summoned to Brunei."

"We? There's nothing I can do there."

"Lim Eu-meh, Jade's mother, has requested your help."

"This is a police matter. I've given them my statement, as have you. What more can I do? Let the police do their job and catch the gang of thugs that kidnapped her."

"You can't be serious. That was not a gang of hoodlums." Robert paused to let the thought sink in. "Why didn't they shoot us? It would have been easier, faster."

"How should I know? Maybe they thought the police would

put more resources on the case if they committed murder."

"You're joking. Right? Come on. They kidnapped the niece of the Sultan of Brunei. It doesn't get more high-profile than that."

"I can't help you."

"That job was professional," Robert said, his face grim. "With military precision, they herded us into a trap using multiple elements and coordinated in real time."

Peter stared back.

"You saw it; you were there," Robert pressed.

"So were you. And what good did it do?"

"Like I told you, I'm familiar with your file. Mrs. Lim is, too."

"I'm not Sherlock Holmes, nor am I James Bond or Jason Bourne."

"What you are is resourceful." Robert leaned forward. "You know as well as I do that the police will not find her. What do they have to go on? Tell me."

Peter's silence was answer enough.

"Neither of us can ID any of them. If the vehicles are ever recovered, they'll be clean."

"Someone will call with a ransom demand," Peter said. "Isn't that the way this works? The police can trace the call or follow the cash. A bank transfer would be better—easy to follow the account numbers."

"You don't understand. It's not about money."

"It's always about money."

Robert shook his head. "Not this time."

"Really? Enlighten me."

"I can't."

"Then why should I go with you to Brunei?"

"Because you care about Jade."

"Well, caring isn't good enough." Peter sighed and rubbed a

hand across his face. Fatigue, combined with the whiskey, was beginning to have an effect. "It didn't help today."

"The Sultan's A340 will be fueled within the hour and the flight plan is being filed. We'll leave in the morning."

"You're not listening. I'm not going to Brunei."

"Yes, you are."

"Are you planning to drag me onto that flight?"

"Mrs. Lim wants to talk to you."

"No disrespect intended, but she knows how to use a phone."

"She'll only speak with you in person."

"Look, Robert, you seem like a nice person. And I'm sure Eu-Meh is as well. She's upset. It's understandable. But she has the assets of her government plus the London police—probably Scotland Yard as well—at her disposal to solve this kidnapping and rescue Jade. There's nothing more I can do."

"She knows."

Peter furrowed his brow. "Knows what?"

"She knows why Jade was taken, and it's not for money."

CHAPTER 11

THE *ROYAL SEEKER* WAS NEARLY MOTIONLESS on calm seas. A light breeze washed across the bridge. Captain Rei checked the radar scope again—no blips. It was approaching time.

The sun had risen but was still low on the eastern horizon. He would have preferred low clouds, but the weather conditions were acceptable nevertheless.

First Officer Chang approached from behind the captain. "Everything is ready, sir."

Rei nodded almost imperceptibly, prompting his First Officer to continue.

"The target coordinates have been entered and confirmed. What are your orders?"

Rei clasped his hands behind his back and gazed through the forward bridge windows at the placid ocean. Just off the starboard beam a rocky outcropping, barely a square mile in area, rose a dozen or so feet above the sea. He had positioned his ship close to this barren patch of ground—one of many dozen small islands, cays, reefs, and shoals in the vast archipelago known as the Spratly Islands. It was all part of the illusion.

"Why do you suppose these islands are coveted by so many nations?" he asked.

Chang was still behind Captain Rei, and he frowned, annoyed with this trivial conversation when far more important tasks required action. "Fishing, I suppose. Perhaps mineral rights."

Hmmpf, Rei scoffed.

"Sir, I request permission—" but Chang was cut off before he could complete his request.

"Fish… oil and gas that have yet to be discovered," Rei sounded philosophical, his voice soft. "Countries don't threaten war over such mundane needs. No. This is about dominance. China must show the United States that it can take these islands and the surrounding waters—for no other reason than because the Central Party says so."

"Captain?"

Rei turned and faced Chang. "China must expand. The west is arid and unsuitable for supporting a large population. The east is overcrowded. Pollution is poisoning our water and our air." His dark eyes squinted as he scrutinized his First Officer. Chang only nodded, unwilling to engage in a pointless discussion.

"The opportunity is east, of course. Southeast Asia, Taiwan, Australia… Japan. It will be an empire the likes of which mankind has never witnessed. Once the western Pacific is dominated by China, our security will be assured."

Chang's countenance was rigid, showing no emotion. He cared little for politics. He was a soldier, trained to follow orders.

"Captain, it is daylight. Once again, we are vulnerable to

observation by passing aircraft and satellites. We should not tempt fate and press our luck any further."

"You would have preferred we fire the missile under the cover of darkness?"

Chang did not answer.

"Your youth is both an asset and a weakness, my friend. Over the years, I have learned the value of patience—a lesson you still have to master. The darkness is not our ally; it is an illusion. Once the rocket motor ignites, the brilliant plume is a million times brighter than a signal flare. It would attract attention for a hundred miles in all directions as the missile climbs higher and higher."

Captain Rei placed a hand on his First Officer's shoulder, addressing him like a student rather than a subordinate. "Now, with the sun just above the eastern horizon, infrared imagers onboard the American satellites will be challenged to detect the superheated exhaust against the rising sun. And if the missile plume *is* detected by their satellites, technicians monitoring the signals will lose precious minutes trying to determine if the detection is really a missile launch or merely a false alarm due to the sun."

Rei paused, a rare smile creeping across his face. "You are smart and ambitious, and you will do fine. Now, it is time."

Deep inside the bowls of the rusted hull, four decks below the bridge, the electronic launch and control center was bustling with activity. The overhead lights were extinguished, replaced with red lamps and diffuse illumination from a vast assortment of electronic equipment—most of it with multicolor flat screens to display graphic data and images with remarkable clarity.

Thick, shielded cables connected the control center to the outside world via radar, several cameras, and antenna for both sending encrypted messages as well as conducting electronic surveillance. Most of the cameras were pointed at the deck area where the missile was erected amidst the three steel drill towers, the images displayed on a dual row of screens.

At another console, a technician was monitoring for radio and radar signals. Even though there were no ships within a radius of sixteen nautical miles, electromagnetic emissions from ships could bounce off the upper atmosphere and travel much farther than line-of-sight. "Normal background emissions," the technician reported.

"Very well," Chang replied. He preferred the control center over the bridge. "Is the deck clear?"

"Clear!"

Chang raised his eyes to a color video feed showing the Hwasong-12 missile cradled among the steel girders and cross bracing of the towers. From a distance, the casual observer could easily miss the green rocket body encircled by the clutter of the green drill towers.

"Time to launch?" he said.

"Sixty seconds and counting," came the reply.

The tension was palpable as all waited, watching the analog clock, the red sweep-second hand looking black under the red lighting.

"Radar?" Chang said.

"Still clear. No surface vessels, and no aircraft on the screen."

"Emissions?"

"Only background. No change."

Five, four, three, two, one…

Suddenly the deck shuddered under their feet, and despite their location deep within the ship, the control room reverberated with a deep roar. Chang imagined that it would be deafening if anyone had been foolish enough to be topside as the missile was launched. Propelled by a first-stage rocket motor fueled with a hypergolic mixture of unsymmetrical dimethylhydrazine and nitrogen tetroxide, the missile cleared the drill towers in seconds and rapidly accelerated in a near vertical arc.

The red-brown smoke trail behind the first-stage motor was dispersed within minutes by the light wind. A video feed from one of the cameras followed the missile until it faded from sight.

"Tracking true," reported the radar technician.

"Very well," replied Rei. "Mr. Chang. Have the wash-down crew hose off the deck and towers. I want all residual propellant cleaned from the towers and deck within fifteen minutes in case we are visited. I'll be on the bridge."

Captain Rei left the control center and hastily climbed the stairs, emerging onto the bridge. Wasting no time, he addressed the Officer of the Watch. "Is our course laid in as ordered?"

"Yes, sir. Bearing one-seven-three. Radar is clear."

Rei placed a pair of high-powered binoculars to his eyes and scanned the horizon. Nothing but blue water and clear sky. "Very well. All ahead full."

The ship's position was held stationary for the launch using sophisticated bow and stern thrusters, linked to the electronic navigation system. It was designed to hold a stationary position—essential for drilling into the sea floor—using GPS coordinates. With no anchors to raise, the two main engines, which had been idling, quickly came up to full power. Each massive power plant—a significant upgrade from the previous engines—turned huge bronze screws, specifically designed for maximum efficiency and speed. Soon the *Royal Seeker* accelerated forward, pushing an ever-larger bow wave as her speed increased.

Cruising at her maximum speed, the *Royal Seeker* would be 100 nautical miles away from the missile launch location in just under five hours. Rei had been assured by the mission planners that it would be that many hours before a Keyhole satellite would pass overhead and capture multispectral images of the area. The search area would be defined generally by radar tracking data from U.S. warships in the South China Sea and the Philippine Sea.

Captain Rei was accustomed to the routine of his seafaring life. Whether for military purposes or private industry, orders were given and followed. It was predictable, and provided for accountability—except that he had never met the mission planners. He did not know who they were, or if their motives were other than they had represented.

At first, he was enticed by the money. The mission would have him at sea for a month, and during that time he would earn more than he could make over two years as captain of a cargo ship working for Hua Ho Holdings. But soon he found motivation in the purpose of the mission—to strike a blow against America and her allies, drive them from the coastal waters off China, and vanquish their military from Southeast Asia.

A loyal member of the Communist Party, Rei believed China had been pushed around for too long. The abuse of Chinese at the hands of the invading Japanese Army in the middle of the twentieth century was bad enough—horrendous crimes against humanity had been committed by the occupying army. Yet, in 1945 and 1946, the Allies, under American leadership, refused to vigorously pursue criminal charges against the Japanese officers and politicians who were responsible for the inhumane treatment of so many Chinese and Korean civilians. Certainly, there were no trials like those faced by German officers in Nuremburg.

In his late fifties, Rei Jianming had been born after the end of World War II. But his immediate family would never forget, and he grew up with first-hand accounts of rapes, beatings, executions, starvation—all at the hands of the Imperial Japanese Army.

President Chen Jinghua had continued a policy of occupying disputed islands in the East China Sea and the South China Sea, including building artificial landmasses on some of the many shoals and reefs. All of the constructed islands were now occupied by Chinese military—Navy, Marines, Air Force. In response, the U.S. supported many legal challenges from Japan, Vietnam, Malaysia, Taiwan, Brunei, and the Philippines. But other than pointless UN resolutions lacking any teeth, and unenforceable legal rulings from the International Court, nothing had come of this posturing.

That is, except for the insistence of the U.S. to sail its military ships through the disputed waters on a regular basis and occasionally fly Air Force spy planes over the occupied islands. Many Chinese citizens believed they were being bullied by America. And with the Japanese government moving away from a purely defensive military doctrine, and Japanese leadership still refusing to apologize for past wartime atrocities, Chinese fear was giving way to a surge of nationalism.

Captain Rei was no fool, and he knew that the missile launched from his ship a few days earlier had sunk a Japanese warship. But he allowed his mind to think of the dead and wounded as abstract statistics—nothing more than a number on a sheet of paper. It was, he reasoned, perfectly within his rights—the rights of his homeland—to correct past wrongs and to regain dignity and self-determination.

But if this was the case, why did the mission planners remain so secretive? The question nagged at him.

CHAPTER 12

THE DECK OF THE *USS MAKIN ISLAND* was bustling with activity. Aircraft—F35B Lightning fighters and helicopters, both attack and transport—were landing, long enough to refuel and rearm, then taking off again. All the while, crew were scurrying about in apparent frenzied motion, but in fact it was a well-orchestrated team action.

The WASP-class amphibious assault ship was large by any measure at 840 feet long with a beam of 106 feet. She was the newest and most modern of her class, the pride of the Marine Corps. She was the centerpiece of the Expeditionary Strike Group participating in this live-fire training exercise—a beach landing and coordinated air, sea, land assault. The training target was an under-developed island at the northern end of the Philippine archipelago: Mavudis Island.

Located about midway between Luzon to the south and Taiwan to the north, Mavudis Island was situated at the eastern edge of the South China Sea—a key factor in choosing this location for the joint Australian-Philippine-American exercise.

The first wave of Marines from the 31st Marine Expeditionary Unit was about to embark in their air-cushion landing crafts, or LCAC. Australian and Philippine troops, in much smaller numbers, were anchoring both ends of the broad landing beach. The American forces would land in the middle, supported by armored vehicles and Marine Corps aircraft.

Sunrise was marked by a naval barrage of five-inch high-explosive shells, fired from two destroyers at simulated enemy troop positions at the edge of the beach, where the white sand gave way to lush, tall grass, bushes, and trees. The battle plan had been developed during some of the bloodiest engagements of World War II and had changed little over the intervening decades, other than to accommodate modern military weapons and machinery.

The annual Balikatan exercises came at a fortuitous time, as it provided cover for the Navy to deploy two attack submarines plus a range of surface warships to the region. Soon, a carrier strike group would also arrive in the disputed waters, providing a significant U.S. military presence.

Today, the seas were light at about one to two feet, ideal conditions for the LCACs to sprint to shore and unload men and materiel. With aircraft darting across the sky like hornets buzzing around a hive, battle-ready Marines were gathering in the well deck, preparing to board their large hovercrafts. The *USS Makin Island* carried three LCACs, and today all three would be deployed.

There was hardly any roll as the amphibious assault ship moved through the water at a few knots, just enough forward speed to maintain steerage. The large door at the aft of the ship was open, allowing bright tropical sunlight to flood the well deck.

Sergeant Larabee led his squad onto the flat deck of the

LCAC and into the personnel compartment. His men were the last to board.

"Hey, Sarg!" a Marine yelled to be heard above the echo of engine and propeller noise in the confined space. "Is it true the Aussies are cooking lobster and steak for lunch?"

"Yeah, man. What's on the Barbie?" another Marine joked.

"Who cares as long as the beer is cold!" a third chimed in.

Larabee smiled. He thought of himself as firm but fair. Blowing off some steam was acceptable, maybe even preferable. Although today was only training, he knew that tomorrow it could be for real. A veteran of three deployments to Iraq and Afghanistan, Sergeant Larabee had witnessed death and destruction. He'd often dealt it out without mercy. With tensions rising between the U.S. and China, he knew they were practicing diplomacy through demonstration of superior firepower—and training.

"Everything you need, Marine," Larabee said, "is on your back or your belt." His comment earned a groan.

The engines spun up to a higher rpm, signaling that the LCAC was about to fly out on a cushion of air. The machine moved slowly at first, and then picked up speed as it moved down the long well deck toward the aft opening.

Larabee was facing toward the rear and had a clear view out a small window. He'd seen this view many times before. Although he understood the physics, it always struck him as odd that he could be on seawater within the ship, and all was normal.

A sonic crack louder than anything he'd ever heard overpowered the chatter and engine noise within the 180-man troop compartment. Instantly, a brilliant white light momentarily blinded him. But just as fast as it appeared, the flash was gone, replaced by the most terrifying image he could imagine.

A yellow-orange fireball filled the forward end of the well deck. Flame billowed and moved like a living creature. It expanded, chasing after him. Larabee felt his body pulling against his straps as the LCAC accelerated hard, the craftmaster knowing that survival depended on escaping the bowels of the ship.

As the seconds passed, Larabee was regaining his hearing. The frightening sound of steel bending, buckling, and failing was background to the explosions of ordnance. Now, the walls of the well deck appeared to be moving, and the ceiling was coming down, threatening to drive the LCAC into the seawater. And still the fireball approached, but not as rapidly as before.

Larabee was jarred to the side when the hovercraft collided with the steel wall, only to have the air skirts serve as a bumper and bounce the large craft back into the lane. Blackness filled folds between the pillows of flame that seemed to be touching the rear of the hovercraft.

And then, daylight! The LCAC shot out the well deck opening like a cork off a Champagne bottle. A moment later, the well deck completely slid beneath the waves as the USS *Makin Island* broke in two. The hovercraft slowed and turned, circling back to the churning sea where the two halves had sunk beneath the water.

CHAPTER 13

COMMANDER JAMES NICOLAOU was hunched over his desk reading the most recent update emailed from Mark Williams. He rose from his chair, headed directly to Ellen Lacey's office. He opened the door without knocking. "Lieutenant, follow me to Conference Room A. Have your team meet us there." Within minutes they were assembled around a polished conference table, tablets powered up and ready.

"Ross and Sanchez are cross-checking briefings from several agencies," Lacey said, explaining their absence.

"Fine," Jim said. He stood ramrod straight, arms folded across his chest. He was the first of his family to be a naturally born U.S. citizen, his parents having immigrated from Greece and naturalized. With thick, black hair and rugged, masculine appearance, he could have made a living as a model. But he'd chosen to enlist in the Navy, preferring challenge and adventure to an easier path. After serving in the SEALs and commanding a team of his own, he was recruited by Colonel Pierson to head the then newly-formed SGIT.

As the analysts settled in, he cleared his throat. "With the attack on the *USS Makin Island*, we are moving quickly toward a shooting war," Nicolaou said. "Now, you've all read the intelligence, including the assessment by Sergeant Williams. The problem we have is identifying who is behind this. We need answers." Jim took a seat and folded his hands on the table. "Speak freely."

Mark Williams spoke first. "China is the obvious culprit—perhaps too obvious."

"Explain," Lacey said.

"Well, why go to so much trouble to remain anonymous? I mean, they'd know we would place China at the top of the list of suspects. It's only natural given their aggressive position regarding taking control of the South China Sea and, to a certain degree, the East China Sea as well."

Mona Stephens added her thoughts. "With Japan positioning for a greater leadership role in defining the policies of the region, including evolving their military doctrine to include some offensive operations rather than remaining strictly defensive, President Chen would have reason to act now."

"So far, you haven't shared any theories that haven't already been thoroughly considered by every intelligence agency. This hasn't gotten us anywhere. I need something more."

"China has been a vocal critic of the U.S. for meddling in the South China Sea," Lacey said, "an area they clearly view as their front yard. The analogy has been drawn to the Caribbean—how would President Taylor respond if the Chinese government began to play a role in regulating naval vessels wishing to make port calls at any of the many islands within a few hundred miles of Florida?"

"I don't accept that analogy," Jim replied, his face drawn taught.

"I agree," Williams added. "It's an inaccurate comparison. In fact, there are no disputed landmasses in the Caribbean, unlike the Spratly Islands, Senkaku Islands, Scarborough Shoal, the—"

Jim held up a hand. "Okay, point made."

Williams nodded, then continued, "In the Spratly chain, China has engaged in island building—another controversial action—and based on pretty solid satellite imagery, fortified their positions including building long runways capable of serving as forward bases. The Chinese government does not deny the allegations of militarizing the Spratly Islands, and insists it is their right and responsibility to ensure safe passage through the region."

"I find it hard to fault their argument," Stephens said. "After all, we have maintained a significant military presence at Guantanamo on the island of Cuba since the end of the Spanish-American War."

"Whether you agree with the Chinese or not is irrelevant," Jim said. "Our job is not to establish foreign policy—that's for the President and the State Department."

"Yes, sir," Stephens said. "We agree the Chinese have motive to drive the U.S. out of the Western Pacific. So, why play games about it? The answer may be as simple as they want to avoid a war. Maybe President Chen thinks he can establish doubt that his government has launched these attacks. Maybe he thinks he can coerce President Taylor into withdrawing forces pursuant to the demand."

Lacey shook her head. "No way. I don't buy that. Whoever is behind this would have to know the President would never give in that easily."

"The loss of life—American and Japanese—has already been high," Jim said. "And since two weapons have been used, we have to assume that more can, and will, be deployed."

Lacey had been here before. Yet she still felt the pressure of needing to supply answers when they knew next to nothing. "So it's a high-stakes game of poker—see who folds first?" she said.

"That's a fair analogy." Jim rubbed his temples, a habit to try to release the tension that was building. "Our other prime suspect is North Korea. Comments?"

"They have the missile technology," Stephens observed. "But do they have the warhead? Mark?"

He leaned forward, resting his arms on the conference table. "Unlikely that they've developed a kinetic penetrator that even remotely resembles what sunk those two ships. The material science know-how and manufacturing expertise is beyond any recognized capability of the North Koreans. However, it is possible they acquired warheads from the Chinese."

"Which brings us back to square one," Lacey said. She leaned back in her chair and let out a sigh.

Jim looked across the faces of his team. "This is as real as it gets, people. You are the first string, the A team. No one is better at gathering and interpreting intelligence. The President is demanding to know who is sinking our ships. Men and women are dying. We have to provide answers."

"What if we can't?" Williams asked the question he was sure was on everyone's mind.

Jim's countenance softened. "You will. No one has more faith in the abilities of this team than I do."

"Yes, sir."

"Okay, what can we deduce from the launch coordinates?"

"The obvious," Stephens replied. "The missiles were not launched from either the Korean Peninsula or mainland China. In fact, we aren't certain they were even fired from any land mass."

"Are you suggesting they were sub-launched?"

"Yes, sir. That is the most logical conclusion."

"Great. Both North Korea and China have that capability, so we are still no closer to identifying the responsible party." Jim stood and paced beside the conference table. "What about the thermal image of the exhaust?"

"You mean the plume from the main rocket engines?" Stephens said.

Jim nodded. "Can we use that as a kind of fingerprint, maybe identify the country that manufactured the rocket motors?"

Mona Stephens frowned. "I'm sorry, sir. We looked into that, and since the characteristics of thrust and weight, at least for a given class of ballistic missile, are not especially unique— as well as the fact that almost every rocket motor uses similar propellants—we can't distinguish Chinese and North Korean intermediate-range ballistic missiles. Not from the thermal signature."

"Have we considered non-government groups?" Jim asked.

"Yes, sir," Lacey answered. "But none of the known terrorist groups have access to this technology. I mean, this is really sophisticated. Just acquiring and launching a theater ballistic missile is a high bar, but think about the targeting. Whoever is doing this has to have access to satellite imagery and GPS to have any chance of scoring a hit."

"What about commercial companies who will sell satellite images? And access to GPS is hardly restricted technology— not anymore."

"All true. But those sat images have to be close to real time, right? The *Izumo* and the *Makin Island* were hardly stationary targets."

Jim nodded. "Have you checked with the Navy? If there are missile boats in the South China Sea, I have to believe the Secretary of the Navy knows about it."

"We have," replied Stephens. "However, the Navy has not detected any foreign submarines in the South China Sea. We have reason to believe that the Navy has at least one fast-attack boat on the prowl in those waters, although my sources at DIA would not go on the record, and the Department of the Navy refuses to comment."

"Even now? Hell, we're about to go to war."

"I'm sorry, sir. Maybe Colonel Pierson can get better information."

Jim nodded. "Make sure your reports are current and comprehensive. I'll package what we have and send it off to the Colonel. Keep at it. You know this is vital. With public pressure mounting, before long we are going to start shooting at someone. Let's be damned sure it's the right party."

CHAPTER 14

SECRETARY OF STATE PAUL BRYAN hustled to the Oval Office. Overweight and overworked, he was slightly winded as he took a seat on the Chippendale sofa. He pushed strands of black hair back in place and then leaned forward to pour a cup of coffee, ignoring his physician's repeated advise to reduce his intake of caffeine.

President Taylor was seated at the Resolute Desk reading a report, the same report Bryan had read less than an hour ago, and the reason for this urgent meeting.

The President looked up. "The USS *Makin Island* was sunk? Are we certain this is not a mistake?"

"It's not a mistake, sir. My staff has confirmed with the Pentagon. Casualties are in the hundreds, and the number is expected to rise. There were a large number of Marine Corp aircraft in the air at the time. Thankfully, all were able to land safely. Still working on the suspected missile launch coordinates—should have that information shortly once the trajectory has been fully analyzed."

"Has this made it to the press yet?"

"No sir, not that we're aware of. When it does, it'll be headline news for days. Initial reports strongly suggest the *Makin Island* was attacked by the same weapon system that sunk the *Izumo*."

"Any claim of responsibility yet?"

Bryan shook his head. "No, sir."

"So, the message is clear. If we don't pull back our forces from the Western Pacific, the attacks will continue."

"That would seem to be the case."

Taylor slammed his fist on the desk in a rare show of emotion. "Dammit. Who's doing this? North Korea?"

"Maybe," Bryan shrugged. "One could make a credible argument that it's China."

"Which countries in the region have the capability to carry out these attacks?"

"Aside from those already mentioned, maybe South Korea and Taiwan. We know they each have short-range ballistic missiles. Whether they have any intermediate range missiles is uncertain. But I see no motive for South Korea or Taiwan to force, or even encourage, the U.S. to withdraw from the region and concede military dominance to China."

"What about Russia?"

"Their eastern bases are north of Japan, and the government of President Pushkin has not vocalized any interest in Southeast Asia."

President Taylor nodded, his eyebrows pinched together. "Summon the Chinese ambassador. See what he'll share with you. I can't believe China would be so brazen."

"Southeast Asia is becoming increasingly dangerous. China's activities to militarize the Spratly Island chain, combined with flying bombers and sailing warships close to Japan and Taiwan, are only a few recent examples of provocative actions that are destabilizing the region."

"Not to mention the North Koreans testing atomic bombs regularly and launching missiles over their neighbor to the south as well as Japan." The President pushed away from his desk and took a seat next to his Secretary of State. "Has humankind gone mad?"

"Sir?"

"Sometimes it seems that we are on a one-way trip to self-destruction."

Paul Bryan stared blankly at his boss. He'd had a similar thought, many times. Aggression was always justified based on past transgressions, with neither side being willing to listen and consider opposing perspectives. An experienced diplomat, Bryan was committed to logical reasoning and compromise, an approach that had helped him achieve success in the past in resolving difficult issues, including with the Chinese.

"I'll get a meeting with the ambassador right away." Bryan stood to leave. "And, for whatever it's worth, I still have faith in humankind."

Gao Jiming liked living in Washington, D.C. The traffic snarls in Washington were nothing compared to the congestion that choked the flow of transportation in Beijing, turning even short commutes into multi-hour ordeals. Plus, the air was many times cleaner in his adopted American home city, and he enjoyed a degree of freedom absent from life under rule by the Central Government.

His wife was also content, especially enjoying social media platforms that were blocked in China. And she looked forward to having their son attend an Ivy-League university. Someday, he would retire from the diplomatic corps and purchase a comfortable apartment in Alexandria, or maybe a small house in the Virginia countryside.

Paul Bryan stepped from behind his desk as Mr. Gao entered. They shook hands, and then the Secretary of State motioned to a more comfortable seating area.

"Thank you for coming on short notice, Mr. Gao. A serious situation is developing that threatens the longstanding peace our countries have enjoyed."

"I have already explained that China had nothing to do with the attack on the *Izumo*. What more can I share with you?"

"There has been a second attack. This time, it was aimed at the *USS Makin Island*, an amphibious transport ship that was participating in joint exercises with the Philippines and Australia. The ship was sunk."

"Mr. Secretary. On behalf of my country, please accept my sincerest condolences—I assume there was loss of life."

Bryan narrowed his eyes as he studied his counterpart—body language, cadence and tone of voice, choice of words. *If he's acting, this is an Oscar-worthy performance.*

"Thank you. I'll be sure to pass along your comments to President Taylor."

"No doubt you requested this meeting to ask once more if my country carried out this aggression?"

"Did you?"

"My answer remains unchanged," Gao said calmly. His expression did not betray any emotion.

"My government was given a message—more of a demand, really. It said that the United States is to remove its military presence from the Western Pacific or face destruction. The message was anonymous."

"Given our ongoing disagreement over the territorial claim my government is rightfully asserting over islands in the South China Sea, it is easy to understand your suspicion. However, if President Chen wanted to send a message to President Taylor, he would do so directly. Besides, our displeasure with American warships sailing provocatively through our territorial waters surrounding these islands is communicated frequently through recognized channels. This is not a secret."

"If not China, then who?"

"I assure you, China has not attacked your Navy."

"North Korea?"

"What makes you think China has any useful intelligence on this issue?"

"Do you?"

"Mr. Secretary. I have grown fond of living in the United States. One reason is that most Americans feel perfectly comfortable speaking candidly—sometimes too much so." Ambassador Gao paused, selecting his words precisely. "I gather that you are of the opinion that China, either directly or by aiding North Korea, attacked those two ships. And I am telling you that my government was not involved. What happened is tragic, but you would do well to look beyond your prejudices."

"It would be most helpful if you would share any intelligence that you have related to the possible role North Korea may have played in this matter."

"No doubt. I will pass along your request. However, it would be highly irregular for my government to share information related to the military capability or activities of an allied nation."

"We both know that the present government of North Korea represents a significant threat to world peace."

"Do you believe the missiles were launched from North Korea?"

Bryan shook his head, his expression like stone.

Gao opened his hands and raised his eyebrows.

"We know the weapons were launched from the South China Sea."

"Then, why do you suspect North Korea? They do not

occupy any islands there."

Bryan settled in his chair. "Very well, I'll be candid."

Gao smiled.

"The flight performance of the two weapons was identical. Both were intermediate-range theater ballistic missiles. As you know, few countries have these weapons in their arsenals. And in the region only China and North Korea have the capability to deploy such weapons."

"I see. Do you have evidence of launch facilities anywhere in the South China Sea?"

"Submarines are not easily detected by satellites."

"Ah, a ballistic missile submarine. Please tell me you have evidence?"

"We are searching. And when we locate the boat, well..."

"For a man who has no solid evidence, you are rather certain of the guilty party."

"Two ships have been sunk while conducting routine exercises that threaten no nation. Hundreds of lives were lost. Those are facts, Mr. Gao. Hard facts."

"Of course."

"Do you have anything to add?"

"I have already answered your questions, truthfully. There is nothing more to say, unless you have further questions for me."

"Mr. Ambassador, this is an extremely dangerous time. It would be prudent if your government would take actions to demonstrate its commitment to peace in the region."

"And what actions would you have my government take? You have already concluded that China is responsible for the sinking of the Japanese and the American ships."

"To begin with, your intelligence agencies could open up and cooperate—"

Gao waved a hand, cutting off the Secretary of State. "Please, don't insult my intellect. Your intelligence community will never cooperate with China. Nor will the American military. You would have us turn over sensitive information in a useless gesture of good will, while maneuvering for a superior position to weaken my government's legitimate territorial claims. This is not cooperation."

Bryan folded his hands. He had gone as far as he could, and, with emotions rising, maybe too far. "President Taylor has instructed me to share with you the following message." Paul Bryan drew a deep breath and exhaled. "The unprovoked attack on a U.S. Navy ship is an inexcusable act of war. All nations involved should expect a response in kind. I cannot be more clear."

CHAPTER 15

RATHER THAN TAKE A TAXI to London City Airport, the management of the Ritz insisted that Peter and Robert use the hotel's chauffeured limousine. With no security screening lines to deal with, they simply walked onto the tarmac and climbed the stairs to board the Airbus.

Shortly after takeoff, the attendant served a light snack, including a bowl of water and a plate of diced chicken, peas, and rice for Diesel. The red pit bull consumed the food as if he hadn't eaten in a week. "The Captain has informed me," the attendant said, "that we will be cruising at 35,000 feet on a course to Dubai. We will land there to refuel before completing the final leg of the journey. Would you care for wine or a cocktail?"

Peter and Robert both declined.

"It's going to be a long flight," Robert said, his first words since boarding. "I suggest we both try to get some rest. I'm gonna try a bed in one of the guest rooms. You should do the same."

Peter nodded, but did not rise from his seat on the leather sofa. Headline news was playing on the flat screen, but he wasn't paying much attention. Although he felt fatigued, his mind wouldn't shut down. He kept replaying the events of the previous evening—the attack and struggle, and finally the kidnapping of Jade. *If only I'd had a weapon, something more than a steak knife.*

He leaned back, allowing the soft-padded leather to embrace his still-aching body. Eventually, he closed his eyes, wondering why Eu-meh had insisted on a face-to-face meeting that required him to travel halfway around the world. What did she know? And why was she convinced the abduction was not motivated by greed? As his mind drifted into a semiconscious state, his thoughts returned to Jade. Less than twenty-four hours ago, they were sharing stories over dinner. He recalled in vivid detail her genuine smile, bright laughter, and cheerful eyes. And then images of the kidnapping played on a loop through his mind, tormenting him with a repeating nightmare.

Consumed in his thoughts and guilt, the hours ticked by too slowly. Finally, after a brief stop in Dubai followed by two light meals separated by short, restless naps, the flight attendant announced they were about to land and instructed his passengers to fasten their seat belts. Diesel hopped onto the seat next to Peter.

When the aircraft came to a stop and the engines shut down, Peter stepped through the open cabin door and descended the stairs to the tarmac. His first sensation was a blast of hot, humid air. Within thirty seconds, beads of sweat dappled his forehead. "I've been in hot weather before, but this is something else," he said.

Robert smiled. "Eight-five percent humidity and ninety degrees. Unless you're born here, I doubt a person ever gets used to it."

A middle-aged Malaysian, skinny and about five foot six, was hustling to catch up with their luggage stacked haphazardly on a small trolley. Mercifully, they didn't have far to walk in the oppressive heat; the waiting limousine was parked in the shade of a nearby hangar.

"Another Rolls. Should've guessed," Peter said in mock surprise.

"Well, think what you will of the Sultan, but brand loyalty is not one of his shortcomings."

The driver held the door open and Robert folded his bulk into the rear compartment while Peter walked to the opposite side, causing the driver to dash around the front of the car. He reached his hand to open the door just as Peter was about to grab the handle.

"Oh, sorry," Peter said to ease the man's worried expression.

"Always let the driver open the door for you," Robert advised, his voice low.

"So I gather."

Panting, Diesel jumped in and positioned his body directly in the cool air streaming from a central air vent located near the floor.

As they rode through city traffic, Peter lost count of the number of luxury automobiles he saw—Mercedes, Jaguar, BMW, Audi, and top-of-the-line limousines from Germany and the U.K. It was not long before they stopped in front of a glass-encased modern structure on the bank of the Brunei River.

Robert led the way—clearly he'd been here before. In the lobby, a sign directly opposite the entrance indicated the building's occupant, Hua Ho Holdings. The floor and walls were surfaced in light-tan marble, and recessed lighting in the high ceiling supplemented the natural light flooding in through the front glass wall.

They signed in at the reception desk and then passed a

uniformed guard to enter the glistening chrome elevator. The guard inserted a key in the panel, turned it, and then pressed the top button—tenth floor.

"Looks like we are expected," Peter said.

Robert nodded. "Mrs. Lim is a very important executive within the company, plus a member of the royal family. Her security is taken seriously."

The elevator opened onto another reception room. They signed in at the desk and then were led through a frosted glass wall into a large office. Peter tried to take it all in, discretely of course, but he was having to turn his head far to one side and then the other, and he still wasn't capturing the entire office. He estimated the area to be at least 3,000 square feet.

"Welcome to Brunei," a feminine voice called from across the office, drawing Peter's attention.

An attractive woman with a slim figure rose from behind a massive desk. Her shoulder-length black hair showed just a hint of copper highlights. She approached with her hand outstretched, cloaked in a long, high-collared dress that extended to her ankles. Even her arms were covered to the wrists. The fabric shimmered like silk and was adorned with an intricate floral pattern. A long string of perfect white pearls was wrapped in a double loop around her neck. She shook first Peter's hand and then Robert's. If Peter hadn't already known she was Jade's mother, he would have guessed her age to be late-thirties.

"Thank you, Robert, for coming quickly. You must be exhausted, but I need you here. I hope you understand."

"Of course," he replied with a slight bow of his head.

She faced Peter. "My name is Lim Eu-meh. But please, call me Eu-meh. Formalities should be reserved for state functions. And this must be Diesel. Jade spoke at length about how your dog saved you from a vicious bear." She lowered her hand and patted the dog on the head.

"It's a pleasure to meet you Eu-meh. Your daughter has told me much about you." She looked deeply into Peter's eyes, and at that moment he felt as if she might read his thoughts. "I'm very sorry about what happened."

"My daughter told me you are a nice man, a good man. She calls you her guardian. You saved her from harm in Oregon, is that right?"

Peter nodded.

"And Robert tells me you fought the kidnappers in London, placing yourself at great risk."

Eu-meh turned her head to Robert, noticing the bruise on his forehead. She added, "You both did."

She motioned to a grouping of plush chairs arranged around a small table. As Robert and Peter were seated, Eu-meh opened her office door and issued quick instructions in Malay, then sat opposite her guests.

"I've read the preliminary report from the London police." She read the confusion in Peter's face. "The government of Brunei shares a close cooperation with the United Kingdom— one of the advantages, I suppose, of being a former British colony." Eu-meh paused while a woman dressed conservatively and wearing a Hijab placed a silver tray on the table. She poured coffee from a silver carafe into porcelain cups decorated with gold filigree, and then silently departed the office.

"Of course, the report included both your statements. Those men had guns—they could have killed both of you."

"We'll find Miss Jade," Robert said, "and bring her home."

Eu-meh's eyes glistened with moisture, but she refused to allow tears to fall. "Robert, you have been a loyal employee for so many years. You have watched over my daughter since she was a young girl. I have no doubt you speak with sincerity. But you do not fully understand who we are dealing with."

"Excuse me," Peter cleared his throat. "You sound as if you know who kidnapped your daughter. If you'll forgive me, why not just go to the police with your information?"

She looked hard at Peter, worry shadowing her features. "Do you know what it feels like to lose someone you love more than life itself?"

Peter felt his emotions stirring, old and painful memories resurrected again by her directness. Memories of a shootout with Janjaweed rebels in Darfur to rescue his son, Ethan. Memories of his wife dying on a hospital bed following a winter automobile accident. Vivid images, sounds, scents—all still real and far from forgotten. He quelled his feelings before replying. "I've suffered the loss of a loved one." He worked his jaw, choosing his words carefully. "And I know that sometimes the best we can do is not sufficient. I didn't always think that way. At one time, I believed that anything was possible; that I could protect those I held most dear, shield them from harm." He shook his head, and held Eu-meh's eyes. "But it's not true."

"Your wife."

Peter's eyes widened and his lips moved to voice the question, but she cut him off. "Jade told me," she explained. "My daughter is a good judge of character. She told me much about you. Many men would have tried to take advantage of a young, rich woman, but you didn't."

"My daughter is about the same age as Jade."

Eu-meh nodded. "Then I know you understand. Your paternal instinct is strong, and I'm asking for your help."

"And I will do all I can, but I still think this is best handled by the police. If you know who abducted—"

"What I know to be true, and what I can prove, are two entirely different matters."

"I see."

"But to be clear Mr. Savage—"

"Please, call me Peter."

Eu-meh smiled politely. "Peter. The night my daughter was kidnapped, I spoke over the phone to Robert. I told him that I know *why* Jade was taken."

"That's a good start. If we know why, then maybe we can figure out who is behind it."

"Please, go on," Robert said.

She rubbed the pearls between her fingers and leaned back in her chair. "Do you understand, Mr. Savage—Peter—what my job is with Hua Ho Holdings?"

"Jade mentioned you're in charge of logistics for the company. Beyond that, I really don't know."

"That is partly true. You see, I am the chairperson of the company. Rather unusual for a woman, wouldn't you say?"

"Yes, I suppose so."

"One of the benefits of being the sister to the Sultan." She lifted the porcelain cup by the handle to her lips.

"In any case," Eu-meh continued, "I oversee the activities of Hua Ho Holdings. One of my responsibilities is to see that the company's long-term strategy is executed. I have many executives who report to me, including logistics. Naturally, I receive regular reports of where our ships are deployed, what maintenance and upgrades are being carried out, and so on. I'm sure you understand."

"The company is engaged in off-shore oil exploration," Robert added.

"That's right. Revenue from oil and gas production has made my country quite wealthy, allowing the citizens of Brunei to enjoy a very comfortable standard of living. In fact, per capita income is relatively high by any measure, and combined with free health care and subsidized food and housing, Bruneians have long life expectancy and are well educated."

"Not to mention many have excellent taste in automobiles,"

Peter quipped.

"We have a fleet of seventeen ships. Nine are purposed for exploration, including drilling test wells. The other eight are supply ships."

"You mean they transport cargo?"

"Yes. Not only to support the exploration vessels, but they also ferry equipment and other materials and supplies to off-shore wells. It is a lucrative business, although not as glamorous as exploration.

"The South China Sea is rich in oil and gas. My company generates steady revenue, and as long as expenses are managed, the profit margin is attractive and predictable."

"Has a ransom demand been delivered yet?" Peter asked.

"No, and I am certain there will be no ransom demand. As I explained to Robert already, Jade was not kidnapped for money."

"How can you be so certain?"

"Three months ago, I noticed an anomaly in our maintenance records. One of our exploration ships, the *Royal Seeker*, was in dry dock being fitted with new engines and props."

"Go on," Peter said.

"I did not recall authorization for such expensive upgrades. That should have come from the Board of Directors. So, I inquired with the engineering manager. He checked his records, and said that I must be mistaken; the *Royal Seeker* was scheduled for a routine overhaul of its engines, not replacement."

Peter sipped the strong coffee and then placed the cup on the table. "Perhaps the engines were too old and damaged, and replacing them was the most cost-effective solution? Maybe the propellers were also worn and in need of replacement?"

"Yes, I had the same thought. But the engineering department would have had a record of that."

"And no such record exists," Peter said.

"No."

"Have you spoken with the vessel's captain?" Robert asked.

Eu-meh nodded. "He denies that these upgrades were done and claims that his ship was in port for routine maintenance only, before putting to sea again."

"Are you certain this isn't a simple case of fraud?" Peter said.

"I am not naïve. Naturally, that thought has occurred to me as well. I have instructed one of my trusted accountants to look into this—discretely, of course. So far, the question remains unresolved."

"I don't see the connection with your daughter's kidnapping."

"Hua Ho Holdings equips all of its ships with locating beacons. The device is similar to those on commercial aircraft. It sends a signal that is relayed by satellite, indicating the location of the ship. This way, we track our vessels all the time. You see, the South China Sea is still dangerous, and piracy is a very real threat.

"I requested the log record for the *Royal Seeker* from the date it left dry dock until a week ago. The log indicated everything was normal and showed the ship followed its scheduled route. Except it didn't."

"How can you be certain?" Peter asked.

"According to the tracking log, one week ago the *Royal Seeker* was within helicopter range. I had my pilot fly me to the location where the ship was supposed to be—"

"Only it wasn't there."

"You are perceptive, Peter. The *Royal Seeker* was not anywhere within sight of the location indicated by the tracking log."

"Where is the ship?" Robert asked.

"I don't know. But late that night, a message was delivered

to my apartment." Eu-meh walked to her desk and retrieved a slip of paper. She presented it to Robert. He read it and then passed it to Peter.

The note was printed on common paper and consisted of only two sentences. It was not dated or signed. There were no identifying markings at all—it could have been printed by anyone. Peter frowned, and handed it back to Eu-meh.

"Now, do you see? If I do not stop my investigation and remain silent, they will kill my daughter."

CHAPTER 16

IT WAS A SHORT DRIVE from Hua Ho Holdings headquarters to Istana Nurul Iman Palace, home to Sultan Omar Muhammad Shah. At over two million square feet and with 1,788 rooms, there was more than enough space for the Sultan's extended family, celebrity visitors, and official state business.

While the driver slowed at the gatehouse, the government soldier stepped out and quickly recognized Eu-meh Lim. He snapped to attention and saluted as the driver eased the limousine forward.

"Park at the security office," Eu-meh instructed the driver. A separate structure from the main palace, the security building housed a garrison of soldiers, all wearing distinctive black berets, whose job it was to ensure no harm came to the royal family. With meeting rooms and offices, barracks, commissary, medical facilities, and armory, the security operation was entirely self-contained. All of the soldiers were handpicked, and all were single with no significant family ties.

The driver held the rear door for Eu-meh, while Robert and Peter were content to let themselves out of the vehicle. Diesel waited in the car with the driver.

"I want to introduce you to my nephew, Pehin Anak Shah. He is the youngest of my brother's three sons, and he's in charge of security—here at the palace as well as for Hua Ho Holdings."

The glass double doors slid open as Eu-meh approached. She strode in with a confident air as if she owned the property—which wasn't far from the truth.

"I'd like to speak with my nephew," she said to the receptionist from five paces away.

"Yes, ma'am." The young woman spoke softly into a phone, and then said, "He'll see you now." She waved to the side but Eu-meh was already in motion.

A short hallway ended at two tall, polished mahogany doors. The brass plaque on the door read DIRECTOR OF SECURITY.

Eu-meh knocked politely and then nudged the door open.

A young man dressed in military uniform and decorated with an abundance of ribbons and medals, stood from behind his desk. "Come in! Eu-meh, always a pleasure to see you. And these must be your friends?"

"I see word travels fast," Peter mumbled.

Eu-meh stepped forward and embraced her nephew. Turning slightly, she said, "This is Peter Savage. And of course, you know Robert."

Pehin Anak Shah extended his hand first to Peter and then to Robert. "Of course. Robert and I have met before." He smiled, his teeth flashing brilliant white. "And you, Mr. Savage. It is a pleasure to meet you. I understand my family owes you a debt of gratitude for saving my cousin while she was touring America."

Peter bowed his head. When his eyes met those of the

Security Director, he said, "Unfortunately, we were not as lucky in London. I'm very sorry."

"Yes, I understand," Pehin said. He clasped his hands behind his back. "You are welcome to the palace, as guests of my aunt. I will make sure your presence is known to the security guards so there is no," he tilted his head, "misunderstanding." Although his eyes twinkled, the rest of his face hardened. There was no expression of sincerity.

"Thank you," Peter said, wondering if there was a threat buried in this last statement.

"Of course," Pehin continued, "as honored guests, you may enjoy freedoms while on the palace grounds that would not be afforded elsewhere in Brunei. I'm sure you understand."

Peter studied the smiling face, again thinking there was more being communicated than the simple statement. "No, actually, I don't understand."

"What he is saying," Robert explained, "is that Brunei is a predominantly Muslim country. Some Western indulgences, such as alcohol, are not allowed."

"Thank you, Robert. Mr. Savage, I advise you to be cautious, and respectful. Strictly speaking, the actions of citizens and visitors alike may be judged by Sharia law."

"There is no reason for concern," Eu-meh said. "Robert understands our culture and our laws. I've no doubt he will teach Mr. Savage accordingly. Now, I would like to put my friends in the corner suite."

Pehin bowed.

The brief meeting concluded, the trio left the Security Director's office. A short drive in the limo, and they were at one end of the palace. From the backseat window, Peter saw a three-story structure with expansive terraces at each level. Rich and diverse plantings rose above and spilled over the waist-high railings.

"This is called the garden apartment," Eu-meh said.

"It's beautiful," Peter said.

"Wait 'till you see the inside," Robert replied, earning a rare smile from Eu-meh.

They strode across a walkway of polished granite slabs— each at least a meter in dimension on each side—that traversed a lush lawn. Peter recognized the roundish, pea-sized leaves and low-growing ground cover as dichondra. The granite walkway continued into the garden where it merged with a large patio, also constructed of the same granite squares.

To lend privacy, the garden was surrounded with a trellis wall. Philodendron, jade vine, Indian clock vine, red trumpet vine, bougainvillea, and other varieties of flowering plants Peter did not recognize grew together in lush abundance. Pots placed at various locations on the patio held other gorgeous tropical specimens blooming in vibrant shades of red, orange, pink, yellow, blue, and violet. And the foliage itself offered a seemingly endless range of shades of green that seemed all the more vibrant in the bright tropical sunshine.

The entrance door was taller than Peter by at least two feet, and crafted of solid teak wood. The surface of the door was decorated with a deep, three-dimensional carving of a peacock in front of a domed mosque. Peter stood before the door, admiring the carving.

"That is the Omar Ali Saifuddien Mosque," Eu-meh explained. "It's named after the twenty-eighth Sultan of Brunei, and many consider it to be the most beautiful mosque in all of Asia."

Awestruck, Peter said, "It's absolutely gorgeous." It didn't escape his notice that all of the door hardware—from the hinges to the latch to the large cover plate—were plated with 24 karat gold, not brass.

Eu-meh opened the door. It appeared to move effortlessly

and not a squeak was heard as the lubricated hinges swiveled. "Shall we?"

Peter and Robert followed her into a large parlor floored in squares of alternating black and white marble, like a checker board. From the parlor, a wide staircase ascended, the treads covered in ruby-colored carpet. "Bedroom suites are on the second and third floors," she said. "Each room has a buzzer, like this one," she pointed to a button inset in a gold plate on the wall. "Press it and the wait staff will respond to serve your needs at any time. Since the apartment is not normally occupied, the butler and day staff will be here shortly."

Eu-meh walked to the right and opened double teak doors that led into a large room. Like the parlor, the ceiling was nine feet high, and crown-molding lining the coffered ceiling exuded elegance, which was subdued slightly by the furnishings. In the center sat a full-sized billiard table, constructed of polished ebony and covered in cobalt-blue felt. To the right, facing the patio garden, were a pair of French doors framed in teak. The panel of each door was made of an intricate pattern of leaded beveled glass. Through the ornate glasswork, the garden appeared as a kaleidoscope image. Around the perimeter of the room were floor-to-ceiling bookcases, separated at the center of the room by a massive gas fireplace framed in carved white marble. On the wall opposite the fireplace was a full-length bar. It took Peter a full two minutes to take it all in. When he did, all he could say was, "Wow. This is unbelievable."

His eyes floated over the selection of spirits along the mirrored wall behind the ebony bar. "I thought alcohol was not allowed?"

"My brother believes in tolerance of other cultures and religions. He does not wish to impose his beliefs upon our guests."

"So it would seem. Tell him thank you."

"While you are here, consider this your home. You should get some rest, and in the morning we must talk."

Peter realized he'd been behaving like a tourist. There was a serious reason he was here. "Thank you… for your gracious hospitality," he said. Diesel, who had remained close by Peter's side, sighed and looked directly at Eu-meh, his amber-colored eyes locking on hers.

She forced a smile and then left Robert and Peter standing in the game room. A thought suddenly came to Peter. "She didn't leave a key."

"Why should she," Robert said. "You're at the Sultan's palace, not the Holiday Inn."

"But—"

"Relax. The butler will be here 24/7. Probably has a room on the ground floor. And besides, this place has a security detail that puts the White House to shame."

Peter walked to the bar and opened a wine refrigerator, removing a bottle of white. "Pinot gris. Chile." He cast his eyes about the bar and opened drawers until he found what he was seeking. He pulled the cork and poured a glass, leaving the cork puller on the bar. "Care for some?"

"Why not," Robert said.

"So, what now?" Peter asked.

As Robert sipped from his glass, he walked to the billiard table and rolled a few balls around the table with his free hand. Peter watched in silence for a minute.

"Well?" he prompted.

"We could start by reviewing all the documents Hua Ho Holdings has on the *Royal Seeker*. Maybe Eu-meh missed something in the maintenance and engineering logs."

"And we'd be wasting time. Whatever is in those records, it doesn't explain why the *Royal Seeker* was not where it's locating beacon indicted it should be."

"So, what are you saying?"

"I don't know." Peter removed two pool cues from the rack and handed one to Robert. "Rack 'em up."

Peter leaned over the edge of the table, moving the cue stick back and forth, then slammed the tip into the cue ball. "What could be on an oil exploration ship that would justify making it disappear?"

Robert stared back. "I don't know. Maybe they found something? And they don't want their log book and records to be seen by Hua Ho Holdings."

"Nah. You don't disappear an entire ship if all you want are the records. It would have been easy to replace the original log book with a forged copy, and the same for the computer records. And, now that I think about it—there's the crew."

Robert took his shot, the number ten ball failing to drop into the pocket. "What do you mean?"

"Well. If you are going to make a ship disappear, what about the crew? I mean, are they all complicit? Or only some? And those who don't play along, what do you do?"

"They'd have to kill them."

"Exactly. And how many of the crew can they kill and still operate the ship?" Peter rammed the cue ball into the three ball, it sank. He lined up for the next shot.

"All of them. Even the captain and executives officers could be eliminated if a replacement crew was onboard."

The clack of billiard balls colliding sounded loud and sharp, echoing off the hard surfaces of the room. For a moment, Peter thought it metaphorical, like a gunshot punctuating the hypothetical murder of the ship's crew.

"Or none. What if the crew was hired by another party?"

"Same difference," Robert replied. "Either way, we have a crew that is not answering to their supposed employer, Hua Ho Holdings."

"Exactly." *Crack!* The five ball fell into a leather pocket. "So, it doesn't matter what is in the company's maintenance logs. The answer lies in what's onboard the *Royal Seeker*."

"Okay, Master Yoda. How do we answer that question?"

"First, we find the *Royal Seeker*."

Robert rolled his eyes. "Yeah, like that thought never occurred to me. Okay, *how* do we find the ship? It's tracking beacon is not functioning, remember? And, in case you didn't know, there are hundreds of ships in the South China Sea."

Peter set the cue stick aside and started punching a number into his phone. "I think I know someone who can help us."

CHAPTER 17

THERE WAS NO MISTAKE. Commander Nicolaou had gone over the data with Lacey and the team. Based on the radar tracking from the *Shiloh*, *Lassen*, and *McCampbell* of the missile used in the first attack, and radar data from a circling AWACs that tracked the second missile, the conclusion was irrefutable.

His secure desk phone rang; the call was expected. "Commander Nicolaou."

"I need answers, Commander." It was Colonel Pierson. "I'm sure I don't have to remind you of the gravity of the situation. And it seems to be deteriorating by the hour. President Chen vehemently denies any involvement in the sinking of either ship, and has publicly accused the United States of fabricating the incidents in order to justify a military buildup in the South China Sea. We are tracking an increased level of troop movements, not to mention a flotilla of nine Chinese warships that is steaming for the Spratly Islands. Satellite photos show that fighter aircraft have already been transferred to the three operational airfields in that island chain."

"We're working the problem, Colonel. This is our top priority... Hell, our only priority."

"Talk to me."

"There just isn't much to go on. We've tracked the two missile launchings to two separate locations near the Spratly Islands. Since we see no evidence of missile launch facilities on any of the islands—even those enhanced in land area and further improved by President Chen's government with airfields and missile batteries—it is very likely that we are looking for a submarine."

"With ballistic missile capability?" In a rare display of emotion, Colonel Pierson did not hide his surprise.

"Yes, sir. Based on the work by Lieutenant Lacey's team, that's the most probable explanation. Both China and North Korea possess submarines with ballistic missile capability."

The phone line was silent while the colonel considered the implications. "Then we're looking for a needle in a haystack, and for all practical purposes we're blind. The only way we'll find that missile boat is if one of our ships stumbles across it."

"Sir, I recommend that the Navy deploy sonobuoys at every choke point in and near the Spratlys."

"That'll take some time."

"Yes, I understand. Which is why it's vital to start ASAP. Both the Chinese Jin class ballistic missile submarine and the North Korean Sinpo class are relatively noisy, and we should be able to detect and track them from a great distance. The commercial shipping traffic will create a lot of background noise, but that can be filtered out with computer software. How many fast attack boats do we have in theater?"

"Not enough. The *New Mexico* is presently on station, and two more Virginia-class submarines are scheduled to arrive in the South China Sea within thirty-three hours. Carrier Strike

Group 5 left the Sea of Japan over a day ago. They're making thirty-five knots for the Spratly Islands."

Jim heard a muffled conversation in the background, then Colonel Pierson addressed him again. "I just instructed my aide to advise the Navy to get every P-3 and P-8 they have from Canberra to Manilla in the air and seed the South China Sea with sonobuoys. If there are any Chinese or North Korean submarines lurking in that vicinity, we'll know within forty-eight hours. I'll relay your assessment to the Joint Chiefs. Keep me updated if you have any new developments." The colonel ended the call.

Jim had a nagging concern that he hadn't been able to shake. If the Chinese were using the ship-killer weapon, they had to know they were risking all-out war with the only super-power navy; a fight they were sure to lose, and at great cost. Could it be that North Korea's Supreme Leader—a reckless ruler who many considered to be mad—was trying to implicate China? But what would that gain for his regime? After all, China was the only benefactor of the isolated and poverty-stricken country. If China were to suffer a blow at the hands of the U.S. Navy, what good would North Korea derive? And if the Supreme Leader was, in fact, receiving the hardened and ultra-dense warheads from China, didn't that make China culpable? *It has to be China—but why? What do they hope to gain?*

At the heart of Carrier Strike Group 5 was the modern aircraft carrier *USS Gerald R. Ford*. Recently commissioned and temporarily based out of Yokosuka, Japan, there was no match for her battle capability and firepower. Soon, she would be within aviation range of the Chinese airbases and naval ships in the South China Sea. Approximately 15,000 men and women from both sides were about to come face-to-face. Would one side blink? Or would someone pull the trigger and fire the first shot inaugurating a Sino-American war?

Jim leaned forward, resting his chin on the palms of his hands, elbows firmly planted on the desktop. Stress and lack of sleep were conspiring against him, and he closed his eyes. He saw the *USS Gerald Ford* steaming into the wind, his vantage point above the carrier and to the side, but keeping pace perfectly as the warship sailed at thirty-five knots.

Super Hornets were taking off, one after another, from the massive flight deck. And then, from the Heavens, a bright streak reached down and connected to the center of the ship. It was like a lightning bolt, only it formed a perfectly straight trajectory. At the point of connection with the flight deck, a massive hole instantly appeared, followed a second later by the horrendous noise—a combination of sonic boom and the bending and renting of steel as the hardened, hypersonic projectile tore a path of destruction through the ship, exiting through the keel. A heartbeat later, secondary explosions added to the cacophony. A huge fireball erupted from the impact hole, fed by almost a million gallons of aviation fuel. Flame ejected through the aircraft elevators, fiery tongues lapping out the side of the hull.

The aircraft carrier seemed to slow. The wake behind the ship as well as the bow wave were diminishing in size. Men were scurrying across the flight deck. A new sound rose in intensity to be heard above the roar of fire and both large and small explosions from ordnance cooking off. The mournful sound rumbled from deep within the ship as the steel groaned and bellowed, fighting against the uneven stresses of blast-furnace heat, and compromised bulkheads and deck plates. Then suddenly, the mighty carrier, pride of the Navy, buckled and separated in two. The cleaved sections quickly slid under the waves, leaving behind a burning slick of fuel.

Jim awoke with a start. He rubbed a hand across his face and then rose from his desk. A walk around the facility would do wonders to relieve his lethargy. He entered the cafeteria and was pouring a cup of coffee when his phone rang, the caller identified on the screen.

"Hello, Peter."

"Jim, hope I didn't catch you at a bad time. Do you have a minute?"

"Just grabbing a coffee and stretching my legs. What's up?"

"I need your help."

"Okay, if I can."

"A friend has been kidnapped, and I need some help to find her."

"This sounds like police business. Domestic crimes are not within the charter of SGIT, or the Defense Department."

"Look, I know that. Just hear me out—please."

Jim listened as Peter recounted the events leading up to Jade's kidnapping.

"Jade's mother," Peter explained, "received an anonymous note demanding she stop searching for an oil exploration ship that apparently is missing."

"Go on," Jim said.

"How can we search for this missing ship? We know what it looks like, so I'm wondering if high resolution satellite images can be used to identify it?"

"Sounds intriguing. You have a real-life mystery on your hands."

"So it can be done?"

"Yes, it can be done. Assuming the ship's not sunk or hidden by cloud cover, that is. But searching and screening images is a tedious and time-consuming task. And depending on the angle of the sun, a ship's super structure can take on different appearances. Unless you have a computer doing the work. And before you ask, no… I can't authorize MOTHER to search through satellite images for you. Besides, my entire team is focused on another priority at the moment."

After a brief pause, Peter said, "I understand. Actually, Jade's family is very well connected. I've no doubt they can buy the computer time as well as the satellite images."

"They'll also need to hire a programmer to write the code, a short program that instructs the computer to examine each image against the specifications and design of the missing ship…"

Jim's voice trailed off as another thought entered his mind.

"Where are you?" he asked.

"Brunei. Jade is a niece of the Sultan."

"And this missing oil exploration ship—where was it last seen?"

"The South China Sea, in waters Brunei lays claim to."

Jim fell silent as the possibility registered in his brain.

"Hello? Jim, can you hear me?"

"This could be important," Jim said. He suddenly lost interest in coffee and was striding back to his office. "I'm gonna call you back. I want to get Lacey in on this. Are you in a private location where you can talk?"

Barely five minutes had passed when Peter answered his phone. "I have you on speaker. Where are you?" Jim asked.

"I'm at the Istana Nurul Imam Palace."

"Palace of the Faith Light." Lieutenant Lacey recited the English translation.

"It's the Sultan's palace in Bandar Seri Begawan. A mouthful, so the ex-pats here just call it BSB."

"Are you in a private location?" Jim asked.

"Yes, I am. Jade's mother—Eu-meh—has invited us to stay in a guest apartment at the palace. I'm there now."

"You said 'us'. Who's with you?"

"A guy named Robert Schneider. Ex-Navy. He's Jade's bodyguard and driver."

Jim noticed that Lacey was typing the name into her tablet. "I'll have Sergeant Williams run a background check," she said.

"Good. Now, you mentioned an oil exploration ship. Do you know the name of the ship?"

"Eu-meh said it's the *Royal Seeker*. It's owned and operated by Hua Ho Holdings."

Lacey was entering the information. "Got it. Here's an image of the ship." She turned the screen so Jim could see it. With the superstructure placed far forward, the middle and stern of the ship was low and relatively flat. Towering above the middle of the ship was a grid-like structure; a crane was farther aft. Beneath the tower was the moon pool, an opening in the hull to allow pipe and drilling equipment to enter the water beneath the ship.

"What do you think, Lieutenant?"

Lacey raised her eyebrows. "I think you are suggesting an intriguing theory."

"See if Williams can run the numbers. I want to know if it's possible."

"Latitude for modifications?"

Jim nodded. "Tower and crane. For now, assume no change to the hull or superstructure."

"Hello? I'm still here, you know," Peter said.

"I'm sorry, Mr. Savage," Lacey said. "But this line is not secure."

"Look, I called asking for help. And now you're playing the security card on me?"

"Relax, Peter." Jim locked eyes with Ellen Lacey as he finished his thought. "We can help you. I believe we now have reason to task MOTHER with your quest."

CHAPTER 18

WITH A SLEEK HULL and angular superstructure that more closely resembled Darth Vader's Imperial Star Cruiser than it did classic warship design, the littoral combat ship *USS Independence* was making thirty knots on a northeasterly heading. Sailing from Singapore and accompanied by her sister ship the *USS Coronado*, the *Independence* had travelled more than 600 nautical miles to the southern reach of the Spratly Islands.

"East Reef is directly to port, sir," announced Executive Officer (XO) Birch.

Captain Moresby was scanning the forward horizon through binoculars. He had read the latest update from USPACFLT. Two ships, thought to be Chinese destroyers, were well north of his current position. Satellite surveillance photos suggested the pair of warships were patrolling the central region of the South China Sea.

Moresby's mission was to sail through the southern

grouping of islands and then along the eastern edge of the Spratly Island chain, exercising what the United States government termed "freedom of navigation." There was nothing new about this policy, but with the current heightened tension between the U.S. and China, Moresby knew this would not be a routine deployment. He had ordered his crew to strictly adhere to international law and Navy policy. In particular, his ship was to approach no closer than twelve nautical miles from any landmass, no matter how small the chunk of coral and sand may be.

"Maintaining minimum approach distance?" he asked.

"Yes, sir," Birch replied. "Closest approach was 12.1 nautical miles. We are passing East Reef now. Cuarteron Reef is ahead. Also to port."

"Very well." Captain Moresby was young, only forty-six. Born and raised far from the ocean in Topeka, Kansas, Bruce Moresby was ambitious, smart, and yearned to travel. From an early age, there was never a doubt in his mind that his calling was to serve in the Navy. He graduated from Annapolis at the top of his class and then began a meteoric rise through the Navy until he was awarded command of his own ship.

"Status of defensive systems?" he said.

"SeaRAM is online and ready," answered the XO. "All guns are manned and ready."

Constructed of steel and aluminum, the littoral combat ships were designed to move fast and traverse shallow, coastal waters. They were not designed to slug it out with larger and more heavily-armed opponents. One well-placed anti-ship missile and the *Independence* would be another chunk of litter on the ocean floor. That's not to say the *Independence* and her sister ship, the *Coronado*, were defenseless. Both vessels carried a Seahawk helicopter for antisubmarine warfare, an unmanned Fire Scout drone armed with Hellfire guided missiles, and

Harpoon anti-ship missiles.

Moresby continued to scan the horizon. As far as he could see, the sky was clear—pale blue with a few scattered white puffs of clouds. The ocean almost merged with the sky, distinguished only by a slightly-darker shade of blue. Thankfully, the seas were relatively calm, and motion onboard the *Independence* was minimal as the sleek vessel knifed through the water.

"Once we pass Cuarteron Reef, Fiery Cross Reef will be the next significant land mass to port, is that right?" the captain asked. He routinely memorized the key features along their intended route.

XO Birch consulted the navigational chart projected on a screen in a console in the center portion of the bridge. It was dotted with dozens of islands, most uninhabited. He moved his finger along their charted course. "Yes, that's correct."

The captain lowered his binoculars. "The Chinese will be especially sensitive to a Navy warship approaching their newly constructed base on Fiery Cross. Plot a course that brings us within twenty nautical miles, but no closer. Then turn to new bearing nine-five degrees. I want to make it clear we are present but are not a threat."

"You think they'll see us on radar?" the XO asked.

"Maybe. But for sure they'll pick up our emissions."

For the next five hours, the *Independence* and the *Coronado* sailed in a close formation. After turning east and speeding away from Fiery Cross Reef, Moresby instructed the XO to conduct a man-overboard drill. It was a thinly-veiled attempt to support the argument that the two Navy ships were conducting a routine training mission.

As expected, their ship-born sensors indicated they were being painted by radar from the airfield and supporting infrastructure China had constructed on Fiery Cross Reef. Whether or not the technicians operating the land-based radar systems were seeing enough reflected energy to interpret as two warships was anybody's guess. Moresby suspected that the angular construction and other stealth features of his ship masked their approach to the military installation. One of his mission objectives was to probe the capabilities of the bases on Fiery Cross Reef and Mischief Reef. The radar data was being recorded, along with their navigational history, for later analysis.

"Standard search frequencies," Birch reported. "They're probably trying to figure out why they see our radar emissions, but nothing else."

"Let's keep them guessing. The electronic warfare guys at the Pentagon will spend weeks reviewing the data. For now, just maintain our heading. Once we turn north and make way for Mischief Reef, it might get tense. According to the satellite images, a couple missile batteries have been installed there. Intel says they're most likely SAMs, but no one is ruling out anti-ship missiles."

The afternoon wore on with no remarkable events. The tropical sun baked down on the ship, and Moresby and his officers were glad the bridge and other interior compartments were air-conditioned. He could only imagine how uncomfortable it would have been to serve on a ship a few decades ago, when the only relief from the tropical heat was an open hatch, a cold drink, or ice cream.

The XO continued to make his rounds, checking in with the crew men and women responsible for the major function of the ship—navigation, engineering, weapons. They had plenty of fuel to circle the Spratly Islands before returning to Singapore, and the engines were running well. The reports were routine.

Other than short breaks, Captain Moresby stayed on the bridge, mostly glassing the horizon for anything—ship or plane—that might represent a threat.

"Scope still clear of contacts?" Moresby asked.

Only five minutes ago the XO had asked navigation that very question. "Yes, sir. Nothing—"

He was interrupted with an urgent update. "Contact. Unidentified bogy. Bearing three-zero-zero degrees. Altitude 18,000 feet. Distance... approximately forty-three nautical miles and closing."

The XO and captain both gathered around the navigation console. The screen showed a green blip representing the aircraft. Well beyond visible range, it looked like it would come close to the *Independence*, but was not on a direct course to intercept the ship. "Too low to be commercial. Can't be one of ours," the XO said. "There's no IFF transponder code showing."

"Don't always trust that. Sometimes the pilot may turn off the transponder, not wanting his aircraft to be identified as friend or foe. Maybe one of our planes is doing some aerial recon on the Chinese bases. Better get on the radio and find out if we have any aircraft in the area."

Birch made a call over the ship intercom to the communications center, while the captain continued to stare at the tactical display. A minute later, he had his answer. "Negative. No U.S. or allied aircraft are conducting operations within a hundred miles of us."

The blip changed direction, tracking now on a straight line for the ship. "Looks like they were listening to our radio signal," Birch said.

"Sound general quarters," Moresby ordered. The klaxon screeched, signaling every sailor to go to their designated battle stations.

Four more lookouts entered the bridge and searched the sky with binoculars in the direction from which they knew the bogey would approach. "Two of you," the XO said, pointing to a pair of crewmen. "Out on the deck and search aft. If you spot anything—airplane or ship—report immediately."

"Increase to full speed. Stay on course," Moresby said, and the XO repeated the order.

A long, tense minute passed before the silence on the bridge was interrupted by Birch. "We're being painted by search radar from the bogey. No indication they have a lock on us."

The captain was still studying the tactical display. The bogey had altered direction a second time and was on a parallel bearing to the ship. One of the spotters called out. "I've got 'em sir! Reflection off to port and slightly aft."

"Can you get an ID?" the XO asked.

"No, sir. Too far away, only a reflection of light."

Glued to the display, Moresby said, "We ought'a know soon. The bogey is on a new bearing that should take it over our bow."

"The crew has probably been ordered to get a positive ID on us."

Six pair of binoculars were pointed at the sky where the unidentified plane was speeding toward the naval vessel. Still only a bright spot of reflected sunlight, the spot was growing larger by the second.

"Looks like four engines," one of the lookouts reported. Several more seconds passed before he added, "Turboprop."

A second and then a third lookout confirmed. Both the captain and XO were also studying the aircraft through the high-magnification optics.

"Patrol aircraft," Birch said to no one in particular. He continued speaking without lowering the binoculars. "Y-8X. At least it doesn't carry weapons."

Moresby wasn't ready to relax yet. "No, but it can track us and report our position."

"We're well outside of the twelve-mile limit for any landmass, clearly in international waters."

"You seem to forget, Mr. Birch, that the Chinese view

the entire Spratly Island group as their territory. From their perspective, we are well *within* their territorial claim."

The XO lowered his glasses and followed the captain into the Communication Center at the rear of the bridge. A heavy curtain blocked sunlight from entering the compartment, which served as the combat and communications nerve center for the ship. It was bathed in dim red light. Several crewmembers, wearing headphones with lip microphones, were hunched over consoles studying their data feeds.

"It's passed us," Birch said, meaning that the patrol plane was now flying away from the *Independence*.

A crewman spoke up. "Picking up radio traffic from the bogey."

"No new contacts," reported another crewmember monitoring the ship's radar. "Bogey is departing. New course... due north."

"All weapons are in standby," came the report from another console.

"Keep them locked down," Birch ordered. "I don't want an accidental firing because the SeaRAM was switched to auto."

A close-in defensive system, the SeaRAM used a search and track radar system to steer missiles onto attacking aircraft and anti-ship missiles. With a range of nine kilometers, and a battery holding eleven rolling airframe missiles, it could track, lock, and fire automatically, using pre-program guidelines to identify and prioritize threats.

"New contact!" The radar technician's voice was elevated in pitch. "Bearing one-three degrees. Moving fast, sir... subsonic... return is too small for an attack aircraft... I think it's a cruise missile!"

"Battle stations!" Moresby ordered. "Set condition zebra. Engage SeaRAM. Set on auto."

Birch turned to Captain Moresby. "That cruise missile must

have been fired from Mischief Reef. I don't get it. How can they have a lock on us? None of our sensors indicate a lock?"

"They don't," Moresby replied without diverting his eyes from the tactical display. It showed a red line, designated Bogey Two, moving toward their ship and the *Coronado*. "The patrol plane reported our position and gave the firing coordinates to the missile crew. If the cruise missile gets close enough, it's internal search radar will get a lock."

Then Moresby issued a new order. "Increase to flank speed." The order was repeated by the XO, and they felt the increase in speed as the ship accelerated. The engines were running at 110% of rated output—acceptable only for short bursts of speed. Which is exactly what was required here. Moresby needed to get far enough away from the cruise missile that its seeker head would not detect them.

It was a race. A cruise missile traveling at 400 knots versus the *Independence* and *Coronado*, steaming forward at fifty knots. Since he couldn't outrun the missile, Moresby's best strategy was to travel at a right angle to its flight path. If he could cross enough distance, the missile would never get close enough to acquire a lock. It would simply fly into empty space until it either ran out of fuel or self-destructed.

"New tone," the radar technician said. "It has a lock! The missile has acquired us and is changing course."

Moresby and Birch watched the red line on the display angle toward the blue arrow symbol representing their ship. They judged the missile would home in on the port side of their vessel—a big, fat target. And with an aluminum superstructure, it would be ravaged by the high-explosive warhead.

"Closing fast," the technician said. "Ten miles."

From another console, the technician reported, "SeaRAM is active. Search radar has a solid track on the bogey... lock acquired... RAM fired... second RAM fired." The computer was programmed to launch a pair of missiles at a high-priority threat such as a cruise missile. "Tracking true… splash down. We got 'em!"

"Radar confirms. Bogey Two is dead."

Everyone let out a sigh of relief. They'd escaped certain death thanks to their defensive systems and training. "Good job, everyone," Moresby said. "But this is not the time to relax. Stay sharp."

He no sooner finished speaking when the radar technician said, "Bogey One is turning, changing course to one-eight-zero."

"The patrol plane is coming back," Birch said.

Moresby nodded. "Probably to make a damage assessment. They only launched one cruise missile because they weren't certain they'd get a lock."

"Recommend we turn south," Birch said. "Our best defense is to put as much distance as possible between us and the missile battery on Mischief Reef."

The captain shook his head. "No. We can't maintain fifty knots indefinitely, and even if we could, it would take hours to get beyond range of those cruise missiles. No, our best bet is to blind them."

"Sir?"

"Take away their patrol aircraft. If they can't see us, they'll have to disengage."

The XO considered his captain's plan, and it made sense. Except the *Independence* was not equipped with surface-to-air missiles. She was never intended to offensively engage enemy aircraft.

"Radar," Moresby said, "what's the course for Bogey One?"

"Headed right at us, sir."

"Weapons, power down the SeaRAM radar, but otherwise keep the system at the ready in standby. Set the seeker select to infrared."

"Yes, sir. Powering down search radar. Switching to heat-seeker mode."

"You want to lure that aircraft in close..." Birch said as understanding dawned on him.

Moresby explained his plan. "When the bogey is close, we'll switch on the search radar to give us a location to aim at, and the IR guidance in the missile warhead will steer for the kill. Radar, shout out when the bogey is nine miles out. Weapons, be ready to power up the SeaRAM radar."

Minutes ticked by, interrupted only by the reports updating the position of the approaching patrol aircraft. "Mr. Birch. Have the *Coronado* move in close on our starboard side. If another cruise missile comes in, I don't want there to be any chance it sees multiple targets."

"Bogey is now fifteen miles out, direct bearing... fourteen miles... thirteen... twelve..."

"Weapons, power up the SeaRAM radar! Set to manual control."

"Sir?"

"You heard the captain," Birch said. "Manual control. Fire when ordered."

"Eleven miles... ten... nine miles!"

"Fire one RAM," Moresby ordered.

"IR lock acquired. Firing one missile. Fire!"

"The bogey's at extreme range, sir," Birch said. "We'll be lucky to get a hit."

The rolling frame missile leapt out of the battery and streaked toward the lumbering patrol aircraft.

"We don't have to knock them out of the sky, Mr. Birch."

Immediately realizing they'd been lured in, the pilot of the Y-8X aircraft banked hard left. At the same moment, the copilot rammed all four engine throttles to the stops and ejected both chaff and flares. The aircraft pivoted hard on its left wing, trading altitude for airspeed.

"RAM is tracking true."

"Bogey changed course," reported the radar technician. "They're trying to outrun the RAM."

"Mr. Birch. New course one-one-zero degrees. Full speed. Let's get out of here and into Philippine coastal waters."

"We missed him, sir," reported the weapons operator. "Bogey is out of range."

"Looks like you scared him off, sir," the XO said.

Moresby's lips were drawn tight. "Let's hope so. Now they know we have teeth and are willing to bite. Maintain battle stations just in case. We won't be in Philippine waters for another two hours."

CHAPTER 19

"HE CHECKS OUT," Mark Williams reported to Lacey, his voice coming over the speakerphone on Commander Nicolaou's desk. "Former Navy. Retired with an honorable discharge after twelve years of service. No criminal record in the U.S. Still pays taxes and claims residence in Seattle."

"Thank you," Lacey said, relieved there wasn't any bad news from the background check. She was still conversing with Jim in his office, considering the merits of his theory.

"These ships are designed to erect long sections of drill pipe, which is why the central tower is so tall. I suppose it could be reconfigured to erect a ballistic missile for launching. And by engaging the dynamic-positioning thrusters, both bow and stern, in theory the ship could be a very stable and stationary launching platform."

"Exactly my thought," Jim added. "The crane could be used to maneuver sections in place. The weight of the missile and fuel is certainly no problem. But it might be conspicuous during daylight. So, I'd guess they would erect the missile under the cover of darkness, and launch at first light."

"Why wait until daylight to launch?"

"That exhaust plume would light up the pre-dawn sky and alert everyone within miles that something unusual was happening."

Jim had been refining his theory ever since speaking by phone with Peter. Until now, the only plausible explanation was that the ballistic missiles had to have been fired from a submarine, either Chinese or North Korean. The hunt for the ballistic missile submarine was still in progress, but this new theory opened intriguing possibilities.

MOTHER was crunching through daily satellite images of the South China Sea going back to the beginning of August. The plan was to locate the *Royal Seeker* and then track her position daily up to the present time. It was an intensive task, given the thousands of ships that regularly transited the South China Sea.

But the potential payoff was significant. If they could establish the *Royal Seeker* was in the vicinity of the launch radius of the two missile attacks, their theory would suddenly have credibility—a lot of credibility.

"Those missiles still had to come from either China or North Korea," Lacey said.

"Perhaps, but India, Pakistan, and Russia also have medium-range ballistic missiles. A group of rogue officers could have arranged to sell a few to a terrorist group. And, unlike operating and navigating a submarine, sailing an oil exploration ship is something a lot of merchant seamen can do. All it takes is money."

"I don't think so. The motive is not there to drive the U.S. from the Western Pacific." Jim considered her observation for a long moment, then nodded.

"That's why I hired you, Lieutenant."

An hour later, Jim had his entire team of analysts assembled around the conference table. Joining the group were five of his best operators—Magnum, Ghost, Bull, Iceberg, and Homer.

First Sergeant Mark Beaumont, known as Bull for his large physique and brute strength, was the second in command of SGIT. Following in the footsteps of his father and uncle, Bull chose to join the Marine Corps rather than be seduced by the street gangs in his hometown of Oakland, California. He was also the team medic.

Next to Bull sat Staff Sergeant Ryan Moore, who went by the nom de guerre of Ghost. The former SEAL appeared thin next to Bull's bulk. Just topping six feet in height and weighing every bit of 200 pounds, Ghost moved with fluid grace, a skill he honed to perfection after years of hunting the remote evergreen forests of northeastern Oregon and Western Idaho.

Another former SEAL, Magnum—aka Percival Dexter, or Percy as his friends called him—sat across from Bull. Magnum had joined the Navy at age eighteen to see the world, believing it would be far more attractive and inviting than his neighborhood in South Central Los Angeles. Standing at six feet one inch, he was a hand taller than Commander Nicolaou and, like all of the team members, he was very fit and muscular.

Although all the SGIT operators were expert in a wide range of small arms, Sergeant Jesper Mortensen was considered the most skilled at long range sniping. He favored the .50 caliber M107 semiautomatic rifle, and held the official record for longest and second longest confirmed kill—a record still classified. Jesper, call sign Homer, was also a lady-killer with a ruggedly handsome appearance, hair that was just a shade lighter than coal-black, and cobalt-blue eyes.

Jerry Balvanz was the newest member of the team. Like Homer, he was recruited from the army, Delta Force. Jerry was tall and lanky, yet lightning fast and strong. Prior to signing up, he'd played college basketball for two seasons and still loved to shoot hoops in his down time. With a head of snow-white, curly hair, he'd been given the call sign Iceberg.

With Jim as the squad leader—call sign Boss Man—the team was at mission strength: six highly-trained and extremely lethal special forces operators. Whatever the mission was, or might be, they were ready.

Colonel Pierson was participating via video conferencing, so he could also see the map images that were the focus of the discussion.

Mark Williams zoomed in on a section of the Spratly Island chain as he talked. "Due to the limited data we have from the first attack that sank the *Izumo*, calculating the initial phase of the trajectory is uncertain. Consequently, the probable launch-location radius is seventy-five miles and centered approximately thirty-five nautical miles south of Alison Reef.

"The missile used in the second attack was tracked for a much longer time by the E-3 Sentry early warning aircraft that was participating in the annual Balikatan exercise. From the flight path, we have worked out a probably launch location here..." Williams pointed to a location on the map very near Sand Cay. "The second missile was fired within a radius of thirty nautical miles of this location."

"There's a lot of ocean and a dozen or more islands within those launch locations," Pierson said. There was no hint of patience in his voice.

"We've eliminated the possibility that the missiles were fired from any land mass," Lacey said. "First, there is nothing in the satellite imagery that suggests launch facilities exist on any island within the probable launch radius of either missile. Second, none of these islands have been improved in any way by China or any other country."

"Could they have underground facilities?"

"No, sir," Jim said. He wanted to get the discussion back on track and following his agenda. "As the Lieutenant said, there is no evidence for improvements on any of these islands, and even if somehow our satellites missed it, which is extremely unlikely, the complexity of an underground ballistic missile launch facility on an island about the size of a Walmart parking lot—"

"If that big," Lacey interrupted.

"Right. Sir, these specks of land range from the size of a tennis court to a large parking lot. Water infiltration and shifting sand and coral would present enormous engineering obstacles. And when you factor in that there is no visible evidence of any hypothetical improvements, well, I think everyone at the table would say it's impossible."

"Very well. Continue."

"At first, we concluded the missiles had to have been fired from one or more submarines. Both North Korea and China have such capability. However, despite laying thousands of sonobuoys in the choke points in and around the Spratly Islands, the Navy reports no contact from submarines of other nationality. And mind you, the North Korean boats are noisy, as are the Chinese missile boats. So it's unlikely that we simply missed them."

"My information says the Navy is still laying sonobuoys, Commander."

"Yes, sir, they are. But as of this time, no contact with foreign boats has been made."

"And you have an alternative theory?"

"Yes, sir, we do." Jim motioned to Williams to advance to the next slide. It was a file photo of the *Royal Seeker*.

"Colonel, this is an oil exploration ship, under ownership of Hua Ho Holdings, a company based in Bandar Seri Begawan."

"Brunei? You're not going to suggest that the Sultan of

Brunei is attacking U.S. and Japanese naval vessels, are you?"

"No, sir. We have no evidence to support such a hypothesis. But we do think this ship is significant."

Jim pointed to Williams, who advanced to the next slide. "This is a rendering of how an oil exploration ship might look if it was adapted to fire a missile, such as a medium-range ballistic missile. You can see that the missile would fall short of the towers. And the crane has adequate height to install a customized warhead atop the second-stage rocket engine."

"Multiple rocket stages and warheads could be easily stored below deck," Williams added, "and then assembled at the tower prior to launching."

"Interesting. But why this ship in particular? What does Hua Ho Holdings have to say?"

"We've not contacted them officially, not yet."

"Excuse me? I know you better than that. You have something you're not telling me, some reason to back your theory that you haven't shared yet."

Jim knew Colonel Pierson well, and wasn't surprised by his deductive reasoning. In some ways, the Colonel was like a father figure to Jim and the entire team. He was protective of the members of SGIT—he felt pride and responsibility in founding the organization and leading the selection of what he considered to be the finest and most talented operators and analysts anywhere. "We stumbled on this, sir. And it may involve the abduction of a member of the Sultan's extended family. But in the interest of time, if I may, I'd like to stay focused on the missiles."

"Understood. Continue."

"The *Royal Seeker* has been missing, her transponder deactivated." Jim motioned to Lacey to continue.

"I ran a simple search routine through MOTHER. We analyzed daily satellite imagery going back to the first of

August, prior to the deactivation of the ship's transponder. Once we established that we could identify the ship by its satellite image—we did this by cross-checking the transponder readings from early August with the high-resolution images of the ship—it was easy to track the daily movements of the ship."

Another map of the Spratly Islands appeared on the monitor, only this one had a red line indicating a course taken by a surface vessel. "This is the movement of the *Royal Seeker*. The date is indicated next to each position point."

There was a stir around the conference table as the assembled analysts and operators saw the data for the first time. "As you can see, on the date of each attack, the *Royal Seeker* was within ninety nautical miles of the probable launch point."

"Brilliant work," Pierson said. "But, there's something more. Something you're holding back."

Jim moved his gaze around the room, making a point of connecting with each and every member of the team. Then he nodded to Williams, and the last slide appeared. "The catch is that the *Royal Seeker* is not the only oil exploration ship sailing these waters. As you can see, MOTHER matched three other ships to the visual profile of the *Royal Seeker*. By cross referencing the tracking transponder of the three new suspect ships, we've obtained an ID on them."

"How did we get that information?" Bull asked.

"MOTHER. She accessed the databases of every oil exploration company known to be active in these waters."

Bull let out a low whistle, amazed at the data processing speed of the super computer.

Jim continued, "The daily paths of all four ships are shown by the dashed lines on this map."

The charted sailing route of each of the four ships, including the one previously labeled as the *Royal Seeker*, crisscrossed a very large section of water, from the Gulf of Thailand east and north to the Philippine Sea.

"Two of the candidate targets were more than 200 miles away from both launch origins at the time the missiles were fired." Jim stood before the wall-mounted flat screen and used a stylus to circle the location of the two ships he had referenced. He continued, "For that reason those candidates are eliminated. Mark, erase those traces, please."

Williams made some keystrokes and two of the four dashed lines disappeared from the map.

"But that means there are two ships that could have been the missile launch platform. One is the *Royal Seeker*. The other ship is the *Panda Star*. It's owned and operated by Sinopec. Both ships are sailing in the South China Sea, within the disputed islands."

Silence befell the room and Colonel Pierson as the conclusion sank in. Finally, Pierson was the first to speak. "You're telling me the *Panda Star* operates under the Chinese flag. That certainly complicates the planning."

Jim exhaled. "Yes, sir, it does."

"Excuse me," Iceberg said. He leaned forward over the edge of the conference table and waited acknowledgement.

When Jim nodded in his direction, he continued, "We can take one target simultaneous with an assault of the other. We've trained for this type of mission with the SEALs, a coordinated assault on separate targets."

"Not this time," Lacey replied before Jim could explain. "The entire South China Sea is ready to explode. The exchange yesterday between U.S. and Chinese forces very nearly escalated into a much bigger conflict. Fortunately, cooler heads prevailed, and both sides disengaged before it got out of control. But, in order to avoid an accidental war, the President has ordered all U.S. military units to stay out of the South China Sea—for now."

"What about my team, Colonel?"

"That includes SGIT. The President doesn't want a war— hell, none of us do."

"There's no way Sinopec is going to allow inspection of the *Panda Star*," Lacey said.

Jim quickly added. "She's right, sir. This new theory only serves to further implicate China. It is imperative that we get onboard both ships to conduct an inspection. If missiles have been fired from the deck, there should be observable signs of scorching. And if rocket motors and warheads are onboard, they need to be confiscated."

"I'm not arguing against your logic, Commander. But I have my orders. Can we learn anything more from satellite imagery? As you said, there will be evidence of heat on the tower and perhaps elsewhere on the surrounding deck if missiles were launched."

Jim cast a questioning glance to Mark Williams. "We can try, sir, but I'm not optimistic. Sunlight playing across the grid-work of steel in the towers will create a complex pattern of light and dark. Plus, the crew could have applied paint to cover up any evidence of extreme temperature blistering or burning away older paint."

"So we predict negative results from the satellite data won't be conclusive, which means it's a waste of time."

"Drones?" Colonel Pierson asked.

Lacey shook her head. "Same problem, unless we get them in close, very close. And even then a negative result won't be conclusive."

"If I were a crewmember," Iceberg said, "and a drone came close snapping photos, I'd shoot it down."

"Wouldn't that give us confirmation that the ship was up to no good?" Bull asked, speaking for the first time since the meeting began.

"Maybe," Lacey replied. "But given the tense situation

between China and the U.S., flying drones close to a Chinese-flagged ship, even though it is not a military ship, is certain to be viewed as provocative and will only escalate the tension."

Jim knew that there were limitations to data gathering from machines. Every now and then there was no substitute for having people on the ground, so to speak. Only in this instance, trained people needed to be on each ship in order to determine which one was responsible for sinking two warships. In Jim's mind, there was no doubt that it had to be either the *Royal Seeker* or the *Panda Star*. Knowing the truth would either exonerate China or provide the compelling evidence to declare war. "Colonel, this is exactly the type of mission SGIT was made for. And if anyone can pull it off, it's the men and women in this room."

"The administration will have to have plausible deniability. Can you guarantee that?"

Jim swept his eyes from face to face. What he saw was confidence and determination. "Affirmative, sir."

Silence settled across the conference room as Jim awaited orders.

"Commander. Assemble your team. I want you in the air within ninety minutes, sooner if you can do it. You're flying to the South China Sea. I'll get authorization from the President while you're en route."

CHAPTER 20

PETER WAS IN THE PATIO GARDEN when Jim called. "We *are* able to track the *Royal Seeker*," he'd reported without offering explanation.

"That's great news! Thank you. It's the first break we've had. I'll let Eu-Meh know. Is the ship within helicopter range of BSB?"

"As of thirty minutes ago, yes. It seems to be staying in the Spratly Islands, not far off the coast of Brunei. I'll have Sanchez coordinate the tracking with you. For security reasons, we cannot allow a direct sharing of data from MOTHER to a civilian computer."

"That doesn't present any problems. I'd imagine Eu-Meh will have a security detail travel with her to the vessel. Hopefully, her daughter is there. Or at least we'll find more clues as to where Jade is being held."

"I'm afraid this is bigger than the girl's kidnapping."

"What do you mean?" Peter said. "I contacted you, remember?"

147

Jim sighed, debating how much to share with Peter. True, they had completed many missions together—all of them classified to a large degree. Yet Peter had no affiliation with the military or intelligence agencies. Quite simply, he was a man with a knack for being in the wrong place at the wrong time. Or maybe that was the right place at the right time, if you were looking at the mission results.

Although the rules were quite strict—information would be shared on a need-to-know basis, and even then, only if proper security clearances had been issued—leaving Peter in the dark could easily be counterproductive. He was the only trusted person on the ground within 500 miles of the two suspect exploration ships. In the end, the need for human intelligence trumped all the other reservations Jim had.

Jim answered, "You did, thankfully. And right now, I'll take luck over skill."

"What are you talking about?"

"I'm sure you've heard about the tense situation developing in the South China Sea."

"Who hasn't? Two warships sunk, and the U.S. and China squaring off for a fight. But what does this have to do with finding Jade?"

"Maybe nothing—maybe everything. Do you have encryption software on your phone?"

"I do. Lieutenant Lacey convinced me to install a commercial app. Not as good as what you have, but better than nothing." Peter shared the name of the software.

"Okay. I'll activate the same app and call you right back." Less than a minute later, Peter's phone rang.

"What I am about to tell you," Jim said, "is classified top secret. This information has the highest security rating and is not to be shared with anyone. Understood?"

Peter dropped onto a bench surrounded by an acre of lawn.

Branches of a flowering magnolia hung over his head, filtering the bright sunlight. It was early morning, and the temperature had not yet risen to a level of discomfort. Diesel was meandering aimlessly, his nose to the lawn, following a trail of interesting scents, never ranging too far from his master and companion.

"Yes, I understand."

Over the next five minutes, Jim filled Peter in on the risks, the difficulty of executing the plan, and the dangers of sparking a war with China. Still, the source of the missile launchings had to be found and neutralized, and the only two leads were a ballistic-missile submarine or a surface vessel of the likes of the *Royal Seeker* and *Panda Star*.

"It is vitally important that both ships be boarded and taken under control simultaneously. At this time, we cannot be certain that only one ship is launching those missiles—it could be that both are working in unison. If we don't time this operation precisely and a radio warning is sent, one ship could destroy any evidence and slip away."

"If that happens, the danger isn't eliminated and war ensues."

"Yes. That's the assessment of Lieutenant Lacey and her team."

"What do you need me to do?" Peter asked, genuine concern in his voice.

"I need for you to convince Eu-meh Lim to board the *Royal Seeker* with an assault force drawn from the Brunei Special Combat Squadron."

After a brief phone call that left Eu-meh with many more questions than answers, she agreed to speak with the Crown Prince, who had authority over all of the Brunei military, and relay Peter's request for the assault team to be drawn from the Brunei Land Forces special ops soldiers. "Under the circumstances, I am confident he will cooperate," she concluded.

"Thank you. It would be best if I could speak directly to the commander of the assault team. I'm certain he will want more information, and I can put him in contact with the appropriate intelligence officer. Naturally, this operation is classified. But given the importance, I've been assured that sufficient information will be provided to enable the commander to adequately plan this mission."

Peter thought he heard a measure of hope in Eu-meh's voice. She had steadfastly refused to believe that any serious harm had come to her only child. Yet with every passing day and no breakthrough, no useful clues, she found her optimism diminishing.

"Come on, Diesel." *We'd better brief Robert. He needs to know, too.*

Back inside the air-conditioned comfort of the guest apartment, Robert was in the billiard room pacing before the fireplace. He ended his phone call as Peter entered the room.

"That was Eu-meh," he said. "She said we have a way to find the *Royal Seeker*?" Although Eu-meh had repeated the essential parts of the phone call she had just completed with Peter, Robert decided to see how freely Peter would share that information.

"We do. I was just coming to fill you in."

Robert listened and asked questions for the next fifteen minutes. Satisfied he'd been fully briefed, he said, "This could be the break we need. With the *Royal Seeker* back under control of Hua Ho Holdings, we have a chance at figuring out why Jade was abducted in the first place."

"I understand the focus right now is on boarding that ship and gaining control. But has anyone thought about getting an investigative unit onboard, too?" Peter said. "There could be vital evidence, and if the investigation is not properly managed by experienced detectives, the evidence could be compromised for use in court, or even worse, completely destroyed."

Robert looked at Peter and nodded slowly. "Good point. I'll mention that to Eu-meh. Maybe they can have one or two investigators board with the assault team." Robert had his phone in his hand again.

"I'm going to resume my walk with Diesel while you make your calls."

With the red pit bull close by his side, Peter strolled across the patio and then through the gardens surrounding the palace. Soon, the heat and humidity would render even a short, leisurely walk unbearable. Diesel already had his tongue hanging low as he panted.

A gardener, a slim woman whose wrinkled face betrayed her age, watched Peter and Diesel approach. When they were separated by three paces, she clicked her tongue against her teeth. Diesel turned her way and tilted his head. She smiled, her eyes twinkling.

"It's okay," Peter said, and Diesel approached, his head down and tail wagging from side to side. Laying her tools down, she leaned over and rubbed both sides of the canine's blocky head, massaging his ears. He leaned into her and she ran a hand down his back, seemingly admiring his sleek coat and copper coloration. She said something in a tongue totally foreign to Peter, and yet he was certain Diesel understood her emotional energy and body language. She liked animals, and showed no fear of the pit bull.

Abruptly, Diesel stiffened. The wagging motion of his tail ceased and he focused on something in the distance. The gardener and Peter both turned their heads, trying to see what had alerted the dog. In the distance, a palace guard was looking their way from within the dark shadows of a cloister. After a moment, the guard turned to leave, revealing a white bandage over the side of his head.

"Diesel, come," Peter said, the friendly exchange had ended, replaced with concern and urgency. He strode purposefully back to the guest apartment. He had to warn Robert.

He pushed open the heavy carved-wood door. "Robert!" he called even as he was clearing the doorway.

No response.

"Robert? You here?"

Peter stopped in the parlor and glanced up the stairs. The apartment was deathly quiet. He looked down at Diesel. The dog was as still as a statue—looking through the open doors into the billiard room, every muscle tensed and ready to propel the animal into action.

"Heal," Peter said, his voice soft. He edged forward through the parlor, Diesel shadowing each footstep. As he approached the billiard room, Robert stepped into view on the far side of the massive game table.

"Are you alright?" Peter breathed a sigh of relief. "Look, we have a problem. I saw one of the palace guards, and the side of his head was bandaged. I think—"

The palace guard Peter had seen only minutes ago stepped into view, a Glock 17 pistol aimed at Robert. He closed the distance in two steps and placed the gun against Robert's head.

"Please, come in," he said. His voice carried a hint of a British accent.

Peter did as instructed. Diesel was edgy but remained by his side.

"Just relax," Peter said, his hands open and displayed in full view. Diesel issued a deep, throaty growl, causing the gunman to divert his eyes to the canine.

"Get that dog out of here," he said. "Or I'll kill your friend and the dog."

Robert winced as the steel barrel was pushed harder against

the base of his head, just below his ear. "Better do as he says."

"Diesel, come." Peter gave a jerk of his head and the pit bull slowly walked out of the room. Peter closed the doors to the parlor.

"I was going to warn you that one of the men who attacked us in London was here."

"Yeah, thanks. But I kinda figured that out," Robert said.

"So, how's that ear? Healing well?"

"Maybe I'll slice off your ears; and your nose. How would you like that?"

"No, thank you, I'd rather not." Peter was edging closer, passing between the bar and the billiard table. The gunman was slowly rotating his position, being mindful to stay behind Robert.

"What do you want?" Peter asked.

"You're both coming with me."

"Well," Peter said. One hand was close by his side, his fingers crawling along the bar. Peter hoped the tool he was seeking had not been put away. "You're going to have a hard time moving both of us out of here without people seeing what you're doing. I mean, two men walking across the palace grounds at gunpoint probably isn't a regular occurrence. Surely it's going to attract attention."

The gunman's eyes narrowed. He seemed to be thinking about this comment. Perspiration dappled his face and threatened to roll off his forehead.

There! Peter's fingers touched the corkscrew. "It's me you want," Peter said. "Let him go, and I won't cause any problems."

"Don't be crazy, Peter."

Peter persisted, continuing to creep forward, the corkscrew out of sight, palmed against his thigh. "Look, I don't know who you are or what you want, but this *is* going to end badly if you don't calm down and put the gun away."

The gunman snorted a laugh. "It's going to be real bad for you when I cut up your face."

Peter was just about at the end of the pool table. He suddenly raised his free hand to distract the assailant, and hooked the corkscrew on his back pocket. "You guys really messed up in London, right? Is that what this is about? Your boss needs answers, and I'm just the guy."

Sliding his feet, he continued to close the distance. "Why did you take Jade?"

"I'm not answering your questions," he sneered.

Peter raised his hands and stopped in front of Robert. Taking the bait, the assailant shoved Robert aside with surprising strength, and then placed the gun against Peter's chest.

"On your knees bodyguard. Hands on your head, fingers locked together. Now! Or I put a bullet in your friend."

Robert followed the orders, already feeling the discomfort radiating from his knees pressing against the hard stone floor.

Peter glanced down at the gun. He understood that one pull of the trigger would send a 9mm bullet blasting through his chest and out his back. Even if by some chance the bullet missed his heart—a miracle given the placement of the muzzle—he would bleed out within a minute. If the notion concerned Peter, it didn't show.

"You know," Peter said, as he held his hands open at his side. He looked directly into the man's eyes: They were cold and devoid of emotion. They were the eyes of a killer. Peter had looked into eyes just like those many times before, and he knew he wouldn't talk him down. "You really aren't very smart. You lost control of this situation when I entered the room. And now it's worse."

"You talk a lot, but don't have much to say." He spat the words out.

Peter took a half step closer, forcing his assailant to bend his elbow in order to keep the pistol leveled on Peter. "Who do you work for? Obviously, you're not loyal to the Sultan. How much are they paying you?"

"Enough!" he twisted the gun barrel into Peter's sternum.

"If you're going to kill me, at least tell me why you kidnapped Jade. What is she to your boss? She's just a kid."

He leaned his face close to Peter's, and began to speak. "I said—"

Ufff! He rammed the corkscrew into the gunman's abdomen, just below the rib cage where the flesh is soft and unprotected. At the same instant, with his other hand he knocked the Glock to the side.

Boom! The report of the shot was deafening in the confined space. Peter winced, favoring his right side. Still, he twisted the corkscrew and pushed harder. The gunman's eyes bulged, and his mouth hung agape. The pistol appeared to be a heavy weight, holding his arm down.

"Here's some advice," Peter said through gritted teeth. "When you have a gun, never allow your adversary within arm's reach."

From only inches away, the gunman looked at Peter, his eyes wide in confusion and fear. Robert scrambled from his knees and yanked the man backwards, wrapping a meaty hand around the Glock, ensuring it remained pointed at the floor as he twisted it from the dying hand.

Peter released the corkscrew, and ran a hand over his side, just above his hip. It felt wet. He moved to the bar and found a white napkin which he pressed against the wound.

Robert laid the man on the floor and removed the spare magazines from his belt. His unfocused eyes were already losing their gloss.

"You okay?" Robert asked.

"Looks like the bullet just nicked me."

"Let me see." Peter removed the napkin. Fortunately, the bleeding had already slowed. "You'll live, but we still need to get a bandage over that or you'll be oozing blood all night." Robert opened cabinet doors looking for a first aid kit. After quickly searching half the bar, he found a box with bandages, gauze pads, and tape. He applied a dressing to Peter's side with ample tape to hold it in place, and then passed a bottled of acetaminophen.

"That gunshot had to have been heard," Robert said. "Won't be long before real guards show up."

Peter swallowed several pills and glanced around the room. "I'm gonna miss this place."

CHAPTER 21

THE GUNSHOT AND SOUND of shattered glass comingled and became one, immediately followed by the tinkling of hundreds of glass fragments on the stone floor.

Peter and Robert fell to the tiles as more bullets streamed through the remnants of glass and lead came that had once adorned the French doors. Chunks of wood were blasted from the billiard table. Other rounds found the stacks of books on the far wall.

Two figures were in the patio garden, converging on the shattered glass doors. They were both wearing uniforms of the palace guard. Sitting with his back against a leg of the once-beautiful game table, Robert raised the Glock and fired off a rapid succession of four shots. Peter watched as the two guards collapsed under the fire.

A shot came from the parlor, quickly followed by a scream. *Aaahh!* Before Peter or Robert had time to react, the double doors burst open and another palace guard crashed through the opening, landing on his back. Diesel was on top of the gunman, his jaws locked around his right arm. A Glock pistol fell out of his hand and skidded a short distance away. He was attempting to reach it with his left hand, but Diesel wasn't giving any quarter. The pit bull was shaking his head, furthering the lacerations on the man's arm.

Peter rose and rushed to aid his companion. He scooped up the pistol, just inches from the guard's reach, and trained it on the man. "Enough!" Peter ordered, the rapid movement sending burning pain through his side. Diesel released his victim and slowly backed away, all the while keeping his eyes locked on the guard.

Only after Diesel broke off did Peter see the bandages on the right arm. The dog had torn into a fresh wound, perhaps one made only a few days ago by a steak knife slashing across the arm.

The billiard room fell into silence, save for the groaning of the guard. He placed his left hand over the ragged tear. Blood slowly seeped between his fingers.

"You were in London, weren't you?" Peter said, looking down at the man.

His question was answered with a look of malevolence.

"Of course you were. Well, I know you're not loyal to the Sultan…"

"What do you know?" came the gruff reply.

"I'm rather certain the Sultan will not be pleased to know some of his trusted palace guards kidnapped his niece."

"You have no idea what has been set in motion, or the reach of power. You'll never leave here alive—never."

"Yeah, whatever you say. I've heard it all before." Peter turned to check Diesel for wounds. He squatted and laid the Glock on the floor, then ran his hands along both sides of his canine. They came back clean, no blood.

Suddenly, Diesel leapt over Peter's shoulder. He twisted his body to see. Diesel was latched onto the guard's left wrist, the hand holding a short, curved blade—a karambit. It hooked inward, reminding Peter of a talon or claw. With teeth crushing the man's wrist, the karambit was useless. Despite the wounds on his right arm, he was desperately slugging Diesel with his free fist.

Peter reached around, trying to locate the Glock. The fist was pummeling the canine's side. Still, he wouldn't slacken his bite.

Boom! Smoke wafted from the muzzle of the pistol in Robert's hand. As the guard stopped moving, Diesel sensed the fight was over. He released and returned to Peter's side. Blood pooled where the man's head rested on the stone tiles.

Again, Peter ran his hand over Diesel, only this time the dog whimpered a little when the hand brushed over the ribs that had been pummeled. "Is he okay?" Robert asked.

Peter tilted his head to the side. "Bruised his ribs. I don't think any are cracked."

"We have to get outta here. Grab the extra mags from his belt."

Each armed with a Glock 17 pistol tucked within his waistband, and shirt pulled out to cover the handgrip, Robert and Peter casually walked out the front door of the apartment, Diesel close by Peter's side.

"Now what?" Peter asked without turning his head toward Robert.

"We go to a safe house."

"You have a safe house here?"

"I do. My apartment."

Peter spun his head. "You think these people are idiots? They're probably already searching your apartment."

"Nope, not likely."

"How can you be so certain? It didn't take long for them to mount an attack on us. And we're inside the palace grounds!"

"The apartment is not in my name, and the alias is buried deep. Plus, I don't actually live there."

Boom! Boom! The two men ran for the cover of a cluster of palm trees. Bullets split the air all around them, but none connected. As they came to a rest, the gunfire became more precise. Bullets were cutting into the trunks, but so far none had penetrated through.

"You have a plan B?" Peter said.

Robert was surveying the grounds. Behind them were more trees and clusters of dense foliage. Beyond that, the entrance to the palace.

"Nothing elegant," he replied.

Peter sank lower and pulled Diesel in tight as another barrage impacted the palm trunks. "We don't have the luxury of being choosy."

Robert shrugged. "We go that way." He motioned with his chin. "Use the available cover and exit through the gate. Then we hail a taxi."

"Oh. Sure. Why not?"

"Look, those guards will kill us if we stay here. So, unless you have a better idea?"

Peter exhaled deeply. "You think they're all gunning for us?"

"Looks that way."

"Can Eu-meh help?"

"Once we escape—"

"You mean *if* we escape."

"We hole up in my safe house while I contact Eu-meh. She could be in danger, too."

Peter ran over the different scenarios in his mind. None of the options were good. "You win. Plan B it is."

Robert nodded. "Angle for the closest cover. I'll draw their fire until you get there. When I hear you fire off two rounds, I'll be running for your position while you cover me."

Peter nodded. "Ready when you are."

"Good luck." Robert eased around the base of the trees and fired off in the direction he believed the attackers were located. Immediately, gunfire was returned, the muzzle flashes revealing the shooters' locations.

Peter and Diesel were up and running. In four seconds they reached another grouping of palm trees, and Peter tumbled to a stop on the far side. He raised the Glock at the same time he came up to a kneeling position. Ahead, Robert was still shooting at a measured pace of about one round a second.

"Clear!" Peter yelled, and he began firing his Glock. The distance was long for a pistol, just shy of 100 yards, he estimated. Still, Peter knew from experience that it took an incredible amount of will power to remain calm and focused when being shot at, even if the shooter was unlikely to hit the target.

In a flash, Robert was running. He moved quickly for a big man, and could have made a respectable tryout performance for professional football. Seeing what was taking place, the palace guards began to abandon their positions and fan out to the sides to get a clear angle on their targets. As they moved away from cover, they became easier marks to hit. Peter tracked one guard and fired. *Boom! Boom! Boom!* After the third shot, the guard stumbled and fell forward, his rifle skittering across the ground.

After the last shot, the slide locked open on Peter's Glock. He ejected the spent magazine and rammed home a full load. Just then, Robert slid in and rolled over, bringing his gun to bear.

When the palace guards left the cover of the cloisters, they became easier targets, although the distance was still challenging. Robert was firing aimed shots from the base of a palm tree at the running guards. Two fell to his gunfire, giving Peter needed cover to make his dash.

Peter looked over his shoulder and spied a large fountain not too far away. He pushed to his feet and sprinted. Off to the side, motion attracted his attention. He turned his head without breaking stride and saw a golf cart angling his way. It looked like one of the grounds-keeper machines, used for moving plants, tools, and insulated containers of drinking water around the large property.

Only this one was driven by a guard. Riding shotgun was another guard. He aimed his rifle and squeezed off a short burst. The bullets impacted the grass some distance in front of Peter, no doubt his aim disrupted by the motion of the electric cart as it bounced over the uneven lawn.

With his eye on the fountain, Peter pumped his legs harder, trying to ignore the pain from the bullet wound as the flesh opened anew. More rifle shots, this time striking the earth closer. He reasoned that as the distance decreased, the gunman would inevitably find his mark. It was a race to the fountain, where Peter hoped he could gain momentary protection. If he was lucky, the golf cart would pass by and offer two or three seconds of exposure during which Peter would have seventeen bullets to fire at the guards. Hopefully, only two or three would be needed.

Unexpectedly, the sound of gunfire from the golf cart ceased. Still running, Peter turned his head. The gunman was dropping the spent magazine and pushing a new one in place. The cart was still closing. Peter swung his Glock toward the cart and squeezed off a shot. In that moment, Diesel launched at the electric vehicle and its occupants. The pit bull was running all out—his head down and tail laid flat. A streamlined, seventy-pound missile of teeth, muscle, and sinew.

Peter slowed and faced toward the threat. Everything seemed to move in slow motion. He saw the gunman raise his rifle and aim—not at Peter, but at the dog. The gunman seemed to shout something, and the driver came to a stop. From the stationary vehicle, the guard raised and braced his weapon against one of the steel tubular supports for the sunshade.

"No!" Peter shouted. Diesel stayed locked on, running fast. The gunman took aim and fired.

Diesel closed the distance.

Peter raised the Glock and began shooting, his stance solid, two hands firmly supporting the pistol. On the third shot, he landed a bullet in the guard's shoulder, throwing off his aim. Peter fired again, this time hitting his chest. He fell backwards, bounced off the seatback, and rolled to the grass.

Diesel sprang into the air, clearing the wounded guard and slamming full on into the side of the driver. The shear momentum of the canine moving at thirty miles per hour carried the driver out of the golf cart. He landed hard, head slamming into the turf. Diesel was on top of him, lacerating his arm amid screams of terror and pain.

Peter sprinted to the scene. The rifle was laying not far from the prostrate body of the gunman. Peter grabbed it and came around the golf cart, his pistol aiming forward. Diesel had the driver pinned to the ground, his jaws locked on the man's right forearm and wrist. The man had his left arm over his face. Any movement from him, no matter how subtle, and Diesel would shake his head and bite down harder, generating more screams.

"Diesel, enough!" Peter commanded, the Glock pointed at the driver. Diesel relaxed his jaws and backed away three steps. Peter reached down and removed the guard's pistol and ammunition magazines. Just then, Robert arrived.

"Heard the gunshots, thought you were at the fountain!"

"I got us a ride," Peter said. Diesel jumped in and Robert

took the wheel, pressing down on the accelerator just as Peter hopped into the passenger seat, holding onto the steel support for added security as they crossed the rolling lawn at the maximum speed the cart would deliver. It wasn't a racer, but still twice as fast as they could run. Quickly they left the other palace guards far behind.

"Where's the gate?" Peter shouted, his ears ringing from the gunfire.

Robert pointed. "Up there. Not too far."

Peter saw a paved road; the one they'd entered on. It crossed at an angle to their current direction of travel. Robert slowed and turned onto the pavement, and the ride became much smoother. The road followed a gentle curve to the right where it entered a broad belt of dense greenery—a wide variety of trees, shrubs, and flowering bushes—all planted with the goal of providing visual and acoustical privacy from the bustling city just beyond the palace grounds.

"Get ready," Robert said. "When we pass around this bend, the guard station will come into view. I don't know what to expect, but the guard must have been alerted by now."

Peter nodded. He shifted the rifle in his hand—a U.S.-made M4 military weapon—making sure the safety was off. The electric drive was practically silent, and Peter assumed the guard at the gate would not hear them coming.

As the greenery gave way, the guard station, a small windowed building just big enough for one man, came into view. The door was closed, no doubt to assist the air conditioner in keeping the interior temperature comfortable—a tall order given that all four sides were almost completely glazed. Thankfully, the gate was open.

Upon seeing the golf cart, the guard opened the door and raised his hand, signaling for them to stop. Instead, Robert mashed his foot down on the accelerator and the golf cart sped up. Peter pointed the muzzle at the building and fired, sending bullets into the windows. The gunfire combined with the shattering of glass had the desired effect, and the guard ducked and threw his body back into the meager safety of the building as the golf cart raced by.

Robert turned the wheel and merged the electric cart into the street traffic. After traveling a short block, he turned the corner, repeating this maneuver many times until he felt they had enough distance from the palace grounds and were not being followed.

He steered into a narrow alley between two buildings and parked the golf cart next to a refuse bin. "Toss the rifle in the dumpster," Robert said.

"Why? It could come in handy."

"Trust me, okay? It's too conspicuous. And you don't want to get caught with an automatic rifle that will be easily traced back to the shootout at the palace. Remember—Sharia law here."

"Fine," Peter grumbled. He looked over his shoulder to make certain no one was watching, then heaved the rifle into the dumpster with bags of smelly garbage and rotten food scraps.

"How's your bandage holding up?"

Peter looked down and raised his shirt. The gauze pad was nearly soaked through but was still in place. "Hurts like hell."

"I've got a decent first aid kit at my apartment. I can close that up and replace the bandage. Plus, I've got antibiotics to knock the bugs back."

Peter lowered his shirt, pulling it over the Glock, which was back in his waistband. "Come on, Diesel."

Out on the main street it wasn't long before Robert hailed a taxi. He gave the driver directions, rather than an address, as an added precaution. After many more turns over an unnecessarily circuitous route, the car pulled to the curb. After paying the driver, Robert, Peter, and Diesel exited the taxi and stood on the sidewalk until the cab was lost in the distance.

"Now what?" Peter asked.

"This way." Robert led the way past several shops and restaurants. He turned into an alley no wider than a car. On either side the buildings rose to a height of three floors. Weaving around bags of garbage, he stopped and pulled down an old-fashioned steel fire escape. It was more staircase than ladder—but very steep, like a ladder onboard a ship. Looking up, Peter saw that the steps stopped at a landing at each floor. With Diesel between Robert and Peter, they climbed to the first landing. Robert inserted a key into the deadbolt, turned the latch, and opened the door. It squeaked, the hinges in obvious need of lubrication. "This way."

A narrow hall extended into the building. Robert stopped at the first door. "My apartment." He motioned with his hand. "Not much, but serves my purpose." He turned a key and opened the door onto a large, dark room. He flipped the light switch.

Diesel sauntered from scent to scent, checking out every corner and along the base of the wall. "Hey, he won't pee in here, will he?"

"Relax," Peter replied, and called his dog over. Diesel clung to Peter's leg. The room was sparsely furnished: A wooden rocking chair, two canvas director's chairs, and a rickety folding table in the center of the space. There was no kitchen, but a partially-open door revealed the existence of a bathroom. A rolled sleeping bag and a small refrigerator completed the furnishings.

"Have a seat," Robert said. "There's water in the fridge." He disappeared into the bathroom, but left the door open.

Peter retrieved a bottle of cold water and sat in the rocking chair. He placed the bottle against his neck and felt the cool blood flow into his head. He had a good angle into the bathroom and watched as Robert opened the medicine cabinet and then, using a screwdriver, removed four screws. Next, he pulled the cabinet forward exposing a secret compartment. He grabbed a white box with a red cross on the lid.

"Let's take a look at that wound," he said.

Peter stood and raised his shirt, then in a quick motion pulled off the tape and blood-soaked bandage.

Robert squeezed an antibiotic ointment onto the ragged edges of flesh. "Rub that in. It's not as bad as I thought." He pulled the tear together, pinching the edges of flesh. Next, he squeezed several dabs of a cyanoacrylate wound-closing glue to hold the cut closed. He finished the dressing with a sterile gauze pad and more tape. "Here, take these. Three a day for five days. It'll knock down any infection before it gets out of control."

"Thank you." Peter looked around again, as if seeing the room for the first time. A cardboard box of dried-noodle packages was in a corner. And next to that was a single-burner camp stove and a gallon jug of water, the cap still sealed. "So this is your safe house?"

Robert left the first aid kit on the table. "That's right. In my line of business, a space like this is part of the planning. Like an insurance policy. You hope you'll never need it, but if you do..." He returned to the secret storage space and retrieved a large navy-blue duffle bag. He lifted the bag onto the table with both hands. "My bug-out bag."

He peeled the zipper back. Inside was an assortment of weaponry. Robert stuck his hand into a side pouch and pulled out a cell phone and powered it on. "They might be tracing calls from my number," he explained.

Peter's impression of the bodyguard had just changed significantly. Whereas he'd originally thought of Robert as merely hired muscle, he now realized the ex-Navy man had a good sense of tactical planning and execution. This safe house was well provisioned, but not flashy. There was nothing about the non-descript apartment to attract attention. And it seemed to be in a relatively quiet neighborhood. Whoever his neighbors were—if he even had any—kept to themselves.

"Yes, ma'am, that's right." Peter assumed Robert was speaking with Eu-meh. They needed a new plan. It was still a high priority to get onboard the *Royal Seeker*. Initially, they'd planned to fly in a Hua Ho Holdings corporate helicopter and land on the helipad of the ship. Under the current circumstances, that might be hard to pull off.

Why were palace guards involved in kidnapping Jade from London? Peter was still mulling over the question when Robert completed his call. "Well?" Peter asked.

"Not much to do until nightfall."

"And then?"

"We take a taxi to the International Airport, just like we were going to catch a flight. Instead, we take the shuttle bus to the P2 Car Park. It's the farthest from the terminal. From there, it's a short walk to the RBA Golf Club." Robert unfolded a map and laid it on the table. "Here's the car park and here's the golf course. This hole is right off the access road," he pointed at the edge of the golf course closest to the airport parking and terminal. A circular green was visible with a water hazard and sand trap on one side. "That's where the helicopter will pick us up. The pilot will set down on the green. Should be easy—there's ample clearance from the palm trees on this side of the green."

Peter considered the plan. It was bold, for sure. But, the approach of the helicopter would not seem out of place next to an airport. And access to the green by foot should be easy. A quick dash from the road, hop on the aircraft, and take off again.

"Okay, makes sense," Peter said. "What about Eu-meh? Is

she safe?"

"She doesn't think any rogue members of the palace guard will go after her, given that she *is* the Sultan's sister. Still, she agreed to go for a long drive to stay on the move. She'll instruct her most senior pilot to fly the helicopter tonight."

"Can she trust the pilot?"

"He's not a member of the palace guard. He works for Hua Ho Holdings, and has been in Eu-meh's employ for longer than I have. On her personal security detail for fifteen years."

Peter nodded. "I suppose that will have to be good enough."

"My thought too," Robert shrugged. "Now, let me show you what we have."

He emptied the contents of his duffle bag on the table. There were pistols, ammunition magazines, and a block of white material wrapped in clear plastic. "Is that what I think it is?" Peter asked.

"C4. It's a great problem solver."

"As in, it makes the problem go away?"

"Yep," Robert replied. "We have time-delay detonators and remotely-triggered detonators. Plus a short length of primacord." He held up a yellow rope, coiled and the ends and fastened with a twisted wire.

Peter reached into the pile and pulled out a black disc. It looked like a hockey puck. "Careful. That's a flash-bang. There are three more in here."

"Looks like you're ready for a zombie apocalypse," Peter observed.

"Hey, I was a boy scout and I take their motto, 'Be Prepared,' seriously. Better safe than sorry and all that."

Peter gently set the black flash-bang down with the others. "No argument from me."

CHAPTER 22

CRUISING AT 34,000 FEET, the four turboprop engines whipped the thin air behind the six-bladed propellers, pushing the large aircraft along at 350 knots. Inside the cavernous cargo bay of the specially-modified HC-130J Combat King aircraft, the SGIT operators were busy planning the mission, although authorization from the President still had not been received.

Jim was pointing to a photograph of the *Panda Star*; his team of operators were circled around the table, listening intently. "Like most oil exploration ships, the *Panda Star* has a helipad for ferrying crew on and off the ship through normal rotations. That will be our drop zone."

Ghost raised his eyebrows. "Not a very large target to land on, especially if the ship is underway."

"Once we are within range, our aircraft will be tracking the radio beacon from the ship. The location of the *Panda Star* will be continuously updated, in real time, and fed to our jump computers." Each operator wore a small but powerful computer on his wrist that calculated the glide path to a pre-determined GPS coordinate. Each man would steer his parachute to follow the glide path. Only this time, the drop coordinate would be moving.

"Relax. Oil exploration ships are not known for their speed," Jim added.

"And if we miss?" Iceberg asked the question, knowing it was on everyone's mind.

"Don't," Jim said.

"Let me get this straight, sir. Night jump, high altitude opening, gliding to a moving target only a little larger than my first apartment."

"That's right, Iceberg. You got a problem with it?"

"Would it make any difference if I said yes?"

"Look," Jim said, "if it was easy, someone else would have been given the job. None of you earned your position in SGIT by being second best. We're going to be gliding down from in front of the ship. At the last moment, flare your chute, circle, and drop onto the helipad."

"Piece of cake," Bull said.

After a long moment with no further questions, Jim continued, "Our mission call sign is "Swordfish." Once on board, we'll secure the deck. Homer and Ghost, you two cover the forward half of the ship. Iceberg and Magnum, you cover the aft. Bull, you will come with me as we search; first the vicinity of the crane for evidence and then move our way to the moon pool. If there are other rocket motors, fueling equipment, warheads—anything that might be military in nature—we are to take the ship and all personnel under our control, and call in the Marines."

"What about the crew?" Iceberg asked.

"We expect most of the crew to be asleep in their cabins. We will not take the bridge unless we find just cause. We are to maintain a very low profile. If all goes well, the crew will never know they were visited in the middle of the night. If you run into a crewmember out for an evening stroll, avoid him or her if possible. If that is *not* possible, use your Taser. Use lethal force *only* as a last resort. Understood?"

A chorus of "Yes, sir!" gave Commander Nicolaou the answer he expected. His team was exceptionally well disciplined, and they had performed admirably through dozens of missions, each of them equally dangerous and challenging.

"Remember, this is a Chinese-flagged vessel. Expect it to be crewed by Chinese nationals. It will not go over well with the State Department if you have to explain why you killed an unarmed civilian."

"How long to complete your inspection?" This question from Magnum.

Jim pointed to a schematic of the ship. It showed the decks in a cross section of the vessel, running from bow to stern. "Bull and I will focus on the main deck. This is where the moon pool is located, and it's where the base of the towers are anchored. I figure ten minutes, tops. We're collecting photographic data mostly, but also paint samples—especially if it looks freshly applied or scorched."

"Exfiltration?" Bull asked.

"You're gonna get wet. On my signal, everyone will converge on the moon pool. Your load-out includes a compact rebreather, good for about five minutes underwater, and a one-man sled. Developed with funding from DARPA, it's small but powerful. It's still in limited testing, so consider yourselves privileged to be the first to use this kit outside of training. Shed your BDUs prior to entering the water to reduce drag." Each operator was clothed in a neoprene wet suit underneath standard Chinese-made fatigues issued to the PLA, or Peoples Liberation Army.

Jim continued, "To further reduce drag and conserve battery power, weapons are to be discarded once we have cleared the ship. We will stay in tight formation about one meter under the surface until the rebreathers are expended. Your GPS has been preloaded with the rendezvous point, which is expected to be about two clicks south from your landing coordinates when you set foot on the helipad. The computer will calculate the route automatically, triggered when you stop descending. So even if you miss the helipad, you will still have the proper coordinates. If you get separated for any reason, follow your GPS." Jim indicated a spot of ocean on a detailed navigational chart.

"Then what?" Bull asked.

"On my order, the *Combat King* will come in low and slow and drop an inflatable fitted with a silenced outboard. Everyone has NVGs, so the Zodiac will not be hard to see. Just in case, it will have a short-range radio beacon. Each of your GPS units will pick up the signal. Once in the Zodiac, we'll motor to new coordinates here." Jim pointed at another spot of open ocean. "At 0430 hours, the *USS New Mexico* will surface and we can all get a good, hot meal."

"And if things don't go as planned?" Magnum asked.

"Then we hold the ship until the Marines arrive. A V22 Osprey is circling here." Jim pointed at a location on the chart. "On my order, the Osprey will fly to our position and a platoon of reinforcements will fast-rope onto the helipad. We will take control of the vessel until the Navy arrives. Questions?"

Ghost spoke up. "What about the other ship?"

"The *Royal Seeker* will receive a visit from Brunei military."

All of the SGIT operators exchanged questioning glances.

"Don't ask," Jim said. "It's need-to-know information. Other questions?"

"What can we expect for backup if the *Panda Star* is really hot?" Iceberg said.

"The man next to you is your backup until the Marines arrive. The *Combat King* will stay on station to provide radio relay and air cover should the Chinese attempt to intervene, although that is not expected."

Jim cast his gaze across his assembled team. In every face he read confidence and determination. "Anything else?"

Only silence was returned.

"Very well. Get some rest. We're still on hold until authorization is received from President Taylor."

Ninety minutes later, and still two hours from the drop zone, Commander Jim Nicolaou received the message he'd been hoping for.

CHAPTER 23

PRESIDENT TAYLOR STOOD before the three tall windows overlooking the garden. He was accustomed to making difficult decisions; it came with the job. All too often, lives were at stake. This call was no different, except maybe in regard to the number of people he was placing in peril. He recalled a poem, one he'd been required to memorize as a young student.

> *Half a league, half a league,*
> *Half a league onward,*
> *All in the valley of Death*
> *Rode the six hundred.*
> *"Forward, the Light Brigade!*
> *Charge for the guns!" he said.*
> *Into the valley of Death*
> *Rode the six hundred.*
> *"Forward, the Light Brigade!"*
> *Was there a man dismayed?*

Not though the soldier knew
Someone had blundered.
Theirs not to make reply,
Theirs not to reason why,
Theirs but to do and die.
Into the valley of Death
Rode the six hundred.

He paused, repeating the line, his voice barely louder than a whisper, "Theirs but to do and die."

With two naval ships swiftly sunk and tensions with China nearing the breaking point, was he being reckless, prideful? Was he repeating the errors of British commanders who, during the Crimean War in 1854, ordered the Light Brigade on their futile charge, dooming two-thirds of the men?

A familiar voice interrupted his introspection.

"Stormed at with shot and shell,
While horse and hero fell.
They that had fought so well
Came through the jaws of Death,
Back from the mouth of hell,
All that was left of them,
Left of six hundred."

President Taylor turned, facing his Secretary of State.

"Lord Alfred Tennyson, if memory serves me well."

"Paul, I didn't hear you enter."

"I'm sorry, sir. Should I wait outside?"

The President waved his hand. "Walk with me. I need some fresh air."

The two men exited the tall glass door opening onto the Rose Garden. Walking slowly, a contemplative President Taylor voiced his concern. "Have I made the right decision?"

"You mean by sending the *Gerald R. Ford* strike group to

the South China Sea? To the Spratly Islands?"

Taylor nodded. He stopped and faced Paul Bryan. "Paul, you've been an integral member of my cabinet from day one. I think you know that I value your counsel."

"Thank you, sir. We've been tested before and have always prevailed. The carrier strike group is the best there is. I have confidence they will succeed."

Taylor frowned. "But this weapon, this ship killer—we have no means of defense." Secretary Bryan wanted to rebut the President's statement, but he knew the truth as well as Taylor did.

"We can't take out the launching sites, so what's the tactical value of sending the carrier into harm's way? Hell, we don't even know *what* the launch vehicle is. It could be a sub or surface ship. It could be a secret silo on one of those islands and we just missed it." Taylor sighed heavily.

To Paul Bryan's eye, his boss had aged ten years in the last ten hours.

"Am I repeating the mistakes made by those arrogant British officers who ordered the Light Brigade to charge entrenched Russian cannon? Four-thousand five-hundred men and women serve on the *Ford*. It's their lives I'm gambling with."

"We can't pull back the fleet, sir," Bryan said. "To do so would concede the entire Western Pacific to China."

"You're assuming China is the power behind the attacks."

"Assuming, for the sake of argument, that North Korea is somehow capable of carrying out these launchings—and mind you, we have no reason to believe they possess the technology to fabricate the warheads—it doesn't materially change the balance of power in that region of the world. The U.S. Seventh Fleet is the only force able to check Chinese expansionism. If we pull back, China becomes the second superpower. Beijing has laid claim to almost all of the East China Sea and the

South China Sea. Her sphere of influence will cover more than half of Asia plus the seas stretching east to Korea, Japan, the Philippines, and south to Malaysia.

"The mineral wealth beneath those waters could represent a staggering fortune. China is thirsty for oil, and many experts think there are enormous undiscovered reserves waiting to be claimed. If that's true, it would be a boon for China's economy."

"I don't see that as a bad thing," Taylor replied.

"No sir, it's not. But the South China Sea is a major shipping route. Five trillion dollars of sea-borne trade passes annually. If China refuses to allow open access under historical freedom of navigation agreements, the impact will be felt by every country that trades with Southeast Asia."

"I've heard that argument before. But isn't this simple fear mongering? Sure, China *may* clamp down on shipping and charge fees for passage, or forbid some ships altogether based on the flag they fly—and they may not. So what? I really don't see this issue as materially different from the Panama Canal."

"I beg to differ. Control of the Panama Canal was transferred to Panama by two treaties, collectively called the Torrijos-Carter Treaties. It was the second of the two documents, the Panama Canal Treaty, that actually transferred control of the canal as of December 31, 1999. However, the first document, commonly known as the Neutrality Treaty, provides that the United States will retain the right to defend the canal from any threat that might interfere with equitable access by ships of all nationality. In essence, the U.S. maintains the right to use military force to keep the canal open."

"I'm familiar with the Neutrality Treaty. And yet we don't see China or Russia complaining that the U.S. should relinquish influence over the canal. What if President Chen made a similar proposal regarding shipping through the South China Sea? Isn't it time that we look at China as a trading partner and not a military threat?"

"Perhaps. However, the legal claims put forth by China to the disputed islands in the South China Sea and the East China Sea are not clear. The number of islands subject to the disputed claims is quite numerous."

Taylor raised his eyebrows. "You're not telling me anything we haven't already discussed—in detail."

"Respectfully sir, it is my duty to remind you of our obligations to our allies—Japan, Taiwan, Malaysia, the Philippines—who also have legitimate claims contradicting those of China. This is a complicated matter that must be resolved through diplomacy and the international courts—not through threat of force."

Taylor had resumed his walk, turning the corner and strolling along the west colonnade, his hands folded behind his back. "As usual, Paul, you make a compelling argument."

They took a few more steps in silence, thoughts weighing heavily on the President's mind.

"Wanna know what really bothers me, Paul?" He didn't wait for a reply. "It's the relative ease with which these life-and-death decisions are made." Taylor turned and gazed across the garden as if his eyes were searching for something that wasn't there. "Hardly a week goes by when I'm not being asked to make a decision that would put our people at risk. Hell, the only remarkable point about the current affair is the number of service men and women that I'm…" The President paused, searching for the right word. "That I'm ordering to charge the Russian cannon, with literally no defense."

"I'm sure all of your predecessors also wrestled with this very issue. But the world is a violent place, and we have to deal, as best we can, with situations and problems that are not of our making."

"You'd make a good professor," Taylor said, turning just enough for Paul Bryan to see his crooked grin. In fact, Paul

Bryan had taught political science at Stanford. But the lure of politics was simply too strong.

"I'd like to believe," Taylor continued, "the voters elected me in no small part because they had confidence I'd do a better job than the former administration at finding diplomatic solutions to conflict, rather than opting to use military might."

"And you have, sir. At the risk of sounding self-congratulatory, you have a pretty impressive record of defusing very challenging international incidents. The Sudan and Eastern Europe immediately come to mind." Bryan was thinking of two particularly dangerous events involving the Chinese in Africa in one case, and in another the Russians attempting to expand their borders through the use of proxy militia.

"Not good enough. It doesn't matter what we've done, only what we do—or plan to do—that counts." Taylor sighed. "I've ordered an entire carrier strike group—more than 7,000 enlisted men and officers—into harm's way. All from the comfort of my office. And then, less than an hour later, I delivered a feel-good speech to high rollers in exchange for their generous contributions to the DNC. I order men and women to risk their lives, knowing many will pay the ultimate price, while I dine on prime rib and drink Champagne."

He faced his Secretary of State. Bryan found it difficult to meet the President's eyes. "Doesn't that strike you as odd? Maybe even perverse?"

"Sir—" Bryan was cut off.

"No, I'm not back peddling. But I am saying that we need to do more to find common ground with our sometimes adversaries, especially China. We need to do better—we *will* do better."

"I'll revisit some Southeast Asia initiatives previously under consideration."

Taylor nodded, liking what he heard. "And put a high

priority on equality and respect. I don't want to be preaching from a soap box or negotiating for a double standard. Look to historical examples of how territorial disputes were resolved amicably while preserving national self-interest. The Panama Canal treaties that you mentioned are a case in point."

"I'll get my people working on it. But in the meantime, we still have a very delicate situation off the coast of China."

"Yes, plus possible involvement of North Korea—maybe even collusion with President Chen."

"It makes for an extremely volatile mix, sir," Bryan said.

Several more steps were taken in silence, and then the President said, "So, we can't afford to fail. We have to find that launcher."

"Colonel Pierson's team at SGIT was made for this type of mission." Bryan glanced at his watch. "We should have their first report in a little more than an hour."

"You know, someday we're going to run out of luck."

"Who's to say luck has any role in this mission?"

"It always does," Taylor answered, his expression dour. "And between you and me, I'll take luck over skill any day."

CHAPTER 24

AS NIGHT DESCENDED ACROSS THE CITY, exertion and lack of rest finally caught up with Peter. He stretched his frame along a wall, using the sleeping bag as a pillow. Mercifully, he fell into a dreamless sleep, the first in many days. Diesel lay against his legs, snoring rhythmically.

"It's time," Robert said, one hand nudging Peter's shoulder.

He sat upright and rubbed a hand across his face. "Right."

Groggily, Peter rose and crossed to the table. Spread across the surface were the tools they would carry on this mission: pistols, spare magazines and ammunition, explosives and detonators, flash-bangs, bottles of water, rope, medical kit, knives, sturdy nylon zip ties, and two backpacks. Robert handed one of the packs to Peter. "The magazines are loaded. I stripped and cleaned the Glock while you were sleeping. Take a box of extra ammo, two of the flash-bangs, the first aid kit, and a couple bottles of water. Which knife do you want?"

Peter pointed to a folding three-inch blade and then filled

his pack. Cinching the top closed, he slipped his arms through the straps and followed Robert out the door. This time, they exited through the front entrance to the building. After walking two blocks, Robert flagged down a taxi and they rode to the international airport.

With Diesel, they would draw too much unwanted attention within the departure terminal, so instead Robert pointed along the road. A blue sign marked the way to a long-term parking lot.

The expansive paved lot was in sore need of repair and maintenance. Cracks and potholes were abundant. This was the low-price parking lot, and unlike the modern parking garage, there was no roof to shelter the cars from the torrential tropical rain that alternated with blistering sun. Still, most of the slots were occupied. The few lights high overhead on posts provided minimal illumination. "This way," Robert said.

They crossed the lot in silence, exiting onto an unlit service road. He followed Robert single file along the side of the macadam. Before long, they turned to the side and crossed through grass and low bushes. Peter recognized the open expanse before them as the golf course. In the dim light, he could just barely make out the flag marking the cup.

Still wanting to avoid attention, they stood off the green by ten yards, each man squatting low in the bushes. There they waited for thirty minutes, surrounded by sounds of distant automobile traffic, insects chirping and clicking, and one commercial airplane landing on the long runway. Peter shifted his body and leaned against the trunk of a palm tree, taking the strain off his knees. He popped two more acetaminophen tablets. And then he heard helicopter blades, whipping the still night air, quickly growing in intensity.

The swirling air was gentle at first but grew quite strong as the helicopter closed on the flat green. Peter was surprised at how the aircraft still sounded distant. Clearly some sort of noise attenuation was engineered into the turbine engines and the rotors.

Only at the last second did the pilot turn on the landing lights to accurately gauge the distance to solid ground. The sleek machine slowed and gently touched the manicured green. The door was pulled open, and Peter and Robert dashed from the cover of their hiding spot with their heads low. Diesel leapt into the passenger compartment a step head of Peter.

The helicopter lifted into the air even before the door was closed. Peter took the nearest seat, and was surprised to see Eu-meh Lim occupying one of the beige leather chairs. He cast a questioning look toward Robert.

"She insisted," he said. "I tried to talk her into staying behind."

"I have every right to board the *Royal Seeker*," Eu-meh said defiantly. "They could be holding my daughter there."

"It's likely to be dangerous," Peter replied.

Eu-meh gave a mirthless smile. "I've been in a car randomly riding around Brunei for the past several hours. All because Robert said my life could be in danger if I was at my office, or my apartment. So, it seems I'm in danger wherever I go."

"The crew are likely to be armed."

"Mr. Savage. This is my daughter we are talking about. My only child. Surely, you cannot expect me to find a safe hole to hide in until she is returned."

If the situation were different and it was Peter's family, he knew what he'd do—what he had done before when Ethan was kidnapped, or Joanna was being held hostage. "No, I suppose not."

Peter took stock of the cabin. It was furnished as a luxury corporate aircraft with leather upholstery, wood panels, and gold trim. Other than Eu-meh and Robert, there were the two crew members: the pilot and copilot. He noticed an MP5 submachine gun—a dependable piece of German engineering—secured next to the co-pilot's seat.

Robert handed to Peter a set of headphones with integral microphone so they could speak to the pilot and each other over the engine noise. "Do you have reliable coordinates for the target?"

"Roger," the pilot said. Peter could hear the conversation with remarkable clarity over the headset. "We have a live tracking feed. Apparently the Americans have a submarine shadowing the target."

Although Peter was pretty sure that was not the true source of information, he decided not to correct the pilot. "What is your ETA?"

Having just plotted their course, the co-pilot answered, "The target is moving slowly, under ten knots. Based on her current heading, south toward Malaysia, we will intercept in fifty-three minutes if they do not change course."

Robert issued his orders. "When you are seventy miles out, drop to the deck, skim the waves. Does this bird have any defensive measures?"

"Only radar threat receivers and flares."

"Better than nothing," Robert said. "Make your final run for the target fast, staying on the deck as long as possible. Then pop up and land on the helipad. It'll be forward above the superstructure."

"Roger that," the pilot answered. "Are we expecting any resistance?"

"If the ship has been modified to fire ballistic missiles, I'm guessing they'll not want to be boarded."

"We should be able to get a quick look on the way in," Peter said, and then added, "This one?" He nodded toward the copilot.

"Loyal to Eu-meh. While you were sleeping I received their personnel records."

Peter nodded. "We go in fast and hard, understand? If any crewmembers have weapons, shoot to kill. Don't hesitate. You hesitate and you die."

Robert appraised Peter. "Sounds like you've done this before."

"Thought you read my file," Peter said.

"What there is of it. The interesting stuff is heavily redacted. Even using the Sultan's connections to MI6 proved to be of little use."

"Well, Robert, what can I say? Trouble has a habit of finding me, and in large doses." He paused for a moment. "I figure we take control of the bridge and then one of us goes down to the well deck to gather up evidence of a missile launch, assuming that's why the ship disappeared in the first place."

"Gotta be it."

"You don't think it could have been taken by pirates?"

Robert shook his head, and Eu-meh chimed in. "If pirates had captured the *Royal Seeker*, they would have issued a ransom demand within twenty-four hours."

Peter leaned his head back against the padding and closed his eyes. He murmured, "When all possibilities have been eliminated, whatever remains, however improbable, must be the truth."

"I see you are a scholar of literature," Eu-meh said. "Maybe there are lessons to learn from the great detective."

"You lost me," Robert complained.

"Peter was quoting Sir Arthur Conan Doyle, creator of Sherlock Holmes."

"You see," Peter opened his eyes and glared at Robert. "If all possibilities can be eliminated, whatever is left, regardless of how unlikely that may be, must be true. In this case, it would seem we have considered the most likely reasons for the *Royal Seeker* to go missing—piracy, lost at sea, mechanical or electrical failure—and yet none of these reasons stands up to scrutiny. So, we are left with only one working hypothesis. And that is, the ship is a floating missile launch facility. Crazy." Peter shook his head. "But that is the logic of Sherlock Holmes."

"Well, that's good, isn't it?" Robert asked. "I mean, those missiles have to be stopped."

"You're assuming we successfully land on the helipad without being blown out of the air on final approach."

"That's the plan." If Robert was apprehensive, he hid it well.

"One of the crew needs to guard the helicopter. That leaves three of us to take control of the ship."

"Yeah, so?"

"It's going to be heavily defended. You said so yourself."

"Once we secure the bridge, we have the advantage. We radio for help."

"Radio who? We don't even know if the U.S. Navy has ships in the area. Honestly, I'd be surprised if they did given the extreme tensions with China at the moment. And we certainly can't call the Brunei military. We don't know who to trust."

"What about my daughter? I don't give a damn about missiles—we have to find my daughter!"

"Well, you should care," Peter said. "Because if those missiles aren't stopped, there's going to be a big war right in your front yard."

Robert shifted his gaze from Eu-meh back to Peter. "She's right. One of use has to search the ship and rescue Jade."

"*If* she's there," Peter said. He didn't voice the remainder of his thought—*most likely, she has already been killed and the body disposed of.*

Eu-meh pursed her lips. "I will never give up hope." Her voice trembled as she fought back tears. "I will find my daughter and bring her home, or I will die trying."

Peter leaned forward against his seat belt, his outstretched hand grasping Eu-meh's. "If Jade is on that ship, we will find her, I promise."

"And how do you plan to do that if we're holding down the bridge?" Robert asked.

"We get the captain and make him talk."

CHAPTER 25

THE AIRBUS H160 CORPORATE HELICOPTER raced north at 175 knots. The pilot was glad he was carrying an extra 150 gallons of fuel—at five meters elevation and flying at maximum speed, the engines were consuming fuel at an alarming rate. It was a dangerous flight, the sea and night sky merging into one featureless body of blackness. The pilots flew by instrument, aided by their night-vision goggles, as close as they dared to the wave tops.

"We were just picked up, being painted by radar," the copilot reported. "Standard marine S-band." He glanced at his own radar return showing the ship dead ahead. "Looks like the target has found us. She's stationary, must've cut her engines. Distance… seven nautical miles and closing."

Robert and Peter heard the entire conversation. "Remember, stay on the deck until the last moment," Robert said.

"Roger that," came the reply from the pilot.

The seconds seemed to stretch out to minutes. No one

spoke, save for the copilot calling out the distance.

"Four nautical miles…"

"Three…"

"Two…"

Peter felt his pulse quickening.

"One…"

Abruptly the aircraft pulled up, shoving Peter into his seat cushion. He gripped the armrests as they banked to the side. The pilot's voice came through the headsets. "She's off the left side. Going around the stern and then we'll land on the helipad. Keep a sharp eye open for missiles and RPGs."

Peter craned his neck, trying to get a good view of the target. The *Royal Seeker* was barely visible. The only lights were shining through windows in the super structure.

"Do you have a spotlight?" Peter asked.

After a moment of hesitation, the co-pilot replied. "Yes—but why?"

"As you circle the aft of the vessel, shine the spotlight on the derrick extending upwards from the middle of the ship."

"They'll know we're coming in," Robert objected.

"They already know!"

After traveling the last thirty minutes with the cabin blacked out, the white-light beam appeared all the more brilliant. The circle of illumination danced over the upper hull, and then found the derrick, jittering over the steel framework before settling on the center of the towers—and the green rocket motor enshrined within.

Peter pressed his face against the window. *Odd, I don't see a single person. No one is on deck.* The helicopter flared and settled on its landing gear. The pilot kept the engines idling while Peter threw open the door and jumped on the helipad, his Glock pointed forward, an extension of his arm.

At the corner of the landing apron was the ladder, which

looked very much like a steep stairway. Peter motioned with his arm for Robert to follow; Diesel was already at his master's side. Suddenly a crewmember's head and upper body appeared at the top of the ladder. He was raising a rifle, but Peter already had his sights on him. The Glock barked twice, and the crewmember fell backwards, the clanking of the rifle falling against the steel steps and landing on the deck below obscured by the whine of the aircraft turbines.

Peter rushed forward and descended the steep steps as fast as he dared. At the first landing, the ladder switched back in a zig-zag fashion. There was a weathertight door to enter the superstructure and, hopefully, the bridge. Looking beyond the railing, Peter saw the three towers grouped around the unmistakable shape of a rocket, faintly illuminated by a crescent moon. It appeared stubby, a result of the girth of the first-stage motor and the relatively short overall height. He pressed his back against the bulkhead and looked over his shoulder. Robert was rushing down the steps.

"Could be more gunmen on the other side of this door," Peter said.

Robert answered with a nod and then holstered his pistol so he could yank the door open with both hands.

Peter knelt low, ready to thrust his gun hand into the opening and squeeze off several shots. He looked up. "Ready."

Bracing his feet, Robert drew in a breath and turned the latch, then forcibly pulled the door, his momentum throwing his back against the bulkhead and out of the way.

Brrrppp! Automatic gunfire and a stream of bullets shot harmlessly through the open hatch.

Boom! *Boom*! *Boom*! Three bullets left the Glock in rapid succession, followed by the muffled sound of dead weight falling on the deck. Peter cautiously peeked around the corner. The passageway was clear. He rose to his feet and looked back up the ladder, expecting to see the third man from Eu-meh's personal guard. The co-pilot was standing there, having just carried Diesel down the ladder, but to Peter's dismay, so was his boss.

"You're supposed to be in the helicopter," he said through clenched teeth.

Eu-meh straightened her back and returned an icy stare. "I came here for Jade."

"You're as stubborn as my father," Peter groused.

"Good. Then you know you can't change my mind." She took a step forward, but Peter extended his arm, blocking her advance.

"We'll go first. You stay in the middle." Peter pointed at the co-pilot. He was cradling the MP5. "Take the rear and make certain no one comes up behind us."

Entering single file, Peter advanced down the passageway. When he reached the prone gunman, it was apparent from the bloody patch in the center of his chest that the man was dead. Peter picked up his weapon—an Uzi—and handed it to Robert.

Another five paces and the passageway ended at another door. Diesel lowered his head, flexing his shoulder muscles, a menacing, guttural growl emanating from behind his bared teeth. His eyes were locked on the door. "This should be the bridge," Robert said.

Peter attempted to turn the latch, but it was locked.

Robert placed the muzzle of the Uzi very close to the latch. Turning toward Eu-meh he said, "Cover your ears and turn away. This will be loud." Peter and the co-pilot followed the advice.

Brrrppp! The stream of bullets shredded the latching mechanism and doorframe, emptying the magazine. Tossing it aside, Robert grabbed his pistol and with one hand pushed the door open. Inside, the compartment was filled with a blue-white glow emanating from instrument lights and LCD screens. One entire wall was filled with windows looking forward. On the opposite side, a row of windows provided an unobstructed view across the derricks toward the aft of the ship.

Robert and Peter rushed in. Several men were standing at their stations, staring at the opening and the men charging through. Their facial features appeared ghoulish from the soft lighting shining upwards from the consoles.

"Who's in charge?" Peter said. He counted five faces. Most expressed fear, but one face was defiant.

Robert repeated the question in Mandarin, and Peter noticed the defiant man straightened his posture. He took a half step forward, away from the console he'd been studying.

"I am Captain Rei," he answered in reasonably good English. "I am in command of this vessel. Who are you? And what—" He stopped, eyes wide as he saw Eu-meh step from behind Robert's bulk.

"You know who I am," Eu-meh said with disgust.

Captain Rei averted his eyes downward.

"Hands up!" Peter ordered. Rei hesitated at first, and then complied. He was only ten feet from Peter, who closed the distance in three paces. "The rest of you—hands on your heads and against the wall. Now!" The other four seamen quickly moved until they were shoulder to shoulder. Robert passed zip ties to the co-pilot, with instructions to bind their hands.

"So it's true," Peter said, referencing the deadly weapon pointed skyward from the middle of the ship. "Who are you working for? China? North Korea?"

"You're too late," Rei said, his voice surprisingly calm.

"No matter. I'll bet the list of U.S. intelligence officers who will grill you is exceptionally long. And given the number of servicemen and women you've murdered, my guess is they won't be very civilized about it, either."

"Where is my daughter?" Eu-meh demanded.

The captain's face contorted into a bitter mask. "You are a disgrace to your people. You've sold your honor and loyalty for a life of luxury! Your daughter—" he spat on the deck, "she's soft and weak, just as you are."

"Where is she!" Robert placed a hand on her shoulder, restraining her forward motion.

"I have nothing more to say."

Peter lowered the pistol until the barrel was pointed at Rei's feet. "The way I see it, I can put a 9mm bullet in your foot, maybe your ankle too. And if you still don't want to answer the lady's questions, I'll move on to your knee caps—both of them." Peter scrunched his lips and shrugged. "We can play this game for quite some time. I've got plenty of bullets, and it will take hours for you to bleed out."

To demonstrate his resolve, Peter squeezed the trigger. Rei jumped, but the bullet just missed the toe of his shoe, instead puncturing the linoleum-covered steel deck.

Beads of sweat dappled the captain's forehead, some combining to form rivulets that slowly traced a squiggly line past his temples and onto his cheeks.

"Where are you holding my daughter?" Eu-meh seemed undisturbed by the threat of torture taking place before her eyes. But then again, she'd already crossed the bridge of civility when her daughter had been kidnapped, convincing herself that she could kill without remorse whoever had taken her child.

Hands still on his head, Rei moved his head from side to side. "She's not here."

"Then where is she?" Peter yelled, and then in a calmer voice, "Or the next round is through your foot."

Peter stared daggers at Rei. The captain read his resolve, and answered, "She's not on this ship. Some men came and transported her to another location. I don't know where."

"You're not being helpful," Peter said. He edged closer, his steel-grey eyes hard and cold as stone. Rei moved his mouth to speak.

"I… I don't know where."

Boom! Rei screamed in pain.

Peter turned to the side, facing Robert. A waft of gun smoke drifted lazily from the barrel of his pistol.

The bullet cut off his little toe. Blood was seeping out the jagged hole in his black leather shoe.

"Why did you do that?" Peter said.

"You're talking too much, wasting time."

Rei was losing it. "I swear! I don't know where Jade is!"

"Then who took her off this ship?" Peter said, just inches from the captain's face. "And when were they here?"

"The guards! Two days ago."

"Captain Rei. You are trying my patience. More importantly, you are testing Robert's resolve. If you don't provide helpful information, I've no doubt he will adjust his aim for your ankle."

Rei's face was terror-filled. "No, no. That's all I know. Four men. They wore the uniform of the palace guard. One had a bandage over his ear. They swore me and my crew to secrecy. Said they would kill any man who even whispered that the Sultan's niece had been on this ship."

"Sooner or later we all die," Peter said.

"That's all I know, I swear!"

"Liar!" Eu-meh shouted. "You're holding something back. Why would the palace guard be involved? They'd never hurt any member of the Sultan's family. You're lying!"

Captain Rei had shifted his weight to the side, favoring the injured foot. His back was against the console. He'd lowered his hands to help support his weight. "No, not everyone."

Peter pressed his pistol against Rei's thigh. "Speak clearly man, or I promise you the next bullet will shatter your femur."

"I heard them talking. One of the guards said their orders came from the Director of Security."

"My nephew? No, that's impossible," Eu-meh's voice faded.

Peter considered the accusation. He knew that a man would say anything to end torture. The question was how far a man could be pushed before breaking. Had Captain Rei spoken the truth, or was he making this up to avoid more pain and disfigurement?

"It makes sense," Peter finally concluded.

Robert nodded agreement. "The palace guard with the bandage on the side of his head, the same one you hacked with the steak knife in London. And the guards we had the shootout with."

Just then, the ship shuddered and a light, as bright as the sun, flooded in through the aft-facing windows. Everyone raised an arm to shield their eyes as they reflexively turned toward the source. The murderous roar of the main rocket engine made Peter's chest vibrate and he felt the steel deck shaking beneath his feet.

Trailing a cloud of rust-colored smoke, the missile lifted and sailed clear of the towers on a trajectory that would take it miles above the Earth.

"I told you," Rei said, trying to hold his balance without placing weight on the foot Robert had shot. "You're too late."

CHAPTER 26

MORE THAN A THOUSAND MILES north of the drama unfolding on the *Royal Seeker*, the American carrier strike group, led by the *USS Gerald Ford*, the newest and most modern of the U.S. Naval aircraft carriers, was steaming south toward the Spratly Islands. Under the command of Rear Admiral William LaGrassa, the strike group, which included an attack submarine, two Aegis-class destroyers and two Ticonderoga-class cruisers, was to demonstrate U.S. resolve by sailing into the South China Sea and within eighteen nautical miles of many of the lumps of earth comprising the Spratly Island chain. But, in particular, the task group was to approach the islands built out by China as military outposts, all the while remaining in international waters, yet transiting close to the disputed territory. It was a dangerous ploy, one that could easily precipitate a military response. The analysts at the Pentagon placed the odds at 50:50 that China would respond with anti-ship or anti-aircraft missiles.

To say it would be a provocative move was a huge understatement, and Admiral LaGrassa was expecting a confrontation. He had been drilling his crew almost non-stop since forming up in Yokosuka, Japan. That was two days ago.

To ensure security, he'd ordered a combat air patrol (CAP) throughout daylight hours, allowing the flight crew to fall back to alert-five status at night. With two F-18F Super Hornets, pilots in the cockpits, fully armed and ready to be airborne in less than five minutes, the admiral believed they were well protected.

Captain Jackson "Jack" Healy should have been asleep in his cabin, but he also felt the strain of the non-stop training, and like the admiral, Healy was convinced they would be challenged by China. The question was, how close would the strike group get before being confronted by Chinese airpower. The United States wasn't the only country with reconnaissance satellites.

Presently, Captain Healy was on the bridge of the *Ford*. He was reading the recent status update when his concentration was interrupted by the Operations Officer. "*Shiloh* is reporting inbound bogey. High rate of speed."

"Launch the alert five Hornets," Healy ordered. "Sound general quarters. Battle stations! Alert all escort ships. I want multiple firing solutions on that bogey!"

The ship's klaxon sounded. Immediately, men and women poured from their berths or dropped what they were doing and rushed to their battle stations, closing watertight doors after the last seaman passed. Over the PA system came the order: "General Quarters. General Quarters. All hands, man your battle stations. Set condition zebra."

"What's the target?" Healy said. "Where are they?"

The Operations Officer was grim. "Too fast and too high to be aircraft. The *Shiloh* is tracking a ballistic trajectory.

Confirmed by *Antietam*."

"Are there any other contacts?"

"Negative. CIC says the scope is clear—no surface or air contacts other than our escorts."

"Order the *Shiloh* to engage with SM3s."

Equipped with powerful radar and SM3 anti-ballistic missile defensive weapons, any of the escort ships had the capability to engage the incoming bogey. But Captain Healy knew that the crew of the *Shiloh* had the most experience, having engaged the missile that sunk the Japanese warship *Izumo*. He silently prayed for a better outcome this time.

Looking into the darkness beyond the bridge windows, the Captain watched as both Hornets took to the air. *I hope they have a deck to come back to.*

"Captain. *Shiloh* confirms firing solution." The Operations Officer paused while listening to a second message. "SM3 launched, tracking true. No other bogies. This appears to be a single missile." Another pause. "Second SM3 fired. Both tracking. Time to first impact... thirty-five seconds."

High in the night sky Healy watched as first one bright white flare, and then a second, raced toward the heavens and the unseen threat.

Onboard the guided-missile cruiser *USS Shiloh*, First Officer Lawrence was in command, although he was certain Captain Wallace would soon relieve him. Wallace had retired to his quarters earlier in the evening, but once the call to general quarters and battle stations was made, the captain would waste no time to assume command of his ship.

In the Combat Information Center, the *Gerald Ford* carrier strike group was shown on the vertical projection map as five blue arrows spaced well apart. Each of the escort ships represented a corner of a square surrounding the carrier, the largest of the blue arrows. XO Lawrence preferred the projection, since from the bridge none of the other strike group ships were visible, each beyond the horizon.

On the screen, two green lines inched toward a red marker designated alpha. The speed and altitude of the threat was also displayed next to the red symbol. The incoming bogey had not become visible to the ship's radar system until it had gained considerable altitude. Now, the goal was to knock out the rocket engine before the warhead separated and began its terminal descent.

"What do we have, XO?" Captain Wallace asked. Lawrence was so focused on the display that he'd not realized his captain had entered the CIC.

"Incoming ballistic missile. So far, the trajectory and radar cross-section are mirror images of the one we encountered during the training exercise with the Japanese Maritime Self Defense Force. We fired two SM3s. Tracking true."

"Did Admiral LaGrassa order battle stations?"

"Captain Healy on the *Ford* is in command for the time being." Lawrence knew that the Rear Admiral would soon take command of the strike group. The timing of the attack was such that the most experienced officers were asleep.

"Time to impact?"

"Thirty-five seconds for the first SM3. The second missile is five seconds behind the first."

"Can we intercept in the boost phase?" Wallace knew that was their best chance of scoring a hit. Before, when they thought it a drill, they'd delayed firing their SM3 intercept missiles until it was too late. The defensive weapon system was designed to drive a non-explosive kinetic-energy warhead into a ballistic-missile rocket motor. If they missed the boost phase, they'd be forced to attempt to connect with the small, hyper-velocity warhead. As they'd already learned, the probability of success was very low.

Lawrence tilted his head and raised an eyebrow. "It'll be close, but we had a fast response time following acquisition."

"Origin?"

"We're still checking the radar data from the *Antietam*, *Barry*, and *Stethem*. All escorts tracked the bogey, and given our separation, we will have good triangulation to work back from. However, and preliminarily, the trajectory points to launch coordinates in the South China Sea."

"Same as the previous encounter?"

"No, sir. In the same neighborhood, but not the same coordinates."

Wallace glanced at the digital time on the vertical projection. The green lines had closed considerably on the red marker. Ten seconds to go.

He stared at the advancing green traces as the time counted down, second by second. The lead intercepting SM3 was closing on the bogey at Mach 15. The data readout next to the red marker indicated it was approaching an altitude of 300 kilometers, and the rate of gain in altitude was slowing, consistent with the missile approaching apogee, the highest point in the ballistic trajectory.

Everyone in the CIC, including Captain Wallace, was transfixed by the display. The green marker and red marker were quickly approaching, as if unseen hands were drawing the colored lines, intending to make them intersect.

Two seconds…

One second…

The lines connected and the green marker vanished. A cheer rose from the assembled crew, and Wallace exhaled. He'd been holding his breath for the final three seconds.

XO Lawrence was exuberant. "Looks like we nailed it in the boost phase!"

"Good job people," Wallace said. He scanned the faces and saw expressions of relief more than joy.

"New bogey, designate bravo," a voice called from somewhere in the CIC. Lawrence swept his eyes until he spied a crewman leaning over a radar scope. The vertical display was updated with a new red triangle marker. The second green line was closing on it.

"What happened?" Lawrence asked.

"We got a good hit on the rocket booster. Must've separated from the warhead moments before impact."

The velocity number next to the red marker was rapidly getting larger. "It's accelerating, sir," said the radar technician. "Passing apogee. Now at Mach 10... Mach 12. One second to impact."

Again, all eyes were on the display. But this time the green line representing the second SM3 first merged with the red marker, and then continued on. "No contact. Second SM3 missed the bogey."

Wallace barked his order. "Instruct all escorts to fire SM3s in five second intervals! Empty their magazines if they have to! We've got to take out that warhead before it hits the *Ford*!"

"Negative contact, sir. The *Shiloh* missed. The bogey is still inbound," the Operations Officer announced. "All escorts are launching SM3s."

The night sky around the *Ford* was illuminated with pulses of intense white light. Brilliant flares raced with incredible speed from the horizon to a point, a mathematical solution, miles above, near the upper boundary of the atmosphere.

"Bogey has accelerated to Mach 13. Still accelerating... Mach 14. It appears to be aiming for us."

"Time to impact?" Healy asked.

"Twenty-five seconds. Now traveling at Mach 16!"

"How long until our defensive missiles intercept?" Healy said.

"First volley missed. Second volley... twelve seconds to intercept."

"Right full rudder. All ahead flank! New bearing two-nine-five degrees."

The huge flat top heeled to port as she angled sharply onto her new course. Without an active guidance system, Healy reasoned the bogey would miss the aircraft carrier by nearly a third of a mile. The bridge officers steadied themselves as the deck tilted.

"Talk to me," Healy said.

The Operations Officer had his eyes glued to a graphical display showing the rapidly-evolving tactical situation. It was continuously updated through a data link with the USS Shiloh. "Four SM3s are locked and tracking true. Five seconds to intercept."

Healy mentally counted down the seconds, the tactical display showing a cluster of four symbols representing the defensive missiles close to merging with the symbol for Bogey Two.

And then, as before, the symbols crossed and continued onward.

"Another miss, sir. Next volley will intercept in seven seconds."

"Has the bogey altered its trajectory?"

"Affirmative, sir. It is still targeting us. Must have an active guidance system. If the SM3s don't take it out, impact will be in nine seconds."

"Release the Sea Sparrow and RAM batteries. Fire at will." With greater range, the Sea Sparrows fired first from just below the deck on the starboard side. A second later, a volley of rolling airframe missiles fired.

"Negative intercepts! Bogey is still incoming!"

"Helm!" Healy ordered. "Left full rudder. Come hard to port. New course one-eight-zero degrees!"

The Operations Officer raised his head. The red marker on the display had nearly merged with the blue symbol representing his ship. "Brace for impact!"

CHAPTER 27

AS THE ILLUMINATION QUICKLY FADED, Peter rushed to the window, craning his head as he followed the missile into the heavens until it became a tiny dot of light. He crossed to Captain Rei, grabbing him by the collar. "How do we stop it?"

"You can't."

"There has to be a way!"

"Once the missile is fired, it is out of my control. America will lose another warship, and another and another, until your government capitulates."

"Robert," Peter said. "Do you see any equipment here that looks like it might be used to launch a missile?"

From where he was standing near the center of the bridge, Robert could see all of the instrument consoles. "No, nothing. This is all standard equipment for navigation, steering, and communication."

"Then there has to be another room, a control center. And Captain Rei is going to take us there." Peter shoved the man forward. He stumbled until he regained his balance, hobbling forward with Peter's Glock inches from his back.

The procession headed down an internal stairway, Diesel healing close by Peter's side. After passing two decks, they followed a corridor on the third. Captain Rei removed a key from his pocket and unlocked the door. It swung open to reveal a compartment crammed with sophisticated-looking instruments and consoles. Four men were seated at their stations, engrossed in the post-launch activities and not paying attention to the party that had just entered. The space was illuminated in a red glow from overhead lights. A large electronic display showed a white triangle moving across a regional map extending from Malaysia north to the Korean peninsula. "You're tracking the missile?" Peter said.

At the sound of the foreign voice, one man turned and stood. "Captain?" It was First Officer Chang. A sidearm was holstered on his hip.

Peter swung his gun. "Don't even think about it."

Chang raised his hands, noticing the two additional armed intruders, including one blocking the doorway and holding a submachine gun.

"How do we stop it? There must be a self-destruct," Peter demanded.

Chang stared back in silence, looking to his captain for direction. "No, there is no way to destroy the missile," Rei said. "I already told you."

Peter stared at the tracking display, the white triangle advancing across the screen. But what was the target?

"That's it," he said. "You have to enter a launch sequence that includes the presumed target location. But hitting a ship— let alone a moving ship—would require a very sophisticated guidance system. That's how you are able to track the missile— you're sending and receiving data. You're steering it to the target."

Both Chang and Rei remained silent. Time was on their side, and in a matter of minutes the warhead would strike.

"Shut down the guidance system," Peter ordered Rei.

"No."

Peter positioned the Glock inches from Rei's face. "Shut it down!"

"You have already lost. The era of American world dominance is over."

"Shut it down or I put a bullet in your head."

"Go ahead. It makes no difference. In a few minutes, the warhead will destroy another ship from your Seventh Fleet. I won't shut down the guidance system."

Chang lunged for the gun in Peter's hand, attempting to lock it in his grip. Diesel, who had been standing in silence to Peter's side, leapt into action. The canine clamped its jaws around Chang's forearm. He cried out in pain but still held a firm grip on Peter's gun hand.

Diesel's weight dragged the combatant's arms down, moving the muzzle away from Rei. The canine increased his bite force as blood flowed over his tongue and lips, at the same time pushing backwards with his hind legs.

Peter lurched forward but checked his momentum and tugged against Chang's arms. It was no use, like trying to pull a seventy-pound anchor buried within mud. He swung his left fist, connecting with Chang's nose.

The explosion of a gunshot sounded very close, startling Peter. At first, he thought it was he who had discharged his weapon, but then Chang slumped to the deck, a hand over his stomach.

Robert redirected his gun at Rei. The other controllers remained seated, each not wanting to be the next victim.

"You can kill all of us," Rei said, "and it won't stop the destruction of your ship. My death, and that of my crew, will only serve to embolden others to follow."

Glancing up to the projection again, Peter saw the map had zoomed in on a portion of ocean just to the west of the Philippine island of Luzon. The white marker indicating the warhead was moving directly to a cluster of five blue triangles. The blue symbols were arranged such that four were at the corners of a square, and the fifth—the largest—was positioned in the middle of the arrangement. They were all pointed south.

Peter spoke over his shoulder. "Robert, what does that look like to you?" The former Navy man stepped forward, never allowing his pistol to waver from Rei's chest.

"That's a carrier strike group."

"Yeah, that was my thought, too. Then this warhead will be aimed for the biggest ship, the carrier."

Not willing to waste any more time, Peter said, "Get the C4. We have to blow this room. Hurry!"

The co-pilot trained his MP5 on their captives while Robert prepared the plastic explosive and detonators. Since it appeared there were four main instrument consoles, plus what had to be an electrical panel supplying power to the equipment, he used his knife to slice the 1.25-pound block into five sections. Quickly, he molded each chunk of explosive around a length of yellow-and-black primacord. As Robert completed the preparation of each charge, he handed them off to Peter, who placed the explosives against each console in a fashion he hoped would do the most damage. The final charge was placed on top of the electrical panel where three large conduits entered the metal box. Robert taped the ends of all five lengths of primacord together with a radio-controlled detonator.

"Ready," he said after arming the detonator.

Peter grabbed Rei roughly. "Tell your men to get out." Seeing what was planned, the three crewmembers wasted no time in hustling out of the control room.

"Let's go," Peter said, and he shoved Captain Rei out the doorway, followed by Diesel, Eu-meh, the co-pilot, and Robert taking up the rear. They hurried up the ladder, and only seconds after leaving the compartment, Robert depressed a button on the radio link.

The deep, thunderous boom was felt as much as heard. The superstructure shuddered, and Eu-meh lost her footing momentarily. With his free hand under her arm, Peter helped her to her feet. It was time to get off the *Royal Seeker*; they had outstayed their welcome.

Rushing up the ladder, they emerged on the helipad. Peter blinked his eyes, unable to believe his senses.

The landing pad was empty.

CHAPTER 28

THE PLAN HAD BEEN TO LEAVE THE PILOT with the corporate helicopter, engines idling, so they could make a speedy escape. *What could have happened?* Peter wondered.

"Now what?" Robert asked while he secured Rei's hands behind his back.

The co-pilot was searching the black sky. "There!" he pointed. A light was low above the ocean, and approaching fast.

"Hope that's our guy," Peter said. Then the deep, rhythmic *whump, whump* of the rotating blades was heard.

As the air stirred in a whirlwind, the Airbus H160 set down. The co-pilot dashed forward and threw open the door. "Had to leave!" the pilot shouted. "Just barely cleared the edge of the ship before the missile exhaust plume overwhelmed the landing pad!"

Robert advanced toward the open door prodding Captain Rei with a meaty hand firmly clasped onto his neck and the pistol dug into his back. With heads lowered, Peter and Eu-meh followed closely.

"Get in!" Robert commanded to Rei. Still favoring his injured foot, he climbed in awkwardly.

Diesel was facing back the way they'd come, but it escaped Peter's attention. He was focused instead on making certain their prisoner didn't try anything while they were bunched at the door to the cabin. But Eu-meh did notice. She tilted her head to the side and peered into the darkness, trying to see whatever had transfixed the dog.

Suddenly, Diesel launched himself across the helipad.

At the crack of gunfire, Eu-meh threw herself to the side, colliding with Peter. He stumbled into the body of the helicopter before catching his balance.

Then the co-pilot squeezed off a short burst from the MP5.

Eu-meh was leaning into Peter, struggling to hold herself upright. Peter grabbed her arms and fought to hold her weight as her legs went limp.

The submachine gun barked again before the co-pilot lowered it. Robert and Peter eased Eu-meh to a sitting position. Her eyes squinted and her mouth was twisted in a grimace. She removed her hand from the side of her chest and it was coated in bright red blood. Her breathing was becoming increasingly labored as blood filled her lung.

"You saw the gunman," Peter said. "You pushed me aside."

Robert prepared to scoop her up and lift her into the aircraft, but she grabbed Peter's arm. "Find her," she said, her voice barely audible over the whine of the turbine engine.

"What?" Peter said.

"Find my daughter." Her eyes opened and she held Peter's gaze. "Bring Jade home."

Peter nodded.

"We need to get her to a hospital!" Robert shouted, and lifted her with ease into the nearest seat.

"Diesel! Come." A moment later Diesel jumped into the

cabin and the co-pilot closed the door. He was still strapping himself in when the pilot increased engine power and lifted off the helipad.

Peter removed the medical kit from his pack. With Robert's help, they eased Eu-meh onto the floor and gently rolled her onto her side. Two bullets had passed through her chest. Both the entrance and exit wounds were frothing. He applied sterile compresses and then wound gauze around. She was dying, and he doubted they'd get her to a hospital in time.

"How long?" he asked.

Robert shook his head. "Too long. There's a helipad on the hospital in Bandar Seri Begawan, and the co-pilot has already radioed ahead."

Eu-meh's lips moved as she struggled to speak, her breath short and wheezing. She was drowning. A raspy sound came out, and then she coughed up blood.

Peter held her hand and leaned close to hear her above the din of noise. "Promise me. Bring my daughter home. She's my only child." Another bloody cough and spasms racked her body.

"I give you my word," he replied. His eyes glistened and he fought back tears. Another senseless death. Another innocent victim. Too many times he'd been witness to this.

So much loss.

So much grief.

Peter swallowed the growing lump in his throat and he squeezed Eu-meh's hand again. "I'm here with you. Hold on, okay? Just hold on, were almost to the hospital." He hoped his lie would give her strength, and yet he could see life was rapidly ebbing from her ravaged body.

Her lips moved silently, and from behind closed eyes she saw a young Jade running in the sunshine, laughing as she fell into her mother's embrace. They spun and laughed, and then Jade moved away like an invisible force was pulling her from

Eu-meh. Then a new image of Jade appeared. She was alone in a room. Her hands were bound and she sat on a thin mattress, her face battered and bruised.

She opened her eyes, and in those eyes Peter recognized fear and desperation, as only a parent can feel when their child is in jeopardy. "Swear to me," she rasped the words. "Don't let them hurt my daughter."

Peter clenched his jaw, grinding his teeth. She recognized his conviction and knew she could trust him. He would make sure Jade was all right. She could let go.

Peter felt her body completely relax. He pressed a finger against her neck, searching for a pulse—nothing. He leaned close to feel if there was a whisper of a breath, but she was still. He eased her head to the floor, and leaned back against a seat. He felt defeated. Everything had been lost—once again. It was the same sense of helplessness and despair he'd experienced when his wife had died. And again when his friend, Dmitri Kaspar, had been shot by militia in Minsk.

Diesel sensed the pain his master was suffering and curled next to him, placing his big, blocky head on Peter's thigh. He looked up, his amber eyes conveying a shared sorrow.

Robert removed a blanket from a storage locker and draped it over the lifeless body.

Peter repeated her words over and over in his mind. And as he did, his anger grew stronger and stronger until it was an inferno of fury. Pure, remorseless rage.

Without conscious thought, his hand moved to the pistol tucked beneath his belt. His fingers wrapped around the grip. It filled his hand, and he felt a reassuring strength from the texture, the shape. He would find Jade. And when he did, he would deal decisively with whoever held her.

CHAPTER 29

THE *USS GERALD FORD*, pride of the Navy, was cornered. The incoming warhead had survived a fusillade of defensive missiles. Unable to either destroy or shake free of the warhead's guidance system, Captain Healy knew his ship was going to be hit. The only question now was would his ship survive?

He'd read the intelligence reports during the briefing prior to the strike group embarking from Yokosuka, Japan. The warheads that sunk both the *Izumo* and the *Makin Island* were believed to be kinetic penetrators—very small, very dense, and hyper velocity. Thought to be only inches in diameter and maybe three feet long, speculated to have been fabricated in an exotic composite structure—an outer layer composed of a material they called hafnium carbonitride surrounding an inner core of super-dense osmium. The physicists claimed this structure was extremely hard, extremely dense, and nearly immune to the high temperature generated as the projectile completed the terminal phase of its ballistic trajectory. No doubt this is why the missile defenses of the strike group had failed to intercept and defeat the warhead.

The brains at the Naval Surface Warfare Center calculated that this type of warhead would deliver a crippling blow to a ship, transferring an amount of energy equivalent to 2.5 tons of TNT. Even worse, this energy would be transmitted from the point of impact on the top deck or superstructure, all the way through the internal compartments and decks, finally exiting the bottom hull of the vessel. It would be akin to a nickel-iron meteor striking a warship.

Flooding would commence immediately and extend upward through compromised bulkheads and decks. Any material directly in the path of the warhead would be vaporized, even steel. Nearby, metal would be melted, and along with the superheated gases, ignite any flammable materials—the most dangerous being jet fuel and ordnance.

Between the structural damage from the kinetic penetrator, heat from raging fires, and thousands of tons of flooding water placing a tremendous mass around the weakened section of the vessel, it was no surprise that the previous two ships had broken in two within minutes of being hit.

But the *Ford* was a much larger vessel, displacing nearly 100,000 tons. Could she survive the warhead strike? Not if her bunkers of aviation fuel, or magazines loaded with missiles and bombs, were ignited. If that happened, it would be a terrifying spectacle. A deadly, hellish inferno would destroy his ship and her entire crew—more than 4,500 men and women.

Captain Healy leaned against the console and stared out the bridge windows. A second had passed since the Operations Officer had sounded the alarm—"Brace for impact!"

Beneath his feet, the deck tilted, and he felt the shift in momentum as the *Ford* heeled into a sharp turn to port. And then, looking much like a bolt of lightning, only arrow straight, a tongue of brilliant white light lanced through the blackness and slammed into the deck.

His ship shuddered, and new alarms sounded.

At first, Healy thought his mind was playing a trick, a cruel deceit. His pulse pounded in his ears as he waited for the frightful secondary explosions to rip out the guts of the mighty ship. And then he realized the warhead had only grazed the starboard side of the flight deck. He leaned forward, placing binoculars to his eyes and peering through the darkness. The flight deck was illuminated by yellow-orange flames, fuel from three destroyed Hornets that had been tied down next to the forward starboard elevator.

"All stop," Healy ordered, "until that fire is under control. Then turn into the wind and give me full speed. I want two more Hornets on CAP. Anything on the scope?"

"Negative, sir. Only our escorts. No other surface contacts. No air contacts."

"As soon as the debris is removed and the fire is out, get a Sentry up. I want to see anything coming before it can see us."

Admiral LaGrassa entered the bridge. Coagulated blood marked a short gash on his forehead. "Are you okay, sir?" Healy asked.

The admiral waved off Healy's concern. "That first hard turn caught me off balance. Status?"

Healy quickly ran through the deployment of the escorts, the ballistic missile attack and response, the lack of any other contacts on the radar, the order to deploy a total of four F-18 fighters to the combat air patrol, plus the launching of an E-3 Sentry early warning and surveillance aircraft. The Sentry would give the carrier strike force excellent radar coverage of the sky and sea to a distance of 200 nautical miles.

LaGrassa nodded in concurrence. "Damage report?"

"Coming in now, sir," the Operations Officer replied. "The

forward elevator took the brunt of the damage—looks like a direct hit. Three Hornets were destroyed. Fire is under control and almost out, then they'll push the wreckage overboard. Fortunately, none of the destroyed aircraft had been armed or fully fueled. Other than the forward elevator and immediate vicinity, it doesn't look like there is any impairment to launching and retrieving aircraft."

"Status of the EMALS?" the admiral asked, referring to the electromagnetic aircraft launch system that replaced steam catapults used in previous generations of aircraft carriers.

"All four EMALS are operational. No damage."

"Thank God for that," LaGrassa murmured.

Captain Healy breathed a deep sigh of relief. "If that warhead had hit center of ship…"

"Get a message out to COMPACFLT, and updates every fifteen minutes."

"What do you think will be the response from the Fleet Commander?" Healy asked.

"This strike group is still operational. And as long as we can project force, COMPACFLT will not alter our orders. Although I would expect they'll deploy the *Reagan* strike group to bolster our strength."

"The *Ronald Reagan* and her escorts would be a considerable addition. From their current deployment between Taiwan and mainland China, they could join our operational formation in twenty hours, maybe less if we reduce our speed. But that would remove their presence in the Taiwan Strait. Might make Taiwan a bit anxious."

"True. But this strike group has come under attack, and based on latest intel there is no reason to believe China is planning an imminent attack on Taiwan. I think those ships will serve a more useful purpose here, as part of this strike group. At least I hope that's the decision COMPACFLT makes."

Healy looked out the bridge window just in time to see the shattered remains of an F-18 Hornet pushed overboard. Crewmembers immediately followed up with a shoulder-to-shoulder walking of the deck to remove all foreign debris that might get sucked into a jet engine.

LaGrassa addressed Healy directly. "Make no mistake—we are steaming into combat. Make certain that message is understood by every officer in this strike group. Any ship or plane that enters our sphere of control that is not positively ID'd as friendly will be presumed hostile. As of this moment, all ships and aircraft are authorized to shoot first any hostile contact."

CHAPTER 30

THE *PANDA STAR* WAS DARK, the only meager illumination coming from windows in the superstructure. But darkness was an ally of modern special forces, and the SGIT team was wearing night-vision goggles, or NVGs. The entire six-man team had landed securely on the helipad and immediately released their chutes. As quickly as the black nylon fluttered away, the team was on the move: First descending from the helipad and then splitting into pairs to perform their specific mission roles.

With Iceberg and Magnum in the lead, they descended the ladder on the exterior of the superstructure. Halfway down to the main deck, where the moon pool was located, Ghost and Homer took up a defensive position on a landing. From this elevated location, they could see over the main deck. They stood on either side of the watertight door that led from the landing to a passageway that connected to berths. If any crewmembers came this way, they would be stopped immediately by the two operators.

Boss Man and Bull peeled off on the main deck, angling for the towers amidship, while Magnum and Iceberg continued aft. So far, no crewmembers had been seen. Whoever was manning the *Panda Star* appeared to be below deck or asleep in their cabins.

Jim took this as a positive sign. Although the lack of exterior running lights suggested a covert nature to the ship's activities, he found a small measure of relief that they had not encountered any guards or lookouts.

Through the NVGs, everything was in shades of green and black. The sophisticated light-amplification sensors and circuitry delivered an incredibly clear and sharp image, and the two men moved rapidly to the base of the towers. There were three in total, surrounding the moon pool. Looking down, the water appeared inky black, and there was barely a ripple.

Bull quickly went to work, removing a numbered plastic bag from a cargo pocket of his fatigues. Using his knife, he scraped some paint and oxidation off a support leg of one tower and into the plastic bag. Then he held the bag next to the location he'd sampled and using a classified camera, equipped with low-light electronics very similar to the NVGs he was wearing, captured a photo without the inconvenience of a flash. He repeated this procedure many times, acquiring samples from all three towers as well as the base of the crane.

Jim was methodically exploring the deck surrounding the moon pool. Although the artificial coloration of the light-amplification headgear made it challenging to identify supposed scorching of the metal, the paint and other residue samples would confirm if application of intense heat and flame had occurred. He passed a first aid kit, several toolboxes, and even a few wrenches large enough to require a two-hand hold, but so far nothing of a military nature had been found.

He continued his search, moving aft, as Bull leaned over

the edge of the moon pool and scraped away more samples. In his cargo pocket he'd already stashed more than a dozen plastic bags containing flakes and powders, all photographically documented. Jim brushed against several large wooden crates. He paused long enough to conduct a cursory examination. The lettering was in Chinese characters that he couldn't read. But he was able to recognize the upward-pointing arrows and interpret THIS SIDE UP.

Continuing his search, he cleared the aft end of the moon pool and was inspecting several fifty-five-gallon drums that he suspected were hydraulic fluid or various grades of motor oil. He removed a glove and ran his fingers across the top of one barrel, next to the bung; it felt slick and had the odor of petroleum.

More barrels were arranged on the deck. His eye was drawn to two barrels that were slightly different in shape, although they were the same size as the others. The rim on these barrels appeared to be reinforced. He moved closer. Printed on each were four letters: UDMH.

"Bull, I've got something here," he said. His throat mic transmitted the message to the entire team.

"Be right there." Bull sealed the bag and moved toward his commander in a low crouch, always holding his weapon ready.

While Jim awaited Bull's arrival, he requested his team to check in. "Anything?"

"Negative, Boss Man," Iceberg said.

This was quickly followed by Homer and Ghost. "Nothing. These guys must be sleeping like babies."

Bull announced his arrival with a gloved hand on Boss Man's shoulder. Jim pointed at the lettering. "Looks like our smoking gun," he said.

"Can only think of one reason they'd have hydrazine onboard," Bull answered. "Photos?"

"Already done. We have what we came for."

"Roger that."

Jim addressed his team. "That's a wrap. Ghost, Homer. Secure the bridge. Bull and I will meet you there."

"We're on it."

"Iceberg, Magnum. You take the helipad."

"Roger, Boss Man."

Jim nodded to Bull and together they dashed for the ladder and ascended. Iceberg and Magnum were twenty meters behind them. The bridge was on the deck just below the helipad.

From the landing outside the watertight entry to the bridge, Ghost eased open the door just enough for Homer to lob in a flash-bang. Two seconds later, it exploded and the two operators stormed the opening, their primary weapons sweeping the bridge, ready to neutralize any threat.

Even through the bridge lights were out to help the officers maintain a degree of night vision, the diffuse illumination from the instruments was more than sufficient to render the space in bright detail through the NVGs worn by Ghost and Homer. The crew, on the other hand, had been momentarily blinded by the bright flash of the pyrotechnic, and they had yet to see the intruders who were now occupying the ship's command center.

"Hands up! Get your hands up!" Ghost yelled. The four men manning the bridge faced in the general direction of the voice. "Hands up!" Ghost repeated.

One man lunged for a drawer. He pulled it open and grasped a pistol. Homer fired a single round from his MP5 submachine gun. At the close range afforded within the confined space of the bridge, he couldn't miss. The man took the bullet in the chest, dropped the handgun, and fell back against the console.

"Hands up!" Ghost yelled again. This time, the other three slowly raised their hands. By now, they were able to see enough to recognize two figures holding weapons.

"On the landing just outside," Jim alerted his two men inside the bridge.

"Roger. Clear to enter. We have three tangos, plus one that Homer dropped."

Boss Man kept his MP5 leveled at the three prisoners as Bull, with his weapon slung over a shoulder, moved forward. One by one, he pulled the hands of each prisoner down and cinched nylon zip ties around their wrists. Hands firmly bound behind their backs, the SGIT operators felt comfortable enough to lower their weapons.

Bull proceeded to examine the unconscious victim. He was sitting, his back against the instrument console, head slumped forward. Bull check for a pulse. None. "This one's dead." He picked up the pistol. On the black rubber grip was the image of a circle surrounding a star. Bull recognized it as a QSZ-92 semiautomatic pistol, standard issue of the Chinese army. He dropped the magazine and cleared the chamber, then stuffed the gun in his belt. More evidence to share with the analysts at SGIT.

Bullets raked across the outer bulkhead, many penetrating into the bridge. Windows shattered and everyone dropped to the deck at the same time. Then the SGIT operators all heard the warning over the squad radio network. It was Magnum speaking. "Heavy machine gun! Must've been hidden in a crate or something beneath the towers!"

"Can you get a good angle and take 'em out?" Jim replied.

"Negative! Armor plate in front of the gun. Can't get rounds on the shooters. Maybe if we had a Barrett. I doubt that armor is thick enough to stop a .50 caliber round." Magnum and Iceberg were both firing their submachine guns at the threat, but the 9mm pistol rounds, even fired from the longer barrel of the MP5, simply pinged as they bounced off the shield.

Jim crawled to the door joining the bridge to the ladder

landing. As he edged his head forward enough to see down to the deck amidships, his courage was rewarded with a burst of gunfire. The bullets all penetrated the bulkhead above him, but it was sufficient to convince him they would never survive a sprint up the steep ladder to the landing pad.

"Bull, get on the radio. Find out the ETA for that Osprey. Let them know the landing zone is hot!"

Bull grasped the handset connected by a coiled line to the radio in his pack. After a short conversation, punctuated with acronyms and jargon, he concluded with "Roger. Swordfish out." Then he addressed Jim. "The Osprey is five minutes out. They'll continue inbound and then hold at 3,000 meters until we tell them the landing zone is secure. They have twelve Marines onboard, ready to hold the *Panda Star* while we exit."

"Do they have a tail gun on that Osprey?" Jim asked.

"Affirmative. A Dillon minigun. But with limited range of fire, they're an easy target."

More bullets gouged through the wall into the bridge, continuing their path of destruction into many of the instrument consoles. The ship shuddered briefly and then all vibrations ceased. The *Panda Star* was dead in the water. It would continue to coast, maybe for several miles, before it came to a dead stop.

"What's the plan, Boss Man?" The question came from Homer.

Jim racked his brain, running through options, discarding those that were foolish. And then it came to him.

"Magnum, you guys have any flares?"

Iceberg pinched his eyebrows at the unexpected question, and then nodded to Magnum. "Affirmative. But there's not much on the deck here that's flammable."

"Yes there is," Jim replied. "Here's the plan…"

After going over the major elements, Jim turned his

attention to his team pinned down on the bridge. "I want all of you to take up firing positions along the row of windows facing down toward the deck. The machine gun is at the base of the towers."

"We're not going to have much luck getting our rounds through the steel structure of the towers," Bull said.

"Doesn't matter. You're going to draw the enemy's attention. Wait until you see Iceberg's flare, then let loose with all you've got."

Staying low, Bull, Homer, and Ghost edged to the bulkhead with the shot-out windows. Jim checked his watch: ninety seconds until the Marine Corps Osprey would arrive. *This had better work.*

Iceberg struck the igniter on the road flare and lobbed it toward the machine gunner's position. It actually landed behind the gun crew, rolling to a stop at the base of a group of fifty-five-gallon drums.

"Fire!"

Four submachine guns opened up simultaneously from the bridge. The effect was predictable. The large volume of automatic fire with bullets impacting the armor shield and all around the gun crew served to force them down. In the brief lull, Iceberg and Magnum rose above their cover. Their angle allowed them to look down the side of the stored drums and, picking out the farthest drum, they opened fire.

At first, their bullets only penetrated the closest drums, those filled with oil and hydraulic fluid. But eventually at least one round penetrated the far drum. With a hiss, compressed vapor escaped the drum—unsymmetrical dimethyl hydrazine, or UDMH, otherwise known as rocket fuel. The vapor was heavier than air, and it formed an invisible cloud that spread along the deck. Extremely toxic, the vapor also formed an explosive mixture with air.

Magazines emptied, Iceberg and Magnum ducked again behind their cover. And not a moment too soon. The hydrazine vapor spread quickly and reached the flare.

A massive explosion and fireball rocked the deck. Steel barrels filled with more than 350 pounds of fluids were thrown overboard. The gun crew was incinerated, their ashes blasted forward in a sooty cloud, while the heavy machine gun was stripped from its mount and tossed forward in a tangled heap.

"Bull, radio the Osprey. Tell them the landing zone is secure. *Panda Star* is adrift, engine controls believed to have been disabled from gunfire on the bridge."

Seconds later they heard the deep reverberations from the huge Osprey propellers beating the air. The Marine Corps transport circled around the bow of the *Panda Star*, keeping distance from the stern, as well as the obstruction of the towers, just in case there were more gunmen waiting to ambush the aircraft. The raging fire cast an eerie yellow-orange glow that illuminated the Osprey. Tongues of flame and sooty smoke reached skyward, reminding Jim of a dragon.

The SGIT operators watched the Osprey approach, even though it had extinguished its running lights. The huge twin engine nacelles were already tilted partially upward, slowing the plane as it approached the helipad. The whirlwind whipped the fire into a raging conflagration that spread to the many barrels of oil.

With the nacelles pointed vertically, the craft hovered, its landing gear inches above the landing surface. The rear door was open, and twelve combat-ready Marines poured out the opening.

Jim exchanged words briefly with the platoon leader. He wore the rank of lieutenant and exuded confidence born from violent battle under difficult conditions. The men were all heavily armed with M4 automatic rifles, grenade launchers, and two squad automatic weapons. The lieutenant issued orders to his men and they quickly dispersed. Exactly what those orders were, Jim didn't know. He didn't have to. His priority was to get their evidence back to command and file his report.

The SGIT team scrambled onto the rear ramp, Jim being the last to board. He stood on the ramp momentarily, surveying the deck of the *Panda Star*. The hydrazine was still burning, although the flames were less intense. The oil drums might burn for hours. He suspected the Marines would order the crew to attack the inferno with firehoses, but since the conflagration was confined to the deck, he doubted the ship was in peril.

What secrets are in the holds below deck? He'd probably never know, although he felt satisfaction that his team had eliminated the ballistic missile launch vehicle. The Seventh Fleet was out of danger.

In only a few hours, he'd learn how wrong that conclusion was.

CHAPTER 31

THE PILOT WAS FLYING A DIRECT COURSE for the Raja Isteri Pengiran Anak Saleha Hospital in the capital of Brunei. It was the best-equipped facility with the most experienced surgeons.

Robert tapped the pilot on the shoulder. When he glanced up, Robert was shaking his head. The pilot's face registered sorrow upon realizing that Eu-meh was dead. He had not known her well by any measure, but she had always treated the members of her security detail with fairness and respect. On a few occasions, Eu-meh had spoken to him directly, asking about his family and complimenting his loyalty and dedication.

"We're going to the palace. That was her home, where her family is."

"But shouldn't we deliver the body to the hospital? Isn't that the procedure we should follow?"

"There's nothing the medical staff can do for her now. At least we can offer the dignity of placing her in the mosque where her family can pay their respects and offer their prayers."

Retreating from the cockpit, Robert removed some shortbread cookies and a couple bottles of water from a locker, offering the snack to Peter. "I'm going to find her," Peter said.

"Come on, have something to eat," he said, ignoring the comment. Peter stared back vacantly. "Well, if you're not hungry, how about Diesel?"

The red pit bull was looking longingly at the offered snack, a long viscous drop of drool hanging from the side of his closed mouth. He extended a paw placing it gently on Peter's thigh.

Peter tore open the plastic wrapping and offered the cookies to Diesel, who eagerly devoured the food. Then, cupping one hand, he slowly poured water into the make-shift bowl and Diesel drank his fill—nearly the entire bottle of water. Peter finished the remainder.

"What are you going to do?" Robert asked.

"The way I see it, Captain Rei is our hall pass, our ticket. He will gain us an audience with the Director of Security."

"They might just kill us."

Peter shrugged. "Not likely. Whoever is in charge will want answers. They will want to know what we know, so they can cover up their actions."

"You sound pretty confident."

"It's not my first rodeo."

"Okay. What do you want me to do?"

Peter motioned with his chin toward the cockpit. "See if the co-pilot can put you on the radio. You want to speak to any reporter you can reach, preferably not in Brunei. Maybe Singapore or Manilla."

"Time to go public?"

"Yeah. Whoever you reach, tell them the complete story. But mostly that Eu-meh was murdered. With this information out there, the Director of Security will have to learn what we know."

"Got it." Robert left Peter to his thoughts while he had a brief conversation with the co-pilot. Soon he had a radio connection to someone at the *Straits Times*, a prominent English-language newspaper in Singapore. After two transfers, he was finally speaking with a journalist. After another ten minutes, he'd retold the events that transpired onboard the *Royal Seeker*, the missile launch and destruction of the control room, and finally, the murder of the Sultan's sister. He finished by telling the reporter they were en route to the Sultan's palace, Istana Nurul Iman, to lay the body at rest in the mosque.

Ever grateful for the scoop, the reporter assured Robert she would be on the first flight to Bandar Seri Begawan to cover the event first hand and then ended the call.

While Robert was on the radio, Peter typed a text message to Commander Jim Nicolaou using the commercial encryption app on his phone. Short and to the point, he reported they'd destroyed the missile launch control room on the *Royal Seeker*, rendering the platform useless. He pressed the send button, knowing they were over the ocean and not within cellular range. But the text message would be queued to send automatically once he did have a signal. *With that problem solved, I can focus on finding Jade.*

Having prepped the reporter, Robert returned to his seat to update Peter. "The story should break in a few hours."

"Good. Now that the *Royal Seeker* is no longer in business, whoever has Jade should let her go."

"You're assuming she's still alive."

Peter nodded.

"And if she's dead?"

"Then we force them to turn over her body so she can be joined in burial with Eu-meh."

Peter's hand once again found the grip of the Glock pistol tucked in his belt. The movement did not escape Robert's notice.

The equatorial sun shone brilliantly off both golden domes as the Airbus H160 helicopter, now low on fuel, settled down on the lawn before the mosque entrance. From the air, Peter was able to appreciate the enormity of the Sultan's palace—over two million square feet, nearly 1800 rooms, five swimming pools, and a banquet hall that could seat 5,000 guests. Closed to the public except for a few days each year when visitors were allowed to enter the banquet hall and the mosque, Istana Nurul Iman palace was the perfect location for a clandestine operation.

A group of palace guards, all wearing their distinctive black berets, was approaching the helicopter in two electric open-air vehicles that looked like side-by-side ATVs. Peter had no doubt their approach was monitored and the palace guard alerted just before the aircraft landed.

Robert exited first, Eu-meh's covered body supported by his strong arms. He didn't wait, instead moving directly for the entrance, two oversized doors constructed of tropical wood with heavy, polished gold hardware.

Peter directed Captain Rei out of the helicopter, one hand on his shirt collar and the other hand pressing the pistol into his spine. Diesel was hugging his master's side. They only made it halfway to the mosque when the approaching guards opened fire. Bullets sizzled through the air, and Peter encouraged Rei to move faster. But with his injured foot, a rapid skip-step was the best he could do.

The pilot and co-pilot took defensive positions on either side of the aircraft, using their submachine guns to hold the palace guards at bay. With their lives at risk, the guards adjusted their aim to the two aviators, and Peter with his hostage pushed through the doors, gaining distance from the gunfire.

He expected to enter a large, open room but instead found

they were in a tiled courtyard, the ablutions area. A fountain was in the center of the courtyard. Just ahead, he saw Robert pass through another doorway, and Peter urged Rei forward.

"Please," Rei protested. "My foot; I need to sit and rest."

Peter pushed harder with the barrel at Rei's back. "Keep moving."

Once through the second door, they entered the open prayer hall. It was an enormous space without a single supporting pillar, the gold dome serving as the roof. Tiles in all colors, but mostly shades of blue, from turquoise to cobalt, covered the walls and ceiling. Gold tiles set in framed sections along the walls repeated what Peter assumed were passages from the Quran. The floor was covered with small, intricately-woven rugs, all arranged in rigorous geometric order. Two sneakers had been kicked randomly at the side. Peter watched as Robert, now shoeless, crossed the floor aiming directly for a semicircular niche at the far wall, just to the side of a stairway that extended upwards.

Robert kneeled before the niche and gently laid the body down. He positioned Eu-meh so her head was just within the opening. Still kneeling, Robert bowed his head and folded his hands on his lap.

Peter approached silently, his grip on Captain Rei still firm. After a long pause, Robert stood. He turned to discover Peter standing nearby with Diesel sitting at his side.

"That's called a mihrab," Robert said, indicating the domed opening in the wall. "It points toward Mecca."

Peter understood the symbolism of the position in which Robert had laid Eu-meh at rest.

"You shouldn't wear shoes in here," he explained. "And I don't think the Imam would approve of a dog sitting on one of the prayer rugs."

The sound of sporadic gunfire was heard even through the

thick doors. Peter glanced at his feet, and then said, "I don't think we should wait around to speak with the Imam. Time to go."

Robert slipped on his sneakers and they left the prayer hall the way they'd entered. They were met in the courtyard by the co-pilot. "This way!" he shouted and waved his arm as further encouragement.

Passing through the outer door, Peter asked about the pilot. "He's dead, next to the helicopter," the co-pilot answered. Scattered across the lawn between the helicopter and the mosque, and then farther out from the helicopter to the two electric open-top vehicles, were a half dozen dead guards. Peter dashed to the nearest and grabbed the radio.

"Follow me," Robert ordered, and the group moved along a covered walkway. "There's a door up here. We can enter the palace. It's too dangerous out here in the open."

By now Rei had gotten pretty good at his skip-shuffle, and the bleeding had mostly stopped. Robert reached for the doorknob and was surprised to find it locked. He placed the barrel of his Glock where the latch entered the doorframe and pulled the trigger twice. The wood splintered around the strike plate, and the door opened without any resistance.

They entered a service corridor. It was lit by an overhead track of recessed lights. Doors lined both sides, and another door lay ahead at the end.

"Kitchen on the left, storage and utilities on the right," Robert explained. They pressed forward, and exited into an ornately-decorated room. A wide stairway, covered in red carpet and with gilded bannisters and railing, was to the right. Overhead hung a crystal chandelier that Peter estimated was at least fifteen feet in diameter. Suspended thirty feet overhead was the gilded ceiling.

Around the perimeter of the room were gold-framed

mirrors alternating with portraits of past sultans. Narrow tables along the walls held vases filled with a rich variety of brightly colored tropical blooms.

"The banquet hall is through those doors," Robert indicated the pair of double doors to the left. As if on cue, the doors burst open and ten soldiers wearing black berets pushed through, rifles pointed at the American intruders and their hostage. Robert instantly raised his Glock.

The co-pilot fired first. A short burst from the hip. His shots struck four guards, killing three and wounding one. But the return fire was equally deadly, and the aviator was cut down under a hail of lead.

Silence ensued. It was a standoff.

The guards parted, allowing an officer to pass through the group—Pehin Anak Shah, the Director of Security. He removed his sidearm from the black leather holster on his hip. "Robert. I am disappointed." He turned to face Peter. "And you, Mr. Savage. You seem to be a troublemaker."

"I've been called worse," Peter said over Rei's shoulder. Diesel rumbled with a guttural growl. "On me. Stay." He issued the command softly so as not to draw unwanted attention to the canine. Diesel silenced, but licked his lips—a display of anxiety and distress.

The Security Director glanced at the wounded soldier, and with a nod of his head, instructed a guard to assist the injured man and the two of them left. He then locked eyes with Captain Rei. "I did not expect to see you here, Captain." Rei's eyes were wide in fright. "And what conclusion should I draw from your presence?"

"Please," Rei pleaded. "I had no choice. They forced me—"

"Silence!" For a few moments, the room was deadly still. And then Pehin spoke again. "I know you have failed. We tracked your missile, of course, and saw the instant it failed to respond to the homing signal. Our satellite imagery shows the American aircraft carrier is still afloat. In fact, it is still quite functional."

"But," Rei stammered, "They had explosives. They destroyed the instruments."

Pehin raised his pistol and fired. The bullet struck Rei in the leg and passed through, just missing Peter. The captain suddenly slumped and slipped from Peter's grasp. The Security Director fired twice more, both bullets hitting Rei in the center of his chest.

"He became an unacceptable liability the moment he failed his mission," Pehin said. His pistol was leveled at Peter. "Now, lower your gun, or you will be the next to die."

CHAPTER 32

"THE SULTAN'S SISTER IS DEAD," Peter said. "She was murdered on the *Royal Seeker* by crewmembers you hired. You might want to think about how to explain *that* to your father."

"My father will find it much easier to believe that you killed his beloved sister." His mouth twisted in a wicked grin as he continued, "Fortunately, when I caught up with you and your accomplices, you were all shot by my loyal guards."

"Your story won't work," Peter said defiantly.

Pehin turned his lips down, mocking Peter. "I don't see why not."

"Because I already talked to a reporter," Robert said. "Someone outside of your reach. Someone who is very eager to share the story of the *Royal Seeker* and the murder of Eu-meh."

"Come now, you don't really expect me to believe that you found time to call a reporter after your helicopter landed on the palace grounds. My men engaged you immediately; you had no time."

"But I did. On the flight here. Used the radio. My entire conversation with the reporter was recorded, and I've no doubt she has already sent out her story over the wire services. Right now, she's following through on the leads I gave her, checking the facts and getting corroboration. I suspect she'll write a follow-up tonight. Of course, a half dozen news agencies will be all over this—not every day that a member of a royal family is murdered."

"Plus the tie-in to the unprovoked attacks on the two Navy ships," Peter added.

"Three, by my count. At the very least two-and-a-half since the *USS Ford* didn't sink. Not yet, anyway," Pehin said.

Robert was outraged. "You think this is a joke? Hundreds of men and women were killed! And for what?"

Pehin pinched his eyebrows. "The American military is responsible for hundreds of thousands of murdered civilians in Syria and Libya. Millions more displaced in what is, without doubt, the worst civilian crisis of the new millennium. In the decades following the end of World War II, American presidents have trampled the rights of sovereign nations, using covert operations to overthrow governments not to their liking. Your past presidents ignored international law when it suited their narrative and then denounced other governments for lesser infractions. President Taylor and your current Congress are no better."

He took a deep breath, and Peter saw the simmering anger calm as the Security Director reigned in his emotions.

"If you do not lower your guns, my men will shoot you here."

"People will have heard those gunshots," Peter said.

"Don't delude yourself. These walls are very well insulated against sound, and the palace is very large. No one is close by."

Although Peter was confident he could take down Pehin,

with five assault rifles pointed in his direction, their death was certain. Peter relaxed his shoulders and slowly lowered his pistol. Robert followed suit.

"Excellent!" Pehin said. "Now we may have a civilized conversation."

"I want Jade," Peter demanded. "Holding her no longer serves any purpose. Let her go."

He considered the appeal for a long moment. "Very well. You may follow me." He turned to the closest guard. "First, search them."

Two guards patted down Peter and Robert, taking the portable radio from Peter and Robert's cell phone. They also picked up the two pistols laying on the floor along with the rifles from the dead guards.

"You don't have a cell phone?" Pehin addressed the question to Peter.

"No," he said. "Left it on the *Royal Seeker*. Was kinda rushed to get off the ship and back to land."

"Hmmm." The Director of Security turned and exited the way he'd come. In the lead, with his prisoners surrounded by the five guards, he crossed through the banquet hall and entered another corridor on the far side. They continued some distance along the hallway, passing more paintings and sculptures, more floral arrangements, all illuminated by huge crystal chandeliers. Their destination seemed to be a room at the end of the lavish hallway where they stopped before a pair of ornate gilded doors.

Pehin pressed the buzzer and then opened the doors. They entered an outer reception room furnished with ruby-red upholstered chairs and matching sofas. "Sit," he ordered Peter and Robert. They sat on one of the sofas, Diesel parking by his master's feet. The amber eyes tracked every movement of the Security Director as he left through a door on the opposite wall. The door was decorated to blend in with the wall décor.

Several minutes passed in silence. Peter and Robert stared back at the guards who never lowered their M4 assault rifles. Finally, Pehin returned. He was accompanied by another person: a woman. He stood to the side as she entered, his head bowed. All of the guards bowed as well, her mere presence demanding the highest level of respect.

She was dressed in a traditional Chinese gown. A jade necklace rested across her collarbones. To Peter's eye, she appeared to be in her seventies, maybe early eighties.

"Stand, and bow your heads in respect," Pehin ordered. Robert and Peter rose to their feet and dipped their chins.

When Peter raised his eyes, he was looking directly at the woman. Her features were Asian, but hardly a wrinkle showed on her face. Her hair was black and thinning. Her eyes conveyed fierce determination.

"This is Lim Guan-Yin," Pehin announced. "The mother of the Sultan himself."

Peter's mouth fell agape. Jade had only spoken breifly of her grandmother. *How was she involved?*

"You may call me by my given name, Guan-Yin," she said. Her voice was neither frail nor weak.

Peter bowed again. "My name is—"

She cut him off. "I *know* your name, Peter Savage. My grandson keeps me well informed." She turned somewhat. "And you are Robert. Although we have not been formally introduced, I have observed you before, from a distance, protecting my granddaughter."

"I am sorry, ma'am," Peter said. "Your daughter was killed by men working for your grandson. Out of respect for your religion, you should know that Eu-meh was wrapped in a shroud and laid in the prayer room of the mosque. We didn't think it would be right to take her body to a public location like the hospital."

Upon hearing the news, her eyes softened and glistened

with moisture. "I suppose I should thank you." She blinked twice, the tears never fully materializing as she seemingly banished whatever grief she had been feeling only moments before.

"Islam is not my religion. Still, I'm sure the Imam will be suitably dismayed at having her unwashed body left in his prayer hall—but not so much so that he'll refuse the Sultan's money." She faced her grandson. "Make certain my daughter's body is properly washed three times and wrapped in appropriate burial shrouds in accordance with the teachings of the Prophet."

"Yes, Grandmother."

"Didn't you hear what Peter said?" Robert asked. "Your grandson is responsible for murdering your only daughter!"

"What would you have me say? She was a casualty. Unfortunate—but also unavoidable, I'm sure. My daughter did not share my vision—our vision," she glanced at her grandson. "So it became necessary to isolate her from the planning and daily operations. It should have been sufficient for her to manage Hua Ho Holdings. But when she began to ask questions and start investigations into things she had no involvement with…"

"I don't believe it," Peter said. "You orchestrated the kidnapping of your own granddaughter?"

"It was necessary," she answered coldly.

"I've met some ruthless people, but lady, you take the prize."

"You stand before me in self-righteous judgment, and yet you are as ignorant as you are arrogant."

"Well, I'd be perfectly happy to leave, but…" Peter motioned to the surrounding guards with guns aimed in his direction.

Guan-Yin squinted her eyes and tilted her head back, appraising the taller American standing before her. Finally, she asked a single question. "Do you know who discovered America?"

"You mean after the North American continent was

populated by the indigenous peoples who crossed from northern Asia?"

"You are reluctant to answer, even though my question was simple and direct. Very well, you are not one to be easily baited, I see."

She took one small step closer to Peter, and looked him squarely in the eye. "America was discovered by Chinese explorers who set sail with a great treasure fleet on March 8, 1421. The fleet was under the command of Admiral Zheng He. We know this with certainty. Zheng's fleet circumnavigated the globe 100 years before Magellan and set foot on North America seventy years before Columbus."

"All very interesting, and under less…contrived… circumstances, I would enjoy discussing this with you. I'm a history buff, too." Peter forced a smile.

Guan-Yin maintained a stony countenance. "Perhaps I should show you my collection of ancient maps."

"Sure. I really enjoy very old classic books, too. How's your collection?"

Pehin made a nearly imperceptible nod of his head and the guard closest to Peter rammed the butt of his rifle into Peter's stomach. He doubled over, hands over his gut, coughing and trying to catch his breath.

"From your juvenile response, I can see you don't understand the import of my statements."

Peter gulped and took three deep breaths before straightening his torso. His side burned again, and he suspected his sudden movement had torn open the gash.

When he cast his gaze upon Guan-Yin, there was no longer any trace of humor in his expression. "Oh, I get it. You believe some ancient Chinese admiral sailed a fleet around the world claiming all lands for the Emperor. So what? The Vikings sailed to Iceland, Greenland, and along the eastern coast of Canada and New England. And everyone knows about the visit from Columbus who sailed for the king and queen of Spain. It doesn't matter who was there first."

Guan-Yin's lips curled in a tight expression of amusement. "On that point, we do agree. But where it does matter is on the question of sovereignty over the islands to the east of China. In the South China Sea and the East China Sea."

"Many countries lay claim to those islands."

"Yes. They find it convenient to ignore the historical record, supported by written historical accounts and detailed maps first drafted by cartographers under the direction of Admiral Zheng. Being quite large, the main fleet split into smaller groups of ships under the leadership of prominent Chinese explorers—Hong Bao, Zhou Man, Yang Qing, Zhou Wen. These brave men were the first to lay rightful claim to these islands in the name of Emperor Zhu Di."

"So why doesn't the Chinese government simply work their claim through the international courts? Why take military action and risk starting a war?"

"The courts are merely political instruments that work at the pleasure of the West—the European Union and the United States."

"And you think war is a better option?" Peter didn't wait for an answer. "You know, I really don't get it. I mean, you are the mother of the Sultan of Brunei. You live in grand luxury, guaranteed that whatever happens anywhere in the world, your comfort will be assured. So why you? What is your stake in this dispute?"

Her eyes flared in anger, showing an extreme of emotion that had previously been missing. "You have no idea of the suffering I have endured at the hands of invaders!" She paused in thought. No one outside of her closest family members knew her complete history, when she was a young girl in Nanking.

She closed her eyes and was transported back in time and space. When she spoke, her words were measured, and barely audible. "I was a little girl when the Japanese army invaded my hometown. They took what they wanted. They gorged on our rice and livestock—chickens, ducks, pigs. And when they had their fill they slaughtered the rest so there would be nothing for the people. The officers thought it good sport to see who could cut off the most Chinese heads using their katanas. They raped my mother, and in doing so they crushed her spirit." A single tear ran down Guan-Yin's cheek. "And when they came back and threatened to rape her again, my father tried to protect her. The soldiers murdered him, and then they murdered my mother. They beat me, and left me for dead."

She opened her eyes and looked up at Peter. "I am Chinese. I will always be Chinese. And I will never forgive the invaders who butchered, enslaved, and demeaned my family, my people, treating them worse than wild dogs. Justice must be served."

Stunned by her story, Peter empathized with the old woman, imagining the horrors she had witnessed and the suffering she had endured. "I am truly sorry for what happened. Humankind has exhibited barbaric cruelty throughout the ages. But what you have done… these missile attacks… that is not the answer. There are better solutions."

"No. I am an old woman. I've lived almost my entire life waiting for justice. To this day, the Japanese government does not accept responsibility for the crimes committed by its military. And the United States has been unwilling to demand repentance from their ally. Your country took swift action against Nazi war criminals—why did it fail to seek justice against the Japanese scientists and officers who committed abhorrent crimes against humanity?"

Peter shook his head. "I… I don't have an answer. I wish I did."

Guan-Yin's eyes blazed again. "I do know why! The

experiments, the data—the West wanted that information, the results of gruesome biological experiments that Japanese doctors and scientists conducted on helpless prisoners. The United States, Australia, England—they were all too willing to simply let the guilty go in exchange for the hideous knowledge accrued from the torture and deaths of thousands of men, women, and children. It is a shared guilt, and a wrong that the West will never admit to."

With nothing to say, Peter and Robert stood in silence.

She continued, "These are crimes for which there is no statute of limitations. Justice will be served, and China will take control of lands it discovered centuries ago. As it was before, in 1421 when the grand treasure fleet sailed a magnificent voyage of discovery to the far corners of the world, China will again be the dominant cultural, economic, and military power in the East. Without the protection of the United States, Japan will bow in humiliation to a greater China."

Breaking his silence, Robert said, "You don't really think the U.S. will withdraw its military from the Western Pacific, do you? As a former Navy man, I can assure you China is in for a fight it can't possibly win."

"Your bravado is misplaced," Guan-Yin answered with certainty. "The Seventh Fleet will withdraw or it will be destroyed."

"Maybe you haven't been keeping score," Robert said. "Your missile-launching ship is out of commission."

Realization suddenly dawned on Peter. "Unless…"

Guan-Yin smiled. "Correct, Mr. Savage. So, now you know. There are powers at play here that you can only imagine."

"I have a good imagination. But that's not why I'm here, and this is much bigger than me or Robert. I came for Jade. Why don't you just let all three of us go?"

"Where is Jade now?" Robert demanded.

"Where she's always been since she was captured in London. She's here, in my apartment."

Guan-Yin motioned with her head and Pehin issued an order to one of the palace guards. The man obediently left the reception room.

"Now that the *Royal Seeker* has served its purpose," she continued, "and my daughter is no longer a threat to our operations, I see no further reason to hold Jade against her will."

"Journalists will be all over this story," Robert said.

Pehin elaborated. "He claims he spoke to a reporter before their helicopter landed on the palace grounds."

Guan-Yin waved the fingers of one hand dismissively. "Merely an inconvenience. We are in the final phase of execution, and nothing can stop me. Success is within my grasp!"

"You're crazy," Robert said. "A certifiable nut job."

Pehin closed the distance to Robert. "You will show respect!" To emphasize the point, a guard rammed his rifle stock into Robert's lower back. He leaned to the side, grimacing.

Robert was still recovering from the blow when Jade was led into the room, her arm held securely by the guard. Her head swiveled from face to face, and when her eyes focused, she recognized Peter and Robert. She broke the man's grip and rushed forward, throwing her arms around Peter. She sobbed.

"It's okay," he said softly. Diesel, remembering Jade, rubbed his big head against her leg.

"Take them to the control room," she said. "It may yet be prudent to have a few hostages, depending on what the American government does."

CHAPTER 33

FLYING NORTHEAST, THE V-22 OSPREY would refuel once before landing at its base in Okinawa. Boss Man and the other operators were feeling good—they'd accomplished the mission, eliminated the threat, and turned control of the *Panda Star* over to the Marines. Less disciplined operators may have relaxed or even celebrated. But not this team.

"Affirmative, Colonel. The *Panda Star* is not operational as a launch platform. The Seventh Fleet is no longer under threat of missile attack."

Colonel Pierson took notes even though the conversation was also recorded. "Good work, Commander. Pass along my congratulations to your team as well. Looks like we dodged the bullet and avoided war with China, at least until the next Asian crisis. Still have to figure out why the Chinese would take such aggressive actions." Pierson paused in thought before continuing, "Have Lieutenant Lacey and her team stay on this. I'm not convinced everything is as it appears. Any questions?"

246

"No, sir. Thank you, sir," but the colonel had already disconnected.

Jim contemplated those last words—*have Lacey stay on it.* It was unusual for Colonel Pierson to express doubt concerning the outcome of a mission. True, Jim also felt uncomfortable over the apparent ease of the mission, not that parachuting onto a moving ship and engaging in a gunfight was easy. *Why weren't they better prepared to repel boarders? It's like the crew was asleep.*

"Bull, what's your take on the defensive readiness of the crew?"

"You mean down there, the *Panda Star*?"

Jim nodded.

"Well, I'd say we kicked their butts. And the Marines we left in charge aren't going to take any crap, either."

"True," Jim replied.

"What's bothering you, Boss Man?"

"I don't know. Just a feeling. There should have been armed men guarding the helipad. And why did it take so long for the crew to get that heavy machine gun firing?"

"Speaking for myself, I'm glad they screwed up."

Before Jim could say anything more, his phone chimed. It was set up so that calls were relayed through the communication system of the Osprey. The caller ID indicated it was Lieutenant Lacey.

"Go ahead, Lieutenant," he answered.

"Sir, I've received an encrypted text message from Peter Savage. It came in on your personal cell number only thirty minutes ago. It's important."

"I'm listening."

"He says they destroyed the control room on the *Royal Seeker*. The ship is no longer operable as a launch platform. However—"

"What? Brunei Special Forces were supposed to board that ship. What the hell was Peter doing there? And what does the Brunei commander have to report?"

Lacey sighed. "Sir, I have no idea how or why Peter got involved in this. Just seems to be his nature. And regarding the Brunei Special Forces, I can't get a clear answer. I suspect they never departed on the mission."

"We had assurances!"

"Affirmative. We're trying to get better information. It's very sketchy right now."

"Let me know the minute you have answers. What else?"

"You're not going to believe this, but Mr. Savage says a missile was fired just before they blew the control instruments. According to him, the missile struck the *USS Gerald Ford*, although it only caused slight damage."

"Peter says a missile was fired? That's impossible. The *Panda Star* was the launch ship."

"Unless—"

Jim finished her sentence. "There were two ships."

"And if there were two, there could be more. Sir, the Seventh Fleet may not be out of danger."

"Have you briefed Colonel Pierson yet?"

"No, sir. I wanted to speak with you first."

"Well get on it! Where is Peter now?"

"His text message said he was en route to the Sultan's Palace. However, the message could have been queued for transmission before he got within cell coverage."

"In other words, he could already be at the palace."

"That's correct."

"Understood. Get ahold of Peter ASAP. Put him through to my phone. I need to talk to him directly."

"Yes, sir!"

Jim gathered his team. "Alright everyone, listen up. As you

know, our mission was to investigate one of two suspected ships that could be the missile launch facility. We did our job, and we know we have removed from service said ship."

A chorus of cheers erupted accompanied by handshakes and fist bumps.

"Hold it down." The roar subsided, all five team members focused on their leader.

"I have just received a report that the second team, which gained entry onboard the *Royal Seeker*, also disabled a launch facility."

"How can that be?" Bull asked. "I thought there was only one."

"That's what we all thought, Sergeant. But we were wrong. And if there were two launch ships, there could be more."

Concerned looks were shared among the gathered operators. "What's the plan, sir?" The question was voiced by Iceberg, but Jim knew it was the question on every man's mind.

"Sit tight, for now. Lacey is briefing the colonel. I expect we will have new orders before we land."

CHAPTER 34

AFTER GUAN-YIN DEPARTED the reception room, Pehin strode to the opposite wall and depressed a section of the chair-rail molding. A hidden door swung open. It had been so well disguised that neither Peter nor Robert had noticed the passage when they entered.

"This way," he said, and he moved farther into the room. Through the open door, Peter heard the hum of electronic machines. Artificial light spilled through the opening. Peter craned his head left and right, enough to see many computer stations with technicians sharply focused on their work.

Two guards followed the Security Director, and the remaining three guards each nudged one of the prisoners forward. They had relaxed considerably since the shootout earlier, when the co-pilot and three guards were killed. Now, they held their rifles loosely, barrels pointed to the side. Clearly, no gun play was anticipated. Perhaps the thought of a stray bullet or two going through a wall and striking Guan-Yin was on their minds? Or maybe, they were reluctant to fire in or near the control room? What equipment was in there, and what purpose did it serve?

All unanswerable questions. But regardless of the reason, the lax security was an opening, and Peter intended to take advantage of it.

Robert was closest to the hidden door, so he was the first to be escorted through, followed by Jade and her guard. That left Peter and one guard still in the reception room.

Peter hesitated, trying to catch Robert's eyes. His guard shoved him with his rifle, and the minor commotion was enough to draw Robert's attention. He and Peter exchanged a brief glance, but it was enough.

"Diesel," Peter said, his tone sharp and commanding. The red pit bull looked up, and he completed the command. "Bad guys!"

The seventy-pound canine with the torn ear immediately ceased his docile behavior and leapt at Peter's guard. Diesel struck the man waist high and lunged for his face and throat. The guard screamed in terror as the mouthful of teeth gnashed in front of his eyes. He dropped his rifle, trying to use both hands to fend off the attack.

Stumbling backwards, mostly from the momentum of the beast flying into him, he fell on his back. Diesel clamped down on a hand, and shook his head violently. Never slackening his powerful jaws, the teeth soon turned the hand into a bloody mess. The guard continued his efforts to push the dog away, but it was no use.

At the instant Diesel attacked, Peter threw his shoulder into the door, slamming it shut. Quickly, he pushed a table against the door and then bolstered his make-shift barricade with the sofa he had sat on earlier.

Satisfied that it would be a couple minutes before the men

in the control room forced open the door, Peter grabbed the M4 rifle, making sure the safety was off and the fire selector was set to semiauto.

"Diesel, enough. On me." The pit bull released the ravaged hand and trotted beside Peter as they hurriedly left the reception room. They jogged down the ornate corridor, passing the banquet hall, and continued another seventy meters until the corridor joined a cross hallway. Peter had to choose—left or right. He went right, thinking he was skirting the banquet hall. So far, the path had been void of other people. *Maybe all the guards were called to the control room?*

Soon they came to another corner and turned right again—and ran straight into a palace guard who was running in the opposite direction. The collision was jarring, but Peter had the weight advantage over the smaller guard who crashed backwards to the floor. Dazed, he still recovered quickly and started to move the muzzle of his rifle toward Peter. Diesel lunged and clamped down on the rifle, impeding its motion. At the same instant, Peter swung the butt of his weapon downward, connecting with the guard's chin. Teeth slammed together with a sickening crunch as the man's head snapped backwards. The guard was out cold.

Continuing to move forward, they eventually found the same room with the staircase and huge crystal chandelier that Peter recognized from earlier. Breathing heavily, he ducked through the doorway that opened onto the staff service corridor. "This should work," he said to Diesel, and he reached into the front of his pants and removed his cell phone. The guards never found it because they only patted down his legs and torso.

He dialed Jim's number, knowing the call would be answered by Lieutenant Lacey—standard practice when Jim was on a mission.

With his breathing coming under control, Peter got right to the point. "I need to talk to Jim, ASAP."

Lacey knew Peter wouldn't call unless it was urgent. "Let me conference in the commander. Bear with me."

Still onboard the Osprey flying east toward the Philippines, Commander Nicolaou felt a mixture of curiosity and concern following Lacey's brief introduction. "What's your sitrep?" he said to Peter.

Not accustomed to military jargon, it took Peter a second to understand the question. *Situational report.* "Been better," Peter replied. "Look, I can barely hear you. There's a lot of background noise."

"Can't help it," Jim said, raising his voice. "That's the sound of the plane's engines you're hearing."

"We need help here. I don't know exactly what's going on, but it's not good. The ship—"

Jim cut in. "Slow down, Peter. Need help where?"

"At the Sultan's palace. The *Royal Seeker* wasn't acting alone."

"Mr. Savage. We already know about the *Royal Seeker*. I received your text message and the commander has been informed. We're trying to confirm the damage inflicted on the *Ford*, assuming she actually was hit. The second ship— the *Panda Star*—was also a launch platform. It is no longer functional in that capacity and is now under the control of United States Marines."

"Don't start celebrating yet. We have a serious situation here."

"What situation? Spit it out," Jim said.

"There's a control room at the palace. I don't know what its function is, but the Director of Security—"

Lacey interrupted. "That would be the Sultan's youngest son, Pehin Anak Shah?"

"Yes. Had a nasty encounter with him and a fierce firefight with his men on the grounds just outside the palace. Eu-meh's pilot and copilot were killed. And Eu-meh was shot onboard the *Royal Seeker*. She died before we could reach a hospital. The Security Director knows all about the missile launch ships. But I think there's more to their plan."

"Who's 'they'?" Lacey asked.

"Lim Guan-Yin. The Sultan's mother. She and the youngest son are calling the shots. The control room is connected to Guan-Yin's apartment in the palace. I escaped, but Robert and Jade are being held there."

"Is the Sultan in on this?" Jim asked.

Peter had been considering that very question. "I don't know. But his name has not been mentioned by either Pehin or Guan-Yin."

"Tell us more about this control room," Lacey said, her voice communicating a new level of concern. "What's its function? Be as specific as you can."

"I only had a brief glimpse. But based on what the Security Director said about knowing the missile fired from the *Royal Seeker* lost its lock and failed to sink the target, I'd wager the function is command and targeting. We destroyed the launch equipment onboard the *Royal Seeker*, so I doubt the control room at the palace is responsible for the actual firing sequence."

"Lacey, find a map of the palace. We need to know where that apartment and control room are located."

"I'll get right on it, but the palace is huge. Even if I can access a current layout—and that's questionable—it will take some time to study the floorplan. And the private rooms probably won't be identified as such on any plans."

"Do what you can. And alert Colonel Pierson. Request he brief the Brunei Special Forces commander."

Lacey objected. "What if the Sultan is involved?"

"It's a risk I have to take. I'd prefer we go in with their help."

"Go in? Sir, it's my duty to remind you that we have not

received orders to enter Brunei. If the Sultan has condoned these actions, we won't get any help from his military. In fact, he'd likely order a robust defense and file a strong complaint with the State Department. He'd rightly say that any military intrusion is an act of war. The Secretary of State will have your head, if you survive long enough to return home."

"Your objection is duly noted, Lieutenant. Now, just get me permission."

"Yes, sir. I'm on it."

"And Peter, see if you can help Lacey's team identify the location of the control room. Since you've been there, maybe your knowledge of the layout will help narrow down the possibilities. Are you in a safe location now?"

"For the moment. I'm still in the palace. The grounds are crawling with guards who have shown a strong interest in shooting me. But inside the palace I've only encountered one guard outside of the control room. Right now, I'm in a service hallway. When the security teams finally get organized, I think they'll search the public areas first, so I should be okay here for a while."

"Good. Sit tight. We need to refuel our transport and then I'll have the pilot turn back for Brunei. Probably sixty to eighty minutes out. I'll let Lacey know as soon as I have a firm ETA."

"Sir, I'm calling the Colonel now. But it will likely take some time to work out the details."

"Move on it! In the meantime, my team will be en route to Brunei."

"Lieutenant," Peter said before the communication was terminated. "I have something to do, and my phone will be silenced. If you call, I may not be able to answer."

Neither Jim nor Lacey liked the implications of that statement. "Just stay put," Jim commanded. But Peter wasn't one to follow orders. He answered to a higher authority... his personal code of honor.

"Jade and Robert need my help."

"Mr. Savage, Commander Nicolaou is right. You are vastly outnumbered and in a sprawling building that is unfamiliar to you, but that the palace security know intimately well. You are at a huge tactical disadvantage… you don't stand a chance. Please, wait for backup."

Peter glanced at Diesel. The pit bull was standing alert, ears forward and eyes focused on a door not far down the service corridor. "I have backup. And the element of surprise. I'm not going to abandon Jade and Robert."

The door opened slowly, but only partway. Peter ended the call and pocketed the phone. He raised his rifle. Then a young man dressed in a white chef's uniform backed out the doorway, pulling a stainless-steel service cart. Piled atop the cart were an assortment of cooking utensils including two food processors, polished steel pots, and ceramic bowls. Given his youthful age, Peter assumed he was a sous-chef.

At the sight of the rifle pointed at his face, the chef stopped and raised his hands. Peter placed a finger to his lips, and then slowly backed away, exiting the safety of the service hallway and re-entering the magnificent room with the huge chandelier. Not wishing to wait for more palace guards to show up, Peter and Diesel quickly ascended the staircase. He didn't know exactly where he was going, but it would be foolish to merely retrace his path back to the control room.

He recalled Guan-Yin's words that it might prove beneficial to have a couple American hostages. *What was she planning? And would she still hold Robert and Jade in the control room? If they were moved to another location, how would he find them?*

At the moment, Peter had no idea how he was going to rescue his friends and escape. But he was certain he had to try.

CHAPTER 35

PETER TOOK THE STAIRS TWO AT A TIME. At the top, he turned left, knowing that was the general direction back to Guan-Yin's apartment and the control room. Again, the wide hallway was deserted. It reminded Peter of a large luxury hotel with its numbered doors extending down the corridor. Lining the walls were a mix of side tables supporting vases stuffed with fresh tropical flowers, pairs of silk-upholstered chairs, and plush love seats.

Their footsteps were muted by the thick carpet under foot. Ahead, Peter heard a sound and noticed one of the doors was ajar. Diesel focused on the sound, too. It took a few seconds to recognize the noise—a vacuum cleaner. And then laughter rose above the mechanical din.

Hugging the wall, they took several swift strides toward the sound. The vacuum noise stopped and was replaced by conversation. The voices sounded feminine and carefree. Peter turned to a nearby love seat and shoved the rifle underneath the cushions. Just as he straightened, the door fully opened and two maids entered the hall. They startled upon seeing Peter, and then one of the women noticed Diesel. His tail was wagging and his lips parted in a way that many viewed as a smile.

"Oooh. Your dog is handsome," she said in heavily-accented English. She was young, maybe twenty. The other woman was older and Peter immediately noticed the familial similarities. *Mother and daughter, perhaps?*

"Hello," Peter replied as he closed the distance to the two women. The younger housekeeper leaned over and ran her hand along Diesel's head and back. His warm tongue lapped her hand and arm, earning a cheery giggle.

"He's beautiful. What is his name?"

"Diesel," Peter replied. "He's a good judge of people, and he obviously likes you."

Diesel's nose found a pocket in the light-weight uniform jacket the younger woman was wearing. She removed a wrapped cereal bar. "Are you hungry?" The canine sat at attention and stared longingly at the food bar. "May I?" she asked Peter.

"Sure. But I warn you, he'll be your friend for life."

She peeled back the wrapper and began to feed small bites to the canine.

"My daughter has always loved animals," the older woman said.

"My name is Peter. You speak English very well."

"Of course. It is taught in our schools. Also, the Sultan has many foreign guests."

"So these are rooms for visitors?" Peter motioned down the long hall.

The mother nodded empathetically. "No one is here now. But next week there will be many visitors. From all over. There are more than 400 guest rooms in the palace." She held up four fingers.

Peter smiled. "Everything is beautiful. Reminds me of photos I've seen of the English palaces."

As the daughter gave Diesel plenty of attention, her mother eyed Peter suspiciously. "I am a guest of Lim Guan-Yin," he said, hoping to place her at ease.

She nodded.

"Actually, I'm lost, and I hope you can help me. I was walking Diesel through the gardens, and came back through a different entrance. I'm not sure where I am."

She smiled at Peter's chagrin. "What is your room number?"

Do they know about the shootout in the garden apartment? He quickly thought up a lie, not wishing to take the chance.

"Actually, I'm a friend of Eu-meh Lim and her daughter, Jade, and have been invited to meet Guan-Yin. Can you point me in the right direction?"

"I can show you the way," the daughter said with bubbly enthusiasm.

"We have work to do," the mother admonished, turning her daughter's smile to a frown.

Facing Peter she said, "Go down this corridor to the end and turn right."

"How will I know which door is hers?"

"There is only one. As the mother of the Sultan, Lim Guan-Yin is revered. Her apartment is the entire east wing. But her offices are on the ground floor. If you are meeting over business, the grand stairway is also in the east wing. You'll see it."

"Thank you. It was nice to meet you." Peter and Diesel started to leave. "Oh, is there a restroom nearby?"

The daughter pointed back the direction Peter had come from. "Just beyond the stairway," she said.

"Got it. Thank you again." Peter and his ever-present companion turned and casually walked away. He had no trouble finding the restroom—the door was marked with a man silhouette. Like every other space Peter had seen in the palace, the restroom was also opulent. Designed to be used by only one person at a time, the large space was divided into two compartments of unequal size. The marble counter and gold-plated sink with matching faucet occupied the larger area.

Peter locked the door and phoned Lacey. She picked up on the second ring. "I have some information on the location of the control room," Peter whispered. "This place is like a hotel, and I was talking to a couple of the housekeepers—"

"Do you think that's a good idea? What if they report you to the palace guards?"

"I don't think they know what's going on. Most likely the security details are rarely shared with the housekeeping staff. Besides, I don't plan on staying around very long. So, like I was saying, they told me that Guan-Yin's apartment is the east wing."

"Where in the east wing?" she asked while pulling up a floor plan of the Istana Nurul Iman Palace. Her contact at the NSA had emailed the map just before Peter called. It was dated back to the construction of the palace, so it would not reflect any remodeling that may have been done. Still, it was the most detailed information she had on the building layout.

"No, her apartment *is* the east wing. All of it. And the control room is adjacent to her office which is on the ground floor. The entry to the control room that I saw was a hidden door, disguised to blend in with the wall of the reception room of her office. Sorry I can't be more specific."

"I've got it. East wing… Assuming the original layout hasn't been altered… Okay. This is extremely helpful. I'll forward this to Commander Nicolaou."

"Good. Now I've gotta go."

"Wait. Are you in a secure location? A place you can lay low until help arrives?"

"I still have a job to do. Don't try to reach me. I'll call back when I can."

Peter turned off his phone and placed it in his pocket. "Okay Diesel, you ready?"

The pitty looked expectantly at Peter as he opened the door, awaiting the next command. "Let's hope the coast remains clear and there really aren't any guests here today."

Swiftly and silently the pair advanced down the wide hallway. Peter paused just long enough to retrieve the rifle he'd placed beneath the cushions of the love seat. The high-pitch whine of the vacuum cleaner was coming from one of the rooms they passed. At the end of the hall, Peter stopped and carefully peaked around the corner. About twenty-five yards away was a solitary gilded door adorned with flower bouquets in wall-mounted vases on either side of the entrance. It was a little farther, maybe thirty-five yards, to the grand staircase that the housekeeper had mentioned.

Knowing that guards could come by at any time, Peter took a deep breath and dashed across the open hallway for the door.

CHAPTER 36

LIEUTENANT LACEY EFFICIENTLY COMPLETED her briefing of Commander Nicolaou in just under five minutes. "All right men, listen up!" He shouted to be heard over the roar of the massive Osprey engines. Their transport had completed a mid-air refueling and, under new orders from Colonel Pierson, was racing west on a new course for Bandar Seri Begawan.

The team gathered around Boss Man. "Bull, log onto the SGIT secure server. Lacey has uploaded a briefing packet including the floor plan of the Istana Nurul Iman palace. That's the home of the Sultan of Brunei."

Bull set to work typing furiously on the touchkeys of a ruggedized mil-spec tablet. Each team member had one as part of their mission kit. Once he retrieved the file, he'd disseminate it over short-range, encrypted Wi-Fi to the other operators.

"Are we gonna go knocking on the Sultan's door?" Iceberg asked.

Jim nodded. "That's right. The intel is still sketchy, but

here's what we know." He ran through the key elements of the situation at the palace, being clear to indicate what was known and what was speculation.

"The palace guards are to be considered hostile. They've already engaged friendlies, killing two. Based on human intel, we know the control room is located in the east wing. Lieutenant Lacey's team has narrowed down the exact location to the ground floor rooms indicated on the floor plan in the docs you're about to receive. Memorize it. This structure is massive in size. The interior may seem like a maze if you are not familiar with it.

"Our primary objective is to secure the control room. Since we do not know it's complete purpose or function, we are to apprehend all technicians and other personnel on the site and render inoperative the main consoles. Questions?"

"Sir, how will we identify the main consoles?" Ghost asked.

"Communications and radar. Our people do not believe there is any fire-control capability at this facility. Rather, they speculate it is the nerve center of the operation to coordinate missile launches from multiple remote facilities. We've taken out two of those launch facilities, but we don't know if there are more."

Homer looked confused. "Sorry sir, did you say two launch platforms were removed?"

"That's right. The second was the *Royal Seeker*, another oil exploration ship very similar to the *Panda Star*. Friendlies boarded her and captured the captain and bridge crew, but not before a missile was fired. Fortunately, they were successful in destroying the guidance-control equipment while the missile was in flight."

Iceberg raised his index finger, receiving a nod of acknowledgement from Commander Nicolaou. "You said that's our primary objective. Is there a secondary?"

Jim folded his arms. "There is. We have reason to believe there are three hostages, perhaps being held in or near the control room. Two are American."

"Is this intel good?" Bull asked.

"It is. The source is Peter Savage. He's inside the palace, although communication is sporadic. But he's relayed key information already. He was also involved in boarding the *Royal Seeker*."

"We'll get him, sir," Homer said. "Just like before."

Jim recalled the many SGIT missions in which Peter had participated—with this same team of operators—and knew he was tough, but equally reckless. "As you all know, the situation with hostages is always fluid. Hopefully, they haven't been moved to a different location. We focus on the primary objective: The control facility must be neutralized. Am I clear?"

He received a unanimous reply. "Yes, sir."

"We're working multiple channels to get assistance from the Brunei Special Forces, but I have no guarantees at the moment."

"Shooters or intel?" Ghost asked.

"Both. Obviously, they will know the layout of the palace and grounds better then we will. And it would be a whole lot better going in with an elite team of shooters, guns hot."

"How are we to tell the good guys from the bad guys?" This question from Magnum.

"The palace guard is a paramilitary force, so their uniform is common to the Brunei military. However, the palace guards wear black berets, and the Special Forces are issued maroon berets."

"Just the color of their hat? That's not much," Iceberg complained.

Jim had the same thought, but he still gave Iceberg a stern look. "It's what we got, soldier. Deal with it."

Bull looked up from his tablet. "Briefing packet is coming across now."

The chatter ceased while everyone studied the electronic files. In less than an hour they'd be on the ground, and they had a lot of preparation to complete.

CHAPTER 37

PETER WAS STANDING before the entrance to Guan-Yin's apartment. Naturally, the door was locked. So far, he'd cheated the odds with minimal contact with others and no significant resistance. His options for breaching the entry were limited—shoot the lock out or try to break the door down by throwing his shoulder into it, repeatedly. The first option was likely to draw attention, and the second option had a high probability of failure if the entry was of robust construction—most likely the case given the importance of the person living there. And repeatedly pounding the door would only further injure the wound in his side.

With no other solutions coming to mind, he lowered the barrel of the rifle and fired a single shot into the latch bolt at the point where it would enter the wood frame, hoping to break the metal bolt and shatter the wood door frame. The report was deafening. But would it be heard a floor below in the control room? Probably not if Pehin had been truthful with his comment about the degree of soundproofing incorporated in the palace construction.

A small circular hole marked the point where the bullet entered, yet the door remained closed. Peter pressed against the handle… no go. He threw his shoulder into the door and was rewarded with the cracking of wood. He slammed into the door again, only harder this time, and the door swung open as if it was never latched in the first place. He nearly fell through the entrance, just catching his balance and managing to remain on his feet. Diesel followed him inside.

Fearful that the gunshot had drawn unwanted attention from the maids and perhaps other staff, Peter closed the door and quickly surveyed his surroundings. The room was generous in proportions and decorated with lacquered carved wood panels in various shades of red, brown, and black. Traditional Chinese tapestries adorned the walls, and beautiful pottery, demonstrating the pinnacle of Chinese artistry, rested atop wood chests and tables.

The apartment seemed vacant, as no one came running to investigate the break-in. Across the room, a staircase led downward. Peter and Diesel covered the distance and descended into Guan-Yin's private office. To the left was another door. Making as little sound as possible, Peter reached the door and pressed his ear against it—silence.

With measured movements, he turned the latch and eased the door open just a crack. He peered through the slit. The reception area lay on the other side. The table and sofa that he'd hastily used to barricade the entry to the control room had been put back in place. He eased the door further, holding the rifle at the ready.

Standing with his back toward Peter was a man dressed in a green military uniform and wearing a black beret. In two long strides, Peter closed on him and pressed the business end of his rifle into the guard's back.

"Don't say a word," Peter ordered. His voice was firm and commanding, but not too loud.

The guard froze, and Peter reached around to relieve him of his weapon. "Do you speak English?"

He hesitated a moment and then answered, "Yes. It is required."

"Good. That will make this easier. On the floor, hands on your head."

Not wanting to risk a rifle bullet in the back, the fearful guard complied without objection.

"Remove the laces from your boots."

The guard stared back at Peter, not understanding what he was being ordered to do. "Your shoe laces," and Peter kicked his foot. "Remove them, now!"

Reluctantly, he untied his boots and pulled the black cord, handing it over as instructed. Diesel was beside the guard, baring his teeth and emitting a low, threatening growl.

"Face down. Hands on your head. Legs together." Then Peter proceeded to wrap one lace around the man's ankles, knotting it securely. He bound his hands with the second cord.

Diesel remained only inches from the man's face, putting on a very convincing threat display. His inch-long canines glistening white.

"I don't know you," Peter said conversationally. "But you seem like a reasonable guy. I imagine you are just following orders. So, here's the deal. If you move or make a sound, my dog will eat your face. Trust me, you don't want him to do that—very messy."

Upon hearing this, the guard's eyes widened in terror and beads of perspiration dappled his face. His lips parted, just a bit, as if he wanted to speak, but Peter interrupted him. "Ah. Not a word. Be absolutely still. He's quite hungry—all he's eaten in the last twelve hours is a granola bar. He'd much rather have meat."

Satisfied the guard was terror-stricken and unlikely to attempt an escape, Peter turned his attention to the location of the hidden entrance. He recalled the motions Pehin had executed to open the door. *Push this section of chair rail, and then...*

The panel opened.

Peter rushed the opening. Two black berets were just inside the control room, their rifles slung over their shoulders. They were facing toward the interior of the center. Peter lowered his shoulder and rammed into the nearest guard. His body whiplashed as he was driven forward, his face colliding violently with a metal console. Unconscious, the man crumpled to the floor.

The second black beret started to unlimber his rifle when the seventy-pound canine collided with him. Sharp teeth ravaged his hand, and then the bones crunched as the jaws drew tighter. His scream of pain soon became one of horror as his mind focused on priority number one—survival. But the more he struggled and fought to free his hand, the more violent became the shaking of the muscle-bound canine head, serving only to lacerate more flesh.

Quickly, Peter regained his balance. His eyes swept the room, the rifle following his gaze. The Security Director, who had been leaning over an illuminated display, apparently in conversation with a technician, straightened his body at the sound of the commotion. Upon seeing Peter, his hand went to his holstered pistol.

Peter snapped off a single shot, the bullet passing through the Director's forearm. His grip slackened and the weapon clanged on the floor.

Through a tight grimace, Pehin said, "That was a mistake. You should have killed me when you had the chance."

Peter shrugged. "Sorry, I missed."

Two other guards were in the process of raising their rifles. "Stop there. Lower your weapons, or I *will* kill your boss."

The men hesitated momentarily and exchanged eye contact with Pehin. Reluctantly he nodded and they placed their rifles on the floor.

Peter finished his survey of the control room and finally spotted Robert and Jade, sitting bound and gagged in a corner. He motioned to one of the guards. "Untie them."

Robert rubbed his wrists as quickly as the bindings were removed. "Glad to see you again. What took so long?" He strode to the closest weapon and picked it up, checking the magazine and then ensuring the safety was off. While Peter kept a keen eye on his prisoners, Robert removed the magazines from the other rifles, stuffing one in his pocket and giving two to Peter along with Pehin's pistol.

"There's one more outside." Peter cocked his head to the entrance and Robert went to strip the magazine from that rifle as well.

Peter eyed the pistol and then shouldered his M4 rifle. "Berretta model 92. You have good taste in firearms." He pushed the slide back only a quarter inch, just enough to show the shiny brass 9mm cartridge case.

Jade rushed to Peter and threw her arms around him. She was weeping. "It's okay now," he said. But he knew it would take time to heal from the grief she was suffering. Her mother was dead, and her grandmother and cousin were responsible.

Jade felt Diesel brush against her leg. She kneeled next to the dog and rubbed his head and ears. Despite her tears, she smiled at the adorable face that once again appeared to be grinning at her.

"Where is Guan-Yin?" Peter demanded.

"She's not here," Pehin answered with a sneer.

"I can see that. Where is she? I came through her apartment, and it was empty."

"I don't know."

Peter looked around and for the first time noticed a collection of four monitors mounted in a row on a long instrument console. The displays showed various images. One appeared to be a photograph taken from high altitude, perhaps from a high-flying plane or satellite. Another was graphical and had red and blue symbols overlaid on a regional map of the South China Sea.

"What is the function of all this equipment?" Peter asked.

Pehin returned an icy glare.

"You control the operation from here, right?" Peter pointed toward one of the screens. "Are these images in real time?"

Robert answered since Pehin refused to. "Based on what I overheard, its satellite imagery. Somehow they've tapped into one of our satellites, and they're downloading data."

Pehin snorted a contemptuous laugh. "Your arrogance has blinded you to logic and reason, causing you to completely underestimate your enemy."

"Well then, please, enlighten us," Robert answered.

Peter's mind was racing, trying to fit the puzzle pieces together. "India!" he blurted. "You bought a satellite and hired India to place it in orbit."

"Very good," Pehin said. "Two satellites, actually. One for detailed reconnaissance and one for guidance."

Peter studied the screens again, squinting his eyes as he leaned closer. He pointed at the collection of blue symbols, still north of the Spratly Islands. "This is the carrier strike force that you attacked. It's the same formation we saw on the tactical display onboard the *Royal Seeker*, just after they fired that missile."

"Too bad you didn't succeed," Robert added. "The *Gerald*

Ford carriers a helluva lot of fire power. Seems to me your little operation here is over."

"Typical American. There is no limit to your over confidence. Look again."

Peter and Robert turned their attention to the screens, trying to discern whatever Pehin had referred to. But nothing was changing. And then a series of red lights illuminated on the console.

Peter shot upright and turned to Pehin. His hand was pressing against the console he'd been standing next to. "What did you do?" Peter demanded.

"The terminal phase has just been initiated."

"But you don't have any more missile ships. We destroyed both of them."

"Yes. Unfortunate, but not unexpected. From the outset, I knew it was only a matter of time before you discovered our ruse. Still, it served its purpose."

Peter's jaw fell agape as understanding set in.

"That's right," Pehin said. "Manipulating your national paranoia was child's play. Naturally, your military and political leaders would draw the conclusion that it was China attacking your ships. After all, only China had both the motivation and the capability to do so. The disagreement over the Spratly Islands proved to be a convenient locus for your mutual mistrust."

"The missile attacks…"

Pehin completed Peter's sentence. "Only provided the provocation. It was never intended, by itself, to be a decisive action. We knew the United States would not withdraw militarily over the loss of a few ships. Instead, your resolve would be hardened. Your anger and lust for revenge would blind your leaders to the truth."

"You *want* a war between the U.S. and China." Peter paused, trying to think what the next move would be. Why was Pehin acting so confident? "But you failed. Our countries are not at war."

Pehin smiled, reminding Peter of a serpent, as the pain from his gunshot arm seemed to vanish, replaced by the exuberance of knowing he had won. "That will change the moment one of your Harpoon anti-ship missiles sinks a Chinese warship. Those red markers—"

Peter studied the display again and quickly counted eight red symbols.

"That is the *Liuzhou* battle group. As you can see, they have been ordered to reinforce China's military presence in the Spratly Islands. And they are just about to be within range of the American battle group."

As a former Navy man, Robert stiffened his back at the perceived insult. "The U.S. Navy is extremely well disciplined. They would never fire upon that task force unless there was very good provocation."

"Nevertheless, in about seven minutes, the Chinese radar will detect a volley of incoming cruise missiles. Their detection instruments will identify the radar seeker frequency as that of an American Harpoon missile. They should have enough time to report the attack before the first missile strikes. Naturally, having been fired upon, they will react in kind." He pointed to a digital clock on the wall. It was showing seven minutes and eleven seconds, and ticking down in time.

Peter mumbled, "And the war will begin."

"How do you know this?" Robert said.

"It's the terminal phase of the plan," Peter answered. "With enough money, anything can be bought on the black market, and Harpoon missiles are no exception. I'd imagine there are several new multimillionaires in India. But that wasn't the only contribution purchased from Indian sources. The guidance system on the ballistic warheads came from India. The warheads themselves from Chinese technology. And the rocket motors, of course, were readily sourced from North Korea. Isn't that right?"

"Very good, Mr. Savage. At any rate, while your intelligence resources were focused on finding and neutralizing our theater ballistic missile weapons, several fishing trawlers armed with the much smaller anti-ship cruise missiles have moved into location. There really is nothing you can do to stop it."

He moved his hand a few inches on the console and turned a dial. The satellite image was enlarged, and as he continued to turn the knob individual ships appeared—it was the Chinese task force. Then the adjacent monitor showed a similar satellite image, only this was the *Ford* Battle Group. "You are welcome to watch," Pehin said.

Peter focused his eyes back on the Security Director. He raised the Berretta and cocked the hammer. Then he punched several buttons on his cell phone with the thumb of his left hand. "Lieutenant Lacey. I want you to listen very carefully. We don't have much time, only a matter of minutes to stop the outbreak of war."

Although she wanted to ask a dozen questions, she had the discipline not to, and she listened as Peter relayed exactly what he'd been told.

Pehin's face grew flush with hatred at the realization of what Peter was attempting to do. "No!" he screamed, and he charged Peter.

Boom!

The clang of the brass cartridge bouncing on the hard floor displaced the fading echo of the gunshot. The room fell into an eerie silence.

Pehin stopped in his tracks, a hand placed over the center of his chest. His face contorted in pain and the realization that assurance of victory had been snatched from his grasp. He fell onto his knees, and then his face, as the life force left his body.

"What was that?" Lacey asked. "It sounded like a gunshot."

"It was. I'll explain later. First, the *Ford* is sailing toward a Chinese naval task force. They must know that, so they'll have armed fighters in the air, correct?"

"I would assume so," she answered, her voice touched with confusion.

"Those aircraft need to intercept and destroy Harpoon cruise missiles that will be launched from fishing trawlers in…" he glanced at the digital count-down timer. "In just over five minutes."

"Fishing trawlers? Where? We have to know the location of those boats!"

"I don't know! But they must be in the general vicinity of the carrier battle group. The Chinese have to believe they are under attack from the U.S. That's the only way this plan works!"

"Understood. The escorts will have the location of all nearby surface ships pinpointed. Hopefully, there aren't too many. I'll get the message out, flash traffic, but still it will take several minutes to reach the theater commanders."

"You have to try…"

"Wait!" Lacey said before the call ended. "How about you?"

"Time to get out of here."

CHAPTER 38

"WHAT ABOUT THEM?" Robert asked, pointing toward the black berets. "I say we tie them up."

Peter nodded. Following the example in the reception room, Robert ordered them to remove their bootlaces. While he was busy binding their hands and feet, Peter conducted a more complete examination of the instrument consoles. In particular, he wanted to identify the pathway of the electrical power cables. If he could disable the power, there could be no further actions from the control room if other personnel came to staff it.

It didn't take long to determine that the conduits extending downward from the commercial ceiling panels almost certainly carried the main power to each instrument cluster. Peter climbed from a chair to the top of a console and lifted the ceiling tile. Confirming his suspicions, the drop ceiling concealed a tangled array of cables. Judging by the shape and insulation, many were communication wires, but some were definitely power cables.

Robert had just finished his task. "What are you doing?" he asked.

"These metal conduits," Peter ran his hand along the nearest, "enclose communication and power cables. We need to sever these, and this equipment will be nonfunctional for at least a day—long enough to get help and close this operation down for good."

Robert wrapped his hands around one of the conduits at shoulder height and pulled, but the metal resisted his efforts. He tried again, more forcefully. Although the conduit bent, it sprang back to its original position. "That's not gonna work. An axe would probably do the job nicely."

"Sure. Did you happen to see one laying around?" Peter said.

"No. A fire axe doesn't exactly fit into the Asian décor Guan-Yin was obviously fond of."

Peter placed the muzzle of the Berretta 9mm pistol against a length of conduit. "Cover your eyes." He pulled the trigger once... twice. On the second shot he was rewarded with a bright blue-white flash indicating the metal bullet had, for just an instant, shorted the high-voltage wires.

Robert followed the example and shot through a conduit with his rifle, also achieving the same brilliant-white flash caused by the electrical short circuit. Together, they severed the remaining four electrical conduits. With no power to illuminate the screens and indicators, all of the instrument clusters became dark.

"Okay, now what?" Robert asked.

Jade came to Peter's side. "I don't want to stay here," she said. "What if she returns?"

"I promised your mother that I would not let anyone harm you. I intend to keep that promise."

Robert clicked the safety on his weapon to on. "So, what's the plan?"

"Since I shot our free pass, I suppose we have two choices: we can stay here, and hope that eventually someone who is not a party to this conspiracy finds us; or we can take our chances and leave the palace. If we can make it past the outer gate, it should be safe."

"Then what?" Robert said. "When word reaches the Sultan, he'll have the police and army hunt us down. We won't make it out of the country."

"If that's the case, we're in greater danger staying here. Our best chance is to escape and contact the U.S. Embassy."

"They'll have police in front of the entrance. They won't let us in."

Exasperated, Peter said, "Look, I'm doing the best I can. If you have a better idea, let's hear it."

"I say we leave," Jade said before Robert could speak. "We have to escape."

Robert's eyes moved from Jade to Peter. "Okay, let's do it. I'll take the lead. Jade, you're in the middle. Single file. Ready?"

After leaving the reception room and entering the outer hallway, they stayed close to the wall. Diesel stayed close by Peter's side, his blocky head moving from side to side, always searching for danger.

They hadn't travelled far before they encountered their first black beret. Robert was faster to respond and had his rifle aimed at the young man. "Don't do it. Just put the gun down, and you will live to see another day."

The man hesitated and then complied. He placed the rifle on the carpet and raised his hands.

"Do you have any other weapons?"

He shook his head. "No. Only the rifle."

"Go, get out of here."

The guard started to turn back the way he'd come. "Wait!" Peter said.

The guard froze. "Is that direction to the exit? To the palace grounds?"

The black beret nodded.

"Thought so. Other way," Peter ordered.

The man turned and hugged the opposite wall as he passed the armed trio. Once clear, he dashed out of sight.

"What was that all about?" Robert said.

"Didn't want him alerting any friends on the other side of the exit."

"Good thinking." They advanced again and reached the exterior door without any further encounters. The double door was massive in proportions—wide, tall, and constructed of tropical hardwood. Robert gently eased one side open.

"Looks clear. Ready?"

Jade and Peter nodded.

"Once we get out the door, I'll go left. Wait three seconds, and if there isn't any shooting, Jade, you and Peter go right."

Robert disappeared out the opening, and Peter mentally counted down the seconds. All was quiet, so he exited and turned right with Jade and Diesel close behind.

Coming from the air-conditioned interior, the tropical heat felt like a blast furnace, and before long Peter was dripping with sweat even though they were in the shade of a covered portico. Carved stone lions flanked the entry. A driveway extended both directions, disappearing around the corners of the palace.

Looking away from the building across the palace grounds, he saw more expansive lawns with gardens dotting the landscape. In some of the gardens, there were fountains. Others had benches to encourage visitors to sit and enjoy the beauty. Some gardeners were working in the distance, but no black berets were visible.

"This way," Robert said. "The entrance to the palace is on the far side of the building. There's a high wall around the grounds, so the only way out is through that entrance. We'll follow the colonnade until it ends and then cross through the gardens."

Together they moved at a brisk pace, Peter and Robert constantly looking around for danger. They stopped at the last white marble column. Robert searched ahead for any sign of guards while Peter frequently checked to the rear. That's when he noticed the surveillance cameras high along the wall. "I hope no one's monitoring those cameras," he said. Robert looked up, following Peter's gaze.

"I don't know. They're constantly changing and updating the security procedures. But so far the coast is clear."

Just then the crack of multiple gunshots and bullets impacted the marble column Peter was leaning against. The trio sprinted around the corner of the palace and into the garden, aiming for the nearest group of shrubs that might offer some concealment—a dense boxwood hedge four feet high. They ducked behind it, Diesel hugging Peter's side.

"Now we know—they're monitoring the cameras," Peter said.

"It's the most efficient way to find us. The grounds are even larger than the palace."

Jade was trembling. "Are you okay?" Peter asked.

She nodded. "Yes, just scared." Her voice was quivering.

"Me too. Stay close. We have to run from one garden to the next so we are not in the open any longer than necessary. I'll be right beside you. You can do this."

She took a deep, calming breath, and Diesel rubbed her leg with his head.

"We have to get to the gate. From there, we can escape into the city traffic and make our way to the embassy. That's the only way. We have to do this."

Three guards appeared at the corner of the building. "We need to get moving," Robert said. "It won't take them long to find us if we stay here."

Bending over at the waist so as not to be exposed above the hedge, they ran for a fountain surrounded by lush lawn. The fountain was constructed in a star pattern, with jets of water shooting up and splashing into the water-filled pool.

They made it to the fountain without being seen. The sun beat down on their already overheated bodies. Diesel's tongue was flushed pink and hanging low. The sound and smell of the water was a strong attraction, and he jumped over the foot-high ledge and into the water, lapping to slake his thirst. Fearful of making a commotion, Peter allowed the pitty to drink.

Voices emanated from the distance, followed by rifle shots. Bullets splashed the water, almost hitting Diesel. Peter sighted over the edge and observed the same group of three black berets. They were standing rather casually as if they didn't realize the Americans were just on the other side of the fountain. Perhaps they thought the dog had strayed from the group in search of water. Peter thought he heard laughter and watched as the three guards stood side-by-side and took aim, acting like they were at a carnival shooting gallery.

"Diesel, on me," Peter said, his voice firm, while he aimed his rifle.

As Diesel hopped over the ledge, the guards fired. And so did Peter. The black berets missed... Peter didn't. One of the guards fell, mortally wounded.

The remaining two guards dove for cover behind the boxwood hedge.

Robert fired a short burst from his rifle at the location he thought the guards to be. The bullets shredded leaves from the thick hedge and broke woody stems but otherwise failed to do any damage. "Go!" he yelled.

Peter and Jade dashed for a large banyan tree. The branches stretched out for 100 feet from the main trunk, supported on many dozen trunks formed from air roots that had dropped years ago. He urged Jade forward. "Get in the center where the wood is thicker!" Diesel followed her, and Peter rolled to the ground, ready to fire on any pursuing guards.

Seeing they made it safely, Robert jumped to his feet and sprinted. The guards from the hedge saw him fleeing and opened up with a withering volley of automatic fire.

Bullets sizzled passed Robert; a few hit the ground to either side as he ran headlong for the protection of the banyan tree. He only had ten more yards, and his legs were pumping hard, his chest heaving to suck in air.

Peter was shooting back at the guards, even though he couldn't see them behind the hedge. In a couple seconds their rifles were empty, and he felt a wave of relief knowing Robert would make it to safety while they stopped to reload.

The big man tumbled to the dirt in a controlled crash, stopping just short of Peter. He was winded and trying to catch his breath. "How much farther?" Peter asked.

Robert's face was answer enough. They still had to circle around the sprawling palace, and they'd only started, maybe completing twenty percent of the distance.

Jade was at Peter's shoulder. Robert had been her bodyguard for many years, and she knew him to be confident, strong, persistent. She read his expression with certainty. "We're not going to make it, are we?"

CHAPTER 39

ADMIRAL LAGRASSA WAS INCREDULOUS for exactly three seconds. He'd just finished reading the priority message sent by Pacific Fleet Command. In his business, one didn't have the luxury of time to ponder orders. Lives were lost or saved in a span of seconds.

He picked up the communication handset connecting him to the air boss located high in the superstructure, overlooking the flight deck. "Get the alert-five Hornets in the air ASAP! And two more right behind them. Loadout for air-to-air."

"Yes, sir," the air boss replied. He relayed the order, and seamen began scrambling to comply. "What are we hunting?" he asked the admiral.

"According to Fleet Command, we have high-level intelligence that anti-ship missiles are about to be fired from ships disguised as fishing trawlers."

Standing on the bridge, slightly behind the admiral, Captain Healy easily overheard his order. "The escorts will take down any cruise missiles coming our way, and if by some freak stroke of luck a missile gets through, our close-in defensive systems will do the job. Not much chance of intercepting with fighters."

Admiral LaGrassa had a faraway look in his eyes. "That's the damnedest part of this. According to the intelligence, they aren't shooting at us, but at the Chinese task force."

"Who?"

"The message didn't say. Only that we are to intercept an unknown number of missiles at all costs. According to the intel, those trawlers are supposed to be somewhere in our vicinity, so it looks to the Chinese like we fired on them. Follow me to the CIC."

Captain Healy and Admiral LaGrassa moved smartly to the Combat Information Center to better direct the expected action, assuming the intel was correct. The admiral entered first. "Radar, what are we showing?"

A technician answered without taking her eyes from her display. "We've got four surface contacts ahead and to starboard."

"Could be our trawlers," Healy said.

"Could be… or not. We won't know for sure until they fire off the cruise missiles. Assuming the intel is correct."

The muffled roar of two Super Hornets launching off the flight deck drew the attention of Healy and LaGrassa. They already had two Hornets, designated Sentry One and Sentry Two, high overhead comprising the combat air patrol. One of the many improvements implemented in the new Ford-class of aircraft carrier was the electromagnetic aircraft launch system (EMALS) which allowed for much faster turnaround between aircraft launches. Getting more planes in the air faster was a huge tactical advantage in a combat situation.

Healy looked at a video feed of the flight deck. Sailors were darting about in frenetic activity. "Two more are preparing to launch. They'll be airborne in three minutes. Fortunately, the warhead just clipped the starboard edge of the flight deck. If it had hit closer to center and taken out the EMALS or penetrated through the flight hangar, we'd be out of business."

"We need a sharp set of eyes on those surface contacts," LaGrassa said. "Have Bluebird monitor their activity." Bluebird was their E3 Sentry early warning and surveillance aircraft. With a powerful radar and the advantage of altitude, the reconnaissance aircraft was the best tool to spot a missile launch. "Authorize the pilot to shift his position if needed to get a better look. I want to know the instant anything resembling a launch is detected. And then immediately direct the nearest Hornets on an intercept vector. The pilots are authorized to lock and fire at will."

Healy checked the location of the surface contacts again. "*Shiloh* is the nearest escort to that fleet of fishing boats. Maybe it would be prudent to have her load in a set of firing solutions, just in case one of them is our missile boat."

LaGrassa nodded. "Good idea, Jack. See to it."

The tension in the CIC was palpable. Although the damage to the *Ford* was minimal, the officers and experienced crewmembers knew that luck played a major role in their survival. Their defenses were completely ineffective against whatever this new weapon was. If it was used against them again, would they be as fortunate?

"Probable missile launch from surface contact," the radar technician reported. "Contact designated Tango One."

Healy spun around to address the communications operator. "Tell *Shiloh* to take her down!"

"Aye, aye Skipper."

"Second launch detected! Probable missile. Surface contact designated Tango Two."

"Order *Shiloh* to fire on Tangos One and Two," Healy

barked.

"Bluebird reporting multiple launches." This report from the communications station. "Five... make that six bogeys. Flight profile matches Harpoon anti-ship missile."

"Transfer targeting control to Bluebird," Admiral LaGrassa ordered. "Get Eagle Flight vectored on those missiles!" As an afterthought he added, "And order the pilots they are to engage with guns or sidewinders only. No AMRAAMs! Can't run the risk that radar lock is lost in the sea clutter and one of those missiles overshoots and hits a Chinese warship."

"Status on Tangos One and Two?" Healy said, his voice elevated to carry over the chatter.

"Sir, both were just hit by Harpoon missiles fired from *Shiloh.*"

Captain Healy looked at the video showing the flight deck. "Why are those Hornets still there? I want those birds in the air!" No sooner had the words escaped his lips when the roar of jet engines reverberated across the bridge. The pilots were forcibly thrust back in their seats as their aircraft raced off the flight deck into a bright tropical sky. They gained altitude rapidly and joined another pair of Hornets to make up Eagle Flight.

Lieutenant Alfred Dickerson was born and raised in Atlanta. He grew up with a brother and two sisters in a modest apartment. His grades were exceptional, and he enjoyed school. But his passion was flying, inspired by stories he'd read about the Tuskegee airmen. Once, he even met two of the airmen during a book signing event. Freddy, as his friends called him, turned down a scholarship to Brown University, much to his mother's disappointment, to join the Navy and become an aviator.

Behind the controls of Eagle Four, Dickerson was in his element. He believed this would be a fairly easy exercise. After all, unlike an enemy fighter, the cruise missile would not employ evasive maneuvers to avoid being shot down. And now he was racing at Mach 1.5 to close on two lead bogies. The other three Hornets in Eagle Flight were cleaning up the trailing Harpoons.

Exactly following the vector he'd been given by Bluebird, he was expecting to close on his two bogies and be within range at any moment. The window to achieve a kill was now less than sixty seconds. Soon, very soon, he would be upon the Chinese task force—and he doubted they would perceive his aircraft as friendly.

With his attention on the powerful search and targeting radar onboard the Super Hornet, suddenly blips representing the two missiles showed on his display. The targets were both at lower altitude, just above the sea, and somewhat staggered— one ahead of the other. He descended, wishing to come in behind the missiles to get a good thermal lock on the hot engine exhaust. The shot had to be good—he probably wouldn't get a second chance.

Flying twenty feet above the sea, the Harpoon cruised at 460 knots searching for target ships in its path using an internal radar. When located, it would then steer a course unerringly to the target, slam into the side of the ship just above water level, and detonate a 500-pound high-explosive warhead.

"Bluebird this is Eagle Four. I have two bogies on my radar. Moving in to get a thermal lock." Still five kilometers away, the missile was invisible to the naked eye.

"Eagle Four to Bluebird. Can't lock, moving closer." Dickerson dropped to only fifty feet. He thought that if he descended any lower, he'd have saltwater splashing across his canopy.

Skimming the water at 600 knots, he quickly shortened the distance to the first missile. "Bluebird, Eagle Four. Have infrared lock on Bogey One... Fox two." A sleek white sidewinder missile shot forward from the wing pylon, a plume of white smoke trailing behind it as it accelerated toward the Harpoon cruise missile at supersonic speed.

Dickerson continued to close on Bogie One for another three seconds. "Eagle Four, splash Bogey One," came the confirming message from Bluebird. He immediately corrected his course, nudging the Hornet to the left until he was behind the second Harpoon. He was four kilometers away and had to get closer to ensure the sidewinder seeker was locked onto the target.

The radio chattered with more confirmed kills. Eagles One through Three had all succeeded in shooting down their targets and turned safely back toward the *Gerald Ford*. Now it was up to Freddy Dickerson in Eagle Four to kill that sole remaining Harpoon before it impacted on a Chinese ship.

"Eagle Four to Bluebird. I'm being painted by search radar."

"Uh, Eagle Four. You're getting close to the Chinese task force. Time to splash that bogey. You're within range."

"Negative Bluebird. Intermittent lock. I need to get closer."

Dickerson urged a little more speed from his engines. "Bluebird, Eagle Four has tone… Fox Two!" A second heat-seeking missile raced forward, chasing after the hot exhaust emanating from the rear of the cruise missile.

Resisting the urge to turn his aircraft, Dickerson held his course low and directly behind the cruise missile until Bluebird confirmed the kill. "Splash Bogey Two."

"Eagle Four, roger that." He pushed the stick left and entered a sharp turn, advancing the throttles to gain elevation and speed. Suddenly the warning alarm blared. "I've been locked! Ejecting chaff!"

"Eagle Four, this is Bluebird. You have two incoming. Break right."

Dickerson ejected more chaff, bundles of aluminum strips

to confuse radar guidance systems, and then he ejected flares to decoy heat-seeking missiles. He threw the stick hard to the left, and then to the right, rocking back and forth as the airframe turned sharply. He pushed the throttles forward to the stops, kicking in the afterburner, and pointed the nose skyward to gain altitude.

The alarm was screaming inside the cockpit, warning Dickerson that his aircraft was still locked by guidance radar from an incoming missile. He pushed the stick forward and dived for the sea… and still the alarm refused to let up.

More chaff and flares were ejected, and then, just as it seemed he would crash into the ocean, he pulled back on the stick. The G forces were tremendous, and he squeezed his abdominal muscles in continuous repetitions to force blood up to his brain. If he blacked out, he'd crash into the sea at 650 knots.

As his peripheral vision faded to blackness, he focused his narrow field of view on the altimeter… 300 feet… 200 feet… 100 feet… he wasn't going to make it.

He pulled back harder on the stick… seventy feet… forty feet.

Finally, the rate of descent slowed. At thirty feet it leveled off, and a heartbeat later the screaming alarm silenced, the two trailing missiles shattering on contact with the sea.

Pulse racing, Dickerson allowed himself one deep breath and then Eagle Four climbed to a safe altitude, leaving the Chinese task force far behind.

CHAPTER 40

DIESEL WAS CIRCLING, whining, yawning—all signs of heightened anxiety. Something was disturbing him, and Peter knew to trust the dog's senses. "Look, we need to get moving," he addressed Robert, but the message was also for Jade.

Robert rolled near a banyan trunk and prepared to hold back their pursuers. He motioned with his head toward a large water feature that was connected to a main palace entrance via a wide stone pathway. On either side of the path were huge planters, also fabricated of stone, each six feet tall and overflowing with beautiful blooming bougainvillea. The water feature itself was a long rectangular pond with ledge stones two feet high. Spaced across the length of the pond were three ringed cones, taller than the planters. Water shot into the air from the top of each cone and splashed down over the circular rings. "That's your best protection. Maybe a hundred yards. Think you can make it?"

Peter looked to Jade, and she nodded. "Okay, I'm ready when you are."

"Listen," Peter said. "We can't just run in a straight line, we'd be easy targets. We need to zig and zag. Stay one step behind me and follow my lead."

"I think I see movement behind the hedge. It's now or never."

Peter and Jade took off, Diesel following close. After covering a dozen yards, Peter abruptly turned right on a diagonal course, and Jade followed. Then he switched to the left, repeating this process randomly. Soon, the crack of gunshots split the air again.

Fearing the targets running in the open might get away, the two guards fired—and Robert returned fire. At first he was uncertain of their location, but then he saw a muzzle flash from one of the M4 rifles, and aimed at that point, and then just slightly to either side. After a dozen shots, he connected, silencing one of the rifles.

The remaining palace guard switched the fire select lever to full automatic and let loose with the balance of the magazine. A hailstorm of bullets ripped through the air. Peter heard the supersonic crack of a near miss, and then he heard what he'd been dreading. "Ahh!" He looked over his shoulder and Jade was tumbling on the turf.

Peter turned back and in four strides was at her side. Blood was already weeping through the hole in her pant leg, a bullet having passed through the outer portion of her left thigh. "Put your arm around my neck!"

He lifted Jade and they half hobbled, half jogged the remainder of the distance to the pond. Rifle fire had renewed just as they reached the stone ledge on the far side. Peter lowered the young woman, a bit harder than he'd wanted to. She landed on her side with a grunt. She'd be safe behind the long side of the pond.

"Hold your hand here, over the wound, to stop the

bleeding."

Peter laid his rifle on the ledge and started to fire in the direction of the hedge. He didn't have a clear target, but he needed to provide some measure of cover for Robert.

The bodyguard was running, and Peter squeezed off another six shots, still with no visible target. He ceased fire, thinking that maybe Robert had killed the remaining black berets. The gunfire resumed. As Peter searched along the hedge, a volley of shots came from a new direction off to the left. Several palace guards must have circled around through the outer reaches of the grounds, undetected as they stalked through the dense foliage. *That's why Diesel was anxious. He knew they were coming.*

Peter swiveled his rifle and fired at this new threat, but the men were moving quickly across the open ground, firing full auto from the hip as they ran.

Holding his rifle close to his chest, feet pounding the ground, his leg muscles burning as he dashed for safety, the strain was visible in Robert's face. Sweat poured off his forehead; his cheeks were bright red from heat and exertion.

He broke left, and then right, showing moves that would make a pro linebacker envious. This wasn't a game, though. He was running for his life.

Peter continued to fire and nicked one of the guards, who fell and rolled in pain. But the others continued forward—emptying a magazine and then reloading to fire again. It was a tremendous volume of fire, hundreds of bullets. And the law of probability eventually played out.

Robert twisted to the right, as if he'd been punched in the kidney. His left hand dropped to his side, and then his upper body tilted in the same direction. Two more strides and he collapsed.

"Robert!" Peter yelled.

The big man didn't move. He lay only twenty-five yards away. Ordinarily, not a long distance. But in the face of heavy gunfire, it might as well be twenty-five miles. Without another thought, Peter let go of his weapon and dashed forward. Bullets gouged dirt all around his feet, several zipping through the air near his head. Still, he charged forward, and then he was at Robert's side.

There was no time to check for a pulse or examine the man's injuries. If they stayed there, stationary, they would both be dead.

Peter pulled on his arm, and Robert's eyes open. "You've gotta help me. I can't lift you on my own." Together they rose and jogged the remaining distance, bullet's whistling by all the while.

Peter laid his friend next to Jade and then dropped below the ledge. The gunfire subsided, with only an occasional shot.

"Get Jade free of here," Robert said through clenched teeth. He'd taken a bullet in the side, just below the rib cage. If there was a bright side, Peter thought it was that his lung wasn't shot up. But what damage had been done to the internal organs, he had no idea. For sure, the immediate threat was loss of blood. Which was also the danger with Jade.

"She's been shot in the leg."

Robert's eyes widened. "How bad?"

Turning his attention to her, Peter eased her hand aside. The blood oozed smoothly and not too fast. "Didn't sever an artery. I need to wrap it. But it'll start bleeding for sure if we try to run." He removed the folding knife blade from his pocket and cut the sleeve off his shirt. He wrapped the wound, being careful not to cut off the flow of blood to her lower leg. She winced as he knotted the bandage. "That should do for now."

Diesel began circling and yawning again, and the signals didn't escape Peter's notice. He pointed at the ground next to Jade. "Diesel, guard." The red dog came in next to her and lapped his warm tongue on her face. Then he turned and faced right, in the direction of the palace. Neither Peter nor Robert had paid any attention to the building, assuming the threat was limited to palace guards pursuing them across the grounds. The significance of that mistake was about to be demonstrated.

Two heavily-armed men exited the palace and immediately spotted the Americans, completely exposed beside the pond. They ducked behind the tall planters and began shooting at Peter since he was the only one not laying prone on the stone patio. The rectangular pond was laid out with the short side facing toward the palace, and the two palace guards were moving to flank the trio.

As bullets zipped past Peter, some gouging chips out of the stone ledge, a few skipping off the pond, Peter heaved his body away from the pond to use the row of planters as a shield. He hoped that Robert and Jade would be ignored for the moment, appearing either dead or seriously injured. Rolling to a kneeling position, Peter opened up with his rifle.

Three more guards came out of the palace and joined their fellow black berets. They steadily advanced on Peter, scurrying from one planter to the next under covering fire.

Peter dropped an empty magazine and slammed home a full one, then resumed firing, but his situation was untenable. He couldn't stop shooting to help move either Robert or Jade to cover at the far end of the pond. But even if he could, somehow, reach the far end of the pond, then he'd be exposed to gunfire from the other palace guards advancing from across the grounds.

In the distance, he heard the rhythmic thumping of a helicopter, but quickly it faded. More rifle cracks and bullets cratered into the planter Peter was behind.

Then there was a metallic clanking sound. Again it was

distant, but steadily increasing in volume. He'd heard that sound before: the sound of a tracked heavy vehicle, like a bulldozer.

Diesel was barking wildly and bouncing on his front legs. The approaching guards were driving him to the edge of control. If he broke free, he'd be killed. As fierce as he was, he was no match for multiple men armed with rifles.

Peter glimpsed his behavior as he rammed home his final ammunition magazine. "Diesel! Enough! Stay!"

Despite the pain and loss of blood, Robert was still conscious and he read the situation for what it was. Determined to fight, even if that meant to the death, he shifted his prone body to a shooting position and aimed his rifle across the ledge of the pond. With sweat dripping off his face and threatening to cloud his vision, he squeezed off shot after shot, taking down two guards. Peter dropped two more.

The black berets from across the ground had closed to within seventy-five yards and were zeroing in on Robert. Peter had to press his body tight against the planter to achieve some protection from the shots fired from the two directions.

Another group of three guards ran out from the palace, adding more firepower to the assault on the Americans. Peter was conserving ammunition now, firing only if he had a decent shot. Robert stopped shooting long enough to replace the magazine in his rifle.

As Peter fired, bullets from across the grounds were hitting the planter behind him. At the same time, bullets from the guards advancing from the palace were chipping stone from the planter in front of him. With the two forces closing in, he couldn't maneuver. He glimpsed a black beret dash from one planter to the next, only a couple dozen yards away. Peter leaned out and fired. The guard tumbled forward, his weapon skidding across the stone patio.

But in that brief moment of exposure, another bullet found

it's mark. Peter's rifle dropped, his left arm now bleeding from a bullet passing through his forearm. He held back a litany of curses, and instead focused on raising the weapon and continuing the fight.

Boom! Boom! Boom! He was out of ammunition.

Dropping the rifle to the side, Peter pressed his back against the curved stone of the planter. He cast his eyes to Jade. She was laying on her stomach, her head raised and looking forward toward Peter and the advancing palace guards who continued to pour out of the building. Tears streaked her face, certainly expecting she was in the final moments of her young life.

Although he'd only known Jade for a few days, she reminded him so much of his own daughter, Joanna. Youthful, innocent, not deserving of this cruel fate. For a moment, Peter closed his eyes and allowed his mind to drift to happier times. Memories of Joanna, first as a child laughing and giggling while hunting for Easter eggs on a chilly spring morning. Then as the young woman she'd become—smart, caring, vivacious.

Opening his eyes and seeing Jade again, he wondered what contributions she would have made to society if only she'd been allowed a full life. *It's not fair. Life is not fair.*

Then he looked at Robert. The expression on his face conveyed defiance, determination, anger. Peter had seen that look before and read it clearly—he would fight to the end. He'd already accepted death, perhaps even welcomed it since it was no longer a stranger, but a known quantity.

Peter's left arm was going numb, but it made no difference. His only weapon now was the Beretta pistol, and he only needed one hand to shoot it.

The fingers of Peter's right hand circled the rubber grip of the Beretta, and it felt comforting. He pulled the gun from his waistband and shifted his body slightly to have a better angle on the approaching guards. He flipped the safety off and prepared to make his final stand. *Hopefully, they won't kill Jade and Diesel.*

Diesel? Peter's attention was again drawn to the red pit bull. The chunky head was swiveling from side to side. *What does he sense?* Peter tried to follow the dog's focus, looking over his shoulder back away from the palace toward the outer wall.

With a screech of grinding metal, the wall collapsed. Two tracked military vehicles powered through the luscious gardens, and then motored at a high rate of speed across the lawn, ripping up the turf and throwing a rooster tail of dirt and dust in their wake. They were headed directly toward the pond where Peter, Jade, and Robert were pinned down. Mounted atop each vehicle was a .30-caliber machine gun. Completely surrounded now, Peter's last glimmer of hope evaporated.

The tracked vehicles looked like large boxes on tracks, and he knew these where M113 armored personnel carriers (APC). The two machines stopped side by side fifty yards from the pond. A dozen troops, dressed in military fatigues and wearing maroon berets, were disgorged from the rear of the carriers. They scrambled around to the front and took up firing positions. To Peter, it looked like every rifle was aimed directly at him.

The palace guards had stopped their advance with the appearance of the two APCs. But the pause was only momentary, and with the vehicles stationary, the guards renewed their advance.

One of the machine guns cut loose with a short burst. The bullets knocked chunks of stone from the tall planters lining the approach to the palace doors. A second short burst of machine gun fire, and the palace guards were hugging the ground, seeking whatever cover was nearby.

Across the lawn, the approaching squad of black berets fired on the M113s, but it was ineffective. The dismounted troops combined with the top-mounted machine guns quickly mowed down the palace guards from across the lawn.

Over the deep rumble of idling diesel engines, a new sound rose. It was the sound of a helicopter. But as the sound grew louder, there was something odd about it. Turning his head skyward, Peter searched for the aircraft.

It came in low over the palace, kicking up clouds of dust and debris as it hovered only 100 feet above the ground. Painted gray and with two massive tiltrotor engines, the V22 Osprey rotated and then landed next to the armored personnel carriers. The loading door at the rear of the aircraft opened while the huge propellers spun, ready to lift off on a moment's notice.

The cyclonic winds from the Osprey engines whipped the uniforms of the fresh troops and made it difficult for Peter to clearly see what was happening. Palm fronds and sere leaves were thrown across the grounds, sand and dust assaulted his eyes. He raised his hand to his forehead, still holding the Berretta, and squinted. Diesel remained fixed at Jade's side, lowering to his belly and turning his head away from the tempest.

Uniformed men inside the Osprey moved onto the loading ramp. They were dressed in the same green uniforms and wearing the maroon berets of the troops from the tracked APCs. They formed a line, shoulder to shoulder, rifles aimed toward Peter.

Then, from farther back on the ramp, a familiar face appeared. He pushed through the line, followed by another military officer. From somewhere a voice was heard clearly over a loudspeaker. In Malay, the voice instructed the palace guard to lay down their weapons. "You have five seconds to comply. If you do not comply, the Special Combat Squadron of Brunei are ordered to shoot you dead."

The black berets needed no further encouragement as they all dropped their guns and clasped their hands above their heads.

"Peter!" Jim Nicolaou shouted, trying to be heard over the roar of the twin engines. Then he spoke into a handheld radio, but it was impossible for Peter to hear the words.

Jim strode up to his friend while the gale subsided as the aircraft engines spun down. "I'm glad to see you," Peter said. He snugged the pistol inside his waistband. "We need help."

"Bull!" Jim barked. A second later his first sergeant appeared at his side. Seeing Peter's blood-coated arm and the blood-stained shirt at his side, Bull reached for his medic's pack.

Peter pointed toward Jade and Robert. "No, not me."

Bull understood immediately and completed a cursory evaluation first of Jade and then Robert. Seeing the wound to Robert's side, Bull shouted, "Need a medevac ASAP, Boss Man!"

Robert was on the edge of consciousness. Bull leaned in close. "I'm going to stop the bleeding, but that's all I can do. We're going to get you out of here right away—get you to the hospital. This ain't nothing. Let me tell you. I've seen a lot worse than this. You're gonna be fine."

Bull moved to Jade but was stopped by Diesel. The dog was on his feet, lips drawn back exposing his canines and growling at Bull.

"Diesel, chill!" Peter commanded. "Come."

Diesel lowered his head and returned to Peter, where he was rewarded with a head rub.

Bull removed the wrap Peter had placed around Jade's leg. "You're in good shape, young lady. To tell you the truth, I don't know why my boss even called me in." He removed scissors from his medical pack and cut back her denim jeans. Then he sprinkled a blood coagulating powder on the front side of her thigh. "I need to have you roll over so I can also put this clotting agent on the back side of your leg."

She moved gently, holding back a cry of pain. When Bull

had finished, he applied a sterile bandage. "The bullet never touched your bone. In two weeks you'll be running on this leg like nothing ever happened."

Jim was talking to Peter when Bull returned to address his arm wound. "Peter, let me introduce you to the Crown Prince of Brunei." Jim moved his hand toward the officer who had followed him off the Osprey. As the Crown Prince passed, Jim lowered his head slightly.

Paduka Begawan Shah stopped opposite Peter, who was still sitting while Bull wrapped clean cotton gauze over his forearm. "You are Peter Savage?" he asked.

Peter stood and bowed his head.

"Stand tall and proud. You have performed a great service to my country."

Peter looked up, locking eyes with the prince. But before he could speak, the relative peace was disturbed again by rotors whipping up the air. A helicopter bearing the royal seal of Brunei landed on the lawn.

All eyes were turned toward the aircraft. The door opened, and out stepped Sultan Omar Muhammad Shah.

CHAPTER 41

THE BRUNEI SPECIAL FORCES stood at attention as the Sultan strode directly to the Crown Prince. His eldest son first saluted and then bowed.

"I cannot believe the treachery that has been festering in my palace during my absence."

"It is true, although I was shocked when word first came to my attention through the American President. He was most insistent, so I left the regional Security Summit in Kuala Lumpur to personally assess the situation. Still, until I saw this with my own eyes," he waved a hand indicating the palace guards who were either dead or under custody of the military, "I thought there must be a mistake. Misinformation."

Jade had elevated herself to a sitting position, her face still streaked with tears. She was rubbing Diesel's head when her uncle approached. He knelt and wiped the side of her face. "I am so sorry for the pain inflicted upon you by Guan-Yin. And I grieve with you over the death of Eu-meh. I loved her as my sister, and you loved her as your mother. From this day forward, I welcome you into my home to be raised as my daughter, if that is what you want."

Paduka directed his father's attention to Peter. "This man has risked his life to rescue your niece and save her life."

The Sultan's eyes bore into Peter, searching for hints of his character and moral fiber. After an uncomfortable moment, he said, "Then my country owes you a great honor, and I am personally in your debt."

"To tell you the truth," Peter said, "I had some help. Robert, Jade's bodyguard, deserves most of the credit."

Robert was laying on his back, awaiting a stretcher. He acknowledged Peter with a wave of his hand.

"Together, you have saved a child of the royal family. Whatever you wish for, if it is within my power to grant, you shall have."

Bull leaned in close to Commander Nicolaou. "Sir, we need to medevac these wounded."

"Excuse me, Your Majesty," Jim said. "All three of these people need to be treated in a hospital. Mr. Schneider has a serious wound with internal injuries and your niece has lost a lot of blood."

"The Raja Isteri Pengiran Anak Saleha Hospital is the best in my country, and it is only a short distance away. They have a heliport. Please, load them into my helicopter. They will have the best care possible."

Two of the Bruneian soldiers carried first Robert to the helicopter and then Jade. Another soldier tapped Peter on the shoulder. "We need to go, sir."

Peter held out his hand. "Just a couple seconds." He looked beyond Jim to the gathering of SGIT operators standing on the ramp of the Osprey.

"I don't know how you did it," Peter said to Jim, "but I can never thank you adequately for bringing the cavalry."

Jim leaned close to Peter and spoke into his ear. "Looks like you hit the jackpot. The Sultan is an exceptionally wealthy man." Jim raised his eyebrows and his lips curled into a rare smile.

"Yeah, well, he may take back his promise when he learns I shot and killed his youngest son."

He slapped Peter on the shoulder, a sly grin still on his face. "Homer!" he called, and the SGIT soldier jogged down the ramp. "Would you escort Mr. Savage to the helicopter?"

"It would be my honor, sir." He turned to face Peter. "If you're ready, let's get you on that medevac." Peter smiled and felt his eyes tearing. Though he knew he'd never be a member of the SGIT team, they'd been through a lot together. They'd forged an unbreakable bond of trust, respect, honor, and loyalty.

After the helicopter lifted into the sky on a heading for the RIPAS hospital, the Sultan addressed Jim. "My son, the Crown Prince, has told me that you were most persistent in your request that the elite Special Forces of Brunei be activated for this mission."

"Yes, Your Majesty."

The Sultan paused in thought for a moment before continuing, "How did you know that this operation was not at my direction?"

"To be completely honest, I didn't. I took a chance. But based on our intelligence, it didn't make sense that you would orchestrate a covert action to precipitate a war between the United States and China."

The Sultan nodded. "It would make no sense at all. And that is what bothers me most. Why would my mother do this? Why would she deceive me? Why place her country at peril and endanger her granddaughter?"

"Don't forget that she's indirectly responsible for the murder of your sister."

His mouth was downturn and his eyes conveyed a deep sorrow that threatened to crush his heart. As the leader of his country, he needed to be strong. But the pain of loss was very personal. He swallowed down the lump in his throat. "It will take time for us to fully investigate these crimes."

"I suspect that the State Department will be willing to lend assistance to your investigation, if you wish. Our intelligence analysts are already digging through the data. Obviously, there are lessons to be learned here."

"Yes. I will speak with President Taylor and request we conduct a joint investigation. But first, I have a funeral to attend to as my country enters a period of mourning."

"Of course, that's understandable." Jim paused, but still had questions on his mind.

"Is there something else?"

Jim cleared his throat. "At the risk of overstepping my boundaries, have you arrested Guan-Yin Lim?"

"The military and police are searching for her. My mother will be arrested and placed on trial for her crimes."

"I understand. Thank you for your cooperation and support on this mission. It is certain that my friends and your niece would have been killed if we did not intervene the second we did."

Bull stood slightly behind Jim and spoke softly. "Everything is stowed away. Ready anytime you give the word."

Jim spoke over his shoulder. "Have the pilot start up the engines." He extended his hand to the Sultan, who accepted with a firm clasp. "My orders are to get airborne and return to base once the objective is achieved. With your permission, we'll get this aircraft off your lawn."

CHAPTER 42

PRESIDENT TAYLER HAD READ the full report over breakfast. Although it was forwarded to the White House by the Secretary of Defense, the report was authored by Lieutenant Ellen Lacey of the Strategic Global Intervention Team. Taylor knew of the remarkable results the SGIT team consistently achieved on issues of deep national security.

Lacey had written that the motivation behind Guan-Yin Lim's elaborate plan was pure and simple—revenge. She and her family had suffered horrendous crimes and brutality at the hands of the occupying Japanese Imperial Army when she was a child. Those scars never fully healed - instead, they festered as time passed. The fact that Japanese military officers were never held fully accountable for their war crimes, added to Japan's refusal to completely acknowledge its criminal actions during their conquest of Asia, further fed her rage.

So when Guan-Yin's life took a rare twist and she married into the royal family of Brunei, she began plotting. In her mind, the objective was nothing short of financial ruin for Japan. With China surging economically and militarily, the timing was right. But the U.S. military was the sole obstacle in the way of achieving success. If the United States could be driven out of the Western Pacific, China would be free to dominate the region as it had for centuries before.

The door to the Oval Office opened and Paul Bryan entered. "Have a seat, Paul." He planted himself on a Chippendale sofa and Taylor sat opposite in a leather club chair. "What do you think of the report on the China affair?"

"As usual, Colonel Pierson's team at SGIT completed a very professional operation. If the Sultan had not been in the Middle East on an extended trade mission, perhaps the situation would not have spiraled out of control."

"Perhaps, but his youngest son did initiate and oversee the operation, and manage to keep it secret from the Sultan for some time—probably months if not years."

Paul Bryan raised his eyebrows. "As the Head of State, the Sultan is very busy. An alliance between the Director of Security and the Sultan's mother would be formidable. It will take time to fully investigate the extent of the collusion and determine if all the traitors have been arrested."

"Yes… There are a few things bothering me, and I wanted to get your opinion before we meet with Ambassador Gao."

"Of course, sir."

"Lieutenant Lacey wrote in the report that it is likely this Lim person—"

"Guan-Yin Lim. She's the mother of the Sultan."

"Right. So Mrs. Lim probably did not believe that sinking a few, or even several, of our warships would force our retreat from the Western Pacific. Instead, her strategy was to trigger a war between the United States and China. Lacey goes on to theorize that the U.S. would quickly fail to aggressively prosecute a war in Asia because of the expense, the difficult logistics, but mostly due to a lack of public support."

"That's correct. I am inclined to agree with her reasoning."

"Even after some of our naval vessels had been sunk? Please explain."

"I'm hardly in a position to comment on the details of military logistics as they relate to a possible Asian campaign. However, several polls point to the growing reality that the voting public is weary of conflict. We've been at a near-constant state of warfare in Afghanistan and the Middle East since 2001. The expense has been enormous, not only in dollars but also in lost American lives."

"We had to respond forcefully following 9/11. No one can fault the U.S. for retaliating against the Taliban."

"Of course. But then we invaded Iraq, and we destabilized Libya and Syria, making a general mess out of the Middle East. Not to mention a humanitarian crisis of Biblical proportions."

Taylor stood and walked around the Resolute desk, gazing out the window with his arms folded across his chest. "I'm afraid I have to agree with you, Paul. So, we're going to make a major shift in our foreign policy. Beginning today, with our meeting with Ambassador Gao."

With trepidation, Paul said, "Yes, sir. What do you have in mind?" Having a substantial change to foreign policy sprung on him without warning was not how he preferred to conduct business. He wanted to help formulate policy, not simply be a tool for its implementation.

"I keep going back to our conversation about how the United States turned over control of the Panama Canal and yet still maintains enough presence—through negotiated treaties—to preserve our national security. I want to achieve the same goal with China. I want this administration to treat China as an equal."

Paul Bryan shifted in his seat and raised his eyebrows. "Well, that will take some work."

President Taylor turned to face the Secretary of State. "Yes, it will. I fully realize that. And I also know you are the best man for the job. We'll begin today, with the Chinese Ambassador. And I want to invite President Chen to a summit at Camp David, to work through the details of a treaty that ensures freedom of navigation through those contested waters."

"President Chen will sense weakness on your part. He will demand nothing short of recognition by the United States that China has sovereignty over the Spratly Islands and the Senkaku Islands. Japan and Taiwan in particular will be very displeased with our pivot. Malaysia, Vietnam, and the Philippines as well, but that should be manageable. How do you propose we explain this shift to our allies?"

"We all know that this dispute is mostly about projecting an image of strength. Those outcroppings of coral and sand are mostly uninhabited, and other than fishing rights, what intrinsic value do they really hold?"

"Point taken, but what about the possible mineral wealth— oil and gas—in the waters surrounding those islands?"

Taylor shrugged. "So? Do we really care? The U.S. is the leading global producer of oil now, and we have enough natural gas to last for dozens of decades. Besides, we have no claim under any legal theory to whatever riches may be under those waters—if any. At the present, this is all hypothetical. It could turn out that the expense of recovering oil and gas from offshore wells there is prohibitive."

"What you are proposing is a huge pivot in U.S. policy. President Chen will be suspicious that we are hiding an alternate agenda. The messaging will be very tricky."

Taylor smiled. "An understatement. We will present our new policy honestly and openly. And we're not softening our stance on fair trade. Yes, at first Jinghui Chen and his advisers will doubt our sincerity. I have no illusions that this negotiation will be easy, but for the benefit of humankind, we've got to do our best. This path we've been following…" The President shook his head.

"We didn't seek a path of war," Bryan said.

"No, we didn't. But I'm convinced we could have adopted policies following the fall of the Iron Curtain that would have made it less likely we end up there."

"I'm not sure I understand. Are you suggesting that the long-term foreign policies of the U.S. have been a net destabilizing factor in geopolitics?"

"It's a theory I've been formulating since before I was voted into office. Now, more than ever, I am convinced we need to act more like a good neighbor than like an overbearing parent. Our foreign policy should be recognized for tolerance, for embracing other political perspectives and religions. For truly supporting freedom of choice, even if that choice is disagreeable to our thinking.

"I mean, why is it that we feel compelled to insist that our way of life is the model everyone should follow? Why do we assert our right to militarize remote outposts and then vociferously object and stomp our feet when other countries do the same? When did it become our charter to not only influence who is the leader of sovereign nations but, in many cases, to use force to effect the change we want?"

"Mr. President, you know my position on these issues, and you know that I fully support you. But I must urge caution. Rapid changes, radical changes, in our foreign policy may have unexpected, and unwanted, consequences."

"Maybe. But change is needed. As long as I am the leader of the free world, we are going to work hard to start making these changes. Quite simply, we must. We've been on a course of self-destruction for decades. Thank God, we've been able to pull back from the brink of annihilation more than once. But our luck won't hold out indefinitely."

The Secretary of State stood. "I knew this job wouldn't be easy." He took a deep breath and locked eyes with the President. "I will do everything within my power to affect this change, beginning with Ambassador Gao."

Paul Bryan was at the door when President Taylor addressed him. "Paul, this will take time and an enormous amount of hard work. Critics will doubt us. Don't lose faith. This is our destiny."

EPILOGUE

"HARD TO BELIEVE THIS IS WHERE IT ALL STARTED," Peter said. He was sitting across from Todd Steed at a table on the shady side of Wall Street, almost at the exact spot where they had first encountered the thugs trying to kidnap Jade and her friend, Amanda. The twenty stitches in Peter's side would be there for another two weeks as the ragged tear healed. And he still had to take antibiotics for ten more days.

Todd took a long drink from his glass of Sinister Stout. "Who would've thought it would all work out the way it did?"

Diesel groaned and rolled onto his side. His amber eyes barely showed under the partially-closed lids. Following a deep sigh, the eyelids closed completely, and within seconds he was snoring.

Peter looked across the table at his good friend. "Jade called this morning."

"Yeah? How's she doing?"

"Good. This has been a very trying and emotional time

for her. But she's dealing with it. I think the betrayal of her grandmother hurts most."

"I can't begin to imagine what that would be like. Your mother murdered, essentially at the direction of your grandmother, who then kidnaps you. That's really messed up."

"The Sultan is trying to balance the needs of his country with the needs of his family, and himself."

"How's he doing?" Todd tipped the glass of stout again, finishing off the remainder. He caught the eye of the waiter and pointed to his empty glass. The waiter nodded, and held up two fingers, indicating he'd refresh Peter's beer, too.

"He's a strong man. Jade is happy to be close to him and his family. It's all she has left."

"She has you, and her other friends, too."

"Sure. But you know what I mean." Peter turned away from Todd, not willing to look him in the eye, afraid of what he might reveal. "I know how she feels. There's nothing like that sense of loss. No way that words can describe it. You need something to hold onto. Something tangible, not just photos and memories."

"Maggie?"

Peter nodded.

"It's been a long time, Peter. There was nothing you could do. We all know that."

"Doesn't change anything," he answered. When he looked at Todd, his expression was mournful. "If I lived for a hundred years, it would still hurt just as much as it does now."

"The mountains?"

Peter turned his gaze to the west, toward the Cascade Mountains, even though a building was blocking his view. "I don't know why, but I feel close to her there. As if being there somehow brings me closer to the past. It's silly and makes no sense. We can never go back in time. But some of the best memories I have of Maggie are from time we spent in those mountains."

"I know." Todd studied Peter. At the moment, his friend appeared confused, uncertain, even weak. That was not the Peter Savage he knew. "She was your wife and the mother of your children. She was a big part of your life."

"She *was* my life."

The pints of beer arrived, and Todd deftly changed the direction of their conversation. "Jade will be okay," he said with certainty.

"I hope so. I plan to stay in touch with her. You know, she reminds me so much of Joanna."

"I can see that. She's got some spunk. And she's not afraid to get out and experience the world. Just like Jo."

"Yeah. Both are strong headed." Peter smiled, like it was an inside joke. But Todd understood.

"I'm gonna say this as your friend. You need to rest and pull your head together. Take some time off and go on a nice vacation. Hey, why don't you take Kate along? You can't keep living in the past."

"Not sure she'd say yes. We haven't been getting along too well since I got back. I think she's not happy that I went off to London with Jade."

"Well, why didn't you ask Kate to go with you?"

"I did. But she had a wedding to go to. She was the bridesmaid. Not exactly easy to get out of that."

"Maybe that bullet hole in your arm has something to do with this?"

Peter glanced at the bandage taped to his arm. The stitches were healing nicely, but he still felt stabs of pain if he moved just the right way. "Yeah, maybe. She told me she didn't want to date Rambo."

"Instead of sitting here, drinkin' a beer with me, you should ask Kate to dinner, maybe go to a movie."

"Yeah, you're right. I'll call her tonight."

Todd pointed his index finger at his friend. "Promise me you'll do this."

"Okay, I promise."

"Listen to me, Peter. You're working yourself crazy, and you're heading toward self-destruction. You need some rest. The projects will wait, and I've got production under control."

"I don't know…" Peter took a long drink from his beer.

"Look, you saved the world from a war in the Pacific. I say you can take some time to rest and relax. Hey, why not call the Sultan and ask if you can borrow his jet?"

"Which one?"

"He's got more than one?"

Peter snorted a laugh. "Two jets that I know of, and a car collection that is said to number in the thousands."

"Hey! You said he told you to call if you ever needed anything. Well, give him a call."

"I'll let you in on a secret. He said that before he learned that I shot and killed his youngest son."

"The guy who was in charge of the palace security and running the day-to-day operations of the missile boats? Let me tell you something: You did the Sultan a favor by killing that man. Otherwise, the Sultan would have to go through the disgrace of a public trial and scandal."

"Maybe, but blood is blood."

Peter's phone rang. He glanced at the screen, planning to ignore it, but the caller ID showed the country code to be 44. Intrigued, he held up his index finger to Todd, and then took the call. "Hello?"

"Dr. Savage?"

"Yes, speaking."

"Good day, sir. This is George McIntire. You might recall we spoke some time ago. I'm the Customer Service Manager for Rolls Royce."

"I remember. You're calling from Goodwood?"

"Of course."

"As in England."

"Yes."

"It must be past 1:00 in the morning there."

"Quite right. And your point would be?"

"No. No point. Just asking…"

"Well, sir. I've been instructed to schedule another appointment for you to specify your new coach. It seems our last appointment was ruined."

"Did Jade ask you to set this up?"

"Oh, no sir. His Majesty the Sultan phoned directly. He insisted I call you, right away. His Airbus 340 is scheduled to land at Eugene, Oregon tomorrow. Will that work for you?"

Peter finished the call. "Who was that?" Todd asked.

He answered with a smirk. "Oh, that was George."

Todd raised his eyebrows. "George?"

"Oh, he works for Rolls Royce. I guess the Sultan isn't too angry with me after all. He still wants me to pick out my car."

"A Rolls Royce? You're going to the factory?"

"I think I might offend the Sultan if I don't."

Todd laughed. "You wouldn't want to do that. And this time, stay out of trouble."

"Like I ever have a choice?"

"You know what you should do…"

Peter nodded as he dialed his phone. "Hi Kate. How would you like to see England?"

AUTHOR'S POST SCRIPT

THIS IS THE PLACE WHERE I ISSUE my standard warning—
Spoiler Alert!—please do not read this until you have finished
the novel. I hope you found the story suspenseful and
entertaining... and maybe thought provoking as well.

All of the military weapons depicted herein are real, with
the following qualifier: The Chinese "ship killer" ballistic
missile, known by U.S. military as the DF26 medium-range
ballistic missile, is not known to be equipped with a hyper-
velocity kinetic penetrator warhead. However, it does carry
both high explosive and nuclear warheads that are guided to
the target.

Defense against ballistic missiles is very challenging, not
unlike what unfolds in *Guarding Savage*. Unless a ballistic missile
is intercepted during the boost phase, when the rocket engine
is still attached to the warhead and the missile is ascending,
success is very low probability. Attempting to intercept a missile
warhead that has passed apogee and is on a downward trajectory
has been compared to hitting a rifle bullet, in flight, with another
rifle bullet fired from considerable distance.

This is why ballistic missiles pose a significant threat—
there simply is no good defense. Oh, and they do move very

fast, making the window of opportunity to intercept extremely short.

Tensions between China and Japan are very real, as noted in the Author's Notes. I've conversed with many educated Chinese who truly believe they have a solid legal claim to the Spratly Islands and Senkaku Islands based on historical journeys by Chinese mariners in the early fifteenth century. There are many original maps drawn by Chinese cartographers, plus other genuine historical records, to support the claim. As I am not in a position to judge the evidence, I choose to remain neutral. But I can say that the argument is, at the very least, credible.

There is a brief reference to the Panama Canal Treaties in a conversation between President Taylor and Secretary of State Paul Bryan. I recall well the signing over of the canal by then President Jimmy Carter. It infuriated my grandfather, a retired naval captain who served in WWII. He simply could not understand why the U.S. would give up control of such a vital passage.

Perhaps, as President Taylor suggests, the canal treaties are a good model for how to manage the seemingly conflicting issues of national security, freedom of navigation, and sovereignty.

On another note, I hope you've enjoyed following Diesel in this tale. He was very popular in *Hunting Savage*, so late in the drafting I decided to bring him back in *Guarding Savage*. You can expect to read more of Diesel's exploits in future adventures—he's turned out to be a loyal sidekick to Peter Savage.

Please follow me online at lightmessages.com/dave-edlund for more information about special offers and upcoming events. I'm also on FaceBook (facebook.com/PeterSavageNovels) and Twitter (*@DaveEdlund*) and of course there is my website *PeterSavageNovels.com*.

Cheers

DE

ABOUT THE AUTHOR

DAVE EDLUND IS THE *USA TODAY* bestselling author of the award-winning Peter Savage series and a graduate of the University of Oregon with a doctoral degree in chemistry. He resides in Bend, Oregon, with his wife, son, and four dogs (Lucy Liu, Murphy, Tenshi, and Diesel). Raised in the California Central Valley, he completed his undergraduate studies at California State University Sacramento. In addition to authoring several technical articles and books on alternative energy, he is an inventor on 97 U.S. patents. An avid outdoorsman and shooter, Edlund has hunted North America for big game ranging from wild boar to moose to bear. He has traveled extensively throughout China, Japan, Europe, and North America.

www.PeterSavageNovels.com

THE PETER SAVAGE SERIES

BY DAVE EDLUND

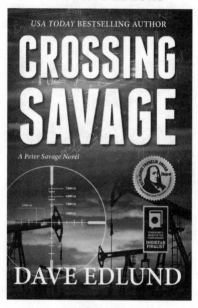

IN THIS EDGE-OF-YOUR-SEAT THRILLER, author Dave Edlund brings readers face to face with the promise of energy independence... and its true cost.

As one by one the world's leading alternative energy researchers are assassinated, Peter Savage and his friend Jim Nicolaou race against the clock to preserve the secret that promises to change the landscape of the world... or start a global war. In the timely, heart-thumping thriller Crossing Savage, author Dave Edlund presents the theory of abiogenic oil production and the terrifying array of unintended consequences that accompany the belief that energy independence can be realized.

PETER SAVAGE CONFRONTS A HIDDEN GENOCIDE, genetic manipulation, and a tipping point in the balance of world power.

When Peter Savage's son Ethan is kidnapped by rebel forces in Sudan while on a service trip, Peter will stop at nothing to get his son home. Recruiting old friends and tapping into the expertise of Commander James Nicolau, Peter puts together an unlikely rescue mission that will pit him against deadly forces. What Peter and his team find in the Sudan is a force far more sinister and dangerous than they could ever imagine. They are drawn into a much larger top-secret government mission, one that leads them to a hidden research site with an army of genetically-perfect soldiers.

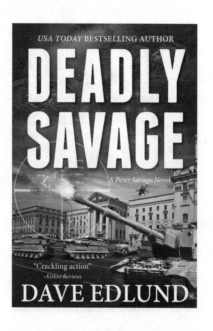

A TALE OF POLITICAL INTRIGUE, BIOLOGICAL WARFARE, and the fragile balance of world power.

When militants invade the Belarusian State University in Minsk, Peter and his father are caught in the crossfire. Held hostage by gunmen who look suspiciously like Russian soldiers, Peter Savage uncovers a deadly plot to kill thousands of innocent civilians—and lay the blame at the feet of the United States government. In a desperate attempt to avoid a global war, Commander James Nicolaou and Peter are called to the front lines of the sinister campaign, and the stakes have never been higher.

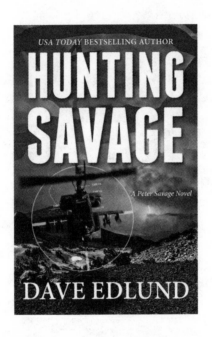

AN UNTHINKABLE ACT OF TREASON and a clandestine pact threaten to redraw the map of the Middle East.

A free-lance hacker uncovers top-secret files about a government cover-up surrounding the 1967 Six-Day War and triggers a murderous rampage. When the files inadvertently land in the possession of Peter Savage, he is targeted by assassins from both sides of the Atlantic and implicated in murders he didn't commit. As the body count rises and with nowhere to turn, Savage makes a desperate decision: he draws his pursuers to the Cascade Mountains, where he leverages the harsh terrain to his advantage. With his own fate uncertain, Peter Savage becomes both hunter and prey.to reveal the truth before full-scale war engulfs the Middle East.

MORE TO COME!

Follow Dave Edlund at www.PeterSavageNovels.com
tweet a message to @DaveEdlund
leave a comment or fascinating link at the author's official
Facebook Page:
www.facebook.com/PeterSavageNovels.